Valerie

GW00771153

Valerie Mendes was born in Buckinghamshire
just after the Second World War began. She arrived
too late to put a stop to it.
Educated at North London Collegiate School
(which she loved) and the University of Reading
(which she loathed) she was first published in her
school magazine when she was six years old.
It was a defining moment in her life.
During her many years in publishing, Valerie
acquired a variety of nicknames. At Oxford University
Press she was The Ogre Queen because she had
inherited a list of Oxford Graded Readers. In one
smaller and rather disorganised publisher she became
known as Genghis Khan. While running *Wordwise*,
her home-based freelance enterprise for eight years,
everybody called her Eagle Eye.
In her private family life, Valerie is Mum
to Sir Sam Mendes CBE and Granny Val to
her beloved grand children.
Valerie is still a meticulous Editor, but only of her
own work. Her own imprint, VMBooks, has published
her new novels, *Daddy's Girl* and *Beatrice and Alexander*,
as well as her Memoir, *Not Only But Also*.
Flight of the Lark, the long-awaited sequel to Valerie's
best-selling historical novel, *Larkswood*, will be
published by VMBooks in 2022.

www.valeriemendes.com

Also by Valerie Mendes

ADULT NOVELS
Larkswood
Beatrice and Alexander

NON-FICTION
Not Only But Also: A Memoir

YOUNG ADULT NOVELS
Girl in the Attic
Coming of Age
Lost and Found
The Drowning
Where Peacocks Scream

PICTURE BOOKS
Tomasina's First Dance
Look at Me, Grandma!

Daddy's Girl

Valerie Mendes

VMBooks

First published in Great Britain in 2021
by VMBooks

A CIP catalogue record for this book is available from the
British Library.

ISBN 978-1-8382490-4-5 (paperback)
ISBN 978-1-8382490-5-2 (ebook)

www.valeriemendes.com

For Somerville College, Oxford
with gratitude and love;
and for John Forster
and Captain Philip Moran
in loving memory

Dance to your daddy,
My little babby,
Dance to your daddy, my little lamb;
You shall have a fishy
In a little dishy,
You shall have a fishy when the boat comes in.

Vocal Harmony (circa 1806)

Devastation

1914

She should not be out in the storm.
Nobody else is.

The grey-black sky, with its menacing toxic clouds, spews bolts of lightning, like giant blue-white toasting forks, into the depths of the sea.

Bent on destruction, waves rear, mount and crash upon the shore.

The narrow cobbled streets gush rivers of rain.

Tiles, after years of patient loyalty, slither off their roofs; chimney pots go crashing to the ground.

Last night, five Cornish fishing boats were lost: tossed and crushed like handfuls of thin biscuit. Staunch, seafaring lives drowned with them, their desperate prayers dismissed as worthless nothings.

Their loved ones, left to grieve, huddle at the seven Shore shelters on the harbour in St Ives. They clutch each other for comfort, cling to each other in hope, scream with the pain of losing.

She should not be out in the storm.

But the woman runs out of a cottage in St Andrews Street, slamming the stable door behind her. She wears a black, ankle-length oiled coat with a protective hood. Swiftly, any old how, she stuffs bulky things into its pockets, her elbows flapping like the wings of a gull. Her eyes, in daylight the colour of bright cornflowers, are now as dark as the sky. Her pursed lips, clenched jaw and hunched shoulders reflect its swirling wrath.

But this woman is beyond anger.

She is furious.

She starts to run as best she can, her boots slipping and sliding on the lethal cobbles, her head down against the driving rain.

Nobody sees her.

There is nobody else about.

She stumbles like a drunk down to the harbour. Noticing the groups of mourners, she stops for a moment to look at them. Then she pushes on.

She hesitates, her body bending against the wind, the hood of her waterproof ripping from her face. Now her dark hair spreads, soaked and flattened by the pounding rain.

She makes a decision.

She turns towards Porthgwidden Beach. She struggles down to the hairline fracture of the shore.

A group of rocks survives the hammering sea.

The woman slithers up to them, flinging herself against them for support.

Now she cannot be seen by anyone. It's as if the sea has

sucked her body underneath the waves, slurped it around and then devoured it whole.

But the woman is still standing. Is she trying to speak? A growl of thunder swamps her voice. Vicious waves lash at her hands, her face, her body, smothering her, eager to drag her down.

But she's still standing there, staring at the sea.

Snatches of her marvellous dark voice echo above the roar.

Is she talking to it, murmuring goodbye?

Is she babbling childish gibberish?

Is she mad with grief?

Snatches of her voice sing like a trumpet over and above the waves.

> *Do not leave me here alone*
> *All alone, skin and bone,*
> *Do not leave me here alone in the storm.*
> *If I wander far from home*
> *All alone, skin and bone,*
> *God be with me where I roam.*
> *I be born.*

The woman closes her mouth. She opens it again but now she is mute as a stone. A wave slaps her in the face. She has no choice but to swallow. The taste of salt fills her mouth. The liquid hits the pit of her stomach, making her want to retch. With the insides of her wrists she scrubs at her eyes, trying to dry them: through the cloudy salt, trying to *see*.

Her eyelashes gum together.

She is almost blind.

With every ounce of strength, she turns away from the sea, forcing her body towards land.

She should not be out in the storm.

But she cares nothing about the elements.

She makes herself walk as if the rain no longer stings against her cheeks.

As if her long skirts are billowing tinder dry, not clinging to her thighs like barnacles.

As if her hair is smooth and elegantly coiled, not dripping down her back.

As if she can remember what it is like to stroll beneath the sun.

The woman reaches the centre of the town.

Raising her head, she pauses for breath, taking sharp gulps of air into her lungs.

A horse and cart wait outside the baker's shop: the horse patient, surviving the weather. Its driver has made his deliveries. He's drinking tea, talking to sympathetic ears, gesticulating wildly, describing his journey, relating his stormy woes.

The fragrant scent of pasties hangs in the air, a reminder of normal life.

The woman in the water-gushing street flicks back her head. Now her eyes are wary, watchful. Pinpricks of her fury subside. Panic replaces them.

She checks right, left, then right again.

Now she is absolutely sure.

Quickly, now there is nobody about.

She gathers her dripping skirts into her hands, squeezing out the water, shivering like a dry leaf in the wind.

Her lips are as blue as her eyes.

4

She makes a dive for the cart, scrabbling on to it. Her long skirt slips and lifts. Her knees draw blood, but she is too cold to feel the pain. Her fingers are numb with shock. She covers herself with sodden old sacking, pulling it over her legs, her breasts, her face.

She closes her eyes. Behind her lids she sees the eye of the storm.

Her heartbeat subsides. She can smell salt on her breath.

She manages to think like a rational human being.

The madness leaves her. She is sane and calm in the new darkness, beneath the weight of drenched blanket, inside her fresh vision of a future full of hope.

If she cannot see anyone, maybe – hope to God, *dear* God – they cannot see her?

Now she is nowhere to be seen. And still there is nobody about.

A fresh bolt of lightning gathers itself to crack the sky in half.

It sets a house on fire. The house squats next to the baker's shop. The delivery man sees the livid flames. It is the final straw. He comes roaring out, clutching his empty trays, shouting against the wind.

He hasn't got time to help put out the fire. He's much too fearful for his own survival. He has a living to make, whatever the weather. A day's earnings to take. A loving wife and three little children with open mouths, waiting to be fed.

He chucks the trays on top of the huddle of sacking. He wipes the spray from his eyes, swearing to himself, vowing to move to middle England, as far away from the cruel sea as he can get.

Then, reeling against the wind, he hauls himself behind his patient horse.

He yells instructions until his throat is sore, pounding at the reins.

The woman stuffs her fingers in her mouth to stop herself from crying out.

The cart lurches away.

Jolt by jolt, she removes her fingers and joins their tips in prayer.

Dear Lord, deliver me. Get me to the station and beyond. And then beyond some more. A great deal more. Only let me survive to tell the tale. Let me escape now and I shall love you for ever and ever. Amen.

She leaves the devastation behind – and takes it along for the ride.

Act One

Ultimatum

1907

"You look *wonderful* in pink," Walter says. "*Divinely* wonderful." His eyelashes flutter over his half-shut eyes. He peers at his model. "I could stand here and paint you all day and *way* into the night."

"Not a chance." Moira wriggles her bare toes a fraction of an inch. "Not a—"

"No, darling, *don't* move. And don't *talk*. It alters the shape of your *cheek*bones."

Moira flings her long, dark pink velvet robe aside. For a tantalising moment Walter sees a slender thigh: creamy, fluffy, so *inviting*. Then it disappears.

He swallows. His brush seeps oil down his hairy wrist.

Moira stands, stretching her arms above her head. Her breasts tilt upwards as if they're smiling. She says, "I've had *quite* enough for one afternoon."

Her voice lilts in his head. That *voice* … Its depth, its husky seductiveness. He'd do *anything* to listen to it.

He puts down his brush, wiping oily fingers against his smock.

"Don't *go*, darling." He uses his wheedling voice, his please-don't-leave-me-when-we're-having-such-a-marvellous-time voice. "We have the house to ourselves ..."

"No." Moira gives him a long, straight look. "That's one of the *many* problems, Walter. We *never* have this house to ourselves. Any minute now one of those lodgers of yours – Harry or Larry or Stinky Percival – will fling open the front door and hurl themselves down to the kitchen. To make even *more* of a mess, *if that's possible*."

He runs his tongue over his furry teeth. He's aware his beloved chums hardly measure up to Moira's exacting standards.

"But *darling.*" He sloshes more pink on to his fleshy-toned brush, bubbling it around. "*We* are snugly up here in our charming little *attic*—"

"Hot and stuffy in summer, freezing in—"

"I can hardly control the *weather*, my angel, now *can* I?"

"No." Moira's seductive voice gathers a touch of frost. The dazzling cornflower eyes confront his. "But there are *many* other things you *could* do a great deal about *if* you put your so-called mind to it."

"But my chums and I, we only *rent* this place—"

"Don't I know it."

He flinches. The long, hard stare starts one of his headaches.

"And before you even *ask*," Moira says, "I'm *not* going to bed with you, not now and not ever, until we have a place of our own. I'm *sick* of telling you so. In fact, I've just decided. I'm *never ever saying it again*." She ducks behind the screen. "And," she adds, her magnificent voice partially smothered, "*I'm sick to death of this filthy house.* The rats, the fleas, the stench of drains, the filthy floors, the greasy pots, the smell of coal, not to mention your Stinky Percival. I can smell his armpits halfway down the *street*. Need I go on, Walter Drummond? *Need I go on?*"

He gawps as the velvet robe flings itself over the screen. His palms begin to sweat. It makes holding a paint brush terribly difficult.

"Of course, you're *absolutely* right, my one and only. I *entirely* understand." He imagines Moira's stockings snaking up her thighs. "Let me take you to the pub, darling. You deserve a drink."

She emerges in a long summer dress, as creamy as her skin, with slinky sleeves, a narrow waist, and a low-cut, heavily embroidered neckline. Its delicate lacy collar climbs her neck like a trellis.

"God, darling, you're *so* beautiful. You've *no idea*."

"As a matter of fact," she reaches for an enormous pale hat with an ostrich feather, instinctively placing it on her head at its properly slanting angle, "I *do* have an idea."

She takes a tiny notebook out of her bag.

"You now owe me for *seven* sittings, Walter. And if you think you're getting away with an eighth without paying me, you're *very* much mistaken. Half of Oxford wants to paint me. And they will *all* pay me at least *three* times the amount *you* do. Or don't, as the current case most certainly is."

Walter's eyes start to whizz in his head. There's no way he can get out of *this* one. He gives Moira what he hopes is a winning smile. "Now the summer term has ended, I should get some proper commissions. At The Slade, Tonks says I'll go far. Did I tell you—"

"*Tonks!*" Moira says the name as if it's a swear word. A delicate gob of spit lands on Walter's hand. Gratefully, he rubs it into his skin. "It's been Tonks this and Tonks that, ever since—"

"Well," Walter interrupts bashfully, "he really admires my

11

work, and he's *terribly* hard to please. The Graduate Prize of the Year, now." He flutters his eyelashes, something he practises in front of the cracked mirror in the hall. "You realise I might actually *win* it, don't you?"

"I'll believe *that* when I see it." Moira takes a powder compact from her bag. She inspects her face, baring her perfect teeth, smiling at herself in admiration.

He wishes she'd smile at *him* like that.

"Well, I only hope you *will*, my angel face. The announcement of the winner may be down from London via the grapevine as early as *tonight*."

Moira snaps the compact shut. The sound startles a small mouse in the wainscot. It wakes up and begins to patter across the floor. Moira glares at it. The mouse vanishes in a cloud of dust.

"And anyway," Moira turns her gaze to the now wilting Walter, "a prize doesn't pay my *fees*, does it? Have you *any idea* how much seven sittings comes to?"

He slides his hand to his smock. His pants feel rather sticky. He says, "I'll ask my dear Papa for a loan to tide me over."

Moira puts her beautiful hands on her hips. Her cleavage deepens. He does his best to keep his eyes off it. He fails.

"Ah, yes, of *course*, your dear *Papa* … I wondered when *he'd* enter our riveting discussion."

He understands what an egg must feel like beneath an energetic cook's whisk.

"Henry's never liked me, never, not once for even a moment. If you tell him you need money to pay me, you don't stand a snowflake's chance in hell of getting a brass farthing."

"Nevertheless, dearest heart," his mouth is as dry as the dusty floor, "I *promise* to do my best."

Moira swishes towards the door. "I've had enough of this nonsense. The Eagle and Child it is. Something long and cool to drink," she adds, "on this deliciously bright, sumptuously exciting summer's evening?"

"Anything." He's imagining Moira stark naked. "I'll buy you anything you want. I'm *entirely* at your command."

Moira turns to look at him, her head on one side: quizzical, appraising, faintly contemptuous. "I reckon you need five hours to make yourself presentable but you've got five minutes."

He runs his paint-stained fingers through his thick, blue-black hair. A smudge of aquamarine streaks his nose. He picks up his briar pipe and stuffs it in his mouth.

"Yes, darling," he says.

One minute she's there beside him, in The Bird and Baby, as they call their beloved pub, at his elbow, just as she always is. She's talking to a friend of hers, admittedly: one of those ghastly Votes-for-Women creatures she's always in such a huddle with. But he can hear her marvellous voice above the din, feel the warmth of her arm against his.

And the next moment she's gone. Vanished, in not even the flick of an eye or a word of explanation and goodnight.

Startled, he feels bereft, as if someone has sawn off his right arm. He reaches for his beer. It's flat and warm. He takes a long swig, mostly for comfort, and drains its dregs. It tastes disgusting. He leans his elbow on the bar to steady himself, his smile as empty as his glass, longing for a whisky chaser. Then he searches the crowd.

Moira's nowhere to be seen.

He looks across the bar.

Wait a minute.

There she is, standing beside another man.

She holds a glass of freshly poured champagne. It froths and shimmers in the lamplight. Where the devil has she got *that* glamorous drink from?

The man beside her is strikingly tall and broad-shouldered, with a confident, swaggering panache in his every move. He wears a cream linen suit with wide lapels, and beneath it a black silk shirt with a dazzling ripple. The outfit must have cost a fortune.

But the worst thing about the stranger is his face. He's so handsome that Walter feels knife-wounds of jealousy drying his throat, his breath searing his lungs.

Moira's unknown companion – Walter has never clapped *eyes* on him before, he knows everybody else in The Bird and Baby, where the dickens has the stranger *sprung* from? – has gold-blond hair swept back from a gleaming forehead, skin burnished from the sun, and eyes the colour of the Mediterranean Sea.

Moira's looking into them as if she's never seen a man before in her entire life.

Someone calls to him. He tears his eyes away from Moira and glances over his shoulder. They are chanting his name.

"Drum … Drum … *Drummond*. Drum … Drum … *Drummond*."

One of his art-school colleagues has just stepped off the train from Paddington. He's run from Oxford's railway station to St Giles as if his boots are on fire. He bursts into The Bird and Baby bearing the good news.

Walter has won the Slade's Graduate Prize of the Year.

Within minutes he's surrounded by friends who clap him on the back, raise him shoulder-high and bring him more drinks than he can swallow.

"Knew you could do it, old chum!"

14

"Congratulations, Drummond! All that hard work paid off!"

"My aunt in Osney says please would you paint her portrait? She's free tomorrow afternoon."

For a glorious hour, Walter smiles, thanks them, basks in their admiration, shakes their hands and drinks whatever he's given. When he looks again in Moira's direction, longing to share his triumph, she and her dazzling companion have disappeared.

At the evening's end, he staggers along the pavement towards Walton Crescent. One by one his companions drift away. He lets himself into his house and stumbles up to the attic.

He lights a candle, filling the room with pinpricks of sunshine and shadow. He carries the dipping flame closer to Moira's portrait, staring at it, pleased with his handiwork. He doesn't need any more sittings. He knows lots of people who'll buy it. He could finish the portrait within the week, sell it, pay Moira more than the sum he owes her – *much* more – and get cracking on something new and equally brilliant.

Winning that prize has placed him firmly on Oxford's artistic map. People will discuss his talents. *The Oxford Times* might publish an article about him. He'll be offered hundreds of new commissions. This is the longed-for beginning of his professional career.

How often had he gone to bed dreaming of such a start?

He gazes around his shabby attic. Now he can begin to earn good money, *real* money. Enough to pay the rent for the entire house. Enough to ask his grubby chums to find somewhere else to live because he can afford his own space. Enough to pay for a maid, so Moira can have her own spotless home and will agree to live with him.

As his own true wife.

No time like the present. What on God's earth is he *waiting* for?

In a drunken trance, he plonks the candle on his cluttered desk. He pulls a piece of paper towards him and dips his pen in black ink.

My darling Moira,

I have won the Slade's Graduate Prize of the Year! Our future together is assured. Will you marry me and make me the happiest man on earth? I love you more than words can ever say.

Your very own, always, and utterly devoted
Walter

He scrawls Moira's name on a dusty old envelope, blows on it to dry the ink, and stuffs the piece of paper inside. Then he crashes downstairs, out into the quiet of the night.

Moira lives on Walton Street, five minutes' walk away, with her best friend Lizzie Farrell, and Lizzie's mother. Moira and Lizzie are devoted to each other, more like sisters, ever since Moira's parents were killed in a tragic accident on an omnibus in Oxford and Mrs Farrell had offered to look after Moira as if she were her own.

Lizzie and Moira, with Mrs Farrell's help, earn their living as competent dressmakers in a house so clean and neat you could eat off the floorboards.

Walter races up to the house, his hands shaking with impatience and excitement. He shoves his envelope through the letterbox, listening as it slithers to the floor.

Then he dances home.

In the attic he grabs Moira's pink velvet gown. He buries his face in it, inhaling its perfume that always reminds him of cloves. He remembers her flashes of creamy skin, her husky voice. He flings himself on to his scruffy bed, imagining her ecstatic answer to his proposal, her radiant smile. How they'll celebrate with wine and love-making.

He eats breakfast next morning in the chaos of the basement with his smelly chums. He stirs his tea, telling his friends to clean themselves up. He'll be giving a party that night for a special girl and a special occasion. They must all take a bath in the tin tub, wash their hair, scrub their clothes and polish their muddy boots.

He's met with sighs, groans and a string of impertinent questions.

"What *for*, Walter? What are you *celebrating*? It's not your *birthday*, is it?"

"No, it isn't," he says. "It's *much* more important than that."

Something flaps at the front door.

He leaps up to the hall, taking the stairs three at a time. His shabby envelope lies on the mat. He bends to pick it up. Someone has crossed out Moira's name and written his own in its place. He stares down at it, prickles of dread running up and down his spine.

He opens the door. He looks to his right on the crescent and then left. Apart from the milkman's horse and cart, the street yawns, empty as a toothless mouth.

He slams the door and tears at the envelope. His note has been returned.

Alongside his passionate declaration of love, someone has written a single word.

NO

In a Wolvercote Garden

1907

"I always knew that woman would spell trouble." Walter's father, Henry Drummond, settles his bony haunches in his favourite garden chair in Wolvercote, north Oxford, after their Sunday luncheon together and lights a cigarette. Exactly as Moira had anticipated, Henry has given Walter money to tide him over, warning him not to spend a single farthing on *her*.

"Yesterday I read an article in *The Oxford Times* about a Miss Moira Mitchell giving a talk at one of those Oxford Women's Suffrage Society meetings. Mrs Bertrand Russell was in the chair, *if* you please. A gathering of harridans if ever I saw one. Give women the vote and watch them take over the world. *Then* where shall we men be? … Nothing would give me greater pleasure than to hear you'd given her up."

"Far from it." Walter's heart thumps with rage. "I'm just finishing her portrait. I've done others of her, but this one's better. I'm proud of it."

He dare not tell his father he's proposed marriage to Moira and been rejected. He remains in obstinate denial about that envelope. Moira must have been in a foul early-morning mood, not thinking straight, probably with a hangover after drinking all that champagne.

He intends to call on her the minute he's put the final flourish to his portrait. While she's inspecting it, he'll get down on one knee and propose to her properly. How can she possibly refuse him?

"In fact," he continues, "it's the best portrait I've ever done."

"That's as may be." Henry inhales, coughs and wheezes. "But winning The Slade prize has given you a head start. Don't squander your success on that Mitchell girl. She'll eat you for breakfast and spit you out the minute she gets a better offer."

"Nonsense, Papa." But he flinches, remembering how other men look longingly at her, how jealous it makes him. "What *have* you got against her?"

"She's too pretty by half. *And* she's clever. She has a cunning way about her I don't trust. She's also a dreadful flirt. The way she wears those clothes of hers—"

"She makes her own dresses! That's why they fit her so well."

"Much *too* well. You can see every nook and cranny—"

"Don't be *obscene*, Papa—"

"You know *exactly* what I mean. She flaunts her body at you, and it's not seemly. You need someone sensible and homely—"

"And as dull as ditch water." He stares across the flowery garden to the edges of Port Meadow, remembering how as a child he'd wanted to draw every frog that hopped away, every flower in bloom, every bird in flight, fascinated by the challenge and excitement of accurate replication.

"Sturdy and reliable don't have to be boring." Henry coughs, pulls a handkerchief out of his pocket and wipes his mouth. Walter sees the virulent spots of blood. "I shan't live forever. Before I die, I want to see you with a decent woman, someone I can trust to bring up my grandchildren in a seemly fashion."

Startled by the blood and the mention of death, Walter says, "I wish you'd think more about your health and less about my love life. Have you seen a doctor for that cough?"

"Don't change the subject, Walter. I'm sixty-three, an old man. *You've* got everything to live for. Marry the wrong woman and you'll regret it for the rest of your life."

"But *you* didn't, did you, Papa?"

"Of course not." Henry mops his forehead with the stained handkerchief. "Your mother was a *paragon* of virtue and loveliness. The fact that God took her from me a week after you were born only made me love her even more."

"I know, Papa." He's heard that exact sentence a million times. When he squeezes his father's hand, it feels cold and fragile. "We've *both* been lonely without her."

"So you be sure to choose a decent, old-fashioned woman. There are plenty of them in Oxford. Steer clear of modern rubbish." Henry closes his eyes. His voice sinks to a whisper. "Choose a virtuous survivor. Four or five grandchildren, Walter, my boy. That's what I want, dancing around my knees."

The moment Henry is sound asleep, Walter tiptoes out of the garden and climbs on to his Raleigh bicycle. He adores the machine. It whisks him around Oxford at a moment's notice, no matter what the weather. From its saddle, he looks back at the Wolvercote cottage. Its roof needs to be freshly thatched, its paintwork renewed, its garden weeded, mowed, pruned. He worries constantly about his Papa: the man who'd made a valiant attempt to be his mother *and* father but had never quite succeeded.

Henry had owned and run a second-hand bookshop in Oxford. Now retired, his cottage is swamped by books, many of them valuable first editions. He spends all morning peering at a newspaper through wobbly pince-nez that pinch his bony nose; then he complains his eyes are tired and he has too much time on his hands. He roams Oxford's streets until he's exhausted, calling on Walter unexpectedly, carrying a paper bag filled with iced buns, demanding a cup of tea. Or he walks from Wolvercote to the nearby village of Wytham to visit his best friend and drink several pints of ale in The White Hart inn.

Walter never knows where he might next find his father. He wishes Henry had a wife who could keep a steady eye on him and entertain him quietly at home.

He cycles back to Walton Crescent. The painting of Moira calls to him as if it's speaking with her own seductive voice. There are a good four hours of working daylight left to him, and then three more concentrated days.

He'll do nothing but paint. He'll barely stop to eat, drink or sleep. On Wednesday evening he'll scour his attic with Vim. He'll change the bed linen, buy fresh flowers and a bottle of champagne. On Thursday morning he'll take a bath and go to the barber on Walton Street. When he looks as shiny as a newly hatched butterfly, he'll call on his beloved and invite her to inspect his handiwork.

Moira will gasp at its brilliance. She'll tell him he's captured her very essence. Then, gracefully, he'll drop to one knee and declare his undying love.

"How *persuasive* you are, my darling Walter," Moira will say. "How *handsome* and *talented* … This attic looks like a new pin. Of *course* I'll marry you."

∞

On Thursday morning, Walter walks slowly towards Moira's house, praying she'll be at home. His clean collar scrapes against his neck. His new shoes squeak. The barber has given him a *very* close shave and his cheeks feel hot and raw. He holds a bunch of cornflowers he'd bought in the Covered Market with his last few farthings.

He rehearses his speech. He'll tell Moira the dazzling colour of the cornflowers matches her glorious eyes.

He thumps on Moira's door in Walton Street. There's a long silence. Then the door creaks open.

"Ah, Lizzie." He tries to smile but his lips refuse to move. Lizzie is slim with soft brown curly hair worn in a knot, pale grey eyes and the demure look of a virgin. "How *very* nice you look this morning."

"Thank you, Walter." She pats her immaculate hair. "I'm terribly busy at the moment. Why are you here?"

He stares over her shoulder, trying to see into the hall.

"Could you tell Moira I'd very much appreciate a quick word?"

"I would if she were here, but she's not."

A knife of disappointment cuts through Walter's heart. "Do you happen to know when she'll be back?"

Lizzie folds her arms. "I've no idea."

"You must have *some*—"

"I don't, Walter. Moira has no idea, so how could *I* possibly know?"

He takes a step away from the voice of doom. Lizzie smells of new linen and moth balls. The midday sun beats on the back of his neck, making him dizzy.

"So where *is* she?" He feels forlorn, like a lost child searching for his mother.

"Somewhere on the Mediterranean. At this very moment

Moira's probably sunning herself on Pierre Tessier's private yacht."

His mouth drops. "I *beg* your pardon?"

"You heard me. Pierre and Moira have been – how can I describe it? – close companions since that night last week when he arrived in Oxford. He's been staying at the Randolph Hotel. He had business at the Ashmolean: a valuable painting to sell. Moira fell for him: hook, line and sinker. I've never *seen* her so enamoured."

"Pierre Tessier …" Walter says the words slowly, as if he's uttering a curse. "Is he the fellow I saw with Moira in The Bird and Baby? Tall, blond …" He hesitates. "Handsome in a flamboyant kind of way?"

"*Very* handsome. He's a French aristocrat, thirty-eight years old and exceedingly rich." Lizzie stares at his much-washed collar. "He asked Moira to go on holiday with him. Said she needed sunlight and wonderful French food. She didn't wait to be asked twice. They left yesterday morning."

"Didn't you try to *stop* her?" The centre of his universe has been ripped away.

She digs her hands into her lace-trimmed pockets. "Of course. I said, 'You've only *known* the man three minutes. You'd be *mad* to run off with him.' But you know what Moira's like when she wants something. Nothing stands in her way." Her hands flutter again to her hair. "Mother and I have to finish a wedding dress *and* veil by Monday. The embroidery involves thousands of tiny pearls. Without Moira, we'll need to work night and day. So if you *don't* mind—"

And she shuts the door in his face.

He turns away into the sun's glare, feeling hot, sick and furious. Moira has betrayed him. He hurls the cornflowers into the gutter and jumps on them, twisting his ankle and gasping with pain. He limps home, taking the stairs one at a time. His ankle screams. His legs creak, his knees knock, his teeth grind.

He bends over, panting, and looks around at his attic. It's so shabby. How can he compete with the blond, impeccably dressed, suntanned, yacht-owning Tessier?

He begins to sob. A genius he might be, but he sure lacks the money to prove it. Well – he straightens his back – now he'll *do* something about it. He's sick of being poor, of asking Henry for handouts and hardly ever having clean bed linen.

Biting his lip, he slides the painting of Moira from its easel, knowing he can't bear to look at it again. But he's determined to earn money from it. He wraps the canvas in a grubby sheet and carries the bundle downstairs. Propping it in his bike basket, he wheels it into town.

A shop that sells ornate antique furniture stands on the corner of King Edward Street. He knows its owner, Graham Maynard. They're regular drinking companions. If Graham likes a painting, he'll buy it. As Walter walks and pushes, he works out how much money he'll ask for it.

Graham could have two more portraits by the summer's end. After all, Walter is The Slade's star pupil of the year. His work is fresh to the market place, a sound investment – one Graham will never regret.

He leans his bike against the nearest wall. Carrying Moira's portrait, dripping with sweat, angry, defiant and burning with ambition, Walter Drummond pushes his fraying shoulder against Graham's beautiful antique door – and begins his professional career.

The New Arrival

1908

Walter gathers up his sheaf of notes and crams on his Panama. He tells the semi-nude model she can relax, put her clothes on and go home.

He enjoys his three teaching afternoons a week in the spacious, well-lit room in the centre of Oxford, close to the Ruskin School of Drawing on Beaumont Street. He likes his groups of enthusiastic but incompetent students who think he's a genius. He stoops towards them as they draw, guiding their hesitant pencils, showing them where they're going wrong – and on rare occasions admiring their work.

But nothing compares to standing behind his own canvas with his brushes and oil paints in his Walton Crescent house. Now he rents it on his own, working in his large ground-floor studio whenever the light is good, in blissful, concentrated solitude.

Of course, he's hardly a recluse. Bridget, his plump and uncomplaining maid, arrives every morning to make him breakfast and luncheon, clean the house, do his washing, shopping and any other chores. He visits his father in

Wolvercote every Sunday for their usual walk, talk and luncheon.

At the end of the day, back aching, head throbbing, eyes burning, he flings down his brushes. He goes out to eat with his grubby chums, or to drink with his neighbours. He knows *everyone* in Oxford worth knowing. And if he's in the mood, there are many elegant ladies, some of whom are also his models, who enjoy sharing his bed. They tell him he's *so* handsome, *great* fun to be with, and *such* a naughty boy.

After Graham had bought Moira's portrait for more money than Walter had ever held before, he'd never looked back. Determined to prove his worth, his speed and his dedicated brilliance, he accepts most commissions. He's courteous and grateful to his clients, helpful to his students and never too drunk to walk home. When childish brawls break out in The Bird and Baby, he makes for the door, intent on keeping out of trouble, his reputation intact.

If he still dreams about Moira every night, hears her glorious voice in his head every morning, hopes to catch a glimpse of her on every Oxford street – well, that's nobody's business but his. He never talks about her to anyone.

Once a month, Henry brings Moira's name into their desultory Sunday conversations, as if he's testing the waters.

"I've no idea *where* she is, Papa, let alone *how* she is or *what* she's doing," Walter says, turning his head away. He'd listen to Henry's predictable "Thank God for *that* then," and deliberately change the subject.

One Saturday in spring, he comes face to face with Lizzie on St Giles, her arms full of cotton remnants. Holding his nerve, he merely tips his hat and says a cool, "Good afternoon, Lizzie," before moving on, even though he's longing to ask, "What news of Moira? Have you by any chance heard from her?"

How he longs to ask.

He refuses to walk past Moira's house and stare into its windows, as if he's a lovelorn adolescent, even if that's exactly how he feels.

That afternoon, after class, he decides to take tea in the café in Oxford's Covered Market. It's a meal he rarely has time for at home, but one that reminds him of his childhood, when toasted crumpets by the fire and sponge cakes topped with icing were the highlights of his day.

He lingers over his fragrant pot of Lipton's tea and munches on a slice of fruit cake. Then he buys a packet of Bells's Three Nuns tobacco, a bottle of old Madeira and some Rowntree's cocoa for Henry; hesitates over a smart leather waistcoat but decides it's too hot to wear in the summer; then turns into the Winsor and Newton art-supplies shop where he always buys his equipment. He needs new brushes and more of those wonderful fat tubes of oil paint: every possible colour, from cobalt blue and buttercup yellow to sizzling aquamarine.

Inside, the shop is cool and dim. He'll have it to himself: there seem to be no other customers. After his busy class and the bustling heat of the market, he draws a breath of relief. He takes off his Panama, runs a hand through his damp hair. Here he can browse, think about his current canvas and emerge with his purchases, refreshed and ready for work.

Except that – wait a minute – he's *not* alone. A woman stands at the far end of the shop. She's talking to the sales assistant. That voice … he recognises it in an instant. He'd sail the stormy seas to hear it, climb the highest mountain, disappear down the darkest coal mine to have it in his ears.

27

It's Moira's.

He squints across the shop. She's no floating mirage. She's standing by the counter, wearing a tight-fitting pale-lilac frock topped by an enormous purple hat, all frothy net and feathers.

He walks towards her, his legs shaking, the beat of his heart barely able to maintain its wild race.

"Thank you *so* much," Moira says to the assistant. "If you could wrap these, I'll take them straight home."

He stands beside her, smelling the scent of cloves. Her dark curls cling to the nape of her neck. He longs to touch her, to pull off the hat and let her hair tumble into his hands.

"*Moira?*" he says. "I can hardly believe my eyes."

He insists on carrying her parcel, grateful he can feast his eyes on her, glad he doesn't have his bicycle so he's free to walk beside her. Buying new oil paints and brushes can wait. Everything else in the world can wait. Finally he's walking beside his beloved girl again. He'd forgotten how *elegant* she is, how she swings her hips as she moves, twisting her sloping shoulders to avoid the crowds.

But she's changed. There's something different about her, although he can't decide exactly what. Her face is fuller. Dark shadows are etched beneath her eyes. Her voice is deeper; its inflexions seem darkened by fatigue.

"Tea?" he suggests. "A cool lemonade? Let me buy you a drink. It's so *wonderful* to see you again." He guides her into the café he'd left half an hour ago. "Where are you living? Are you …" He hardly dares to say the word 'married'. "Lizzie told me you were on holiday. Is that Tessier fellow with you?"

Moira flinches. "No, he isn't. It didn't work out." She settles in her chair, smoothing her sleeves, adjusting her hat.

"I'm back with Lizzie and Mrs Farrell. Where else should I be?"

Walter's heart fills with joy. He wants to dance around the café, flinging his hat in the air, whooping with relief.

He tries to control his voice. "I'm glad to hear it, Moira. It's marvellous to have you back."

"Is it?" Her eyes fill with tears. "How kind of you to be so forgiving, Walter, so tolerant. I thought you might not want to see me again. Lizzie keeps saying, 'I told you so'—"

"Well, your disappearance was rather *sudden*."

"I know." She pulls at the fingers of her cotton gloves. "I left everyone in the lurch. I'm sorry. I couldn't help myself." She gives him a straight look. "But I've learned my lesson and I'm back. I'll never leave Oxford again."

She's surprisingly vague about what she has actually done during their year apart. He wants details but she tells him little. She'd spent the previous summer in the south of France, and had lived for a time in Paris, in an apartment on the Avenue des Champs-Elysées.

Then, abruptly, she clams up. "I don't want to talk about it," she says, raising her cup to her lips, but putting it down without drinking. "You don't need to know ... Tell me about yourself."

So he does, babbling about his work, his commissions, his teaching and his house, as if he only has one brief chance to impress her in case she vanishes again.

They walk through the centre of Oxford and pause in Walton Street. He hands her the parcel.

"Why the art paper and watercolours?"

"I discovered I could draw and paint. On holiday in the Mediterranean. It's something I've always wanted to do, but

29

never had the time. That is, not until …" She touches his arm. "Why don't you come in and look at some of my work? I brought twelve watercolours home with me." She hesitates. "And something else from France, too. Well, not some*thing*, some*one*. You might like to meet him."

"Oh?" His poor old heart misses another beat. Is she telling him she left Oxford with one beau and returned with another? Will he have to face a rival so soon? Before he's even come to blissful terms with her being back? Surely not … *Please God not.*

He summons his wits.

"I should love to meet whoever's with you." If it really is a rival he'll want to knock him to the ground.

The living room at the front of Lizzie Farrell's house is small and oppressively hot, as if it's captured the warmth of the afternoon and is holding on to it for dear life.

A peculiar smell greets him: one he vaguely identifies as sour milk. But as the kitchen's at the back of the house and there are no signs of teacups or milk jugs, he has no idea where it's coming from.

Lizzie sits on the narrow sofa, stitching a lace hem on to a linen skirt. She nods to Walter, saying a brisk, "Good afternoon," and responds to Moira's signal by getting to her feet.

"Would you excuse me? I need to finish something in the workshop."

Moira stands by the hearth, reaching up to remove her hat. She pats her hair and then steps to one side. She gestures to a wooden crib, half hidden by the length of her skirt.

"Here he is, Walter, the person I want you to meet. My son. He's six weeks old today. He's fast asleep."

30

Walter gasps and tries to swallow. The walls of the room zoom around his ears and away again, as if he's mounted a swing at St Giles Fair which has flung him to kingdom come. He slumps on to the nearest chair and stands up again, his legs shaking.

"Good *God*, Moira ... *That* was quick work."

"I know." She flushes. A mixture of guilt and triumph, sadness and joy flit across her face. "Pierre and I, we never *meant*—"

"I don't suppose you did."

"And giving birth ... The pain was ... It went on for days ... I nearly died."

She bites her lip and glances at the crib.

"But now he's here, a tiny human being, it's the most wonderful thing that's ever happened to me. When the midwife put him in my arms, I knew at once I'd bring him home to Oxford."

"I'm exceedingly glad you did!"

He hesitates. The implications of this astonishing revelation dawn on him. Part of him is deeply shocked. A child out of wedlock, and from Moira of all people. He'd never even *imagined* her as a mother, not with her confidence, her style.

But: a baby. This could give him the upper hand. For the first time, she's really vulnerable, even at his mercy. What if he plays her protector, *their* protector? What power over them he might have.

"May I take a closer look?"

"Of course." She bends over the crib. "He may be illegitimate, but who gives a pinch of snuff? I've never cared two hoots about the mealy-mouthed gossips. All I know is, my baby couldn't possibly be closer to my heart."

With a swift, practised movement, as if she'd been

31

making it all her life, she lifts the blanket-wrapped bundle into her arms and swings it round for him.

He looks down at a pudgy face, a small fist emerging from its blanket, a pink, toothless mouth opening and about to howl, damp wisps of blond curls – and two dark blue eyes looking directly into his.

Someone has pushed him off a cliff. He falls down a mountainside into a pit of instant and devoted adoration.

"Moira! You *are* a clever girl. He's absolutely *beautiful*!"

He touches the soft, round cheek. The howl stops. The baby stares up at him. Walter smiles back.

"His name's Felix." Pride gives her voice a new and lighter edge.

He takes the bundle from her. For the first time in his life, he holds the wonderful weight of a baby in his arms.

"That's beautiful, too. Felix is from the Latin *felicitas*. It means happiness."

On the Home Front

1908

W alter races back to Walton Crescent, his heart on fire, his head buzzing with plans.

Bridget has left for the day. His house feels cool, quiet and empty: absurdly large for its solitary occupant. In contrast, the house on Walton Street was bursting at the seams with women, workshops, sewing machines. There was barely room to swing a cotton frock, let alone a bouncing baby.

He leaves his tobacco and Henry's gifts in the hall. He rushes up to the attic. It'll make a *marvellous* nursery. There's room for a crib, a nanny's bed, space for the child to crawl on the floor, for those cupboards to be filled with toys.

He flings a window open. Warm air gusts into his face as he lets his imagination run riot. He'll buy a copy of *The Oxford Times*, and look through the SITUATIONS WANTED AND VACANT columns for a qualified nanny: someone experienced and reliable, but with a sense of fun.

On the first floor, Moira can have a bedroom of her own, at least when she and the baby first arrive. That will be a crucial factor in her agreeing to live with him. He'll insist they're merely sharing the house as good companions.

She can use a second bedroom as a studio, where she'll be able to paint to her heart's content. She'd shown him her canvases. They're perfectly acceptable background art: fruit or flowers, on wooden tables in soft sunlight, the kind of paintings people hang on their walls and never bother to look at. But she takes them seriously – and he fully intends to encourage her.

It's extraordinary, he tells himself as he leaps downstairs to the kitchen and searches the pantry for bread and cheese. His house is *ready* for Moira and Felix, as if it had been expecting them.

He'll smarten up the sitting room, buy a comfortable Chesterfield, ask a decorator friend to hang new wallpaper. Bridget can cook and clean for them all. He'll increase her pay, and she'll be delighted.

It's as if he'd been preparing for this great event, waiting for it, longing for it to happen. Now all he has to do is persuade Moira she wants it too.

He knows it might be a long, hard struggle. He'll throw his heart and soul into the battle until she agrees. Then, oh then, the day can't come soon enough: *then* there will be no going back.

Moira will be his and his alone.

It takes him three months of planning and persistence.

Week after week he arrives at her door with scented flowers, expensive leather Woodstock gloves, baby clothes for Felix, a furry teddy bear from De la Mere's in George Street, chocolate éclairs for tea.

He buys himself a cream linen suit and a navy cravat from Arthur Shepherd's on the High Street. He arrives for every visit looking as spick and span as a ship on her maiden voyage. He courts and cajoles, describing the glories he's offering.

One memorable afternoon he takes Moira by the hand. He makes her inspect all the changes he's made to his house: its new furniture, flowery curtains, spotless kitchen. He begs her to imagine the life he plans for them, full of space, cleanliness and light. He's sure she's tempted. Having her own bedroom and studio are the icing on the Walter Drummond cake.

By early October, when the skies have darkened and the Oxford trees have almost lost their leaves, he knows it's not a question of *whether* she'll say yes, but *when*.

Her excuse that she doesn't want to move Felix to another new home no longer holds water. The child thrives, cheerful and confident. He has a ready smile and eyes that change from blue to sparkling hazel. He grows in strength and shape beneath Walter's adoring gaze. Felix recognises Walter's voice and smile. He grasps his fingers and squeezes them ever so tight.

It's obvious that in Walton Street, Moira doesn't have an inch of space or a minute of spare time in which to paint. She resents helping Lizzie with the dressmaking and feels guilty when Felix wakes them all at night, hungry for food.

Walter knows his game of cards is playing his way. Ever the perfect gentleman, he kisses Moira's hand as he leaves and looks into her eyes.

"Will you say 'yes' very soon?" he whispers, so as not to wake the child. "Come to live with me, and we can be a proper family."

"I don't know." Moira's eyes are cold, her hand unresponsive. "Please stop pestering me, Walter. It's a big decision."

He slams out, his mouth dry with rage. How *dare* she

claim he's pestering her, after everything he's done. He marches into The Bird and Baby to spend the evening getting blind drunk on warm beer.

The following morning he wakes with a headache and an infuriating cough.

He's reached the end of his tether. Miserable and out of sorts, reluctant to face his canvas, he cycles to the chemist where he buys bottles of Eno's Fruit Salts and Veno's Cough Cure. He sits in the Covered Market café, drinking coffee and slurping several large spoonfuls of his medicines. The mixture is revolting. It can't possibly be doing him any good. He remembers how he'd plied Moira with tea that extraordinary first afternoon, unable to take his eyes off her. How *patient* he's been since then. Courteous, generous, understanding – even, some might say, heroic.

He watches a pair of lovers kissing in a corner. Overwhelmed by jealousy, he makes a bad-tempered decision. That afternoon, after his art class, he'll arrive at Moira's with an ultimatum. He'll demand that she make up her mind *on the spot*. The model who'll sit for his class that afternoon – a ravishing blonde called Alexandra, with black come-hither eyes and skin that shines like silk – has made it clear she'll jump into his bed any time he wants her.

The truth is, he *does* want Alexandra, but not as much as he wants Moira. But the chaste life he's led since Moira's return – he can hardly keep it up forever, *can* he? He's a man of flesh and blood, not a cardboard saint.

Later, he stands in her front room, his hat in his hands, trying to look calm, urging himself to spell out his demands. Felix sleeps peacefully in his crib. Moira fiddles with her sewing, then tosses it aside.

She looks up at him. "You're very quiet."

"The thing is," he blurts out in a rush before he loses courage, "I've come to a difficult decision. I won't be calling on you again."

She catches her breath. "Why ever not, Walter? I thought you *liked*—"

"I do. I more than *like* seeing you and Felix, as you well know. I adore you both. Since your return, the two of you have become the centre of my world. But I can't go *on* coming here to cajole and plead like a lovesick fool." He takes a deep breath. "I'll ask you one last time. Will you bring your beautiful Felix and come to live with me?"

Moira stands up. She walks towards the window, her long skirt trailing across the floor. He notices she looks thinner, more vulnerable. He longs to catch her in his arms, smother her with kisses, undress her, take her to his bed.

Surely she can't refuse him. Not any more.

She turns to look at him with one of her straight, dark, uncompromising stares.

"I'll come to live with you on one condition."

His heart jumps into his mouth. "*Anything*, Moira … Name it … Tell me."

"That you don't ask me to marry you."

He kneels at her feet. "I *promise* not to, ever again. Just having you with me will be more than enough." He stands up, takes her in his arms. "My darling Moira … *When* will you come to live with me?"

"Tomorrow afternoon," she says. "I've already packed my suitcases."

"Not that Mitchell girl!"

1908

The only fly in Walter's magnificent ointment is his father.

He must tell Henry his glad tidings, and as soon as possible. He'll have to see him the following morning, before Moira and Felix arrive, in case his father decides on the spur of the moment to drop in for his iced-buns tea.

He cycles to Wolvercote and finds Henry sitting at the breakfast table, inspecting the outside of his boiled egg.

"Morning, my boy!" Henry jumps to his feet. "This *is* a nice surprise. It's not Sunday, is it? I'm so absent-minded I can't even remember the days of the week."

"No, Papa, today's Friday. Please sit down and finish your breakfast." He pours himself a cup of coffee, loading sugar into it. It tastes tepid and disgusting. "I've some news for you. You probably won't like it, but I wanted to tell you before you heard it from anybody else."

"Out with it, my boy." Henry waves his spoon. "I hope you won't be leaving me for a teaching post in London."

"No, Papa." He stares at his reflection in the coffee pot.

It could do with a good clean. Not his face, the pot.

He clears his throat and squeaks, "It's about Moira."

Henry stares at him. "Not that Mitchell girl!"

"Yes, Papa."

"I thought she was abroad—"

"She was, but now she's back in Oxford. She's been staying with Lizzie Farrell." He adds as fast as he can, "But now she's coming to live with me. She has a baby son called Felix. She'll bring him too, of course."

"A baby *son?*" Henry gasps. "Is it *yours?*"

"No, Papa. I only wish he were. Moira and I, as yet, we've never … at least not yet."

As he hears the details of the liaison, Henry pushes back his chair and dances with rage around the breakfast table, hardly listening, his face purple, his eyes bulging. Then he slumps at the table, picks up his spoon and crashes it down on his egg. Its shattered white and yellow innards curl over the cloth and lie in a congealed heap.

"*Now* look what you've done." Walter butters a piece of cold toast. "You'd better eat this instead."

Walter's patience and Henry's fury continue for half an hour. Finally Walter gets to his feet, sick of listening to his father rant and rage.

"I must go, Papa. I've a hundred things to do before my new family arrive." He clears his throat. "I'm sorry you feel so strongly about the way I choose to lead my life, but it makes no difference to my love for you. I hope our weekly meetings will continue. I'll see you on Sunday as usual."

Henry wipes his mouth. "If you must."

"I suppose it would be too much to ask whether I could bring Moira and Felix with me? I should love you to meet them."

"I *forbid* you to bring them here. I can't *possibly* condone what you're doing. As for who you're doing it *with*, words fail me. You couldn't have made a worse choice in all the world. Nothing good will come of your living with that woman, you mark my words. You'll rue the day you met her."

Walter cycles home, his teeth clenched, determined not to let Henry's bitterness cloud his triumph. The arrival of Moira and Felix will mark one of the happiest days of his life. Henry is an ancient stick-in-the-mud, a bigoted conservative. When Moira asks how his father has taken the news, he'll make light of the episode. He's too ashamed to admit he couldn't talk any sense whatsoever into the man he loves.

The day becomes a whirl of activity. Bridget – initially very shocked to hear his news, but glad of the extra wages – flies from floor to floor, giving the house an extra polish. Fires and candles are lit. Supper is cooked and left to cool in the pantry.

Moira and Lizzie come and go in drizzles of rain, carrying boxes and parcels, clothes and crockery, toys, shoes, pots and pans. Two delivery men arrive, carrying a small antique mahogany bureau. It belonged to Moira's mother, so she refuses to part with it. Walter assumes that she managed without it in Paris well enough, but he says nothing. It's carted upstairs to Moira's studio, and placed underneath the window where it immediately looks at home.

Finally, Felix himself is trundled over the road in a new perambulator, his cheeks rosy, his damp woollen hat squashed over his eyes.

Walter lifts the child out of his pram. Felix, whose nappy

needs changing, sticks a thumb in his eye, which makes Walter stumble over the threshold. He collides with the hall stand which is not where he'd left it two hours ago.

"This is your new home, Felix Mitchell," he says.

Felix grabs a hat from the hall stand and crams it on to Walter's head.

"Here you may eat and sleep and laugh and play to your heart's content. If there's anything you ever want, you are to let me know ... Welcome aboard."

With Felix balanced on one hip as if he's an experienced father, he reaches for Moira's hand and raises it to his lips.

"Finally, my darling girl ... I've waited for this moment all my life."

Christmas Festivities

1908

The house in which Walter has lived for the past three years now changes character around him.

Suddenly it smells of women, wet washing and soiled nappies. It feels full of life. It sounds different. Moira constantly talks to Felix: not private baby babble, but long sentences as if her child is an adult who understands everything. Even when Walter is working in his studio, he can hear the echoes of her marvellous voice reverberating from room to room. He listens to her singing as she paints, or giving instructions to their nanny, or the sound of her footsteps flying up and down the stairs, or to the wheels of the pram as she trundles Felix into the street for their daily walk.

Sometimes Moira's Votes-for-Women friends arrive to take tea in the kitchen and discuss their next meeting. Or Lizzie knocks at the door, bringing a new frock for Moira and clothes for Felix. Their nanny knows Bridget's family and is a constant source of salacious gossip. There's always some hustle or bustle going on.

For the first seven nights, overjoyed to have Moira with him, he keeps his distance. At the end of every evening he retires to his bedroom, allowing Moira to go to hers, determined not to force the issue and possibly scare her off.

But he leaves his bedroom door ajar and lies in bed, praying she'll come to him.

The evening she does is one he'll never forget.

She taps on his door. Her dark hair tumbles down her back. She wears a knee-length blue-silk peignoir. It's semi-transparent. She looks so beautiful, so vulnerable and feminine he feels frozen with longing.

"You've been really kind and patient with me, Walter. Wonderful with Felix. You're the most generous man alive. How can I ever thank you?"

"You know exactly how."

"Yes." Her peignoir slips from her shoulders. "Indeed, I do."

Throughout the autumn, Walter continues to spend Sundays with Henry, who's stopped turning up for tea.

One Sunday in late November, he decides on confrontation.

"How long can you keep this up, Papa?"

"Keep *what* up?" Henry pretends to search for his newspaper.

"This not talking about Moira, not asking after Felix. It's ridiculous, and it must stop. I want you to come to us for Christmas."

"I can't. My Wytham friends have asked me for Christmas Day."

Walter clenches his fists. "Then come to us for supper on Christmas Eve. Come at six o'clock so you can see Felix. Spend a couple of hours with us. Moira will roast a goose.

I'll arrange for a cab to drive you home. *Please*, Papa." His eyes begin to burn. "We may not have many more Christmases together."

Henry jams his pince-nez on his nose. He looks like an angry parrot.

"All right, I give in. If you must live with that Mitchell girl, I suppose I'll have to get used to it." Henry lights a match, his hands trembling. "Christmas Eve it is."

"That's *wonderful*, Papa. Shall I come to collect you?"

"Thanks, but I'm perfectly capable of getting to yours on my own."

"Very well. Moira will be delighted. I'll tell Felix his grandpapa will be coming to see him. He can call you Grandpa Henry. Gramp for short."

"Strictly speaking, I'm not even a distant relative."

"Who gives a fig for strictly speaking? Live your life by your *own* rules, that's what I say. I'm Felix's father in everything but name. And ecstatically happy to be so."

Henry leans forward in his chair. "That Mitchell girl, she really has struck gold. Does she have any idea how *fortunate* she is?"

"Who cares?" He changes the subject. "What have you been reading?"

Henry takes out a handkerchief and coughs into it. "I've been hunkered down over an article by this journalist chappie. Claims there's a war brewing in Europe."

Walter strokes his right knee. Badly injured it was, that afternoon on Port Meadow. He'd been seven years old and almost drowned in the river. A stranger had fished him out in the nick of time, taken him to hospital. He'd broken his knee in several places. It had never healed properly, which meant he couldn't be a soldier or a sailor or anything heroic.

"Well, *I* can't fight, can I?"

"No, don't remind me. Almost lost you. Only wish *I* still could!"

"Really? Dress up in a hideous uniform and ponce about with a pistol strapped to your shoulder?"

Henry glares at him. "It's called fighting for your country, dear boy. Taking arms against a sea of troubles."

Walter snorts, lighting his pipe, glancing at Henry over its drift of briar tobacco smoke. "So now you think I'm Hamlet, eh? ... If I'm Hamlet, where do *you* fit in?"

Henry wheezes with laughter. "I'm the bloody ghost on the battlements."

"Not quite, you're not!" He puts down his pipe. "Not before you've had supper with me and the most beautiful woman in the world."

"My goodness!" Moira says that evening. "I thought Henry couldn't stand the sight of me! How on *earth* did you persuade him?"

"He agreed to come almost at once. I was astonished."

"Maybe he was just waiting to be asked?"

He stares across at the seductive creature who now shares his bed without being asked and gives him so much joy.

"Or maybe he's curious to see how beautifully we get along."

Preparations for their special Christmas supper begin. The house is cleaned from top to toe. While Walter paints and Felix sleeps, Moira goes shopping with an empty perambulator. She returns laden with flour, eggs, brandy butter and dried fruit for their Christmas cake, bottles of wine and spices for its mulling, cheeses and an enormous ham, potatoes and parsnips for roasting, and cranberries for the sauce. She orders their goose from the Covered Market:

an enormous bird that will feed them for two days. She'll collect it on the morning of Christmas Eve, and put it straight into the oven. She even buys a copy of Mrs Beeton's *Household Management* and sits for hours consulting its recipes.

At the end of term, Walter spends several afternoons shopping at Morton's Grand Christmas Bazaar on Cornmarket. He buys hand-painted wooden toys and a cheerful-looking gollywog for Felix, a silver pendant and matching bracelet for Moira, a winter suit and woollen waistcoat for Henry, and crystallised fruit, dark chocolate and Mocha coffee. Then he adds an enormous box of baubles, and hauls a small Christmas tree home from the market.

He spends that evening decorating the brave fir, admiring how its branches sparkle by the sitting-room fire. He's never celebrated the holiday properly before. In the past, Henry did all the work. He'd merely sat back and enjoyed his efforts.

When Christmas Eve dawns in the pouring rain, Moira leaves the house early under a large umbrella to collect the goose.

Walter spends the morning finishing a portrait and the afternoon arranging his gifts beneath the tree. By six o'clock the mouth-watering scent of roast goose permeates the house. Fed, washed and ready to be shown off, Felix burbles happily in his crib by the fire. Flushed from cooking, Moira changes into a ravishing red velvet dress and lifts her dark hair into an elaborate swirl.

Walter relaxes in his sitting-room chair. At last he has a family he longs to share.

∞

Henry's always punctual, if not early, for every appointment. He'd taught Walter its importance. So when Henry doesn't appear on the dot of six, Walter thinks it extremely odd, but assumes his Papa must be caught up in other Christmas festivities.

The minutes tick by. He lifts Felix from his crib, dancing him around the room: a nightly exercise during which the baby crows with delight.

When Henry hasn't appeared by seven, Walter begins to sweat with anxiety. He opens the front door, gazes along the wet street, gasps at the freezing air, shuts the door and paces the hall, dodging the perambulator and his bicycle.

"For goodness *sake*, Walter." Moira stands in the doorway. "You're making me dizzy. We must eat or the food will be ruined."

"I don't understand. Papa is *never* late—"

"Well, he's certainly late tonight. Maybe he couldn't face meeting me after all."

"Nonsense. He's a straightforward fellow. If he hadn't wanted to be here, he'd have told me."

Moira gathers up her skirts. "Let's eat, unless you want to celebrate with burned goose." She flounces down to the kitchen. "Come on, Walter. Don't just stand there."

He swallows everything she puts before him, not tasting a morsel, staring at Henry's empty place. At eight o'clock he drinks a third glass of mulled wine, throws on his raincoat, and climbs on his bicycle.

It's still pouring.

"I expect Papa has got the days muddled up." The blasts of cold air freeze his eyeballs. "I'll cycle over and make sure he's fine. If anything *is* wrong – maybe he's fallen down the stairs, if he needs a doctor – I'll stay with him. Don't wait up."

The gas lamps along his way flicker with sporadic life.

He cycles towards Wolvercote, over the bridge, battling squalls of sleety rain and vicious wind, praying Henry's cottage will reveal lights in the windows, with inside the warmth of a fire and an abject apology: "Great heavens, dear boy! I'm *terribly* sorry! Must have got my days mixed up … Here, these small gifts are for you."

But the cottage hunches in darkness.

He lets himself in, calling out as he does so. He's met by silence, the drips of rain as they fall off his hat, and the wildly worried beating of his heart. He lights the gas lamp on the hall table. Next to it sits a wicker basket. Three carefully wrapped parcels nestle waiting for him. Walter peers at their labels, each addressed in Henry's flourishing hand:

Felix, Walter, Moira.

A lump rises in his throat. He turns into the darkness of the living room, the lamp in his hand.

Henry is lying on the floor by the fire. The poker has slipped from his grasp. The dying embers of the burned apple logs murmur and hum.

He kneels at his father's side.

"Papa … Papa … Wake up, my dearest Papa! What are you doing here? … You should be with us!"

He takes Henry's hands in his. They are cold as ice. He touches his father's motionless cheek, feels for a pulse, knowing there will be none. The rain from his hat and coat drip on to the lifeless body.

So do his tears.

Two days later he slumps over a cup of Bovril in the Covered Market café, still numb with grief. Every time he closes his eyes, he remembers his Papa's face: the puffy yellow skin, thin strands of hair, blue-veined eyelids, open mouth.

He's eaten nothing all day but he can't face food. Even the meaty scent of the Bovril makes him queasy. He has so many urgent matters to arrange – the funeral, the flowers, the hymns, the wake, the sale of Henry's cottage and his books – but no energy for any of them. He dreads going home, having to face Moira's stern gaze and hard-nosed questions.

He sips the Bovril, forcing himself to swallow. He's Henry's sole inheritor. He'll be able to buy a house, a car, clothes, take a holiday. Yet all he wants is to have Henry sitting opposite him with his cigarette and wheezy cough.

How will he ever spend Sundays again without thinking hour after hour about his beloved Papa?

Somebody taps him on the shoulder.

"Walter Drummond?"

He looks up to see a pair of shining dark eyes, round rosy cheeks and a wide-brimmed hat.

"I'm Alexandra Cox. One of your models. Do you remember me?"

Blood rushes to his face. She's the ravishing blonde with come-hither eyes and skin that shines like silk.

"Of course. How nice to—" His voice fails. "Please. Won't you join me?"

"Thank you. You looked so unhappy, I felt I had to say hello." Alexandra sits opposite him. She's wearing a coat so tight he fears it might explode from the straining flesh. "I heard about your father. I wanted to say how sorry I am."

His eyes fill with hot tears. "He tried to be mother and father to me, you know. He was an old-fashioned man, but he was my best friend. I loved him very much."

"I'm terribly sorry." Alexandra leans across the table, takes his shaking hands in hers. "Why don't you come home with me? I live just round the corner on Holywell Street with my mother, but she's at work in Cowley. She won't be back until after six. I promise to make you feel better. Drink a glass of wine with me. Just for half an hour."

What a contrast with how cold and reticent Moira had been, when he'd told her Henry was dead: "I'm sorry, Walter, of course I am, but I never really *knew* him. Be honest. He never wanted to have anything to do with me."

He takes out his handkerchief, mops his face, dries his eyes, flicks back his wonderful head of hair. "Do you know what?"

He gives Alexandra a smile that's sad, wistful and just a tad flirtatious.

"I'm going to say yes. That's the best offer I've had all day."

Secrets and Lies

1911

Walter waves goodbye to the last of his art class. He dashes out of Beaumont Street and into the Ashmolean to talk to a friend about a new commission.

As he emerges from the coolness of the museum, he's more aware than ever of the heat. It's a baking-hot June afternoon: too hot to do anything but relax in the shade of a tree-filled garden. Except that in Walton Crescent, he only has a shabby backyard just large enough for a coal shed and a washing line.

He thinks longingly about taking a gentle stroll in the University Parks, sleeping under a tree for an hour. He's been working so hard recently, he deserves a rest. Perhaps he'll call briefly on Alexandra on his way home. His adorable, compliant Alex. Always overjoyed to see him. Or on Jilly. Or Melanie. Each girl has modelled for him. Each has become an enthusiastic mistress. He can't decide which one of them he likes the most.

He walks slowly down the steps of the Ashmolean and hesitates. He has a new portrait of Moira sitting on his easel at home: a surprise present he's managing to keep a secret and hopes to finish without asking her to sit for him. It's excellent work, the best he's ever done.

But it's so hot, a break might do him good.

He catches a glimpse of an elegant woman outside the Randolph Hotel, just across the road. She looks deliciously cool and fresh in her pale blue frock and stylish hat. She's holding the hand of a young boy who wears a smart sailor-suit and smiles into her face.

He blinks. His mouth drops open. Good God! It's Moira with Felix. She hadn't told him she was going out, or that she'd be taking Felix anywhere ...

And wait a minute. A man stands beside Moira, talking rapidly, gesticulating, looking into her eyes. Then he bends and kisses Felix on both cheeks. Now he's clasping Moira's free hand, raising it to his lips: intent, passionate.

Walter stares across at him, his eyes burning. He'd recognise that blond hair anywhere, that tanned skin, those swaggering movements. Nobody else wears such expensive clothes with such panache.

It's Pierre Tessier. Moira's been seeing that French fellow again.

Walter's first reaction is to leap across the road and confront them, but Moira has already turned away. Still holding Felix's hand, she starts to walk into the centre of town. He shrinks back against the stone wall of the museum. Tessier has bowed to Moira with a flourish and disappeared into the hotel.

Startled and furious, a thousand questions whirling in his mind, Walter races home, oblivious of the heat, the crowds, the street-sellers, pushing everyone out of his way.

How had Moira and that French fellow arranged to

meet? He hadn't noticed any letters for her. Was this the first time? If not, how often have they seen each other? How *dare* Moira meet another man behind his back? Have they told Felix who his *real* father is?

Sweat drips down his face. The thought of Felix loving another man more than him is beyond contemplation. Who has cared for Felix from the very week he arrived in Oxford? Loved him, nurtured him, read to him, sung to him, fed him, clothed him, danced him in his arms, given him the best any child could expect? *He* had, with never a word of reproach to Moira that she was saddling him with another man's child.

How *dare* that Frenchman step in now, pretending he cared?

Walter hurls himself through his front door and dashes up to Moira's room. He opens her bureau, churns among its papers, looking for love letters. There's nothing: only lists of drawings and commissions, household duties, recipes. Moira has either destroyed anything private or locked it away.

He tears down to his studio. He stares at the unfinished portrait on his easel. She smiles serenely out at him, more beautiful than ever.

Panting with rage, he slumps on to the chaise longue, his head in his hands, his heart leaping and diving. He must calm down, think straight. Invent a plan.

He'll ask Moira where she and Felix had been that afternoon. Will she tell him the truth? If she doesn't, tomorrow he'll watch her every move. If she goes into Oxford, he'll stalk her. If she enters the Randolph, if by any ghastly chance he manages to catch her with the Frenchman again, urgent action will be needed. He'll either have to talk to her straight, have the matter out with her, get her to promise she'll never meet Tessier again, or …

Or what?

He has mistresses, but that's different. He's a man. He's allowed to take comfort in another woman's arms. It's not as if he's doing any *harm*. Whereas Moira has an absolute duty to remain his and his alone.

The difference between his feelings for his mistresses and for Moira is this: if he thinks about Alexandra or Jilly or Melanie being with somebody else, he merely wishes them every happiness.

If he even *contemplates* Moira kissing another man, he burns with a jealousy so dark and bitter it's positively frightening.

Of course, sexually, things between him and Moira have cooled since those first ecstatic weeks. He tries to remember why. Henry's death started it. Moira seemed incapable of offering him sympathy. He'd felt so miserable and lost without his Papa, particularly on Sundays.

"Move on with your life, Walter," she'd told him, and gone off with her Votes-for-Women friends, laughing and chattering as if nothing had happened.

Should he move away from Oxford? Get her to leave the city with him, go to live somewhere else, where it'll be impossible for her to meet Tessier? He'd have to invent some cast-iron excuses for their move.

And where would they go? Perhaps he could persuade her she needed a holiday? Then, once they'd left Oxford, he'd make plans for them to stay away for ever.

He paces up and down his studio. After he'd organised the repair of Henry's cottage, they could have moved into it. He loved the cosy rooms, the wild garden, the memories of his childhood near Port Meadow. But Moira said she felt Henry's ghost in every corner. She refused point blank to live there.

So he'd sold it, in tears when the contract was signed. He has money to buy a place of their own, but over and again he's hesitated. Whenever he and Moira had seen somewhere new, they'd argued about it. A bad-tempered inertia had taken over. They'd stopped looking. But their rented house is too small, the backyard dull and poky with no space for Felix to play.

Sooner or later they'll be forced to find a proper home.

Perhaps now is the right time? Seeing Tessier again had been a grim warning.

If he wants to hold on to the woman he loves and the child he adores, there's not a moment to lose.

The early stages of his plan work only too well. When he asks Moira over supper that evening what she'd done during the day, she says she'd taken Felix to the Covered Market to buy him new shoes. He duly admires them, his heart sinking.

The following day, he catches Moira waiting for the postman, pushing a letter into her pocket, dashing up to her room. He keeps his studio door open all morning, straining to hear her movements. At lunchtime, she leaves the house, saying she's going shopping.

Following her, he watches her glide into the Randolph Hotel.

For two hours he waits in the hotel bar, drinking coffee and a large brandy until, her cheeks flushed and her hat at a new angle, she emerges on to the steps, alone. She wipes tears from her eyes before she crosses the road and drifts towards Walton Crescent.

Walter is engulfed in a wave of jealousy so bitter he can hardly breathe.

So Moira and that French fellow *are* lovers. What *else*

could they have been doing for two hours in a hotel room? He takes refuge in Alexandra's arms. She notices he's hardly his usual passionate self, asks him what the matter is. His mind – and indeed his body – seem to be elsewhere.

Apologising, he says he's hot and tired. He rolls off the bed. Sweat trickles down his back. He puts on his damp shirt and crumpled linen jacket. He can't stop thinking about Moira. They haven't made love for weeks, maybe months. Far too long.

He must do something drastic to stop the rot.

That Sunday he persuades her to go out with him in his car.

After selling Henry's cottage, he'd bought a top-of-the-range Ford sports car, with a beautiful coach-built body, from Coxeter's in Oxford for five hundred and fifteen pounds. It was his only large purchase and he's mighty proud of it. At first it was thrilling to pile his family into its smart leather seats. During the summer of 1910 they'd driven to small villages all over Oxfordshire.

But the journeys began to pall. Felix is not a good traveller and quickly feels carsick. No sooner have they left Walton Crescent than he wants to go home. He's a restless child who loves playing with his toys on the nursery floor or running in the University Parks. He only sits still to eat, and then only for five minutes at a time.

Walter drives Moira to the Blenheim Palace gardens.

He carries a picnic basket with sandwiches, strawberries and champagne. They walk across the grass and over the bridge to Rosamond's Well, where he spreads a mohair blanket close to the waters of the lake. The summer's heat has already baked the green grass into gold. Above them hangs an Italian-blue sky, cloudless and still.

Moira looks pale and listless. The colour only returns to her cheeks after she's swallowed a glass of champagne.

He says, "We should do this more often. Spend time together alone. We're always so busy, what with work and Felix and everything."

"Indeed." Moira stares across the lake, her face expressionless. Is she even listening?

"I've been thinking." He looks intently at her, desperate for her attention. "Why don't we take a holiday? How would you like to visit your aunt in Cornwall?"

Moira turns her head to look at him. "Aunt Beatrice in Newlyn?"

"Why not? I've *always* wanted to meet her. We could drive to Cornwall, stay with her for a few days, then go further down the coast to St Ives. I had a wonderful holiday there with Henry. Artists work all along the harbour. You could take your paints. The beaches there are beautiful. Felix could race around to his heart's content. We could teach him to swim. I'd love to go back."

"And when exactly were you thinking of going?"

"The moment term ends in a few weeks' time."

"Impossible." She turns her head away. "My exhibition opens in a fortnight at the Ryman Gallery. It'll run for two weeks. I'll have to be at the gallery every day to meet buyers." She adds, "It must have slipped your mind."

"Indeed it had not—"

"You've also forgotten that Lizzie is marrying Christopher Dawkins in July. I'm to be Matron of Honour."

"Of course I haven't forgotten."

He'd been so busy worrying about Tessier, searching her room for letters, stalking her when she goes out, he can barely remember what day of the week it is.

"I'm looking forward to both events." He refills their

glasses with a shaking hand. "We could go *after* Lizzie's wedding, couldn't we?"

She glances coldly at him, reaches for a strawberry. Curving her lips around the ripe fruit, she gives him one of her long, stern stares.

"I suppose we could," she says. "As long as we plan on coming back."

He drives them slowly home, perspiring and slightly drunk.

She complains the road is full of dust, it's getting in her eyes. He promises to buy her a pair of modern goggles. He feels proud of himself. He's managed not to mention that Frenchman's name, and he's sowed the seeds of his holiday idea. If he can find a cottage by the sea, somewhere cool in summer and cosy in winter, somewhere private, intimate and absolutely *theirs*, how happy he'll be, for ever and ever amen.

Over the following weeks he talks about his Cornish holiday idea whenever he can. He tells Felix that making sandcastles is glorious fun. He buys him a wooden bucket and spade. The child bangs the two together all day long and half into the night.

He helps Moira with her exhibition. He trundles twenty-two watercolours to the High Street gallery, astonished by how hard she's worked to assemble the collection – and wildly jealous of its enthusiastic reception. He bribes a friend to tell her at the preview, which he also helps to organise and wholly pays for, that in St Ives her paintings will sell like hot cakes for exorbitantly high prices.

She listens intently. She seems impressed.

Gearing himself up for Lizzie's wedding, one morning in July, he's astonished when Moira tells him over breakfast that the ceremony planned for the following weekend at St Giles Church has been cancelled.

"What on *earth* has happened?"

"I'm furious." Moira rattles plates on to the table. "Lizzie thought long and hard about accepting Christopher's proposal. She'd spent a *fortune* on her wedding dress. It's soft ivory satin, trimmed with old lace. But Christopher had second thoughts, says he's not the marrying kind. Lizzie has been in tears for two days. Nothing will cheer her up."

"Perhaps it would help," he thanks his lucky stars, "if you asked Lizzie and Mrs Farrell to come to St Ives with us? We could drive down there first, get ourselves settled. Then if we like it, you could ask them to join us." He gives her a winning smile. "That would cheer her up, wouldn't it? Nobody can be in tears sitting in a deckchair beside the sea. Certainly not while eating Cornish ice cream."

"Do you know what, Walter?" Moira meets his eyes over the rim of her cup. "That might just be one of your better ideas."

Two other unexpected factors play into his hands.

One is the weather. The unbearable heat continues. It roasts Oxford's streets and its occupants, scorches the grass in the University Parks, dries up the city's rivers and canals, buckles the railway lines, makes the drains stink and fills the air with dust. By the middle of July, desperate farmers are already harvesting their crops in case they are burned to a crisp.

Felix develops a form of dry eczema, patches of which scatter his body. His arms and legs swarm with dark-pink scabs. The doctor blames the weather, recommends Cuticura soap and ointment. Bathing the child becomes impossibly painful. He's often awake all night, scratching his skin sore.

By the middle of August, Moira is at her wits' end.

One evening, when the house is so hot they've left the front door open, hoping for a miraculous breeze, she rustles into Walter's studio.

"How far have you got with your latest?"

He dunks a brush in turpentine. "This is almost finished. The paint's drying faster than I can apply it. Damn this infernal heat."

"I agree. I've had enough. Felix isn't getting any better. If I have another sleepless night, I'll go mad. Lizzie will follow us to the coast once we've found somewhere to live and tell her we like it. You'll be glad to know it's Cornwall here we come."

"At last!" He takes his beloved girl in his arms. "I *know* you won't regret it, sweetheart."

He smooths an oily hand over Moira's damp forehead, his heart bursting with relief.

"We'll go the day after tomorrow. Nanny can have a month off. Ask Bridget to make us a picnic lunch. And tell Felix that soon he'll be beside the sea."

He lifts Moira off her feet, swings her around the burning studio.

Now it will be goodbye to Oxford and the bad old ways. They will *never* come back. Their Cornish life will become their paradise.

And Moira, the woman who has somehow always eluded him, will be his and his alone.

Act Two

Sprinter

1936

A bitterly cold morning grips an iron fist.

Across the frozen sweep of parkland dipping away from Blenheim Palace, every blade of grass stands to attention, stiff and pearly white. Paralysed by snow, trees spread their branches, waiting for the thaw. The sky lours, an implacable steely grey. Against its stillness seagulls call for food, swooping over the glassy lake, outraged as they skid with flapping wings on to its ice-bound waters.

The sound of laughter rings over the bridge. Two horses trot nimbly into sight, their hooves cracking against the gravel path, their breath swirling in the frozen air. One is larger, older, more experienced, her coat a glossy black. The other, younger, is the colour of ripe chestnut, a white stripe streaking his nose.

Their riders are women: trim, immaculately dressed in tight black jackets and white jodhpurs, their faces pink with exertion, their cheeks flushed with delight. For an hour they've been riding their favourite mounts and now they're returning to Blenheim Palace, eyes shining, thighs gripping, gloved hands guiding. Once off the path and on the grass again, their trot becomes a gallop.

An open sports car roars through the arch of Blenheim's gate at the end of the long drive. It zooms towards the Palace. Its driver spots the horses and their riders. Joy and recognition flash across his face. He grins, increasing his speed, waving an arm, honking the horn, shouting a greeting.

His eyes fix on the riders, not on the way ahead. The car skids over an icy bend. For a single perilous instant it looks as if the driver intends his car to make straight for the horses. The glossy black one takes no notice, bravely gallops on. The younger chestnut panics, alarmed and terrified. He bucks suddenly, rearing his head. His front legs claw the air. His neigh – ferocious and desperate – cracks across the snow.

Her rider gasps and shudders. Her hands falter on the reins. She cries out, letting them slip altogether. She falls headlong on to the frost-hardened grass and lies there, limp as a wet autumn leaf.

Her companion shrieks for help. The car screeches to a halt. The driver flings the door open and pounds towards her.

The runaway horse, freed of his burden, tosses his head. He gallops across the grass to the end of the drive. Then, skidding and stumbling on the icy cobblestones, he crashes out through the Triumphal Arch into the centre of Woodstock.

That same morning, eighteen-year-old Eleanor Drummond and her parents, Walter and Anne, are attending Sunday service at St Mary Magdalene's in the centre of Woodstock. Only Anne is inspired by deep devotion. Walter and Eleanor sit beside her not because they are particularly religious, but because they like keeping Anne happy, enjoy meeting their neighbours, appreciate the feeling of community and adore singing hymns together in special harmony.

Father and daughter look strikingly alike, although Walter's dark hair is greying at the temples. Both have deep-set, violet-blue eyes that light up with ready laughter, sharp noses and full lips. They share a similar sense of humour, wear their clothes with nonchalance and take each new day joyfully as it comes.

Florence Budd, the baker's daughter, pounds away on the organ with extra panache, her massive bosom heaving, her face pink with triumph. Everyone sings the hymns with unusual relish: their familiar words are considered afresh, every syllable clearly spelled out into the chilly air.

The Rector – genial, kindly, everyone's friend – offers ritual prayers for the recovery and health of King George V. He'd said them before, eight years ago, in 1928. But this time things are different. This time, everyone knows, their prayers, however fervent, will not help.

Eleanor finds it hard to concentrate, either on the hymns or the sermon. She's in her first year of reading English at Somerville College, Oxford, and her head is full of plans. The Hilary term began only two days ago when Walter drove her to College with her bags, books and files. Yesterday she'd taken Collections, an exam based on her vacation reading. She's only returned to Woodstock to celebrate her mother's fortieth birthday before she returns to her small room in West with its single bed, dainty fire and daily scuttle of coal.

Eleanor loves the Spartan feel to her College room, its view on to the green lawn of the quad, its sense of quiet purpose. She can hardly wait to return.

The moment the service ends, she takes her father's arm.

"Let's escape before we're waylaid by neighbours. I want

to get back to College as soon as we've eaten, and I still need to wrap Mummy's birthday present."

Walter pats her hand. "What have you bought her?"

"Some cushion covers she can embroider. And some beautiful silk thread."

Anne Drummond is already deep in conversation with a friend.

Walter taps his wife on her shoulder. "I'll see you back at the house, dear. I'm going to work on my painting before luncheon."

Father and daughter turn into the aisle, and push their way out of church.

Walter begins to hum one of the hymns, *"Oh, God, our help in ages past."* He catches Eleanor's eye, gives her his swift, infectious smile. "But I don't think even He can help the poor old King. It's happened so fast. Last year we were celebrating the Silver Jubilee. Never been to so many marvellous junkets in my life."

During the service a bitter wind has sprung up. Billows of powdery snow gather on every ledge, flinging icy dust into their eyes. Hunched against it, they dash across the memorial garden and turn on to Park Street. Their much-loved eighteenth-century house lies a few minutes' walk away.

The sound of a horse's hooves cracking on cobblestones startles them, making them glance over their shoulders. A riderless chestnut horse comes careering down the street, his head tossing, his eyes wild.

Walter grips her hand. "I know that horse, Ellie. It's Sprinter, from Blenheim." He pulls away. "I must stop him or he'll kill himself."

Before she can say a word, her father hurtles across the street and flings himself at Sprinter's head.

It's the last thing the horse needs. Born and bred at Blenheim, Sprinter knows its gardens, its bridges and its pathways – but he does not know Woodstock. The throng of people in the street, their staring faces, their shocked voices disturb him. The cold white stuff blowing into his eyes skews his vision, making him throw back his head. The reins no longer restrain or guide him. He's known nothing like this freedom, ever before. Then this man rushes up to him, wearing a silly hat and flailing his arms.

Filled with sudden fury, Sprinter lashes out. He kicks the man hard: first in the stomach, then the head. Then, for good measure, he kicks again.

The cold white stuff is coming down even faster. Skidding, Sprinter tramples on the fallen limbs. Then, snorting with triumph, frothing at the mouth, ignoring the cries of alarm circling his head, he gallops on.

Eleanor stares at her father lying in the middle of the street. She's locked into a nightmare, unable to move. Her lips are so cold she can't move them to call out. Her voice rises only to a squeak.

In seconds, an anxious crowd gathers around Walter: a huddle of coats and hats, pushing and shoving, murmuring concern.

Someone shouts, "That's Walter Drummond, ain't it? Good Lord above! Is he *dead*?"

The words spur Eleanor into action. Slithering on the icy cobblestones, she elbows her way through the crowd.

"Excuse me, that's my father. Please let me pass."

She kneels at Walter's side, the icy cold snaking to her thighs.

He stares into her face, his hands flailing. "Ellie? What happened? Why am I lying here?"

"Sprinter kicked you, Daddy. The horse has gone berserk. He's probably halfway to Combe by now, creating havoc."

Blood dribbles down Walter's forehead into his eyes. "Where's your mother?" He clutches his stomach. "I want my Annie. Why isn't she *here*?"

Eleanor looks up into the anxious eyes and worried faces. "Please, could someone find Mrs Drummond—"

Anne weaves her way through the crowd. "What's happened? Why is your father lying there? Who hit him?"

"Kicked, Mummy. A runaway horse. Daddy tried to stop him."

"*Typical!*" Anne clutches her husband's hands. "For God's *sake*, Walter! Trust *you* to rush in. Why are you *always* so foolish?"

"I'm sorry, Annie." Dazed and pale, Walter stares into his wife's face without focusing. "I had to stop the horse."

Anne smooths her gloved fingers over the spurting blood, trying to halt it, smearing it away from Walter's eyes. "Can you stand up? Eleanor, take your father's shoulder. Get him on his feet."

He slumps between the two women, a dead weight.

"I'm all right." His lips are blue with shock. "Just bruised, is all. I'll probably have a blinding headache for a week."

Anne nods at the gawping crowd. "We're fine, thank you. That's my husband's hat. Could you let us through? We live just down there on the High Street."

A woman's voice calls out. "Reckon he's been badly hurt, ma'am. Seen a kickin' like that once afore. Your husband will need a doctor, real fast."

They half-carry, half-drag Walter down the street. A neighbour has darted ahead of them and alerted Vera, their housekeeper. She's waiting for them as they struggle towards her.

"Great heavens, sir! What *have* you done?"

He stumbles into the house, undoing his coat with trembling fingers. "It's only a scratch, Vera. Looks worse than it is. I'm just a bit shaky, is all. I'll take to my bed for an hour. A stiff whisky would go down a treat."

"Bring me some hot water, please, Vera." Anne throws off her hat and coat. "A flannel and some bandages. And a cup of sweet tea."

As Walter clutches the banisters and hauls himself upstairs, Anne turns to Eleanor. "Run round to Dr Fagg. Say you're sorry to disturb him on a Sunday, but this is an emergency."

She summons the doctor. But when he arrives, Walter flaps him away.

"Sorry to disturb you, Doc, on a Sunday and all. I'm fine. Just got a bit of a headache. No need to examine me. My wife has patched me up. She'll give you a bell in the morning."

They sit with him in turn, half expecting him to leap to his feet, declare he's quite better and will go to his studio.

Eleanor remembers a morning several years ago when she'd found him working on a canvas, feverish and dripping with sweat.

"Nothing like hard work to get rid of a touch of flu," he'd told her. "Never been one to loll around like an invalid."

They eat Anne's birthday luncheon in reluctant relays, the roast lamb and golden potatoes growing cold on their plates. Eleanor wraps her mother's present. She puts it under several others in the drawing room, pretending it's been there all day. Nobody cuts Vera's home-made birthday cake with its crisp white icing and luscious fruity heart.

Walter dozes. He wakes with a start, saying he has a raging thirst and a thumping headache. Then he falls again into a fretful sleep.

Eleanor stands at the drawing-room window of the silent house. The wind drops; the snow dies in mid-air. The freezing afternoon darkens into dusk. By four o'clock, the streets lie deserted. Lights shine out on to the snow. Curtains flick across windows. Sunday is not just quiet: it's dead.

"I'm exhausted." Anne rustles into the room to flop into a fireside chair. "Vera's keeping watch. Be a dear girl and pour me a brandy."

She swirls the liquid around the glass.

"Cheers! God Almighty, Eleanor. This is no way to turn forty."

"You haven't opened your birthday presents."

"No." Anne gulps and frowns. "I'm not doing that without your father. We always open them together after luncheon. They can wait. He's sure to be better tomorrow."

At six o'clock Eleanor realises she can't leave her mother and Vera to manage the night watch on their own. She'll send a telegram in the morning to Miss Lascelles, her tutor at Somerville. There's only one College telephone and nobody answers it after five in the afternoon.

In her cold room, her hand shaking, she writes a message:

UNABLE TO RETURN TO COLLEGE STOP FATHER INJURED IN ACCIDENT STOP APOLOGIES STOP HOPE TO RETURN TO SOMERVILLE TOMORROW STOP ELEANOR DRUMMOND

70

She leaves the note on her desk and goes into her parents'
bedroom, moving across the floor to sit beside the bed.

"Ellie." Walter's eyes flicker at her. "I'm glad you're on
your own." The hand he reaches out to her is burning hot.
"I need to tell you something."

"Hush, Daddy. Go to sleep. Tell me in the morning."

"No." A spasm of pain crosses his face. "I must do it *now*.
I always meant to explain to you and your mother."

"Shall I fetch her?"

"It's *you* I need to talk to." He swallows. "I love you very
much."

A helpless laugh of relief chokes Eleanor's throat. "That
goes without saying—"

"You don't understand. I've let *far too much* go without
saying, for far too long." He raises his head, his eyes fierce,
his grip tightening. "Promise me one thing."

"Anything. Name it." A tide of alarm swamps Eleanor's
relief.

"Find Moira for me." His grip slackens; his head falls on to
the crumpled pillow. "Just find her for me. Tell her I'm
sorry."

"Moira?" Eleanor frowns. "Moira *who*? I've never *heard*
of her. I don't *know* anyone called Moira."

"You'll know her when you see her." His eyes close, his
hands lie limply by his side. "She's much too beautiful for
you to miss."

"I don't understand, Daddy." Eleanor bends towards
him. The wound on his forehead is bleeding again. The
smell makes her feel nauseous. "Where should I look? When
did you last see her?"

"I have a terrible pain in my stomach. Moira will know
how to stop it. She'll tell me with her marvellous deep voice."

"I promise to find her for you, Daddy. Don't fret, now."

She stands up, feeling faint. "Your bandage needs changing. Vera will bring a fresh one." Heat from his body pulses towards her. The fever has come on so fast. "Lie quietly. I won't be long."

On the landing, Eleanor hesitates, longing for the privacy and silence of her room. Dragging her feet, she walks downstairs.

As she and Anne go back to him, she sees with a shock his bed is empty. One of the pillows is stained with blood. He stands by the window. He's pulled the curtain aside and stares into the night, tapping his fingers on the sill. Eleanor flings an arm around his shoulders.

"She's out there somewhere, Ellie," he murmurs. "How many times have I stood at this window, longing to see her?"

"I'm over here, darling!" Anne's voice, sharp with anxiety, rings across the room. She rips off the stained pillow-case, replaces it with a fresh one. "Come back to bed. Give that wound a chance to heal."

He turns to face his daughter, desperation in his eyes. He looks hunted and guilty, as if he's a fox who's killed a dozen chickens and gets caught in the farmer's torchlight beam.

"Your mother couldn't possibly understand." He clutches her arm. "Don't breathe a word."

"Please, Walter, be sensible." Anne tucks him in. "Get some sleep. I'll sit with you for the night. You'll be right as rain in the morning."

Anne and Walter, meeting each other's eyes, clasp hands.

Eleanor sees the look that passes between them.

She closes the door and leans against it, her heart filled with foreboding.

Omens

1936

Sean wakes that morning with heavy eyelids and dread rolling around his stomach. Something is wrong ... Or something is *about to go* wrong.

He'll have to go down to the stables. And on a Sunday, too. It should have been his day off to spend with his beloved girl.

But Kath will understand. She always does. It's one of the many things Sean adores about her. If he needs to work, he needs to work. It's not about the money, nothing like that. It's about having to *be* there. To serve His Grace, the Duke of Marlborough. To be the best he can possibly be at the job he's been given, in the place he loves with all his heart.

Sean flings his heavy blanket aside. His chimney-smoke breath swirls in the freezing air. From his cottage within the grounds of Blenheim Palace, he can hear the bells of St Mary Magdalene's tower start to chime.

One. Two. Three. Four. Five

Outside it's still pitch black. Luckily, he knows his way in the dark.

By nine o'clock that morning, he's beginning to relax. The stables are immaculate. The horses are groomed and quiet; some are even sleeping. He hums to himself. Although it's still bitterly cold, shreds of frosty sunlight paint the stable doors with dappled light.

His stomach rumbles. He must eat something or he'll faint. He sits on some clean straw in a scrap of cold sunlight and unwraps his bread and cheese. Oat bread, heavy and filling. His Kath makes it in the hot, crowded, often bad-tempered Palace kitchen. Cheese, churned and spicy, fresh from his friend, Dan the Dairyman. Best of all: hot, sweet tea.

Sean eats and drinks. It's heavenly.

He must have nodded off, he can't remember, but suddenly he's wide awake again, jolted into life, his eyes dry and burning. He's holding the flask of tea but now it's empty. It's pointing directly at his face, like a gun.

There are sounds. Pounding, grinding, shouting.

He leaps to his feet, his body tense with dread.

He manages to make out the words, *"It's that bloody Sprinter—"*

Sean opens his mouth. "What—"

"He's only gone and thrown Lady Helena."

"Christ Almighty!"

He races for his truck.

"They think she might have broken her neck."

Sean hauls himself into his vehicle. "Where—"

"And there's worse."

He clamps his freezing hands over the wheel. "Tell me."

"Before Sprinter started on his way to Combe or God alone only knows where, he kicked Walter bloody Drummond through his nasty little head."

Sean belches the truck into sputtering life.

He swallows his bile and then his mirth. But it escapes. He throws back his head and laughs. Then he bends double with the joy of laughter, the marvellous irony of it. The blackness of the morning shimmers into duck-egg yellow.

His Uncle Robert, a stalwart policeman, once told him over their Christmas figgy pudding that the only way to deal with dead bodies is to laugh.

Sean knows it will be terrible.

He'll drive like a lunatic, out of the Triumphal Arch and into Woodstock, screeching his brakes and ruining his tyres. At the bottom of Market Street he'll slither left – "Mind out of my bloody way, can't you? This is an emergency, you stupid old crone!" – towards Combe, trying to see the horse, craning his neck.

Please God, let him spot Sprinter in a field. Any old field will do, just soon, please make it soon, before the mad creature kicks anyone else, maybe kills a child. His Grace would never forgive any of the stable boys if *that* happened. They could *all* lose their jobs. His Kath would marry him if he were living down a rabbit hole, but the two of them have made so many good plans for their future.

He tries to stay calm and think straight. He'll stretch out his hand for his gun while he's driving. The minute he spots the wild creature, it'll be screech the brakes, stop and run, stop and breathe, calmly now, steady does it, aim and *shoot*, before Sprinter can get at him first.

The horse is young, but once he's a dead lump of meat,

75

he'll be much too heavy to lift. Sean will go back to the Blenheim stables and shout for help.

By that time, word will have got around. The Palace will be buzzing with the news, and on a Sunday too. Their one day of blissful Woodstock quiet will explode. There'll be an ambulance waiting for Lady Helena, with everyone fluttering around it like gaggles of frightened chickens.

Cock a doodle doo … Cock a doodle doo … For Christ's sake shut up, can't you, cock a doodle doo …

Once he's found Sprinter and shot him between the eyes, he'll get two of the best stable boys to help. They'll go back to the field in Combe and winch the horse into the truck, all of them sweating like pigs on a midsummer's day.

And then for the worst part. Telling Sprinter's mother that her magnificent offspring is dead. Talking to her, explaining, soothing, stroking her nose, trying not to sob with her, explaining again. Releasing Sprinter's body to the butcher who, ruthlessly, stony-faced, will cut the marvellous horse into pieces.

Chop, wham, blood spurting, the colour of wine but the stench of blood.

Then the whole of Woodstock can share a glorious thick, rich, meaty casserole. It will feed some families until Friday, if they hold back.

He can smell it now. The meaty stews smouldering in Woodstock's kitchens. Chimneys beckoning plumes of navy smoke into the night sky. Woodstock mouths chewing. Everyone feeling fed and full – and finally rejoicing. Singing into the darkness of the winter's night. Playing their pianos with their bellies full of food. Falling asleep where they are, sitting in their chairs. Carrying their children upstairs to the one double bed and six other bodies sharing the same space.

Sean bursts into hot tears of relief. They spill their way down his cheeks. Bashfully, he wipes them away with the back of his hands. He'd never want his Kath to see him crying like a baby.

Dark and Chill

1936

Eleanor and Vera eat supper in the kitchen, forcing themselves to swallow tomato soup and cheese on toast. Eleanor takes a tray to Anne, making sure she eats some of it. Together they sit at Walter's bedside until midnight.

Anne hears the clock chime in the hall. She orders Eleanor to bed.

"One of us must get some sleep. I'll call you if I need to."

Eleanor's room is dark and chill. She flings herself on to her bed, too exhausted to undress, knowing she should be back in College by now, with her books, her friends, and the dying embers of her fire. Yet Somerville seems hundreds of miles away, floating in some faraway make-believe world that dances before her eyes.

She remembers seeing the lights shining in the Principal's window on dark nights as she walked across the lawns for her evening meal, the feeling of security they gave her. The College's plain but substantial meals in the long, wood-panelled dining hall with its scent of gravy. The din of voices grumbling about the price of theatre tickets and Fuller's walnut cake.

It's a world whose rules must be obeyed. Don't entertain men for tea in your room without permission. Always wear your Somerville gown when out and about after dark. Be back in College before eleven at night. If they break a rule, the girls have to pay strict fines. Last term she'd mistakenly stayed out after nine o'clock without putting her initials in the book. It had cost her two shillings.

She remembers her very first morning at Somerville College: girls everywhere, mulling and crushing, their faces clean and shining, their coats brushed. Some are more confident than others. They have voices that bray like trumpets, leather-gloved hands that have never washed dishes, eyes that flirt at the raising of a man's hat. Others hang back with a single shabby suitcase by their side, their hats perched at an awkward angle. Their new brogues have been specially bought for the Michaelmas term.

Eleanor, Walter and Anne climb out of his car. Eleanor's heart throbs with excitement. The morning she's been waiting for has finally arrived.

Anne says, "Good gracious, *what* a ghastly crowd! I've never *seen* so many girls in one fell swoop … I need to powder my nose."

Eleanor takes her arm. "I'll find out where the lavatories are." She looks at her father. "Will you wait here for us, Daddy? Will you be all right?"

"Yes, *indeed.*" Walter's eyes glisten with joy. He looks around at the girls: all those ravishing faces, clean, shining, young. "I'll be right here when you get back."

But when they return, he's nowhere to be seen.

Then Eleanor spots a ring of girls, surrounding

somebody. The girls are laughing. The somebody they're surrounding is her Daddy. He's talking and smiling. He's sitting on her pile of suitcases, sketching the face of the most beautiful girl in the throng. Tall, thick-set, wearing a soft blue-green tweed coat, she has flawless skin, a cascade of coppery curls and eyes as yellow as a cat's.

He glances up at Eleanor and Anne.

"*Darlings!*" he says. "*Look* who we have here ... Eleanor, meet Perdita Willoughby-Jones. Perdita, this is my daughter, Eleanor."

Perdita reaches out to shake Eleanor's hand. "How do you *do*? I hope we shall be friends."

Walter puts the finishing touch to his sketch. "Friends?" He gives the sketch to Perdita, bowing over her gloved hand. "You'll be the very *best* of friends, to be sure."

Perdita looks at the sketch. "But that's *me!*" she gasps. She looks up at Walter. "That really is exactly *me*, isn't it?"

"It absolutely is." Walter's eyes mist over. "I'll just *have* to do you in colour."

"Oh, *colour* would be *amazing*, Mr Drummond. Just let me know when—"

Anne takes her husband firmly by the arm. "Some other time, Walter dear. Some other time."

Eleanor pulls off her clothes, shivering until her nightdress covers her limbs and her head hits the pillow. She falls into a restless sleep, half-hearing her mother talking to Vera, doors opening and closing, a tap running, footsteps on the stairs.

Towards dawn, as snow falls silently against the window, covering the pane in diamonds of hard frost, she hears a stifled cry. She dashes across the landing. Anne sits by the bed, clutching Walter's hand. She raises grief-stricken eyes.

"He wanted to say goodbye. He wanted me to wake you. It happened so fast. I'm so sorry. Now all I can do is say it for him."

Slowly, stiffly, Eleanor walks towards the bed. She looks down at her father. His hair clings to his forehead, damp with sweat, half-obscuring the wound. He lies on his side, his arms flung out across the bed, as if he were pleading for help. His violet-blue eyes are open, their colour clouded and misty. He looks startled, as if death has taken him in mid-sentence. His face seems even paler, making the blood on his bandage more virulent.

"Are you sure—"

"*Quite* sure." Anne sounds as if her throat is being strangled. She lays her fingertips on Walter's eyelids. The violet-blue light disappears. She bends to kiss him. "Your father was trying to tell me something. Then he gasped. And it was all over."

"I can't believe it." She can hardly get air into her own lungs. "Dr Fagg—"

"Vile, slovenly, *stupid* man. Blind as a bat. We should have taken your father straight to hospital." Anne clutches her arm. "I'm going to be sick."

"Sit down, Mummy." She wants to pull Walter into her arms, smother him with kisses, bring him miraculously back to life. "I'll bring you some tea. Let's have some air. It's horribly stuffy in here."

She heaves the curtains aside, struggles to open a window. A layer of frozen snow crunches along the ledge. Fingers of pale sky point towards the dawn. The bitter air floods her lungs.

"Find Moira for me."

She bites her lip, swallowing her sobs. It's too late now for anything.

Anne weeps, huddling in her chair, rocking to and fro.

Eleanor kneels beside her. "Don't cry, Mummy. I'll look after you. Everything will be all right. Only don't cry. You know how Daddy hated it when——"

"But he's not here, is he? I can cry for an entire week and your father will never know."

Dr Fagg arrives, red-faced and apologetic, his neck-tie stained with egg. He prods at Walter's body, asking questions. Anne orders him out of the house. At the front door, he presses a bottle of tablets into Eleanor's hand.

"Give your mother two of these at bedtime. It will help her sleep. If you need me, you know where I am. I'm *profoundly* sorry, Miss Drummond. Your father must have sustained *multiple* internal injuries."

Walter's body is taken away for examination. Weary, dead-eyed men in uniform tramp silently through the house, leaving behind the chill of the street, clumps of melting snow and the smell of disinfectant.

Vera spring-cleans Anne and Walter's bedroom. She changes the bed linen, lays fresh logs in the fire and washes the windows, as if the cleanliness might energise Walter's spirit and bring him home.

Eleanor stumbles out to the Post Office. She rewrites the telegram, changing its message to **FATHER KILLED IN ACCIDENT STOP**. The postmistress stares at her, round-eyed, saying she's terribly sorry, Mr Drummond was a *lovely* man, always a kind word for everyone.

Worried neighbours, gossiping of runaway horses and Mr Drummond's injuries, tap at their front door. Vera dismisses them, her eyes red, her hair shoved into its cap, and slams the door.

Anne takes a hot bath but has no strength to get dressed. She wafts around the house in Walter's crumpled dressing-gown, her hair hanging down her back in a conker-brown plait. She hovers near the fire, poking at the logs until they die.

Eleanor sits alone in her room, shivering with shock. If she starts to cry she won't be able to stop. Walter had been her touchstone. Separated from him for the first time when she went to Somerville, she'd seen him every week during the previous term. He'd driven into Oxford, parked his beloved canary yellow Bullnose Morris in Beaumont Street, and taken her shopping in the Covered Market or to tea at the Cadena Café. She told him about her week, her friends, the latest gossip.

"Last night, we were in Rosemary's room drinking cocoa and discussing underwear. Lucilla said she's never washed a pair of stockings in her life. She just goes out and buys new ones. But then her father is one of the richest pork butchers in England. Why can't *you* be more like that, darling Daddy?"

Walter had roared with laughter. "I'll buy you six pairs of stockings immediately, Miss La-De-Dah Drummond." And he had.

Everything she'd ever done had been for Walter's approval. So she could watch his eyes gleam, feel the clasp of his fingers, hear his whispered, "*Brilliant! Well done, Ellie! That's my girl!*"

At breakfast next morning, the copy of *The Times* that Walter always read from cover to cover, is delivered edged in black.

King George V had died at five minutes to midnight. A pictorial history of his reign leads with a photo of "his late

83

majesty" broadcasting to the nation: his beard dapper, his cuffs spotless, his face intent, a pale carnation in his buttonhole. The picture of royal dignity.

A small photo is published of the new King, "Ambassador of Empire". Although forty-one, he looks younger: a slight figure, swamped by his decorated uniform, his thick blond hair immaculately parted, his pale eyes glittering and anxious.

Is he "fitted for a great task"? Could anyone be? Don't people *grow into* the roles they are given?

Eleanor stares blindly at the headlines, worrying. Now *she* will have to grow into a new role. The state funeral will go according to its meticulous plan, with hundreds of people on official duty to help. Her heart throbs with loneliness. How do you bury your own father without cracking into a thousand tiny pieces?

The Uncut Stone

1936

"That will be all, Wilkins."

"Do you have everything you need, sir?"

"Everything." The man glances across the table at his three companions. Their brandy glasses are full, their cigars smoulder. The air hangs heavy with smoke and tension.

"Make sure nobody disturbs us, Wilkins."

"Yes, of course, sir."

"He has *gone* to bed, hasn't he? With or without Mrs Simpson?"

"With, sir ... Quite definitely *with* ... They were heard—"

"Excellent!"

Wilkins clicks himself away, out of sight but not out of hearing. Never that. He of the fountain-pen brigade. *Someone* has to take sober notes in legible handwriting.

Cigars are tapped. Delicate glasses are held between fat fingers. Fleshy lips sip.

The man hoists himself to his feet. He sways, ever so gently. On his upper lip, beads of perspiration catch the light.

"Let us now, on this auspicious evening, raise a toast. To our Proper Plan ... We need a code name for it." He clears his well-fed throat. "Suggestions?"

The chandelier twinkles benignly over the fat-fingered fixers.

One of them says, "Why don't we call our enterprise *The Uncut Stone*?"

The men guffaw. One slaps his thigh. The second twirls his moustache. The third clutches his belly, hooting with mirth. The chandelier jangles in response.

The man who'd suggested the name blushes with pride, his face glistening like a ripe Victoria plum. "*The Uncut Stone* it is."

Cigars are raised to lips. The fog in the room deepens. Plumes of smoke caress the chandelier.

"Now, shall we get down to the business of the evening?"

"It's really very simple." This is a new voice: the man whose hair shines thick and silvery under the foggy light. "We *allow* that jewel-heavy bitch to *think* she's going to make it as Queen Wallis. We *allow* our party-loving, doe-eyed, drink-sodden, so-called King of England and ruler of Empire to become *completely* obsessed—"

"As if he isn't already!"

"And deeply involved. So deeply in the mire of 'love' he can only enmesh himself up to his neck and beyond his eyeballs. *And then we pull the plug.* So *they* go down their love-sick drain into the muck-heaps of Hitler's Germany."

"Which is *precisely* where they belong!"

There is a moment's silence. Eyes meet, lock and smile. Only the cigar smoke drifts.

"And *The Uncut Stone* can take her precious jewels with her."

"Can anyone part her from them? They say she even *sleeps* with them. They're draped around her *everywhere*:

breasts – not that she really *has* much up-front – thighs, around her ankles, hanging from her scrawny neck, dangling on her lazy wrists, decorating her ugly great hands—"

More guffaws. Another silence.

"*Her* greed, *her* jewels, *his* nursery obsessions, *his* money, *their* filthy perverted drunken nights."

The man swigs at his brandy until every drop has vanished down his throat. "They can all go down the plughole, companions in arms." His voice hardens with fury. "But not with their hands around our beloved country's neck. If those two arrogant fascist perverts think they're taking our country with them, they can think again."

The group's mastermind clambers to his feet. He refills the empty glasses, his fat hand shaking. He's surprisingly tall, with broad shoulders, thick legs and an air of natural authority. A captain of cricket. A head boy. A good runner, a sensible drinker – and an expert at undressing shy ladies at four o'clock in the afternoon. Any shy lady will fit his bill, as long as she's plump as a dove and safely married.

"Right you are, my dearest companions. We must get to work and fast."

He scrabbles in his pocket for a small, leather-bound notebook and a top-of-the-range Parker pen.

"First we must plan the weekend at Blenheim Palace. Everything stands or falls on those few precious days in that most beautiful of houses. A Friday to Monday in June … Are we all agreed? That will be when we make Mr Simpson an offer he cannot possibly refuse."

He flings on to the table a coin of the realm.

"That's for starters. I want *anyone* who is *anyone* to put into our mutual purse all they can afford – and then a whole lot more."

The glasses are raised and lowered, the men get to their feet.

"All those in favour of *The Uncut Stone Affair* say 'Aye'."

The chandelier twinkles agreement above the din.

"Aye, aye, aye!"

"I like the sound of this affair!"

"Aye, aye!"

"To Hell with Everyone!"

1936

Vera – sturdy, loyal, practical, devoted – comes to Eleanor's rescue. They sit over coffee to discuss the details. They need to arrange a date for the funeral with the Rector, decide an order of service, and meet with the funeral director.

Vera clatters her cup on its saucer. "You must ring your father's art group, dear heart. They'll be expecting to have their class with him this afternoon. Why don't you speak to Rosie Perkins? Explain what's happened and she can tell everyone else."

She leans forward to take Eleanor's hand.

"You should be wearing black, out of respect. I've dug a black cardigan out of your wardrobe, and a black skirt. And that summer coat of yours. I took it to the shop on the corner. They'll dye it black for you. I said it was urgent."

"What would I do without you, Vera? You think of everything."

Tuesday is consumed with telephone calls and visits. Eleanor won't let herself think about how she feels. She has to be sensible and cool-headed. She discusses the date and order of service with the Rector; the coffin and flowers with the funeral director; the menu for the wake with Vera.

Keep hold of reality, she tells herself. This week will be the worst. Grin and bear it.

Anne does neither. She's not so much grief-stricken as furious. Her tears stop; her mouth closes in a thin-lipped silence. She lies in bed, hollow-eyed, staring out of the window, refusing to eat.

When Eleanor finds the courage to say they should make arrangements for the funeral, Anne punches a pillow and hurls it across the room.

"Do whatever you want. Let's get it over with."

"I thought Friday morning. Would that be—"

"Fine. Tell Vera I'll wear my black suit and the feathery hat with the veil."

"You'd better wear a coat, too. The weather's atrocious—"

"I don't care if I freeze to death. In fact, I'd welcome it."

Eleanor ploughs on. "The wake ... We should ask people to come back here—"

"Don't ask *me* to play lady hostess!"

"But everyone will expect—"

"To *hell* with everyone!" Anne's eyes blaze with fury. "Your father cared more about a stupid colt than seeing me safely home. He was the most thoughtless, bird-brained ... Never a care about tomorrow. The *pointlessness* of his death is the only remarkable thing about it."

Eleanor creeps into her own room, guilt and anxiety settling on her shoulders like dust. *She* had pulled Walter out of church to speed up the celebrations and get back to Somerville. If they'd emerged a few minutes later, Sprinter would have vanished into his panic-stricken world – and her beloved darling Daddy would still be with her.

On the Train

1936

The man is running so hard and so fast that every breath in his lungs brings blood to his eyeballs. He curses and swears, endlessly berating himself. He is so disorganised. He never wears a watch. He leaves everything to the last minute. He'd known he was cutting things fine – very fine – and now he's sure that luck can no longer be relied upon. He has pushed things just that little bit too far.

Trains wait for no man.

The train he wants, he needs, he must God help him *catch*, will puff away without him.

But it doesn't.

"Is this the train to Oxford?"

The man sounds like a lunatic, as if he's just fallen from the bitterly cold morning sky; as if he's never spoken the English language before; as if this is the only time he's ever needed to catch anything.

The guard shoots him a glance of bitter disdain. He nods briefly, crooks a contemptuous thumb in the direction of the steaming dragon lying in wait to devour all who have the courage to board her.

The man takes off his hat and bows. He thinks: Wait a sodding minute, this is the wrong way round. *He* should be saluting *me* for using his service.

He orders his legs to make a leap for it. He manages to cling on to his battered, paint-spattered hold-almost-nothing suitcase, praying it won't split at the seams. The moment the train door has been slammed by the owner of the contemptuous thumb, the wheels hiss and churn. Hiss and churn. Hiss and churn.

Felix Mitchell collapses on to the first seat he can find. He's oblivious of an elderly gentleman whose newspaper he's flattened; of the elderly gentleman's wife whose delicate nap he's disturbed; of the elderly gentleman's parrot who *had* been preening herself in her new brass cage.

Felix hears only the screech of his lungs. His feet sweat in their paint-spattered shoes. He's put on his old shoes by mistake. The new ones, specially bought at great expense for today's occasion, are still waiting expectantly by his front door in St Ives, Cornwall.

He leans forward over his knees and begins to sob. Great long lurching noisy slobbering sobs. On and on they go. He can't hear or stop them.

The elderly gentleman's outrage turns to curiosity. After five minutes of listening to and looking at this catastrophe on legs, he leans towards his wife. Pointing at the quivering lump, he raises an eyebrow.

"Dear, do you think, dear, we ought to *do* something? Dear?"

Before his devoted consort of thirty-eight years can say a word, the parrot begins to shriek. *"Do it, do it, for Gawd's sake, do it!"*

"I do rather agree with Penelope," says the elderly gentleman's wife. Taking command of the situation, she stands up and pulls the emergency cord.

The train from Paddington to Oxford grinds to a screeching halt.

Everybody groans. There's a moment of petrified silence. It's most unusual, so close to Paddington, for the train to stop.

A man arrives in uniform. Navy with gold trim, the outfit makes him look a hundred times smarter than most of the people he's guarding. He exudes an air of bossy confidence.

Felix is escorted to his own private compartment and left there to make as much noise as he likes.

It takes an hour for his sobs to subside.

Gradually he regains consciousness. He mops his eyes. He opens them.

Where am I? I want my Daddy. Alive and kicking, not six foot under. What use is he to me six foot under?

Where is my Mummy? Where, where, where is my Mummy?

The man in uniform quietly opens the door of Felix's private compartment.

"Feeling better are we, sir?"

Felix splutters and nods. He dabs the wet handkerchief on his damp face.

"*That's* the way, sir ... *Very* well done ... Brought you a nice cup of tea."

Fishery Cottage

1936

By Wednesday afternoon, Eleanor can't bear being at home a moment longer. She flings on the dyed black coat, telling Vera she'll be out for a couple of hours.

She fills her lungs with the sharp, frost-filled air. She's off to see her best friend, Kathleen Maisey: plump, down-to-earth, cheerful, Kath will talk to her as always, with sanity and discretion. Now both eighteen, they'd met at Woodstock's elementary school and became inseparable.

Kath lives in Fishery Cottage, next to Blenheim's lake, where her father works as head gamekeeper. Her older sister, Maud, is a lady's maid for a wealthy family in London's Mayfair. Maud feeds Kath the latest gossip about the people she calls "my high and mighty toffs". It's through her that Eleanor learned about Edward's obsessive affair with Wallis Simpson.

When Eleanor went to Oxford's High School for Girls to study for the Higher School Certificate, and the entrance exam for a place at an Oxford college, Kath stayed in Woodstock, leaving school to work as a senior kitchen maid in Blenheim Palace. Wednesday afternoons are her hard-earned time off.

Eleanor skids over the frozen cobblestones, past the hairdresser, the butcher, the baker, the sweet shop, St Mary Magdalene's – past the spot where Sprinter had attacked her father, which she dares not look at – and through the Palace gates. She pauses for a moment to admire the spectacular spread of bridge, lake and cloudy sky. Then she turns right to follow the gravel path that dips to Fishery Cottage.

There's nobody about.

A great spotted woodpecker, high in the conifers, hammers insistently, doing his best to hasten the arrival of spring. The flat branches of the cedars are heavy with snow. A pheasant croaks in the grass, making her jump. The marvellous colours of his plumage – scarlet, blue-green, orange-brown – shimmer against the whitened landscape. How Walter would have admired the bird's confident beauty.

She remembers their walks in Blenheim. He'd suddenly tighten his grip, making her stop and look: a cluster of trees had taken his fancy, or the glimpse of a carpet of bluebells, or the way the sunlight shot a dazzling shaft through soft grey clouds.

She remembers one summer afternoon as a child, running down this same path, holding Vera's hand. Walter was sitting beside the reeds at the lake's edge, his easel propped, scribbling his charcoal over paper. He'd heard her calling him.

"Daddy! Daddy! Here I am!"

She'd raced across the grass, the magical drone of bees lulling in her ears. Walter's face lit up at the sight of her.

The memory is so vivid she could touch him.

"Daddy! My darling Daddy! Here I am!"

Fishery Cottage looms through the mist. The waters of the lake lie frozen at the boundaries of its garden. The bare branches of the weeping willow dip and curtsey beside it. Smoke from its chimney rises in grey curls into the sky. Lights gleam at the windows.

Kath meets her at the door with open arms. "My darlin' Ellie! Sean told me what happened. What a time you've had! That Sprinter spelled trouble, from the moment he were born. Come in and warm yourself."

Eleanor buries her head in a swirl of fair curls. And as she feels Kath's arms around her, the tears she's stemmed since that terrible dawn finally burn her eyes.

"It's been a nightmare."

She stuffs her wet handkerchief into her pocket. She watches Kath bustle around the room, pouring tea, handing her a plate of home-made macaroons.

"I woke up this morning and for one glorious moment I thought everything was normal. Then I remembered." Her voice darkens. "Mummy's gone to pieces. She's either furious and silent, or hysterical. I don't know how to deal with her."

"And *you* should be at Somerville. Do they know—"

"I sent my tutor a telegram. And I've made an appointment to see the Principal on Saturday morning, the day after the funeral. I'm dreading it. Miss Darbishire's a good head of College and a brilliant Wordsworth scholar – but I barely know her."

"Will she be hard to talk to?"

"I won't know until I try. She wanted to see me with Mummy, but *she's* in no fit state to do anything. Miss Darbishire won't have much sympathy if I tell her I can't leave my mother to fend for herself ten miles up the road. But I can't just go back to Somerville and pretend nothing's happened."

"Didn't Miss Darbishire's father die when she were a child?"

"Yes, but things were different for her. Miss Darbishire was only eleven and her father had been ill, so she had plenty of warning. Daddy's death was so swift and brutal."

"My Sean burst into tears when he told me how he had to shoot Sprinter in a field. Now, he's had the grooms check on every horse in the stables, and put a stop to any rider who hasn't the proper experience. Lady Helena had only been ridin' for a few months. Nobody warned her that Sprinter could be difficult. She's still in hospital."

"I'm sorry." Eleanor grimaces. "But shutting the stable door after Sprinter's bolted won't bring Daddy back."

"May I change the subject?" Kath spoons sugar into her cup. "You might not want to leave your mother, but on Monday I'm off to London to meet Maud. We want to see the late King's lyin'-in-state. Will you come with me? It'll do you good to get out of Woodstock."

"I don't know if I can leave Mummy. I'll need to ask."

"If you think *you've* got problems, spare a thought for the royal family. Maud says none of 'em think Edward wants to be King and he won't stay the course."

"Good *God*, Kath! Give the man a chance. He hasn't even buried his father and he won't be crowned until next year. You can't write him off just yet."

"The problem's that Wallis Simpson—"

"But Edward's had affairs with married women all his

adult life, and they never last. Freda Dudley Ward, Lady Thelma Furness. Isn't Mrs Simpson just another?"

"Evidently not." Kath looks across at her with thoughtful eyes. "Maud says Edward's besotted. If he and Wallis are separated, he writes to her all the time. The day after the King died, he rang her every hour!"

"But she's *married*, Kath. Nothing *serious* can come of it while Ernest Simpson is still her husband."

Kath stares into the fire. "If Mr Simpson doesn't mind sharin' his wife with the King, what else might he not mind doin'? That's what *I'd* like to know."

A Fleeting Glimpse

1936

On the morning of the funeral, Eleanor wakes to the sound of tapping. When she sits up and calls, "Come in," her mother pushes at the door.

"I've been behaving like a monster." Anne hovers by the window. "I'm sorry, Eleanor. Forgive me."

Eleanor stares at her mother. Already dressed, her hair coiled into a smooth bun, she looks immaculate and stylish, in a white blouse and black suit with a tight-fitting jacket and a pencil-slim skirt that flows to within four inches of her ankles.

"Of course." In her worst nightmare, her mother had stayed in bed all day while their guests came and went.

Anne brushes imaginary dust from her sleeves. "Today I'll be a model widow. I won't shed a single tear. I'll be quiet and dignified, so proper that you and your father," her voice shakes, "will be proud of me."

"And you look beautiful. Give me a hug."

Anne stumbles towards her. "Mind you," she gives a shaky laugh, "when everyone has gone, I'll cry like a baby."

"So shall I." Anne smells of Dior, her perfume for important occasions. "We'll be big babies together."

"You're a good girl, Eleanor. I'm lucky to have you."

The coffin arrives on the dot of eleven.

They follow on foot. Vera totters behind them, fluttering a handkerchief. The rain stops, as if to let them pass. The pavements of the newly-washed street shine like grey-streaked mirrors.

Walter had been well-known in Woodstock; word of his death spread fast. St Mary Magdalene is packed. The service, full of his favourite hymns, races past.

Rosie Perkins, Walter's favourite art-class pupil, had asked to say a few words. She trots to the front of the church, her navy coat trim and smooth over her curvaceous body, her blonde curls peeping out beneath her hat. She looks carefully at Anne.

"I make no secret of the fact I adored Walter Drummond." Rosie's voice trembles. Anne clasps her gloved hands together. "He was the kindest, most generous-spirited man. Many of us own one of his paintings: those lovely landscapes that echo the glories of Oxfordshire with such calm radiance.

"But Walter wasn't only a good painter. He was a brilliant teacher: astute, kind and so encouraging to small talents. He will be sorely missed. Every time I pick up a paintbrush, he'll be in my thoughts."

As the organist heaves a gentle requiem, Eleanor stands up, her shoulders aching with strain. Something calls to her: a mute, imperative summons to look behind her.

She turns her head and stares towards the back of the church – straight into the hazel eyes of a man she's never

100

seen before. He has a thin, angular face, red lips and high cheekbones. He holds his hat in his hands. A swoop of straight, dark-gold hair falls untidily across his forehead. He pushes it out of his eyes, continuing to hold her gaze.

She blushes, turns away, tries to look busy: bending towards her mother, acknowledging a neighbour's condolences. When, almost against her will, she searches for those hazel eyes in the coldness of the graveyard, the stranger, after that fleeting glimpse, has disappeared.

She shrugs away the memory, throwing a handful of earth on to the coffin.

"Darling Daddy. Rest in peace."

By two o'clock that afternoon, Eleanor's face is locked into a permanent, meaningless smile. Her jaw aches, her feet are sore. Anne and Vera are pouring drinks, offering sandwiches, answering questions with weary patience.

But as the afternoon drags on, in some people's eyes she spots something more ominous than sympathy. Their bank manager, Robin Parker, and family solicitor, Michael Humphreys, talk quietly together. She sees the looks of pity and concern they dart at her mother – and flickers of alarm race down her spine.

Walter's last will and testament will be read on Saturday afternoon. She hasn't had the courage to raise the subject with Anne. She decides to slip away from the remaining visitors. Walter's studio huddles at the bottom of the garden. Since his death she's treated it as out-of-bounds.

Now she needs a sanctuary.

Inside, the small, untidy wooden shack is icy cold.

She switches on the two-bar electric fire, stands there shivering. Every small detail is exactly as Walter left it.

Landscapes of Blenheim in all its seasons hang on the walls. Piles of charcoal sketches flutter on the floor. Some lie on an ancient chaise longue, covered in faded green velvet, together with Walter's battered felt hat, a silk paisley scarf and a pair of paint-stained gloves.

Paints, bottles, jars, brushes, pencils, oils and watercolours straggle over every surface. His blue-linen painter's smock, smeared with ink and paint, dangles from a hook. Several pipes, their stems well-chewed, lie on their sides, clinging to their fragrance. His desk spews clutters of teaching notes, sketches, pens and bottles of ink.

She flops on to Walter's chair in front of his easel, staring at an unfinished landscape: a lake, glassy with ice, and Blenheim's magnificent bridge sweeping over it, edged with snow. Gulls swoop low on the horizon. And, like some ghastly ironic prophecy, two horses with their riders trot into view.

As she stares at the swirls of oil on canvas, at the brushes soaking in turpentine, feeling her father's spirit everywhere, she hears the echo of his voice:

"Find Moira for me. Tell her I'm sorry."

She picks up her father's shabby tobacco pouch, taking a pinch of the stuff in her fingers, relishing its familiar sweet-and-sour scent.

"Moira's not here, Daddy. God only knows who and where she is – but she's certainly not in here." She puts down the pouch. "And what were you sorry *for*, I want to know. *What were you sorry for?*"

The Bear Hotel

1936

Felix Mitchell is only slightly drunk.

After that cup of tea on the train – thick, sweet medicine – and the courteous sympathy – it seemed genuine, the man in uniform had piercing blue eyes that looked into his, offering understanding and comfort – he staggers on to the Oxford platform and takes a very deep breath.

The air smells of soot and green fields.

He reckons it's around midday. He marches across the station forecourt to the Royal Oxford Hotel and orders a beer. The air stinks of tobacco. His hands shake. His palms are damp. But his heart is beginning to gather strength.

He asks the barman how he can get to Woodstock, and catches a rattling old bus. It bumps over icy puddles, the surrounding fields white with snow, the sky a matching colour. Two old women behind him never stop clacking. Why the hell can't they just *shut up*? It's not as if *anything* they're babbling about is of the *slightest* interest. The price of eggs! As if *anyone* could waste their energy discussing those tasteless shells that fall out of a hen's hindquarters.

Although if *he* had a couple of eggs right now, he'd know what to do with them.

The bus's wheels rumble, shaking the hat off his head. It rolls into the grubby aisle. A woman bends to retrieve it, giving it to him with a smile. He glowers back at her. The teeth vanish, the smile fades.

In Woodstock, he heads towards the centre of town. He doesn't have to ask anyone. Besides, there's that sign. He sees it emerge behind a horse and cart.

The Bear Hotel

He knows it's the most expensive hostelry in town. If it costs him a year's money, he doesn't care. He hopes that Walter will have left him *something* in his will. He intends to spend every penny of it in The Bear.

By now he's stone cold sober. His mouth tastes of cabbage. He swings his paint-spattered hold-almost-nothing from one sweaty palm to the other.

And in he goes.

They give him a small room overlooking the square, the stocks – imagine being locked in *that* contraption – and the town hall. It will serve.

The bed looks soft and inviting. The sheets are pristine. Why can't *his* sheets ever look like these? Perhaps, tonight, he'll manage to sleep. In any event, if he can get through the ceremony tomorrow, he'll be out of Woodstock as fast as his shabby shoes will carry him.

He washes his hands in a bowl of cold water, holding the soap to his nose. It smells of lavender and old ladies, but nice ones, intelligent ones, who have time to read and paint and garden, not merely jabber about the price of lardy cakes.

He examines his hands. There's paint underneath his nails. He scrunches his fingers into a ball to hide the stains, and opens his door. Down the narrow stairs he slithers. Their steepness could be lethal, especially if you'd had one too many. Tonight, he'll need to take care.

He walks into the bar.

Felix chooses a corner seat, tips his shabby hat over his eyes and nurses a beer. It tastes better than the one in Oxford. He's starving but he can't even think about swallowing food. If he does, up it'll come in undigested lumps all over the carpet.

Does he fall asleep? He can't remember. He may have dozed off, but then he hears voices. Two men have walked into the bar, bringing with them the tangy smell of the open road.

"Shall us sit 'ere?"

"We allus do."

"What'll you 'ave?"

"The usual … Thank ee kindly."

"So … How *are* you?"

"Oh, you know … Fair to middlin'."

"Come on now. You can do better than that."

Laughter of a reluctant rumbling kind and then a pause.

"They're buryin' You-Know-Who tomorrow."

"Aye." Silence. "Not afore bleedin' time, either. Scuse my language, but not afore bleedin' time."

"Aye." Sounds of slurping and sighs of satisfaction.

"This small town of ours." The voice reeks with righteous gusto. "It'll be a better place without him. He was the filthiest, most disgustin' man I ever met in all my born days. Walter bleedin' stinkin' Drummond. The most disgustin' creature in the whole wide world."

Somerville College, Oxford

26 October 1935

It's a glorious autumn morning, and a Saturday. The glow of an Indian summer is about to fade, but for this moment, this magnificent last herald of warmth and contentment holds Oxford in its hands.

The city looks its best. It's still early, the streets are quiet. The crowds have not yet gathered, jostled and pushed. If you know where to look, in the sacred corners of gown, not town, there's no more beautiful place in all the world.

Walter certainly knows not only where to look but where to hide. He knows how to scamper from quadrangle to alleyway, his sketchpad as his cast-iron alibi. Everyone knows him. The porters of the Oxford colleges at their elaborate gates; the traders in the Covered Market with their piercing voices: he gives them all a nod and a wink.

It's so easy. It's so *delightful.*

On this particular morning in Woodstock, he says a fond farewell to his darling Anne. He'll be very late back that evening, he has various business meetings, don't wait up.

106

Used to his ways, she never asks awkward questions. He jumps into his Bullnose Morris. He's off and away.

What bliss! That delicious sense of *freedom*. He has the whole of this glorious day and then the long evening at his command. He has an intelligent – if rather plain – daughter to collect from Somerville. What's more, today of all days he also has his daughter's best friend, Perdita Willoughby-Jones.

He'll have to be *particularly* careful about this *extraordinary* challenge he's set himself. His many other wicked dalliances – Walter checks his dapper moustache in the driving mirror – pale into insignificance when he thinks about seducing Perdita. In the past he's always avoided having anything remotely sexual to do with any of Eleanor's friends. He's not crazy, is he? He doesn't want to *court* trouble where he needn't find it.

But there's something about Perdita he can't resist. *She's* the bee's knees, the cat's whiskers, the icing on the cake of all his conquests. Most of them are barmaids or flower sellers. Girls too frightened to open their mouths for anything but his own insatiable tongue. And too poor to be anything but grateful for his tireless generosity.

Oh, yes. He can be so generous!

Only he knows how to give a girl a *really* good time – and that poignant little gift at the end of it.

A posy of violets. "Press these in your Bible and think of me, angel mine."

"Wear this little brooch here, near the flawless skin on your neck. That *neck* of yours. Never have I *seen* such a neck."

Ladies of Oxford, on this glorious autumn morning, here I come!

He starts thinking about Perdita again.

He's becoming obsessed with the girl. He's even drawn

imaginary sketches of her stark naked. Some in charcoal, several in coloured pencils. The coppery tones of her hair, her cream complexion.

Of course, he's always extremely careful to push the sketches into his hideaway. Nobody will ever find them. And he feels so joyful and clever with his own little secret.

How far will he manage to get with Perdita on this most beautiful of days? Will she be an easy conquest? Will she say no? Will she make him wait? How patient is he prepared to be?

He reaches the roundabout. He starts to sing *Cherry Ripe*. His mellifluous hum buzzes around his little car – his own small but wonderful world – like the sound of bees in Blenheim's grass by its magnificent lake.

It's like chanting hymns with that rather plain daughter of his – but more enjoyable. In church he has to be careful what he's thinking, just in case God can read his thoughts. We wouldn't have Him read *our* thoughts, now *would* we?

Soon he'll be able to see Perdita's fantastic little face again.

"Cherry ripe, Cherry ripe, Ripe I cry …"

He plans ahead.

He'll gently touch Perdita's shoulder as he gallantly escorts her and Eleanor to the Cadena Café, making sure he walks between the two young ladies at all times.

"Full and fair ones …"

Watch her lips curl around her coffee cup.

"Come and buy …"

While talking mostly to his darling daughter about her week.

᯿

Fuller's walnut cake. He must remember to ask for Fuller's walnut cake. He makes a mental note. And buy *some*thing for Anne. What do you buy a woman who already *has* everything and spends her time playing bridge with her stupid fat little friends?

A driver in another car honks at him as they pass each other at the bottom of the Woodstock Road. He honks back. That's old thingy, whatsisname, right? One of the porters from Balliol. Great chap, always ready for a pint at the end of a long and most rewarding day. Having one's tongue down a young girl's throat is *very* thirsty work. Remember that time when …

He chortles, slaps his thigh with a gloved hand. That *was* a good day! And this glorious Saturday might turn out to be its match!

Walter parks his Morris in Beaumont Street and checks his watch. He has a spare half hour. With a nimble hop, skip and jump, he flits across Wellington Square, doffing his splendid new hat here, there and everywhere. Even the blackbirds envy him. When he reaches Little Clarendon Street, instead of turning right he spins to the left.

He decides to do something he very rarely does because it brings back painful memories. He'll cross Walton Street into Walton Crescent and dart past the house he once shared with Moira.

Sometimes, in such spare half hours, he broods on his past lovers, wondering why in the fifty years of his life he's had so many. The house he shared with Moira – he strides past it, glancing in its windows – looks much the same. They had some happy times there. But he'd been right to haul his family off to St Ives, for their own protection. He bites his lip as he walks up the road again.

Of course, he *regrets* what happened in Cornwall. Sometimes he's overcome by guilt and remorse – and a longing to see Moira again that cuts deep into his heart. If he had his time there again, he'd *never* have behaved like that. It was all Moira's fault. Look how hard he'd fought to keep their small family together!

And then there'd been Rebecca. What an amazing stroke of luck to have found her that evening in London. After Moira, he thought there'd never be another woman. He couldn't take the pain of it, the desperation of loving another human being so much.

But Rebecca had swept him off his feet. Within an hour of their meeting she decided she wanted him in her bed. Next morning she'd asked him to move into her studio in St John's Wood, so he'd never be lonely again. He'd jumped at the chance. He'd hated living alone, he'd pined for Felix.

Walter had never known such a confident, voluptuous woman as Rebecca. She'd adored sitting for him in the nude. She'd sculpted his head and shoulders in bronze. He was astonished at the result. When she asked him to marry her, he'd thrown caution to the wind. How could he put his life on hold for a lover who'd vanished one morning into a Cornish storm and might never return?

And then, just when he'd settled into blissful married life, Rebecca had died on him. Sickened and vanished from his life in seven days. Who could *blame* him for behaving as he did after being hammered to the ground by such bad luck?

He dances up to the portals of Somerville.

Life as a widower had been impossible. Meeting Anne in Blenheim … He knew she'd be a safe, conservative, devoted wife. Much too unadventurous in bed for *his* liking, especially after Rebecca's clever tricks and passionate lips, but there were other ways he could quench his voracious appetite.

"Daddy!" Eleanor chirps with delight. "Right on time, as always!"

"My *darling* girl!" He gives her a fatherly hug. Over her shoulder his eyes meet Perdita's. "I have such *plans* for us. First we'll have delicious coffee and cake at the Cadena. Then we'll do some shopping. I need to buy your *adorable* mother some fur-lined gloves. Then we'll have a spot of luncheon."

He gives Perdita a ravishing smile.

"And *then* we can go to the picture house on Walton Street to see a splendid musical. They're showing *Top Hat* with Fred Astaire and Ginger Rogers. How does that sound?"

"Perfect, Daddy darling. As always." Eleanor turns to her friend. "Isn't he the best father in the world?"

Perdita's gloved hand sends a frisson of delight up Walter's arm. "I'm sure he is," she says. "But he'll have to *prove* it, won't he?"

As the day bubbles along, he becomes bolder and more flirtatious. Eleanor – how divinely naïve his daughter is – notices nothing, he makes sure of that. If he winks at Perdita, it's behind Eleanor's back. If his hand brushes Perdita's, Eleanor, walking the other side, can't possibly see it. When he pulls out a chair for Perdita, Eleanor assumes he's being a proper gentleman, not admiring the curve of her best friend's bottom.

His real opportunity comes when they're sitting in the back row of the picture house. Just before the Pathé News, Eleanor slips away to powder her nose.

He seizes his chance. "Let me take you for a champagne

supper," he whispers in Perdita's ear. "Meet me tonight on the corner of Walton Crescent at half-past nine. It'll be dark by then. Nobody will spot us if we're careful."

Her lips hardly moving, Perdita murmurs, "An invitation I can't possibly refuse, Mr Drummond. I'll be there."

"Excellent." His heart thrums with excitement.

"And what should I wear for this grand occasion?"

His fingers daringly brush Perdita's thigh.

"As little as possible," he says.

Somerville College, Oxford

5 November 1935

It's as if the whole of Oxford is on fire. Every back garden boasts its own funeral pyre. Small boys race up and down their street, trundling small carts. Their bonfire-night guys may be roughly made, but they are easily identifiable. Royalty and academia are the most popular.

Behind her elegant desk lamp overlooking the quiet courtyard, Helen Darbishire, the Principal of Somerville College, works on. She never quite gets to the end of those papers she must sign. In order to give them her unique inky signature, she has to read them first, but when she's tired her mind wanders to Wordsworth's "bliss of solitude" and she has to start all over again. And then there are the letters she must write: endless, diplomatic, carefully worded. You never know who might read them. And the decisions she has to make!

A volume of Wordsworth's poems sits at her elbow. Through thick and thin, his poems guide her, steer, cheer and save her intellectual life. They're her only real escape from being a Principal.

But she's not allowed to open her much-thumbed volume until a tiny voice in her head says, "You've had quite enough for one night. *Demain, c'est un autre jour.*"

There's a tap at the door. She immediately knows whose knuckles that tap belongs to.

"*Come!*"

The door opens. The man is tall, thick-set, comforting: her Head Porter.

"Scroggs!" With great relief, she lays down her pen. Give the thing a rest, for heaven's sake. *How* many miles does it motor every day?

"May I have a word, Miss Darbishire?"

"Of course. When have I ever said 'no' to you?"

She stands, stretching her arms, her back. Every muscle aches. She moves slowly from behind her desk to face what she knows is bad news.

"It's about The Fox, Miss Darbishire."

"Ah … I thought it might be."

"He's moving in for the kill, as it were. You know what I mean."

"Indeed I do." She takes a deep breath. "Who does he have in his sights *this* time?"

Scroggs says bravely, "Miss Perdita Willoughby-Jones."

The Principal staggers slightly. "*Miss Willoughby-Jones?* But her family are one of our most generous benefactors. They live in – let me see now – isn't it—"

"Norham Gardens. One of them big houses by the University Parks." Scroggs appears to sag. He jabs a thumb at the elegant sofa. "May I, ma'am?"

"Please. Make yourself comfortable."

He squats on his haunches. "Seen 'em together, I have, with my own eyes."

She groans. "You'd better give me chapter and verse."

"It were like this, see? I been watching Miss Willoughby-Jones and Miss Drummond, like, whenever The Fox takes her to the Cadena on a Saturday. That's for starters. There's no knowing where they'll end up.

"Well, see, Willoughby-Jones, she's *always* on the scene. Last night I saw all three of 'em coming out the Phoenix. The Fox and that Perdy, as the girls call her, they were holding hands, walking the other side of Miss Drummond. *She* hadn't got a clue. Nice lass, that one, she'll go far."

Scroggs mops his face. His handkerchief is a smart silk scarf that one of last term's students gave him as a parting gift.

"She's a good egg. But that father of hers, he's a rotten flaming—"

The Principal cuts in very fast. "I know." Her mouth tastes of bitter lemons. "Do you think anything *serious* has happened?"

Scroggs looks at the ceiling. "'Fraid so, ma'am. That sorry I am. 'Fraid so."

The Principal's soft voice hardens. "Then we must end the whole thing before it happens again."

Scroggs heaves himself to his feet. He shifts his weight from one tired leg to the other. "Do you wish to see the aforesaid now, ma'am?"

"No. Let me sleep on it." She stoops over her diary. "Shall we say eleven o'clock tomorrow morning?"

"Right on, ma'am. I'll make sure the above-mentioned is waiting outside your door." He hesitates. "Will she be sent down?"

"But of course. Immediately. Clear her room and put her in a cab." Tears spark in the eyes of the brave, the stalwart, the not-so-innocent Principal of Somerville College for

Girls, Oxford. She says, "Foxes can be filthy animals, can't they?"

Scroggs turns at the door. He meets her eyes. The bonfire of anger burns between them, giving them both a smattering of comfort.

"Filthy? I should say! This Fox is *vermin*."

"And *Miss* Drummond?"

"Like I say, ma'am. Innocent as the day she were born. Leastways, she is for now. The poor wee lass."

Talking to Helen Darbishire

1936

The morning after the funeral, Eleanor climbs into her father's Bullnose Morris and drives to Oxford.

It takes her half an hour to persuade the engine to start. Patches of road are still covered in black ice; she drives with the utmost care. This is the first time she's had to negotiate the roads in winter weather. Walter had taught her how to handle the car the previous summer, as a reward for getting a place at Somerville.

"Take the next right after the roundabout. Splendid. That's my girl!"

She'd always longed to drive. She learned quickly, motoring around Woodstock's bumpy lanes in the early twilight, thrilled to be behind the wheel, delighted by her new feelings of independence.

"Always use the mirror. Always give hand signals. Excellent. You're a natural-born driver, Ellie. Some women are, some aren't. Your mother would be hopeless, and she knows it."

Her driving licence became one of her prized possessions: admired by her school friends, a formal acknowledgement that she'd entered the adult world.

The car's back seat is full of Walter's clutter: drawing pads, boxes of charcoal, crumpled maps, a scarlet woollen scarf, a picnic rug harbouring clumps of ageing yellow grass, empty tobacco tins, a pair of Wellington boots, smeared with dried mud. Anne regularly tidied up after Walter in the house, but refused to touch either his studio or the car. She'd shrug.

"If *you* don't mind working in a hovel and driving around in a dustbin, I'll have to put up with it!"

Eleanor's feelings of dread at meeting Miss Darbishire increase with every hour.

She parks the Morris in Beaumont Street, realising she's nervous as a kitten. She remembers her excitement on arriving at Somerville that first morning. Now she has neither the energy nor the inclination to fight her corner. She'll never be able to convince the Principal she should abandon her studies.

Because last night, after the guests had left, after she'd emerged from Walter's studio, Anne had broken down, sobbing in her arms.

"Promise you won't leave, Eleanor. *Promise me!* I feel so lonely and abandoned. Don't go back to College. Stay with me. I can't live without you."

"Don't cry, Mummy. Of course I'll stay with you. Somerville's not important. But you certainly are."

In the Drummond family, promises made are promises faithfully kept.

She taps at the Principal's door.
"Come!"

She pushes against it. The room, spacious, beautiful and

118

elegantly furnished, is lit by sets of tall windows overlooking the gardens.

"Miss Drummond!" Helen Darbishire – plump, kindly, blue-eyed, fair-haired – stands from behind her desk and moves towards her with outstretched hands. "I was very sorry *indeed* to hear your tragic news. I'd hoped so much to meet your mother." She tugs at the pale blue cashmere sweater beneath her tweed jacket. "Please, sit here ... Now, tell me *exactly* what happened."

Eleanor makes a brave attempt to explain, fumbling over the words. She likes Miss Darbishire but feels uneasy in her presence. The Principal has a curious immobility about her. Stories abound about students who'd read their essays aloud to her while for twenty minutes she sat absolutely still, her eyes closed. Convinced that the Principal had fallen asleep, the students were astounded at the end of the essays when she opened her eyes to ask pertinent questions about sections of their work.

Now, however, the Principal listens with equal care and attention, her eyes on Eleanor's face.

"I've told my mother I'll stay with her. I can't renege on my promise."

"I entirely understand." Miss Darbishire's eye lashes flutter with sympathy. "You're not alone in your predicament. During the Great War, I heard of many similar tragedies. Girls who lost their fathers, and were forced to abandon their studies."

"I see." Perhaps the Principal will be more sympathetic than Eleanor has anticipated? "The thing is, *they* died fighting. *They* were heroes. My father's death, by comparison, was such a *trivial* event—"

"But tragic nevertheless. He was trying to prevent the runaway horse from damaging itself or other people."

Eleanor's mind begins to spin. It's as if she's standing in the Woodstock street, spattered by snow, helplessly watching her father slither across the road. "Yes, but——"

"Then, in his own way, your father acted heroically."

"My mother thinks it was a pointless way to die. She's furious. It's why I can't leave her. I'm worried she'll do something silly if I don't keep an eye on her." The enormity of what she'll be giving up suddenly strikes home. "I can't believe I'll have to abandon my studies. I was *so* looking forward to this term. And I've worked very hard——"

"Indeed you have. Your entrance essay for our General Paper was outstanding. We'd have accepted you on its strength alone. And last term, you got through Pass Moderations with flying colours. You didn't do *that* by lying on a sofa eating chocolates."

"No, quite the opposite." She remembers the previous term when her exams consisted of four papers: Pliny's *Letters* in Latin; French; Classical Logic; and Greek literature in translation. She'd had weekly tutorials on the minor Elizabethan poets, attended lectures by C. S. Lewis, the war-shattered Edmund Blunden and Tolkien delivering on *Beowulf*. Every night she'd fallen into bed, her mind whirring.

"If you rejoin us tomorrow," the Principal leans forward, her eyes shining with eagerness, "you could still see your mother every week. I'd make arrangements for you to meet in College. Would that be an acceptable compromise?"

"I'd find it impossible to concentrate. I'd always be worrying about Mummy – and she'd feel I'd abandoned her."

"I don't want to pry into your private affairs, but is it a question of money?"

She flushes, remembering the anxiety in Michael Humphreys' eyes. "I don't know. I *hope* it won't be."

"If you *are* in financial difficulties, the College might be able to help."

Unable to trust herself to speak, Eleanor shakes her head. Carrying a begging bowl around Oxford's management committees would be the final straw.

Miss Darbishire sighs. She takes refuge behind her desk.

"I don't need to remind you that Somerville's one hundred and fifty girls have been hand-picked, Miss Drummond. You're among the chosen few. It's a considerable honour—"

"I *know* that!" Now she's on the brink of tears. Only the sound of her own indignant voice stops them in their tracks.

"Then may I suggest you go home and think carefully about your decision? Getting a degree, being qualified to teach, will be an excellent way to support your mother. Talk to her again. I'd be delighted to see her." The Principal's blue eyes lift and gaze into hers. In them shines sadness and disappointment. "How does that sound?"

"I'll try, but I can't promise anything." Eleanor stands up, her legs shaking. "Believe me, I didn't want *any* of this to happen."

"Of course you didn't." The Principal is also on her feet. "Neither did I." A plump hand strokes at a stray wisp of hair, as if she's brushing away her own dark memories. "Death asks nobody's permission." Her voice falters for a second, but briskly resumes its even keel. "You've only had one bite at the Somerville cherry. It's my job to fight for your continuing nourishment."

"I'm most grateful." Eleanor holds out her hand. "But for the time being, it's goodbye. I'll collect my things. And I'll think about everything you've said."

Back in Beaumont Street, she sits behind the wheel of the Bullnose Morris and bursts into tears. She's trapped between two dark seas. She'll be criticised if she *does* return to Somerville – "How could you be so cold-hearted, Eleanor? Your own mother needs you, and you turn your back on her!" – and condemned if she doesn't – "How could you throw away such an opportunity? Think of those *years* of study, those exams you passed. Remember how proud Walter was when you got your place!"

Staring into the driving mirror, she dries her eyes. Her face looks blotchy, her hair's a mess. She can't go home looking like this. She'll pack her cases, clear her room, drive to the gates of Somerville and pile her stuff in the car. Then she'll have coffee at the Cadena. Pull herself together before facing Anne.

Luckily, her corridor in West lies empty. Everyone is either in the library or shopping.

She dreads meeting her friends, having to face their sympathy and questions. Thank goodness Perdita hadn't returned from her skiing holiday in St Moritz, or there'd have been more questions, especially about Walter! Perdita had been fond of Walter. *Really* fond. Sadly, she'd decided she couldn't cope with the disciplines of studying. She'd left suddenly, even before the end of the Michaelmas Term.

In her absence, the scout has made her bed and tidied her room. The fire is freshly laid but unlit. Shivering, she throws her things into her suitcases. She sits on her narrow bed, clenching her fists, summoning the energy to drag the cases down the flight of stairs and out to the gate.

Someone taps at the door and pushes it open.

"Glad you're still here." Scroggs beams in the doorway. "Miss Darbishire told me to find you. I were that sorry to hear your news. Can I give you a hand?"

"Thank you so much, Scroggs."

122

"Let's hope you'll be back with us in the twinkling of an eye." He smells of petrol and Marmite. "Never say never, that's what my old Mam used to say. I'll carry these two big 'uns, you take the rest."

They load the suitcases into the Morris. Summoned by another porter, Scroggs vanishes into College.

A voice behind her calls her name.

"It *is* you, isn't it? Spiffing to see you again!" Robert Clark puffs up. "My dear girl! What *are* you doing? Why have you packed everything up?" He looks at her more closely. "What *is* the matter?"

She'd met Robert at a party during the Michaelmas Term. They'd liked each other on sight. Reading English at Christ Church, Robert is from a wealthy Cambridgeshire family. They'd spent many afternoons together, walking by the river or across Port Meadow, discussing their English essays, the lecturers, their tutors and university gossip; drinking tea at the Cadena.

Now he throws a friendly arm around her shoulders. "Where have you *been*? I've just asked after you at Somerville but they wouldn't tell me anything. Anyone would think I was an intruder, loitering with intent!"

In spite of her misery, she grins. With Robert beside her, she parks the car in Beaumont Street again. As they walk to the Cadena, she tells him about her week.

"Rotten luck, Ellie! You're *such* a top-hole girl. Dashed difficult and all that … Here's me thinking you had a spiffing Christmas! I *am* sorry." They cross the road opposite the Randolph Hotel. "Rudyard Kipling has died since I last saw you – and of course the poor old King. And now your pater. Life's a rum old cove, ain't it? Snap! And the whole thing's gorn down the blooming plughole."

∞

But the brief window of sunshine offered by Robert Clark closes and darkens fast that same afternoon.

It's clear from Michael Humphreys' face, the moment he walks through the door, that something is seriously wrong. Usually relaxed and smiling – over the years the solicitor's become a good family friend – he has a stiffness and formality about him that makes Eleanor more anxious than ever.

They meet in the drawing room, with the comfortable chairs grouped around the fire. Vera serves tea in the best china. Michael asks her to stay for the reading of the will. He leaves his cup untouched and opens his briefcase.

"Shall we get down to business?" He looks both panic-stricken and well-rehearsed. "This is difficult for me. Walter was a good friend. I've known about all this for some time. The problems" – he hesitates, shuffling his papers, fidgeting with his neck tie – "are ones both of finance and other matters."

"For goodness *sake*, Michael." Anne's voice is tense. "Put us out of our misery and spit it out. What does the will *say*?"

He clears his throat. "This house, Anne, is yours—"

"Of course it is!" She throws back her head. "I was born and bred here. My father left it to me in *his* will. There's no *way* Walter could touch it, even if he'd wanted to."

"Which I'm perfectly sure he didn't," Michael says quickly. "The problem is … that's *all* he's left you."

There's a long shocked silence. Eleanor's heart sinks.

Anne says bleakly, "It can't be."

"I'm afraid it is." Michael's eyes are on her face, anticipating trouble. "The paintings in his studio and on these walls are yours. All his other worldly possessions belong to you. And the car. And he's left Vera two hundred and fifty guineas."

"Good *heavens*!" Vera takes the envelope Michael gives her

with shaking hands. "I've never had so much money in my life!"

"But," Michael continues, his voice a lawyer's monotone, "after the payment of death duties and funeral costs, the remainder of Walter's money goes to a man called Felix Mitchell."

Anne shrills, "Felix *who?*"

"Felix Mitchell. I can only tell you his name. I can't divulge anything else."

"But who *is* he?"

"I'm sorry, Anne, that's all I can say." Michael hurries on, determined to get to the end of the dreadful business. "There's one last bequest. Walter owned a small cottage in St Ives, in Cornwall. He's bequeathed it to you, Eleanor, to use as you think fit."

This takes her completely by surprise. Colour flushes her cheeks.

"Cornwall?" Anne twists a handkerchief between her fingers. "A *cottage?* I'd no idea Walter owned *any* property. When we met, he had a shabby rented flat in north London." She looks across at Eleanor, her eyes blazing with disbelief. "And he *hated* the sea. When we went on holiday, it was always to the Lake District. Nothing would drag him to a beach anywhere in the world."

Michael drinks his tea in several long gulps. "I'm sorry to be the bearer of such bad tidings, Anne. Believe me, if I could have done anything to change Walter's mind, I would have done so. But it's not my job to question or interfere, merely to implement my client's wishes."

"You might have *warned* me. I'd have been able to discuss the matter with Walter. What kind of a friend do you think you are?"

"One that can keep matters strictly confidential. In my professional opinion—"

"*Hang* your profession! I need a brandy!" She adds reluctantly, "Will you join me? Vera, would you like one?"

"Thank you." Michael looks as if he needs one. "I don't wish to hammer home the point, Anne, but you'll need to see Robin Parker. Put your affairs in the best possible order. I don't know any details of your own bank account, of course. But in Walter's, there will be nothing left."

"I don't *have* a separate account!" Anne swirls the golden liquid around her glass. "I'd better enjoy this brandy while I can. We'll soon be living on bread and gruel."

Vera takes her drink and leaves the room, holding her precious gift. Michael sips his brandy. The colour returns to his cheeks. He looks at Eleanor.

"If you'd like to meet next week, I'll give you the details of your inheritance. An estate agent in St Ives is looking after it. He'll give you the keys, show you the ropes."

Anne pours herself another, larger brandy. "Would you *believe* it?" She shoots Eleanor a venomous look. "My daughter's now a woman of property while I'm penniless. *There's* a turn-up for the god-awful books!" She stands up. "I think you'd better go, Michael. I'm *this* close to smashing my brandy glass over your professional head."

Eleanor throws on her hat and coat. She slams out of the house.

She marches into Blenheim, and races down to the edge of the lake.

She bends to clutch at a handful of pebbles and slings them into the water.

"*That's* what I think of you, Walter Drummond." Another handful terrifies the moorhens "That's what I bloody well think of you ..."

"Will there be anything else, sir?"

1936

Felix Mitchell sits quiet as a stone in the corner of the bar in The Bear Hotel. He sits so still for so long that the barman comes over, concerned that his skin-and-bone customer might have died in his shabby boots without anyone noticing.

"Will there be anything else, sir?"

"What?" He rouses himself, glancing at the barman under the rim of his hat.

"We're closing the bar, sir. I believe you have a room upstairs. Is there anything—"

"No, thank you." He clambers to his icy feet. "Wait a minute. May I have a whisky? Make it a double." He staggers towards the bar. "Had a bit of a shock."

The barman doesn't want to hear. He hands over the drink, gulps one himself and turns down the lamp.

For his part, Felix never wants to talk about Walter to *anyone* in Woodstock. The only exception is Walter's daughter, Eleanor Drummond.

He'd planned to meet her. Leave her a note telling her he'd be at the funeral. Could she spare him five minutes, afterwards?

But hearing those men … Their voices clang like church bells in his ears. Listening to their brutal words has changed everything. Now all he wants is to go to the funeral, get the whole thing over and done with. Then catch the trains home, one after the other, as fast as they'll let him.

How on earth has the man he loves beyond all others acquired such a vile reputation? What on God's earth had Walter done?

Felix lies flat on his back, staring at the ceiling. It's two in the morning but he can't sleep. The words he heard in the bar thunder through his head. The bastards must have been lying. Perhaps there's a second funeral in Woodstock later in the day? Another group of mourners? More tears, but not shed for his own beloved?

He counts on his cold fingers underneath the linen. In nine hours' time, he'll attend the service. Within the little space of nine hours the man he loves will be covered in lumps of frozen mud.

Those idiots he overheard. Where are they now? He longs to confront them, take them by their scrawny necks, drag them to a river, push them in and sit on their heads until they bubble their final obscenities to the dying crescent of the watery moon. How he'd bay with laughter then. Oh, how he'd laugh.

At six o'clock, still wide awake, burning with anger but frozen with cold, he throws his bedclothes aside. He hears signs of life in the street. A horseman clatters up. His steed whinnies and stamps. A milk cart rattles by; a street sweeper whistles. A second horse canters down the road. Its bad-

128

tempered rider swears at the patiently waiting groom, demanding ale and food: he's famished, there was a roadside robbery, times are rough as well as cold, he's sick to death of the master who serves him ill.

Felix hears all the commotion, then climbs stiffly out of bed. He takes the flannel beside the bowl of water and douses himself. He starts to scrub and scour every inch of his skin. Wet and naked, raw as a peeled radish, he stands by the window, looking out.

He's got to face it: get dressed in whatever clothes he's stuffed into his hold-almost-nothing bag. Chomp through breakfast. Push his way through the church-goers. Watch as Walter's coffin trundles past his shoulder.

God give me courage for I need it now.

His stomach growls.

Feed me, why don't you? Warm milk with honey. Make me swallow it. Where is my Mummy? My Daddy will soon be under the cold earth.

He'll shut his ears to everything people around him say, just in case it gets worse. He'll stand and sing hymns at the ceremony, pretending they're for a distant relative he barely knew and doesn't even like. He'll saunter back to the hotel as if it were a daily stroll. He'll tip the waiter, raise his hat and check out of The Bear.

Then he'll make a run for it. Dash through Woodstock to the main road. Hitch a ride on a cart. Maybe fling himself on top of one, if the driver isn't looking. Reach Oxford station. Leap on the first suitable train. Keep everything tight, so tight together – until he reaches Driftwood.

How he longs for his oak door, the silence as he closes it, the wooden stairs, his new shoes waiting for his sweaty feet, his untidy bedroom with the sheets that smell of turpentine, his marvellous paint-spattered attic.

Home sweetest home. He stares at his white face in the

mirror on the wall. He makes himself a promise.

He'll speak to nobody.

He'll listen to nobody.

He will become nobody.

Until he reaches home.

A Small Brass Key

1936

After Michael Humphreys has left, Anne rages around the house, kicking the furniture, hurling cushions to the floor. At eight o'clock she takes to her bed.

"I'm nursing *my* wounds," she tells Eleanor, her voice icy. "Your father's slapped me in the face. After twenty years of marriage! I dedicated myself to him, gave him the best years of my life. He had the freedom of this house, my loyalty and devotion, an intelligent daughter, all the support for whatever artistic project he adopted, tea parties for his art groups." She stares across the room. "And *this* is how he repays me. I've *never* been so humiliated!"

Huddled by the fire but still shivering, Eleanor asks, "Will you see Robin Parker?"

"I suppose I'll *have* to, before the bailiffs arrive." Anne punches a pillow, flings her head against it. "We need to find money from somewhere. There are only so many meals you can skip before you starve. I can't get a job, I'm not trained to do anything but run this house." Her voice tightens. "I'll probably have to sell it.

131

Imagine that! I've never lived anywhere else in my life."

"No," Eleanor says firmly. "This house is our only asset. There must be another way. We'll sell everything we can, but not the house."

How she loves the place – and how she'll fight for it. It's one of the prettiest and certainly it's the oldest house in Woodstock. Its central hall leads on either side to an elegant drawing room and a spacious dining room. Beyond them lie Vera's kitchen and scullery, their small garden and Walter's studio. Upstairs are four bedrooms and a large, cool bathroom, and on the second floor some attic rooms used for storage: mostly Walter's clutter, and space for live-in servants.

When he'd been with them, every inch of the house was full. Walter only had to be in a room for five minutes and it would be deluged in strewn newspapers, smoked pipes, a clutter of friends or students and the sound of voices and laughter.

Now, the three of them float in a pall of tidiness and silence.

"Vera offered me her two hundred and fifty guineas." Anne's eyes spark with tears. "Isn't she the kindest? Of course I said no. But how can I pay her wages with nothing in the bank? And I couldn't *possibly* manage without her. She does the work of three people and never complains."

"I have some jewellery." Eleanor stands up, pushing her frozen hands into her woollen sleeves. She peers out of the window to reassure herself. Normal life does still exist beyond her nightmare. People walk to the pubs and shops, talking, laughing, without a care. She envies them.

"Those pearls Daddy gave me last August on my eighteenth. I can sell them to tide us over. I noticed a similar necklace in an Oxford jewellers. It was on sale for two hundred pounds. I'll try to get the same."

"But you *adore* the pearls. They look *enchanting* on you."

"We must be practical. Anyway, I've only worn them three times: once on my birthday and twice last Christmas. I didn't dare take them to College in case they were stolen." She rushes on, to hide the choke in her voice. "And there must be six or seven paintings in Daddy's studio that'll fetch a decent price." She turns to face her mother. "We must be strong and resourceful."

"I feel weak and helpless." Anne wrings her hands. "I expect that Felix Mitchell fellow is drinking himself silly in a pub somewhere, celebrating his good fortune."

Keen to avoid discussing him, Eleanor says quickly, "I'm going to London on Monday with Kath, if you don't mind my leaving you. She wants to see King George's lying-in-state. I'll take the pearls and sell them in Bond Street. And there's The Topaz Gallery in St John's Wood. Daddy sold lots of paintings there. Maybe they'll buy a few more."

"You're being so *sensible*, Eleanor." Anne dabs her eyes. "And you're not going back to Somerville, are you? *Promise* me."

"I promise. I'll write to Miss Darbishire. If I can't even pay my fees, returning to College is out of the question."

"I'm *so* glad, darling. After the *horrendous* news this afternoon, I couldn't *stand* any more. I'm *sure* it's the right choice."

"Do I *have* a choice to make?"

On Sunday, she wakes early, lights the fire in her freezing room, takes a quick bath, pulls on her oldest clothes. She unpacks her suitcases, files her College papers, stacking her books. Then she writes two letters: one to Helen Darbishire, the other to Robert Clark. Before Vera or Anne have woken, she slips out to the postbox.

Back in her room, she takes out the precious pearls. The single-stranded necklace glows lustrous in her palm. Tomorrow she'll wear her best suit and smartest winter coat. Put on the bravest face. And sell the pearls as if she doesn't give a jot.

In the kitchen she makes a pot of tea, takes a cup to her mother.

"I'll be in the studio all morning. I'm going to tidy the place up, sort out Daddy's paintings. Decide what we can sell."

"Rather you than me, Eleanor. Are you going to sell the car?"

"Definitely not." She stares down at the thin figure huddled beneath the bedclothes. "I need it. I'll have to find a job. It won't come to me. The car could be my lifeline."

"Oh, God!" Anne sits up, her face pale, her eyes anxious. "You'd leave me all alone in this great big house!"

"Don't talk nonsense, Mummy." Eleanor's patience is wearing thin. "You have Vera, and I haven't even *begun* to make a decision. Now drink your tea, have a bath and eat a decent breakfast. And go to church, like you always do——"

"As if nothing's happened?"

"Life must go on. Moping won't get us anywhere." She adds slyly, "And staying in bed all day is terribly bad for the complexion."

That seems to do the trick.

Walter's studio is in such a mess, Eleanor scarcely knows where to start. It's hard to throw anything away. But she makes herself stick at it. Her anger over the terms of his will certainly helps. Every time she feels sentimental, her fury spurs her on.

There are six paintings good enough to sell: all landscapes

of Blenheim, done at different times of the year. The lake in summer, glittering with light. Autumn woodland, full of golden shade. The invoices in his desk give her guidelines on how much he'd have charged for them.

And then, rummaging through the single desk drawer, she finds a battered red-leather purse. She hauls it out. The leather's stiff, its colour stained from a rich crimson through to dark brown. The purse is topped by a rusty brass clasp. She snaps it open.

Inside lies a small brass key.

She frowns. It's a very odd find. She'd never seen Walter use it. So why had he kept it? There's nothing in the studio that even *needs* a key. Which piece of furniture in their house has a locked drawer?

She slides it back into place. She has neither the time nor the patience to deal with it now. When their money problems are sorted, she'll find its proper home.

Bond Street and The Topaz Gallery

1936

On the train to Paddington next morning, Eleanor and Kath have the carriage to themselves for an hour. As they lurch through the outskirts of Oxford and across the snow-bound fields, she tells Kath about Walter's dying demand that she find the mysterious Moira. The very name of the woman is beginning to haunt her dreams. About the equally mysterious Felix Mitchell and his inheritance. About their devastating lack of money, Anne's misery, her own decision to leave Somerville – and her astonishment at being given a cottage in St Ives.

Kath listens carefully, her eyes dark with concern.

"Mummy went to church yesterday because I insisted. Then she invited her best friend to tea. I heard her telling Sylvia Dunkley about our predicament. It was *such* a mistake. Mrs Dunkley's one of Woodstock's biggest gossips. Everybody will have heard about us by now."

"But your mother needs a friend, Ellie. Better that than not havin' anyone, now she has no husband." Kath tries to cheer her up. "You could always get a job at the Palace. Or how do you fancy trainin' to be a lady's maid in Kensington?"

"That would *really* thrill my mother, wouldn't it? Me in service, miles away from home? Oh, the humiliation! Oh, her despair!" The girls laugh.

Eleanor squeezes Kath's hand. "What would I do without you?"

The train is twenty minutes late arriving at Paddington. By the time it finally puffs to a standstill, Kath is fretting and anxious.

"Maud will think I've missed the train. There'll be *thousands* of people in Westminster. We might not be able to find each other."

Kath jumps on to the platform. Eleanor joins her. The girls hug briefly.

"See you at Lyons Corner House in Oxford Street at two," Eleanor says.

Kath vanishes into the mass of coats, hats and belching smoke.

A moment of terror grips Eleanor. She's totally alone. She has no darling Daddy, no College term to look forward to, no lectures to attend, no party invitations to accept. She has no career mapped out, and no idea what will happen to her over the next few months.

All she has is a strand of pearls and a nagging mother.

She walks down the platform. People jostle her shoulder, a dog leaps at her handbag. A man walks towards her, raising his hat. He leers at her with black teeth. She ignores him and the whiff of stale garlic on his breath.

When was she last in London? She tries to remember.

A memory explodes in her head. Last summer, she and

Walter arrived in London to go shopping. Walter needed a new suit. They'd just stepped off the train when a man clapped him on the shoulder. The two men embraced. The other man looked at her, his eyes hard and black. "Well, I *never*, Drummond! *She's* very young!"

Daddy had said quickly, "May I introduce my daughter? This is Eleanor."

"Oh! Sorry!" The man smirked at Walter and vanished into the crowd.

She remembers the embarrassment on Walter's face. She'd thought it rather odd.

To shake off her loneliness, she decides to walk the rain-drenched streets from Paddington to Bond Street. She's dreading the next few hours. Londoners seem to move more quickly than her neighbours in Woodstock. Nobody meets anyone's eyes. Nobody says, "Good morning."

She paces up and down Bond Street several times, peering into jewellers' windows, trying to decide which looks the most friendly, summoning the courage to step inside. When she finally chooses a shop and pushes at the door, its sumptuous purple-velvet, brightly-lit interior makes her feel shabby. Her boots are spattered with mud, her coat is damp.

She lays the box of pearls on the counter, pulls off her gloves, lifts out the necklace. Under the bright lights, it looks small and vulnerable, as if its marvellous lustre has been sucked away. In that single instant she loves it more than ever. She'd have given *anything* to be able to slip it back into her bag and rush out of the shop. But her legs refuse to move. She reminds herself: Anne and Vera need to eat. Only yesterday, the butcher had waylaid Vera in the street, reducing her to tears over an unpaid bill.

She manages to say, "Good morning! I wonder whether I could sell you this?"

The jeweller, a tall, thin man wearing a glossy silk jacket, pulls out his magnifying-glass with the faintest sneer. He prods at the necklace with immaculate fingernails, as if the pearls are lumps of meat on a butcher's slab. His nostrils flare with distaste.

"Hmm." He lays the glass on the counter. "The pearls are rather small."

"It's a very good piece." She's furious and defensive. "They're natural, not cultured pearls. I saw an identical strand in Regent Street." The jeweller's eyes narrow. "In the window for three hundred guineas."

The jeweller sucks his teeth. "I can't offer you *anything like* that amount." He pushes the necklace towards her. "Prefer to take them elsewhere?"

She feels like a pauper. "How much could you——"

"One hundred and fifty guineas. Not a penny more."

She accepts. The thought of surviving such humiliation again – perhaps for an even smaller amount – makes her feel faint.

Smirking triumphantly, he slides the pearls under the counter with a practised swish of his lily-white hands.

Back in Bond Street, she hails a cab.

"Could you take me to The Topaz Gallery, please, in St John's Wood."

She stares out at the gloomy crowds as the driver crosses Oxford Street and heads north. Every flag flies at half-mast. Everyone wears mourning for King George.

She opens her bag and counts the crisp notes. She's never had anything like this amount of money before – and certainly not to carry around a big city in broad daylight. It's as if she's robbed a bank.

She takes a five-pound note from the pile and puts it in her wallet. She seals the other notes in their envelope. She has an appointment to see Robin Parker on Wednesday afternoon to open her own bank account.

Start as she means to go on.

The Topaz Gallery is an elegant Regency terraced house: well-kept, with cream-painted walls and a small front garden paved in grey stone. She climbs the flight of steps and rings the bell. There's no answer. Her heart sinks. She should have made an appointment. When she tried to yesterday, she found herself in tears, full of self-pity.

She presses the bell again.

A voice calls, "I'll be with you in a half a sec."

The door opens. A portly man with dark, greasy hair and a handlebar moustache gives her a mechanical grin. He wears a green smoking jacket and smells strongly of cigars.

"*Good* morning, Miss. Can I help?"

This is the first time she's spoken about Walter to a stranger. Her voice shakes.

"I'm Eleanor Drummond. My father, Walter … Do you remember him?"

The eyes register recognition. "Course I do … Poor old Walt. Kicked the bucket. Only fifty. Tragic." He holds out a podgy hand. "Name's Daniel Rogers. How d'you do, Miss Drummond. Won't you come in?"

Daniel ushers her into a long, narrow hall with whitewashed walls and gleaming wooden floors.

"My gallery's through there." She glimpses an enormous room hung with paintings, its central table gleaming with bronze sculptures. "Come into my office."

The back room, lit by a grimy window, is crammed with files and papers. Canvases and framed paintings are stacked all over the floor. Piles of invoices droop across a large desk, along with dirty cups. A half-smoked cigar smoulders in its ashtray.

"Sorry about the mess. I have a clear-out once a year. Within days, it looks like this again." He slumps into a battered leather chair behind his desk, waves her into another one. "Make yourself comfortable. How can I help?"

"My mother and I." She clutches her handbag for comfort. "We've been sorting out Walter's studio. There are six or seven paintings good enough to sell. I wondered—"

"*Did* you now! Sorry to say I haven't bought anything from Walter for at least three years." Daniel picks up the cigar, pouts his mouth around it.

She stares at him, mesmerised by the redness of his lips. "But *why?*"

"His stuff wasn't shifting. Came to the conclusion I couldn't sell him any more."

It's as if he's kicked her in the stomach. "Daddy came to *see* you last December. I was at College, but Mummy told me he was in London on business for more than a week. He left with six paintings and brought none of them back."

Daniel shakes his head. Flakes of dandruff settle on his shoulders like the first delicate drifts of snow. "Sorry, Miss Drummond, but I didn't buy 'em. I'd have made an entry in my black book." He points to a bulging tome sprawling on a shelf. "I keep spit-spot accurate records, in spite of the chaos."

"I see." Her heart drills a painful pinpoint in her chest. "*Why* did his paintings stop selling?"

"Hard to say." He shifts his weight in his chair, which groans beneath the strain. "Tastes change. I can only listen to the marketplace. I can't dictate what my clients want, I can only try to keep up with 'em." He chews at his bottom lip. It flushes an even darker crimson. "To be perfectly frank," his eyes meet hers. "Shall I explain, Miss Drummond?"

"Please. I really need to know."

"Walt's work began to lack *energy*. It's hard to say exactly when the rot set in – I'm sorry, that's unkind, I take it back – but a certain zest, passion. It went missing. I told him to take a holiday, look at new landscapes, find something *fresh* to paint."

"What did he say?"

"He was none too pleased. I returned three landscapes. He left in a bit of a strop. Understandable, I suppose. Sadly, I never saw him again." He leans forward. "I *do* mean sadly, Miss Drummond. I liked Walt. We were friends. But first and foremost, I'm a businessman. I never accept work if I don't think I can sell it."

"When did you first meet him?"

"Dashed if I can ... Wait a minute. Of course. That's it! ... Rebecca brought him to one of my previews."

"Rebecca?" The name sticks in her throat like a piece of apple core.

"Walt's *first* wife, Rebecca Holmes. The sculptor. You must have heard of her."

She feels dizzy. "Daddy's *wife*?"

The cigar hovers in mid-air. "Good Lord! Hope I'm not speaking out of turn. Don't you *know* about her?"

"I've no idea who you're talking about."

"Rebecca Holmes. Lovely woman. Handsome, vivacious, older than Walt, very talented. She sculpted a *marvellous* bronze head and shoulders of your father. I adored it. Then I got an amazing offer from a West End dealer. Couldn't refuse."

She clutches the arms of her chair. Her handbag slithers to the floor. "Walter and this Rebecca." Blood pumps into her cheeks. "How long were they married? And where is she now?"

Daniel crushes his cigar with pudgy fingers. "They were only hitched for a year. During the war, it was. Ghastly time, specially in London. Never knew where those blasted bombs would drop. Your father produced his best work while he was with Rebecca. His nudes were voluptuous without being pornographic. Curvaceous *and* tasteful. It's not an easy line to draw or paint!"

He chuckles at his own joke, flicking a greasy strand of hair into position.

"Sadly, Rebecca died. She caught influenza, winter of 1916. Turned into pneumonia. All very sudden – and absolutely tragic for Walt. He never got over it. That's when he became a landscape painter. Said he couldn't bear to look at women's flesh any longer … I say, Miss Drummond! Are you feeling quite well?"

She pulls out her handkerchief to wipe her forehead. "I'm fine." Her fingers feel numb, her thighs are damp. She makes herself ask, "Did Walter and Rebecca have any children?"

"Good Lord, no! Rebecca wasn't the maternal type. Her bronzes were her babies. And Walt needed a lot of mothering. Look here, Miss Drummond, you have gorn awfully pale. I have some excellent malt whisky if you'd—"

"No, thank you." A whiff of cigar smoke has become trapped in her mouth. She's desperate to escape the dank room *and* its portly owner. "I really must be going."

"I hate to send you away looking so peaky." He scrapes back his chair. "Have a quick look round my gallery. Give you a good idea what my clients *are* buying."

Lyons Corner House, London

That same day

Daniel's walls glitter with amazing talent. Large abstract paintings sizzle with colour: confident and modern. Extraordinary portraits look out at her with dancing eyes. Walter's recent work couldn't hold a candle to them. She's amazed she had the audacity to visit the gallery at all.

As for the portly Daniel Rogers: he'd obviously known Walter better than she ever did. What else – and *who* else – lies in wait for her?

Ten minutes later, Eleanor stands on the pavement outside The Topaz Gallery, her head reeling. She turns left and walks rapidly away from the gallery, she hardly knows where. The rain has eased to a fine drizzle. Cabs trundle past her, driving towards London. She watches them disappear. She has an hour to kill before meeting Kath and Maud. She'll sit over a coffee, try to gather her thoughts.

St John's Wood High Street looms into view: snooty dress shops whose exorbitant prices make her gasp. Furriers too posh for labels. High-class grocers from whose doorways waft the scent of cheese and spices. Announced in all their windows:

WE WILL BE CLOSED TOMORROW FOR THE FUNERAL OF HIS LATE MAJESTY

She finds a coffee shop, filled with groups of friends. They chatter to each other in French and German, turning to look at her as she finds a seat by the window.

She sits over her coffee. A couple of newcomers order soup. Its scent rises, and suddenly she remembers an incident, here in London, that she'd pushed from her mind. It now surfaces like a swimmer coming up for air.

It was five years ago, one Saturday in summer. She and Walter had been to an exhibition in Camden Town. Afterwards they found a small French restaurant in Regent's Park Road. They sat by the window, eating a fragrant *bouillabaisse.*

Suddenly her father gasped, clattering his spoon into its bowl.

"Just seen someone I know." He'd leaped to his feet. "I'll only be a moment."

He'd shot out of the restaurant like a bullet. A woman wearing a long silver-blue cloak stood outside an antiques shop on the opposite side of the road. He tapped her shoulder. She turned to look at him, her profile sharp and beautiful. He shrank with disappointment, stepped back, bowed stiffly, muttering. The woman smiled, shrugged and turned away. He mopped his forehead, swaying.

At their table again, he looked haggard: as if someone had sucked the wind out of his sails and forgotten to pump it back.

"Got it wrong, I'm afraid. Wasn't who I thought."

"Who *did* you think she was, Daddy?"

He picked up his spoon, toying with the soup. Crumbling his bread into damp pieces. Eating nothing.

"Only a friend."

Briefly, he met her eyes. His were overcast, as if they'd absorbed the shadows of a thundery day.

"Before I met Anne," sweat bubbled on his forehead, "I knew lots of people here. Lost contact when I moved to Woodstock. You know how it is."

He spoke little on their journey home, as if he were sheltering behind a glass wall which gave him much-needed protection.

When they reached home, he parked the Morris and turned towards her.

"That woman I thought I knew. No need to mention it to your mother. Trivial incident, nothing happened, eh? Keep it between ourselves, Ellie. Agreed?"

"Of course, Daddy." She blushed, feeling like a conspirator in an affair she didn't understand. "Just between ourselves."

Now she stirs the dregs of her coffee as if she might find answers in the bottom of the cup.

Had her father been looking for Moira? That woman in blue, hovering in Regent's Park Road like an exquisite dragonfly swooping over water: had she reminded him of the woman he had somehow, somewhere, lost?

Back in Oxford Street, she pushes her way into Lyons Corner House. She spots Kath and Maud sitting at the back. Kath waves.

Maud stands to greet her. "I were that sorry to hear your news, Ellie. How are you keepin'?"

They shake hands. Maud looks polished by London life. Her job as a lady's maid in Mayfair suits her. She wears a thin film of make-up, skilfully applied, cherry-red lipstick, a fashionable coat that shows off her curves, and a daringly perched hat. Beside her, Kath looks like a country bumpkin and Eleanor feels like one.

She grimaces. "Thank you, I'm bearing up."

It's a relief to be with friends. She squashes herself on to a chair. "How was the lying-in-state?"

"The queues were long and frightful. The whole thing were real gloomy." Maud gives a brief laugh. "I'm glad I saw it, but honestly! All them droopin' heads, all that mournin'. Makes you want to put on your glad rags and dance the night away."

Ravenous, the girls order eggs and chips; then tackle apple crumble with thick custard, and cups of scalding sweet tea.

"I'm paying for all of us," Eleanor says firmly. "I've just sold my pearls. The minute I get home, I'll be sorting out the bills, putting the money into a bank account and starting to count the pennies. This is *my* celebration."

She listens, fascinated, to Maud's gossip.

"The Prince of Wales had been plannin' to run off with Mrs Simpson and to hell with everyone. *Then* his father died, so he was forced to put his plans on hold." Maud scoops the last of her crumble. "Course, you can't believe *everythin'* you hear, but I reckon there's truth behind the rumour."

"Have you *seen* Mrs Simpson?" Kath asks.

"I were in the hall once when Wallis arrived for a posh dinner. She were dressed to the nines in a slinky frock, and glitterin' with jewels. She's glamorous to look at, but her voice is hard as nails. She thinks everyone should *curtsey* to her."

"Did *you* have to?"

Maud drops her voice. "Wallis Simpson were born illegitimate in Baltimore from some impoverished 'grand' family. She ain't never done a day's work in her life. She's got two husbands still livin', but pretends the first one

147

doesn't exist. Curtsey I *don't* think! She ain't got no money of her own, only what her husband Ernest gives her – and now, of course, Edward."

Maud crooks her little finger as she sips her tea.

"And what does *he* do the minute he's King? Cuts the wages of his staff by ten per cent! They're that angry, especially when Wallis is seen wearing *another* string of emeralds."

"Perhaps," Kath suggests, "he's tryin' to economise?"

"He's got plenty of money," Maud says grimly. "Wallis is behind the petty meanness. Some staff have worked for the royals all their lives. Now they're scared that Wallis will tell Edward to sack 'em." She looks at her sister. "Be warned, my girl. Don't you never work for that woman. If she asks you, pick up your skirts and run."

Looking for an Answer

1936

Eleanor reaches home feeling stiff and weary. The fresh Woodstock air is a relief after the stench of London's horse-drawn carts and muddy traffic. But she dreads facing Anne with her news from the gallery. As for being Walter's second wife, that can *certainly* wait.

The evening has settled in. Woodstock's shops are closed, its streets stand empty. But Eleanor is startled to see the house is plunged in darkness.

Vera meets her at the door, a finger on her lips.

"Your mother's in there," she points to the drawing room, whose door is firmly closed, "with Sylvia Dunkley and two of Sylvia's friends."

Eleanor throws off her hat and coat. "Why are they in the dark?"

"They've lit a pair of candles." Vera rolls her eyes. "They're having a séance."

"What?"

"Come into the kitchen. You must be famished. This is the *last* thing you'll want to hear."

Eleanor eats supper and listens.

"Mrs Dunkley arrived, unexpected like, at two this afternoon. After an hour, your mother comes out, looking all flushed and excited. Mrs Dunkley had two sons who were killed in the Great War within a year of each other. She regularly 'speaks' to them 'on the other side'. She persuades your mother that 'talking' to your father will reveal why he's left his money to Felix Mitchell – and who he is."

"Good *grief*, Vera. Séances are rubbish."

"But would she listen to a word? She draws the curtains, sets up a table, puts on her best black frock, does her hair, proper flustered. Got herself into a right state."

Eleanor pushes her plate aside. "Will she listen to *me*?"

"You can try, dear heart. Trouble is, if you get too fierce, she'll disappear to Mrs Dunkley's. I'd rather she stayed here, so I can keep an eye on her."

Depressed and exhausted, Eleanor crawls up to her room. She opens her bag and digs out the envelope. She counts the crisp notes. Then she makes sensible plans.

She and her mother meet over breakfast next morning.

"How was London?" Anne asks listlessly.

"Crowded. Rainy. Gloomy. Everyone was in mourning. I was glad to get home."

"Did you sell the pearls?"

"Yes. At a jewellers in Bond Street."

"Hmm." Anne gulps her tea. "Hope they gave you a good price."

"Good enough. I don't have the experience to haggle."

"And that gallery." Anne straightens her back. "How was it?"

Eleanor says quickly, "Closed for the royal funeral. I'll go

150

back another time." She moves the conversation on to the attack. "Vera tells me you held a séance with Sylvia."

"So what if I did? It's not against the law."

"It may not be *illegal*, but it's certainly a waste of time."

"Then perhaps *you'd* like to tell me who this fellow Felix Mitchell is."

"You know I can't."

"So kindly let *me* find out! By doing it *my* way!"

"It's a crazy way. I don't want you to be more upset than you already are."

"I know." Anne's expression softens. "You're only trying to look after me. By the way, a letter came for you yesterday. It's over there."

Standing by the window, Eleanor tears it open.

"It's from Miss Darbishire. She thinks I'm still in shock and incapable of making a rational decision."

"And what does *that* mean?"

"She wants me to reapply for my place and start my course again in the autumn. She can't guarantee I'll be successful, but my application will be given priority. She wants me to think seriously about my future."

"It's her *own* future she's talking about, not yours."

Eleanor flushes. "That's not fair, and you know it."

Anne shrugs. "How can a woman like that know *anything* about real life? She has never married, never had a child. She lives in her own little ivory tower. She can't know what it's like to love someone for twenty years and lose them in a heartbeat."

"You're being *most* unkind—"

"All those books, all that abstract knowledge. Do you *really* want to spend your life as a boring old blue stocking? Teaching snotty-nosed children in smelly classrooms?"

Eleanor meets Anne's eyes with difficulty. She's beginning to hate her. "Not much, but it's an honest way of earning a living. Not that *you'd* know anything about that."

Anne chews and swallows. She has nothing left to say.

"I shall tell Miss Darbishire I'm thinking about her very kind offer."

Anne finds something. "How can you *afford* to return, now we're little better than *paupers*?"

"Sell the cottage in St Ives? I'm going to see Robin Parker tomorrow. I worked it out last night. I can afford to pay Vera's wages and our household bills for the next six months."

Anne's cheeks flame with two bright red spots. "God Almighty! All this scrabbling around for the nearest penny. It's so *humiliating*—"

"We have a problem and we're solving it."

Anne puts down her cup. "Tell you what … Could you call on Jonny Giffen? That big linen press in the spare room. It's Cuban mahogany, been in our family since 1775. I adore it, but I can store the sheets and blankets somewhere else. Ask Jonny to take a look at it."

"Shall I also tell him why?"

"Sure. He's a kind-hearted soul. He was at the funeral." Anne blinks back tears. "Tell him the truth. I trust him. And he might just give us a more than decent price."

The Tuppeny Chew

22 August 1931

"It's poor little Eleanor Drummond's thirteenth birthday today." The man hunkers down with his companion, mopping his face.

"Aye, it is that."

"Makin' a proper song and dance about it, is You Know Who."

"Aye, he is that."

"Bought hisself a new car. Bloomin' bright yellow, like a silly bird. Bullnose Morris from that Longwall Garage."

"I *ask* you!"

Pause. The men drink. The beer foams comfortably around their mouths and dribbles on to their beards.

"It's goin' to make everythin' worse, ain't it, what with her bein' thirteen and all."

"You reckon?"

"Aye. Seen it afore now, I 'ave."

"'*Ave* you now?"

"Aye, I 'ave that."

Pause.

"Does you think we'd better *do* summat? Give 'im a kind of a warnin'? Gentle, like, but me and my missus, *we* reckon summat should be done."

"'Appen to agree."

The two men shake hands on it.

"Praps after we've supped up, you and I could take a gentle walk in the Park, 'ave a few words together in private, like."

"Aye, we could that."

Pause.

"Shouldn't take long. Promised the missus I wouldn't be late 'ome. Think I know someone who could sort out this 'orrible mess for us."

The following evening, Walter Drummond, strolling along, unaware of everything but the black obsessions in his heart, finds himself being pushed down Woodstock's Market Street by someone behind him who has his hand on his neck.

Before he realises what's happening, he's up against a mossy wall in a dank alleyway. He can't see the writing on the wall because he has his back to it.

"I'm going to spell it out to you straight, Squire Drummond," the man mutters.

His voice trembles with hatred. He's wearing a large felt hat and a scarf pulled over his face, but even so his breath stinks of garlic.

"My dearest daughter, the joy of my heart, I caught her in tears the other week and she told me all about you. I know what you've been getting up to in that cellar of yours, underneath that oh-so-pretty house your lovely wife allows you to squat in."

Walter's knees crumble into splinters. "I'm sure I haven't

154

the *faintest notion* what you're talking about. *Kindly let go of*—"

"And if you don't *stop it right now*," the man continues, "you won't live to see your own dear daughter's fourteenth birthday. Not by a *long* chalk."

A large hand takes hold of Walter's neck and, ever so slightly, squeezes it.

"Are you listening to me, Squire Drummond?"

Walter's about to suffocate. His eyes bulge with terror. His hair beneath his velvet hat streams with cold sweat. He gulps. He's allowed to come up for air. He remembers how he almost drowned when he was a child.

"I hear you," he says. "Can I go home now?"

The man vanishes, as if by magic, leaving behind only a glob of spit on one of Walter's shoes. One minute the stinking alleyway feels full of menace. The next it's silent and empty. Walter remains, a quivering mass of guilt and shock.

Whose daughter had he been messing about with? It had only been a bit of harmless fun. He makes sure his girls have a good time. Crazy to make such a fuss.

He limps home.

"Is that you, darling?" Anne calls from the drawing room.

"It is, my sweetness and light."

"Won't you join us for a hand of bridge?"

He checks his face in the hall mirror. It's a strange shade of pale green. His eyes are bloodshot. His collar is black with soot.

"Got a bit of a headache, my angel. Think I'll go straight to bed."

Quiet as a mouse, he slips out to his studio in the garden. He doesn't need to put on the light. He creeps towards the chaise longue, pushes it aside with his hip. He presses a floorboard. The trapdoor opens.

He slides into it, climbs down the rungs, slithers along the underground passageway until he reaches the cellar door. He's inside the cellar in a flash.

He reaches in the pitch dark for the shelf, the matches and the candle. The guttering flame reveals a pile of seductive pillows, a pair of silky knickers, a few drawings of stark naked women, a towel, a feathery fan and two dead roses.

He scrabbles in a corner for the bricks he'd used to create the gap in the cellar wall. He'd better use them again, only this time in reverse.

Not right now. Anne might waltz into the bedroom and wonder where he was. He'll start filling it in tomorrow. For, say, an hour at a time over the coming week. That should do the trick.

Then that vile busybody, the bastard, he'd have nothing on him, would he? Only the hysterical words of a girl whom nobody would believe. He, Walter Drummond, would be innocent as the day he was born.

He gets out his pocketknife and slashes at the drawings. When they lie in tatters at his feet, he starts on the underwear.

Five days later, he's in the immaculate office of his friend and solicitor, Michael Humphreys.

He's partially recovered from the unexpected events of that very brief, very dark encounter. It might never have happened. An unfortunate incident. They'd got the wrong man. He'd worked with some bricks and mortar very fast indeed.

He checks his fingernails. Immaculate. Nobody would ever know.

∞

"Good to see you, Walter." Michael spoons sugar into steaming cups of coffee. "What can I do for you?"

He gulps. It's a lot stronger than Vera's mediocre brew. The powerful aroma gives him courage. He fills his lungs with determination.

"Need to make a will, old boy. Simple as that."

Michael puts down his cup. "Oh? You're not *ill*, are you, sir?"

"Course not, old boy." He adjusts his fetching cravat, admires the shine of his shoes. "Never had a day's illness in my life." He hesitates. "Except for that tragic accident when I was a child. The one that prevented me from fighting in the war——"

"Ah, yes, *that* one."

"How I should have *adored* to do my bit in the trenches. But you know how it is. Getting on a bit now. The knee aches and all that. You know, old boy, I should've done these formalities long ago. For my darling Eleanor." His eyes mist over. He's frightfully good at making their violet-blue light a bit misty. "For my darling little girl." He looks directly at Michael. "And, of course, for Felix."

"Ah, yes. I get your drift."

Michael pulls a folder, labelled LAST WILL AND TESTAMENT, out of his desk.

"Right, then. Let's begin at the beginning. That's always the foolproof way."

Relief seeps out of Walter's heart. Now he can make proper plans.

His Eleanor and his Felix: they might actually meet in St Ives. They'll talk about him, sit in his cottage together, in his own hideaway. Stand on the balcony. Watch the sunset, hear the roar of the waves. Touch hands.

And maybe, just maybe, they'll fall in love.

An Inky Inscription

1936

It's her Money Day: Wednesday 29 January 1936. Eleanor will spend it talking about the stuff. First with her solicitor, Michael Humphreys, then with her bank manager, Robin Parker, and finally with their family friend, Jonny Giffen.

She's terrified. She'll be treading entirely new ground. Walter always handled every penny of their lives. Anne has never signed a cheque and wouldn't know where to start. So Eleanor will step into Walter's shoes and become the purse strings of the family.

She pulls on her best navy suit and cream silk blouse. Does she look smart, organised, professional? Is her hair tidy, are her seams straight, do her shoes shine? She peers in the mirror. A pale face stares back. She pinches her cheeks. She should copy Maud and buy some make-up. Try to *look* the part.

But she's not sure what part she wants to take. Who *is* she, exactly? Her mother's protector? A Somerville student? A budding businesswoman? A shy eighteen-year-old whose dead father has become a bewildering mystery?

But the moment she walks into Michael's immaculate office and they shake hands, she sees in his eyes not only sympathy but a new respect – and she feels reassured.

"How's your mother?"

"Bearing up … She doesn't know I'm here." She gives Michael a wobbly smile. "She thinks I've gone to pay for Daddy's funeral, settle some domestic bills. It was easy to give myself an alibi. Walter's affairs need putting in order – but I have to do it tactfully. I want to protect Mummy from any more bad news."

"She's had enough to last a lifetime."

"She's very cut up about this Felix Mitchell fellow. I need to talk to you about my cottage." She bites her lip. "But I didn't want to rub salt in the wounds."

"Everything we discuss here will remain strictly confidential." Michael glances at his file. "The Cornish property details are very straightforward. Walter took out a short lease from the Fourth Earl Cowley in August 1911. Your father loved the place and extended the lease. In 1930, he bought it freehold from the Earl for three hundred pounds. He came to see me after the deal, full of delight. Then from 1911 until the summer of 1914 he lived there full time. It's fully furnished. You could move in tomorrow."

"I still can hardly believe any of this."

"When your father left St Ives, he put the cottage in the hands of an agent." Michael checks his notes. "James Lanham. His instructions are to keep it dry, warm, aired and in good repair. It's directly on the harbour and gets deluged in sea spray. The Cornish name for it is 'spindrift'. It needs to be cared for all year round or it can become extremely damp."

He meets Eleanor's eyes.

"It's yours to live in or to sell, whatever you want."

He opens the file.

"Here's a photo Walter took of it in 1914, just before he left. He added the inscription five years ago when he made his will. The address is on the back."

Eleanor stares at the grainy sepia photo. A row of wet, higgledy stone houses crouch together in a narrow street, cheek by jowl, as if for comfort. Puddles drench the cobblestones; rain drips from the tiled roofs. A young boy wearing clogs, baggy trousers and a massive cap pushes a young girl in a one-wheel handcart, grinning as they share a joke. Her curly fair hair falls to her shoulders. She holds a skipping-rope and her small feet are bare.

The photo captures a fleeting moment of Cornish history, poignant and beautiful.

On the back, Walter has scrawled:

The Hideaway
3 St Andrews Street, St Ives, Cornwall
A gift for my one and only Eleanor
Love you always
Daddy

Her throat dry and raw, she asks, "So which of the cottages is mine?"

"That one." Michael jabs a finger. "Walter gave the cottage its name, but the photo doesn't do it justice. What you *can't* see is the back of the row of cottages, which look directly on to the sea. There's a small balcony leading from your living room. None of the others have one, so it's a useful selling-point. The cottage used to be called The Balcony Studio." He ferrets again in the file. "Here's a map of St Ives and the agent's address and phone number.

Lanham operates from the High Street, which runs through the town centre. Let him know when you plan to arrive. He'll have everything ready."

"On Monday, in London, I sold my pearls, but the money I got for them won't last us long. I must think long-term. I'll probably *have* to sell The Hideaway to give us an income, and maybe to fund my studies."

"But you'll go to see it first?"

"Yes, after Easter."

"If you *do* decide to sell, I'll be delighted to handle the legal side. I have the deeds safely locked away, and Lanham will help. He's very well-established in Cornwall. He'll know what price the cottage could fetch."

"It feels weird." She shifts in her chair, the photograph and map on her knees. "I know so little about Daddy's life before he came to Woodstock, before he met Mummy. He never talked about it. The trouble is ..." She can hardly get the words out.

"Go on."

"The cottage, the whole set-up ... He must have had an entire *life* in St Ives. Did he have a wife and children? Were Mummy and I his 'second time around' – or even his third?" She perseveres. "Did you know he'd been married before?"

"Yes." Michael has the grace to blush. "His first wife died. But he loved you and your mother very much."

She longs to ask, "And does the name *Moira* mean anything to you?" but her courage fails. Could there be a connection between the mysterious Moira, and Felix Mitchell?

She stands to shake Michael's hand again. "Thank you for your help. I'm sorry my mother was so rude to you. You've been a very good friend."

"Go down to St Ives." He smiles at her. "And be sure to tell me about your hideaway when you get back."

161

At two o'clock, she's ushered into Robin Parker's office on Market Street. It only takes her half an hour to explain her position, hand over the money and arrange for her own bank account to be set up. Robin, brisk, genial and efficient, wishes her well.

She stands outside the bank, breathing a sigh of relief. Jonny's antiques shop, Giffen Antiques, is only a minute's walk away. She decides to go straight there, while her courage and stamina hold.

She pushes at the door and stands against it, hearing the jangle of the bell and the ticking of a grandfather clock. She breathes in the musty smell of antiquarian books, oak furniture and beeswax polish. The room is alluring, filled as it is with carefully restored mementos of other people's lives.

Jonny Giffen, now thirty-eight – only two years younger than Anne – had moved to Woodstock with his elderly mother ten years before, after his own father's death. Within a month he'd opened Giffen Antiques. He and his mother had often been to supper with the Drummonds, Jonny amusing them with stories of his childhood.

"My dad used to run a second-hand furniture stall in London's Caledonian Road. I grew up surrounded by brass and copper pots, oak dressers, glass, porcelain and clocks and, if Dad had visited Bermondsey market in the early hours of the morning, pieces of stolen silver. They swiftly changed hands while the police turned a blind eye to all transactions, provided the traders were off and away by dawn!"

Jonny has a lifetime's experience in antiques, an attractive face, a gentle, persuasive manner and a highly-trained eye. He's also an excellent businessman. He understands that people in the 1930s have smaller families and live in smaller houses than their Victorian ancestors, with fewer servants. They want furniture that's pretty but practical: tables that seat six, not twelve; wardrobes that don't overwhelm bedrooms; sturdy kitchen equipment that's small and easy to clean.

Once a month Jonny climbs into his van and drives to Aberystwyth in Wales to replenish his stock. There he attends auctions and visits private dealers, buying furniture from ancient Welsh farmhouses: stools, rocking chairs, nests of tables, Sunday-best china, and creaking bedsteads that have long forgotten the weight of slumbering bodies.

Now Eleanor stands looking at a porcelain teapot, with pink roses and pale green leaves trailing the base and spout. She hears footsteps leaping up from the basement. Jonny Giffen bursts into the room, his coppery curls bouncing. His gravelly voice with, now, only the faintest Cockney accent, cries, "Eleanor! Good to see you again. How *are* you?"

He grasps her hands.

Her relief at seeing his handsome face and shining green eyes threatens to overwhelm her. She stutters, "Fine, thank you——"

"Have you come to buy a ravishing piece of Meissen, perhaps? A present for your mother, to cheer her up?"

"Nothing like that. In fact, quite the opposite."

Tears sting her eyes. She pulls her hands away, steeling herself to say the dreaded words.

"We're in big trouble, Jonny. Daddy has left us without any money."

"Good *God*, Eleanor! I had *no idea*——"

She rushes on before the tears take over. "Mummy said … We wondered … I've come to sell *you* something, if you'd be kind enough to buy."

∞

163

Without another word, Jonny leaps towards the door. He locks it, turns the sign to CLOSED, pulls out his handkerchief and pushes it into her hand.

"What you need is a cup of sweet tea."

He takes her elbow, guiding her through the shop and up the stairs.

In the cosy living room he says, "Make yourself comfortable. I won't be long."

She sinks on to a sofa, wiping her eyes, glad of a moment's privacy. Suddenly she misses Walter more than ever. Seeing his handwriting again, reading his inscription: they've made everything worse.

She hears Jonny talking to his mother, the rattle of cups, the chink of cutlery. He carries a tray into the room, puts it on a low table in front of her.

"Talk to me, Eleanor. I want to know *everything*."

Half an hour later they're on their way to her house.

"Are you sure the shop can spare you?"

"Course it can. You need to sell. I'm only too happy to help. Buying your linen press is the *least* I can do."

They slip upstairs before Anne or Vera hear them.

In the spare room, Jonny runs expert fingers over the linen press. He opens the two doors, slides the shallow drawers in and out. The scent of lavender fills the air.

"It's a beautiful piece, Eleanor. The mahogany is in excellent condition. Useful *and* handsome." He touches her shoulder. "I'll give you fifty guineas for it, in cash."

"Jonny! Thank you *so* much. Mummy will be *beside* herself."

"Good. Surprise her over supper. Come back to the shop and I'll give you the money now. If you hurry, you can put it in the bank while it's still open."

Back at Giffen Antiques, before he's reopened the shop, Jonny disappears upstairs. He comes down with an envelope, and presses it into her hands.

"It's all here. Every last guinea."

"I can't thank you enough, Jonny."

"Only too glad to help. It'll sell like a hot cake." He meets her eyes. "I'll arrange for my men to collect it on Friday. Sit down a moment."

He gestures to a newly upholstered chair.

"I have a proposition for you. How do you fancy working here, for me, *with* me, in this shop?"

"But—"

"You don't know anything about antiques? I can teach you – and I'm sure you'll be a fast learner."

"I do desperately need a job."

"Mum has been helping in the shop, but by one o'clock she's exhausted. Why don't you come to work here every afternoon, between two and five-thirty? We close on Wednesday and Saturday afternoons, but if you could also work here on Saturday mornings, that would be wonderful.

"I've got Darren to help with the heavy lifting and the restoration work, but he hates dealing with customers. I'm often away at auctions, buying new stock, or in London, seeing private clients. I've been thinking of hiring an assistant for months. Then you show up on my doorstep, like a godsend. You'd be perfect. And I'll pay you, of course. One guinea a week."

He smiles at her, reaching across to grab her hands.

"What do you say?"

She's astonished but delighted. He's just paid her an enormous compliment. "I'll need to ask Mummy."

"Why? Does she run your life?"

165

"Pretty much. I've given up Somerville for now – maybe for ever, I'm not sure – because she needs me around."

"So? She'll still have you, won't she? You'll only be over the road in the afternoons. How can she possibly object? You'll still have time to keep up with your College work. I'm not asking you to burn any boats."

She stuffs Jonny's envelope into her handbag, snaps it shut.

"You're a breath of fresh air, Jonny Giffen – and you're right."

He grins. "You mean we have a deal?"

"Looks like we have."

"Terrific! So when can you start?" His eyes are dancing with anticipation and delight.

"Give me a couple of days to talk to Mummy, get her used to the idea."

"Shall we say next week? Could you start on Monday afternoon?"

She looks around the shop: at the porcelain teacups, the leather-bound books, the shining silver spoons. A pair of feathery barn owls, perched in their glass case, peer down from a walnut bureau, their eyes round and black, waiting for her answer.

She turns to Jonny. For the first time since her father's death, a sense of purpose floods her heart.

"Monday afternoon," she says, "sounds very good to me."

Giffen Antiques

1936

As the short dark days of February and March lengthen into spring, Eleanor's life gathers momentum. She crams her week with a whirlwind of activity that allows her little time to mourn.

She becomes joint housekeeper with Vera. Their young daily maid refuses to return after Walter's death, confessing she's "that fearful" of entering a house in which someone has died – and anyway her "auntie in Banbury" has offered her a job. She's not replaced. There's no money to pay her wages.

As the weeks tick by, Eleanor feels increasingly alienated from Somerville, and from the self-important world of the university. She dreads facing other students: having to answer their questions, explain her absence, talk about Walter. She and Anne hardly ever mention him, but he hangs like a shadow over their lives, eerily ever-present – particularly at mealtimes when they sneak furtive glances at his empty chair.

Her afternoons are filled with Jonny's antiques. She

enjoys the work, looks forward to being in the shop, away from Anne's brooding melancholy. His passion for antiques is infectious. She learns fast: about prices, periods and the crucial details of how to greet customers, when to let them browse, how to tempt them to buy.

For the first fortnight Jonny stays by her side, describing every item in the shop.

"This bedside table is an 'old friend'. I bought it in a job lot and never managed to sell it. It'll disappear eventually. This wonderful rosewood bureau is mid-seventeenth century." He runs his fingers over it. "It has three secret drawers. We call the central one a 'bible well'. See if you can discover each of them and find out how they open."

By the third week, he has enough confidence in her to travel to Aberystwyth, leaving her on her own, although Mrs Giffen hovers upstairs with cups of tea at the ready.

And at the beginning of March, while Jonny is at a Christie's auction in London, Eleanor makes her first major sale. A young American couple, on honeymoon in "your wonderful rainy old England", spend two hours buying furniture for their New York apartment. They decide on a Regency mahogany bow-front secretaire bookcase, a pair of William and Mary walnut chairs, and a George III gilt-wood mirror. They pay top dollars and ask for the consignment to be shipped to America.

As she closes the door, she feels a rush of pride at how she's handled the sale – and also a pang of envy. How happy the couple look. Will *she* ever find someone special to share her life?

Reaching home that afternoon, she catches sight of herself in the hall mirror. It's a shock. She looks frayed and shabby. She can't bear wearing her old black clothes any longer.

Every morning when she pulls them on, she's reminded of Walter's funeral, the heartache of missing him. What's the *point* of making her life even harder?

She checks her accounts, counting the pennies. Next morning, she cashes a cheque at the bank and drives to Oxford. She buys a lightweight spring coat, two smart suits to wear in the shop, shoes with a small heel, underwear, and a small but glamorous hat. She also buys some make-up at the chemist – and as a final treat the hairdresser shapes her long curls into a smooth bob.

Even Anne is impressed. "You look *enchanting* in that suit. It brings out the colour of your eyes."

On his return, she tells Jonny about the lucrative American sale. He gives her a delighted hug, and slips an extra guinea into her hand.

"A well-deserved bonus. The first of many, I'm sure. Always knew you could do it, Eleanor. You're a gem." His eyes flicker with admiration. "It's such a *relief* to see you wearing *colours* again. And I *love* the new hair!"

She blushes, enjoying the clasp of Jonny's fingers – and startled by the sudden throb of her tired heart. His praise reminds her of Walter's: *"That's my girl!"*

On Wednesday afternoons, when the shop is closed, she continues to meet Kath.

Under the watery sunshine and high clouds of early spring, they walk in Blenheim or drink tea at Fishery Cottage. Kath and Sean are now formally engaged, planning an engagement party and their future together.

Delighted, Kath's happiness fills Eleanor with quiet joy.

On Saturday afternoons, she takes Anne out in the Morris to remind her there's still a thriving world beyond their front door. They eat luncheon in Burford or Oxford, making valiant attempts to talk. She tries to persuade Anne to see a film or a play, visit an art gallery or a museum, even to walk across the University Parks. But the response is always: "It's much too soon for me to go gadding about."

Anne often sleeps all morning, appears for luncheon looking pale and listless, shambles around the house in the afternoons, stabs half-heartedly at some ancient needlework and continues her séances with Sylvia Dunkley three evenings a week. She never talks about them, and refuses to wear anything but black.

"I look hideous and I'm sick of it, but I must continue to show respect for my husband. Queen Mary will wear mourning for nine months."

Sunday is the worst day of the week. They go to church out of habit. Anne says she no longer believes in a God who's abandoned her, but she doesn't want anyone to know she's lost her faith.

Their neighbours stop pitying them and begin to treat them with a new respect. Quietly and without fuss, the Drummonds are fighting adversity. They demand admiration – and receive it.

In the middle of March, on an exceptionally mild Sunday afternoon, they carry buckets of water, dusters and polish to the bottom of the garden. They clean the Bullnose Morris, inside and out.

"There you are," Anne says two hours later, kicking at the bags of rubbish. "Over to you, dear daughter of mine. This car is no longer your father's, even if I still am."

On many heart-breaking nights, Eleanor hears her mother sobbing in her room. She wants to offer comfort, but knows she can't without breaking down herself.

During that winter, she longs to take refuge in her textbooks, but a vital thread has snapped. Without a tutor, her studies lack urgency and timetable. She tries to read but becomes enmeshed in another vivid memory of Walter. One evening as she leaves Jonny's shop, a man walks by smoking the tobacco he loved. She breathes in its scent, unable to move, wishing with every fibre of her being she could see her Daddy again. Whoever said time is a great healer?

One morning when Anne is at the hairdresser, she remembers the tiny key in Walter's studio, in that red leather purse. She flits around the house, trying it in every lock. It belongs nowhere.

Walter is still the first person she thinks about when she wakes – and the last as her head hits the pillow. In her dreams she hears his voice and the desperation of his last request: *"Find Moira for me. Tell her I'm sorry."*

I'll find her if it's the last thing I do, Daddy.

Promise.

Even if I'm scared stiff at discovering what you were sorry for.

Blackmail

1936

Eleanor spends one Sunday afternoon with Robert Clark. His gossip about university life seems tedious and irrelevant. She no longer cares about who's been sent down, what he's studying, what he plans to do when he leaves university.

That evening she finally decides not to go back to Somerville – much to Anne's vociferous relief. With a new sense of liberation, she flings herself into working with Jonny. He often asks what she thinks about a piece of furniture, valuing her opinion. He shares problems about an account or a difficult customer. They've become a working partnership. She feels at ease with him, and looks forward to his company.

The following Tuesday afternoon is exceptionally busy, while Jonny is away at a London auction. Mrs Giffen patters down with Eleanor's cup of tea at half-past four, leaving her to price a set of Welsh tableware. She's standing at the back of the shop when its bell jangles. She turns to see Rosie Perkins shutting the door.

Glad to see a familiar face, she walks swiftly to greet her.

"Mrs Perkins! Lovely to see you again. It seems a long time since—"

"Indeed." Rosie shakes hands but her eyes are frosty. "You're *very* well turned out, I *must* say!" She inspects Eleanor's smart business suit, her shining shoes. "I heard you were working here. You're obviously enjoying it."

"Very much. Have you come for something special?"

"I'm not here to buy." Rosie glances at the shop door, at the stairs leading to the basement, then up to Jonny's flat. "My business is strictly personal. Could we talk in private?"

"I can't leave the shop unattended. Why don't you come for a drink with Mummy and me at six o'clock?"

Rosie gives a snort of mirthless laughter. "I don't think your mother would be too happy to hear what I have to say."

Eleanor's heart freezes. "Then could you wait until we close? I'll meet you outside the shop at half-past five."

They stand on a street corner as lights are turned off, owners lock doors and make for home. Dark clouds thud across the sky; the air fills with spatters of rain.

Eleanor turns up her coat collar. "How can I help?"

"I'll come straight to the point, Miss Drummond." Rosie's voice is quiet but determined. "Your dear father. I miss him a great deal. Walter and I were very fond of each other."

"I'm aware of that. You spoke most movingly at his funeral."

"You don't understand." Rosie flutters a nervous hand to the curls peeping beneath her hat. "Walter and I were more than *friends,* Miss Drummond. We loved each other deeply. We'd been having an affair."

"*What?*"

"My husband walked out three years ago, disappeared to Australia. He sends me money when he remembers, but it's never enough. I have a little boy. Children eat *mountains* of food. They need shoes, toys, clothes. My Mark, he's five years old. He was very fond of his Uncle Walter. Your father was an *exceedingly* generous man."

"But he's not with us. I'm sorry——"

"No, Miss Drummond, you can't just apologise and leave it at that. Walter helped me financially. I'd be most grateful if you could make sure his help continues."

Eleanor gapes. "I *beg* your pardon?"

"You heard me."

"I've no intention of giving you a penny. It's not only that I won't, I can't. Why do you think I'm working for Mr Giffen? I have to make a living."

"Very well, then." Rosie hunches her shoulders. "I'll take my problem to your mother. I'm sure you wouldn't want knowledge of my affair to reach *her* ears, would you, now?"

"I most certainly would not!"

"That's what I thought." Rosie flicks rain off her tight sleeves. Her curls look bedraggled, but her eyes shine with triumph.

"What *exactly* do you want, Mrs Perkins?"

"I need a lump sum," comes the prompt reply. "Enough to put in the bank, earn interest, give Mark the education he deserves. He's a bright lad. I'm ambitious for him. Shall we say three hundred guineas?"

"That's utterly ridiculous! I don't have anything like that kind of money." The words stick in Eleanor's throat. "I'm not under any obligation to you. I don't even know if you're telling the truth——"

Rosie throws back her head. "I can give you some intimate physical details——"

174

"I don't want to hear them."

"No, you probably don't! My darling Walter was hungry for my love. And I was only too delighted to give it. If your mother had looked after her husband properly, he wouldn't have needed to find devotion elsewhere."

Eleanor wants to smack Rosie's softly rounded cheek. "This is nothing but filthy blackmail. Go home, Mrs Perkins. Find yourself another protector. Leave me and my mother alone."

"Very well then. But don't say you haven't been warned."

Rosie turns abruptly on her heel.

Eleanor stands rooted to the spot, watching the comely figure in her high heels and tight-fitting coat mince across the road. She imagines the conversation the woman might have with Anne. Dodging a car, she dashes after her and taps her shoulder.

Rosie turns to look at her, tears glittering on her cheeks. "Thought better of getting rid of me, have you?"

"I'll give you twenty-five guineas." The bitter words sound mean and paltry. "Come to the shop on Thursday afternoon. And if you *ever* come back for more, or drop the merest *hint* of this to my mother, I'll tell her about you. I'll also make sure the whole of Woodstock knows what a rotten little blackmailer you are."

Eleanor races home, up to her room, tearing off her new hat and coat, now damp with rain. She sits on her bed, kicking off her shoes, furious she'd given in. Everything she's earned at Jonny's and more will now have to be paid to that … that …

How *could* Walter betray his family? Rosie's neither beautiful nor intelligent. What had they *talked* about? How

175

had he found time to spend with her?

But what choice does she have? If she decides to do nothing, the moment her back's turned, the wretched woman will start knocking on Anne's door. She tries not to imagine her father tucked up with his plump Rosie.

God in heaven. What *else* had he been doing? *And with whom?*

Next morning, Eleanor spends an uncomfortable fifteen minutes with Robin Parker, explaining she needs some cash to clear two debts Walter had incurred in London several months ago. Mercifully, her bank manager asks no questions.

Neither does Rosie when Eleanor hands her the money in the doorway of Giffen Antiques. She'd waited impatiently all afternoon, determined not to let the woman enter the shop. She watches Rosie push the envelope into her bag.

"This is the very *least* you could do." Rosie glances at Jonny who's dealing with a customer. "I can see you're busy. This will be all for now. But don't think you've seen the last of me."

Furious and humiliated, Eleanor slams the door.

Jonny notices something's wrong. When his customer has gone, he asks, "Are you all right, Eleanor? The woman in the doorway. Wasn't it Mrs Perkins? Didn't she give a eulogy at——"

"I've dealt with her." Eleanor's tempted to add, "I've just handed over every penny you've given me for working here," but she chokes back the words. Jonny might offer to refund the money, which she could never accept.

She's covered her father's tracks.

How many more times will she need to do so?

And who else will be involved?

Someone to Share the Driving

1936

One Saturday morning towards the end of March, when the customers have gone and it's one o'clock, Eleanor flicks the shop's sign to CLOSED.

She glances at Jonny, who's bending over some art-deco ornaments, and summons up her courage.

"Can I ask you a favour, Jonny? ... Well, two favours, actually."

He looks up at her, pushing his chestnut curls out of his eyes. "Fire away."

"After the Easter weekend, in April, may I have a fortnight off?"

"Of course." He straightens his back. "I can hardly hold you captive." He moves towards her, suddenly anxious. "Is your mother ill? Are you taking her on holiday?"

"No. I'm going to leave her with Vera for the first time since Daddy died. I haven't told her yet, but I can't put it off any longer."

"Your Cornish cottage?"

"Yes. If I decide to sell, the agent will want it on the market before the summer."

"Very sensible." A smile lights his face. "And exciting! How will you travel?"

"That's the other favour. The cottage is furnished. I think some of Daddy's paintings may still be there. If they are, I'd like to bring them home, which is why I'm planning to drive." She meets his eyes. "Would you come with me in the Morris? Maybe find a few antiques along the way?"

"Eleanor!" He throws back his head and laughs. "You sly minx! You've got it all worked out."

"Not exactly." Her cheeks are fire-hot. "It's a long way to go. Daddy taught me to drive, but I've never gone really far on my own. It would be lovely to have someone to share the driving. What do you think?"

"It's a *great* idea. I'd be delighted. I'll close the shop for a fortnight. Give Mum and Darren a break. Heaven knows they deserve one." He grabs her hands. "Have you worked out a route?"

"Not yet."

"Booked an hotel?"

"I'll ask the agent to recommend somewhere. I could stay in The Hideaway, but I'd like to see it first." She shivers. "It might be full of Daddy's ghost."

"Will you drive down in a single day?"

"I don't know how long it'll take." They're standing close now. She notices the flecks of silver in Jonny's coppery hair, the enchanting laugh lines around his eyes. "I'll work out some details over the weekend." She adds shyly, "Thank you *so* much."

He releases her hands. "The pleasure will be mine, Eleanor … We can swim in the sea, walk along the cliffs. We'll put The Hideaway on the market if you want. But

178

we'll also fill our lungs with sea air and eat cream teas. It'll be wonderful!"

"Leave me out of it, why don't you!" Anne says that afternoon as Eleanor drives them into Oxford.

"You didn't *want* to come." She allows a bullying lorry to overtake. "You couldn't care less *what* happened to The Hideaway. You said——"

"I *know* what I said."

"Then why make such a fuss?"

"I don't want to be left in Woodstock on my own."

"You won't *be* on your own. You'll have Vera."

"It's not the same." Anne stares out of the window. "I feel old and boring and discarded, like a threadbare sock."

"You're only forty, you're not boring, you're certainly not discarded. Look how faithfully I've cared for you."

"Only because you *have* to. And now you'll be away for *weeks* on end."

"A fortnight is hardly——"

"To me," Anne's voice trembles like a spoilt child, "it'll feel like an eternity."

"You know what?" Eleanor grits her teeth. "You could try the patience of a saint."

After an uncomfortable lunch, during which Anne grumbles, and then sulks, Eleanor leaves her in a dress-shop while she dashes into Blackwell's Bookshop on Broad Street. She quickly finds a *Touring Map of Britain*.

That evening she traces their route with her finger. They'll drive from Woodstock to Witney, Faringdon and Swindon; then to Wootton Bassett, Lyneham and Chippenham to Bath; then to Radstock, Wells, Glastonbury, Bridgwater, Taunton and Cullompton to Exeter, where they'll break the journey and stay the night. The following day will take them to Okehampton and Launceston – by then they'll be in Cornwall – across Bodmin Moor to Bodmin, onward to Redruth, Camborne and Hayle, and finally to St Ives.

If they leave early on Tuesday the 14th of April – the day after Easter Monday – and stay the night in Exeter, they'll be in St Ives by Wednesday afternoon. She'll write to James Lanham. Her heart flickers with excitement.

"Well, *well!*" Kath says over tea at Fishery Cottage, her eyes twinkling. "You and Jonny Giffen, eh? You make an interestin' pair!"

Eleanor blushes. "It's nothing like that, Kath. He's a good friend—"

"But you've asked him on a Cornish holiday!"

"I don't want to go alone. I have to inspect the cottage, put it on the market. Jonny will help. It'll hardly be a romantic interlude."

"Don't you be surprised if he makes a pass. He hasn't got a girlfriend, has he?"

"He's never mentioned anyone special."

"There you are! He's single, good-lookin', with a thrivin' business. I bet he'll be wantin' a wife."

"Well, it certainly won't be me." Eleanor drains her cup, anxious to change the subject. "How's the royal love affair going? Anything from Maud?"

"She's *full* of it! She says the Americans think Edward is our idol. He can ride a horse, dance, fly a plane, mix with commoners and deal with diplomats. He's a young people's King in a young people's country."

"Except for us, it doesn't feel anything like that, does it?"

"It sure doesn't. Maud says Edward's bein' real difficult.

Now he's King and all, he's got to live in Buck House, but he thinks it's gloomy and oppressive. He goes roarin' down to Fort Belvedere with Wallis Simpson every weekend. He never goes to Sandringham or Balmoral and his staff feel ignored."

"He's trying to be his own man. To have a private life that's got nothing to do with being King."

"Which is impossible, as well he knows. When he's separated from Wallis, he sends her love letters on black-edged stationery, full of baby talk, like a sixteen-year-old with a schoolboy crush. Lord only knows where it will end."

Eleanor crosses off the days in her diary as they tick towards Easter. Foreign tourists flock into Woodstock, and Giffen Antiques thrives. But at the end of each working afternoon she and Jonny plan their journey, longing to leave.

She takes the Morris to the local garage. They replace all four tyres, check and fine-tune the engine, declare the car fit to travel.

In reply to her letter, James Lanham says he'll have the cottage: *"ship shape and Bristol fashion"*. He recommends she stay at the Porthminster Hotel. *"It has splendid sea views and an excellent reputation."*

Giffen Antiques is open on Easter Saturday, but closed on Easter Monday, so at one o'clock on the Saturday Eleanor flicks the sign to CLOSED. She turns to smile at Jonny.

"See you Tuesday morning," he says. "I'm *so* excited. A whole fortnight together ... Let's leave at eight sharp." He moves towards her. There, in the middle of the shop, suddenly, they're in each other's arms.

"I can hardly wait." His lips brush her cheek. "Have you been counting the hours?"

"You know I have."

Jonny's eyes dance. "I'll be outside your house, ready and waiting."

She races home to start packing.

On Easter Monday, Anne accepts an invitation to spend the afternoon and evening with Sylvia Dunkley. Vera has also disappeared, to stay the weekend with her sister in Bournemouth. Eleanor has the house to herself.

At four o'clock the phone rings.

"Eleanor? It's me." Jonny's voice comes sharp and desperate. "I'm at the Radcliffe Infirmary."

She catches her breath. "What's wrong?"

"It's Mum. She's had a fall, tripped on the stairs … She's done something awful to her hip. She's in terrible pain. She was wearing those disgusting old slippers of hers. I've warned her about them a dozen times."

"Will she be all right?"

"I don't know. She's very shaken up. They're going to take some X-rays. She may need an operation. Obviously I can't leave her. I'm so sorry, but Cornwall's out of the question." His voice breaks. "You do understand, don't you?"

"Of course." Her head thunders with disappointment. "What will you do?"

"No idea … I need to think."

"Is there anyone else you could travel with?"

"Maybe." Eleanor thinks wildly of Kath. But she won't want to leave Sean, and she'd need permission from the Palace. "Probably not."

"I was *so* looking forward to our trip. I feel *terrible* letting you down."

"Please don't, Jonny. It's not your fault." Her mouth tastes sour. "The Hideaway has waited for me all

182

these years. A few more weeks won't change anything."

"It's good of you to be so understanding. I must go."

"Of course. Give your mother my love."

"I will. See you soon. I'm *so* sorry."

She stumbles back to the kitchen. She stares at the neat pile of ironed blouses waiting to be packed. She should ring the Porthminster Hotel, cancel her booking, speak to James Lanham, explain her delay.

She also knows she won't be getting on the phone to anyone.

Tonight she'll study the route to St Ives until she knows the sequence of towns off by heart. She'll set off tomorrow morning at dawn, while both Vera and Anne are still asleep. Before she leaves, she'll push a note through Jonny's door:

I'm going to Cornwall on my own. Please do NOT tell Anne. I'll ring you from St Ives. I hope your mother is on the mend. Love, Eleanor.

She stares around the kitchen: at the steaming iron, the immaculate blouses, the dresser with its shining plates, the geraniums, bright-headed and expectant on the window-sill. She takes a deep breath, trying to quell a sudden wave of terror.

She's facing a long journey alone in the Morris.

Staying overnight in some unfamiliar boarding house.

There are hundreds of miles to her destination ...

This will be the biggest challenge of her life.

Act Three

Heavy Weather

1936

On Tuesday the 14th of April, Eleanor is wide awake at five o'clock.

She has already stored her suitcase in the boot of the car. She throws on her clothes, runs a comb through her hair and picks up her handbag. Into it she pushes the battered red purse with its tiny key.

She tiptoes down to the kitchen. She makes a flask of sweet tea, cuts some ham-and-cucumber sandwiches and a slice of fruit cake: breakfast after she's driven for several hours. She pulls on her boots, coat and hat. Then she slips through the kitchen and out of the house.

The crisp morning air meets her lungs; the thrill of freedom fills her heart.

She skitters to the garden's end and the car. The chirrup of dawn chorus spatters the air. A thin mizzle of rain fails to dampen her spirits. The steering-wheel and seat feel cool to her touch. She closes the car door quietly. Vera's room overlooks the garden and *she* can hear a bat squeak five miles away.

For a dark moment she feels furtive and guilty, but she pushes the guilt aside. It's too late for any second thoughts. She needs to sell The Hideaway. This isn't a self-indulgent jaunt, but a necessary expedition, planned with meticulous care. As for travelling alone: Walter taught her to drive so she could put the skill to good purpose.

She digs out her list of towns and props it on the dashboard, staring at the first three names:

WITNEY   FARINGDON   SWINDON

The engine starts immediately. She breathes a sigh of relief.

"Right, Miss Drummond. Let's get this show on the road."

The thin mizzle of rain grows steadily worse. By the time she gets to Faringdon it's thickened to a downpour. The windscreen wipers creak. Hunched over the wheel, concentrating with every bone in her body, she peers through the spray raised by other traffic, trying to maintain a steady pace.

She battles through Swindon, Wootton Bassett, Lyneham and Chippenham. Then she turns into a narrow country lane, thirsty and ravenous. She longs to climb out of the car and stretch her legs, but knows that within minutes she'd be drenched.

She consults her list: Bath, Wells and then Glastonbury, where she'll stop for luncheon. Long-distance driving is hungry work. She winds down the window and gazes at the sky, black with louring clouds. She misses Jonny's dancing eyes, his infectious laugh and easy banter. He'd have made light of the weather, taken over the wheel, driven confidently at twice her speed.

188

She wonders how he is. At his mother's bedside, surrounded by doctors and nurses? Perhaps *she* should be there, instead of in the middle of nowhere?

She reaches Exeter in the late afternoon, her back aching, her head throbbing. The rain has turned to silvery hailstones that bounce on the car's roof, crackling in angry showers across the windscreen, lying in treacherous white sheets along the road.

She spots a traditional guest-house and pulls into the drive. Snatching her case from the boot, she dashes inside, hailstones lashing her face like pellets of ice. She accepts the last available single room, where she falls into an armchair. Then she soaks in a hot bath and eats supper in her room by the fire. By nine o'clock she's very sound asleep.

Next morning Eleanor breakfasts early, pays her bill and is out of the guest-house by eight o'clock. The Morris feels chilly and damp. As she climbs into it, she realises she'd forgotten to tell The Porthminster that Jonny won't be with her. It's too late now for phone calls. She'll press on, make her apologies when she arrives.

She checks her list again: Okehampton, Launceston – the border town of Cornwall – and across Bodmin Moor to Bodmin itself. The rain has stopped, but the roads heave with puddles. Grey early-morning fog swirls on the horizon.

In spite of the weather, she makes good progress. Yesterday's driving was so tough it's given her confidence. Over Bodmin Moor, golden heads of roadside gorse spark through the mist, lighting the landscape. As she drives through Cornwall, she winds down the window. A gentle warmth penetrates the car. She throws her hat on to the seat, peels

189

off her gloves, rakes her fingers through her hair. She starts to sing: *"The Wings of a Dove"*, *"Sweet Lass of Richmond Hill"*, *"Daisy, Daisy"*.

She catches a fleeting glimpse of a grey sea and sings more loudly with increasing excitement. She'll drive straight on: through Redruth, Camborne and Hayle, and at last into Carbis Bay, with St Ives clearly signposted ahead.

The hotel emerges from the mist. She parks the Morris and sits for a moment, gripping the wheel. Then she pulls on her hat, checks her reflection in the mirror. She climbs out of the car, grabs her suitcase from the boot. Her legs tremble with fatigue, hunger claws at her stomach.

She crosses the wet road and pushes at the door of The Porthminster Hotel.

Meeting James Lanham

1936

Eleanor's hand shakes as she dials Jonny's numbers. There's no answer, either from the shop or the flat. She puts down the receiver, picks it up again. More shaking and dialling.

"Mummy? It's me."

"Eleanor!" Anne's voice sings with relief. "Where *are* you?"

"St Ives. At the hotel. I got here half an hour ago. I've just unpacked."

"Thank God you're safe! How was the journey?"

"Yesterday was difficult because of the rain, but the Morris held up beautifully. Listen, I need to tell you. I'm on my own."

"*What? So where on earth is Jonny?*"

"He couldn't come. His mother had an accident. He's taken her to hospital."

"You mean you've driven all that way by *yourself?*"

"I had no choice."

"Of *course* you had a choice! I'd *never* have allowed—"

"That's why I didn't tell you."

"You're *impossible*, Eleanor! Whatever will you do next?"

"Go to see The Hideaway." The phone line crackles as if it's laughing at her. "I've tried to ring Jonny to find out how his mother is but there's no answer. I'm worried. Could you—"

"All right, if you insist." Anne sounds impatient and furious. "I'll call round and ask after her. Tell Jonny you've arrived."

"Thank you."

"I blame *him* for letting you go—"

"Please *don't*. He didn't know until it was too late. It was entirely my decision. He's been a really good friend." Frightened of what Anne might say, she adds, "I *forbid* you to fall out with him. He was terribly disappointed he couldn't come. *Please*, Mummy—"

"All sweetness and light, then." Anne makes an effort to be civil. "What's the hotel like?"

"Large, a bit old-fashioned but rather nice. It's right above the beach. I'm in a ground-floor room with a sea view, except everything is shrouded in mist. It's like looking through a grey blanket."

"Have you had luncheon?"

"No. I'm starving—"

"Go and eat, Eleanor. *Do* look after yourself. Ring me tomorrow."

It's not until she leaves The Porthminster and walks down the hill into St Ives that she realises she's shaking with nerves. Her pride in managing the journey seeps away. Now she has to face the consequences.

The narrow street, shining with rain, tumbles steeply into town. Rooftops glisten through the mist. Below the hill to

192

her right, she can just make out a stretch of pebbly beach. Seagulls shriek and swoop above her, vanishing into the fog. She smells the dank sea-air, tastes its salt, hears the grumbling roar of the ocean. But both sea and horizon are enveloped in cloud.

Shoppers haul slowly up the hill, laden with bags. Nobody looks at her twice. She's totally anonymous. It gives her a wild feeling of freedom.

She stops at the first café she finds, choosing a piping hot cheese-and-fish pie – "It's fresh cod, Miss, delicious, caught only this morning" – washed down by a cup of dark tea.

Then she's out of doors again, looking for the High Street and James Lanham.

But at the estate agent's door – AUCTIONEERS AND VALUERS – her courage drains away. She stares in the window. Perhaps first she should find The Hideaway? Get her bearings in town? Anything, rather than spell out who she is.

Anything but discover the truth she's driven all those miles to find.

She'd almost decided to walk into town when the shop door opens. A short, stocky man with a leathery face and thick white hair stands in the doorway.

"Are you by any chance Miss Drummond?"

"Yes." She's trapped: caught in a tightly-webbed net like a pilchard flailing in the sea.

A hand grasps hers. "Welcome to St Ives! I'm James Lanham. My word! I'd have recognised you anywhere. You're the spitting image of your father."

"How do you do?" She has no breath in her lungs.

"I was *very* cut up to hear of Walter's death. You must

miss him terribly. Kind-hearted, well-meaning fellow. Wonderful painter, too. He made the most ordinary things look exquisite. We were the best of friends."

She tries to swallow. "I'm glad."

"Everything's ready for you at The Hideaway." Sharp blue eyes look into hers. "How was your journey?"

"Very long. The driving was hard work." Her voice trembles. Lanham's description of Walter has brought her to the edge of tears.

"You travelled on your own? … Come, Miss Drummond, steady yourself." He touches her shoulder. "You're here now, safe and sound. We'll have you sorted in no time. Won't you step inside?"

A small, cluttered office greets her, its walls lined with photographs of Cornish properties. The room is crammed with desks, two at each side, their surfaces heaped with files.

Lanham disappears into a back office. He returns carrying a tray with cups of coffee and a plate of biscuits. "Cornish gingerbread. My wife makes it every week. It's probably the only reason our clients come to see us." His eyes twinkle.

The delicacy melts on her tongue: light, buttery, with a subtle kick of ginger. "I can see why." The coffee is strong and refreshing but her cup rattles on its saucer. "I wanted to thank you for looking after The Hideaway."

"It's been a pleasure. I enjoyed doing business with Walter."

"The thing is…" She sits on her hands to stop them shaking. "My mother and I … We knew nothing about The Hideaway until Walter died. It came as a shock."

Lanham chokes on his biscuit. Red-faced, he brushes at the crumbs. "I don't know how he managed to keep the place a secret. Although given what happened there, he probably didn't want to talk about it."

"What *did* happen? *Why* did he keep his life here so secret?"

"It's a long story." He drains his coffee. "Shall we take a stroll? I'll give you the keys to The Hideaway, show you the ropes. I can tell you something about your father along the way."

"We first met in August 1911. The hottest summer I can ever remember."

They are out on the High Street, moving downhill towards the swirl of misty sea. He walks with a slight limp. She slows her pace to keep in step.

"Walter arrived from Oxford. He wanted a place to rent, initially for a holiday. He was new to the area, said he wanted to find his feet before he bought somewhere permanent. *If* he decided to stay.

"We had a photo of 3 St Andrews Street in our window. He loved the place, rented it for a year. Then we extended the arrangement into a long lease from the Fourth Earl Cowley. Many years later – 1930 it was – Walter bought the property freehold."

She struggles to ask, "Was he on his own?"

Lanham doffs his hat to four ladies clustering outside the church. They smile at him, chirruping like sparrows. "Of course not." He's breezily matter-of-fact. "He arrived with his family."

The grey sky lours on to her shoulders. "His *family*?"

"Of course. Walter was always a devoted family man."

She stops in her tracks, facing Lanham in the middle of the street. Behind her lies a tree-lined garden, filled with apple blossom. To her left stands the church with its elaborate tower: soft brown, pale grey. Ahead, she can glimpse the harbour. Its small boats bob on the tide like bright postage stamps on a jade-green envelope. She's standing in a complicated jigsaw puzzle made of sharply coloured pieces, the most important of which have gone missing.

"Mr Lanham, *my mother and I* are his family. Did Daddy have another wife, other children? If so, where are they now?"

He looks at her, the corner of his right eye twitching. Tiny rivulets of sweat trickle down his face. He pulls off his hat, runs his fingers round its rim until it spins.

"I can't tell you, Miss Drummond. Walter asked me never to talk about it. I deal in property, not in the family problems of those who buy and sell it."

A flush of anger spreads through her body, as if she's been dangled over a blazing fire and left there to roast.

"My father's dead." Her voice seems to come from a long way off. "I've driven more than two hundred and sixty miles to meet you. You were one of Daddy's oldest friends. Yet you *still* refuse to tell me the truth?"

"Correct. I'm not allowed to spill the beans. Anyway," he shrugs, "it's all in the past. Let sleeping dogs snooze on, that's my motto."

She stares at him. She wants to pick him up, shake him until he rattles, stand him on his head until the information he *could* reveal comes spewing out.

Instead, she swallows back her fury.

"Very well. Just one more question, please, if you can bear to answer."

"Of course." He responds to her icy sarcasm with an apologetic smile. "I don't mean to be mealy-mouthed."

"When did you last see my father?"

196

Lanham mops his face with a crumpled handkerchief. "He used to come down here every year, to check on The Hideaway. Give me instructions for repairs." He jams his hat back on. "I last saw him in December, just before Christmas."

So *that's* where Walter had been. Not London, but St Ives. She should have guessed.

"He had some paintings to sell, here at the Portman Gallery on Fore Street. I bought one for my wife. We thought very highly of his work. Very highly indeed."

"Thank God for that!" She remembers Daniel Rogers and her humiliating hour in St John's Wood. "It's been really hard, having to clear Daddy's studio. Wondering whether his work is any good."

"My dear girl!" The beads of sweat vanish. "If *that's* what you're worrying about, I have a wonderful surprise for you." He glances at his watch. "Sorry to rush you, but I have to meet another client. Shall we walk on?"

"Take me to The Hideaway." She squares her shoulders. "I can't wait a minute longer."

She recognises St Andrews Street from Walter's photograph.

The line of higgledy cottages glints back at her through the mist. An inquisitive face peers through a window, clutching a ribbon of net curtain. A boy and a girl, dark-haired, bright-cheeked, race over the cobblestones, bowling a hoop. Seagulls stand like sentries on the rooftops, flicking their heads. It's as if she's come home to a sepia landscape she's known all her life. But now, for the first time, she's a part of it.

Lanham pulls some keys from his pocket, unlocks a shabby front door and throws it open.

"Welcome to The Hideaway, Miss Drummond. Please come in."

Eleanor takes the biggest breath of her life. She peels off her gloves. She clenches her fists so tightly her fingernails bite into her palms.

And she steps over the threshold.

The Hideaway

1936

A spacious living room stretches ahead of her. She can see straight through to the far end, where the wide French windows overlook the churning green-flecked sea. At her feet, a narrow flight of stone steps leads down to the basement.

The room itself is lightly furnished: two easy chairs, a deep sofa, an oak table, its surface worn and scrubbed; a fireplace, unlit but laid with coal and in front of it a striped red-and-turquoise rug. In the corner nestles an antique mahogany bureau.

But her attention is caught and held by the clusters of paintings on the walls, each meticulously framed and hung, as if they're on professional display.

She doesn't recognise a single one.

For a frantic moment she fears none of them are Walter's. That he's filled the cottage with other people's work. But as she moves closer, she can see his familiar black signature on dazzling, intimate portraits. Faces, old and young, look out at her, full of marvellous detail, their eyes shining with life. In among them hang vibrant still-life watercolours: anemones hovering in a vase; lemons clustering in a bowl; a single decorated dish standing on a table in a rainbow of light.

Instantly she knows the watercolours are not Walter's.

She searches for their signature. But they have none.

Behind her, Lanham coughs politely. "May I show you the kitchen, Miss Drummond?"

"Of course." She grips the side of the table. "I've never seen Daddy's portraits before. I didn't know——"

"Wonderful, aren't they? Strong, youthful, energetic work. Disappointing he never returned to them … Come downstairs. I'll show you the range and how it works."

She follows him into the basement. It has a spotless terracotta tiled floor. Light filters in from an enchanting porthole window.

"I lit the slab – that's what we call the range – early this morning, so you'll have plenty of hot water. The coal is stored in this cupboard here," he opens a wooden door, "and that's the lavatory," he taps another door.

"If you want a bath, it's kept here, under the sink. You can easily pull it out and fill it. Upstairs, there are two small bedrooms and the studio where Walter always worked. I'll leave you to explore those at your leisure. Now, if you'll excuse me——"

He limps back upstairs ahead of her and presses the keys into her hand.

"There's no telephone, so if you need one, come to my office, use mine. If I'm out, my daughter Agnes will look after you."

Lanham opens the front door and steps into the street. He turns to face her, his eyes filled with sympathy and respect. "Walter told me all about you. You were the apple of his eye. He was so proud of you, passing your exams, getting into Somerville."

He raises his hat.

"Whatever you find out about your father over the next few days, don't let it tarnish your memories. He was a good man. It was a privilege to know him and to count him as my friend."

"Is your name Moira?"

1936

Eleanor closes the door, throws off her hat and coat, and moves swiftly across the room to the French windows.

She throws them open and steps on to a small balcony. It overlooks a narrow walkway, a thin strip of pebbly beach and the choppy green waters of the sea. She can hear the dull roar of the tide, seagulls calling in the heavy sky. The sea wind pulls at her clothes, tugging her hair back from her face.

This is the view, these are the sounds, this is the wind that must so often have greeted Walter. This is his cottage, yet his paintings here are so different to anything she's ever seen, it's as if they've been created by a stranger. She can sense none of Walter's spirit; she can't see or feel anything familiar.

Perhaps the bedrooms might reveal an essential clue?

She turns on her heel, closes the windows and moves back through the room. Her legs shake, her palms sweat. She climbs the narrow wooden stairs, imagining Walter doing just the same: laughing, talking to his family, getting up in the morning, dashing down for breakfast, carrying his latest canvas under one arm and a pile of linen in the other.

There are three doors on the landing, all of them closed. One by one, she swings them open.

The first room must have belonged to a child. A small wooden desk and matching chair stand against the window. A single bed, without a coverlet, hunches against the wall. She wonders whether the youngster was a boy or a girl. How old had they been when they left? What were their names? Were they blonde or dark? Vivacious or quiet? Questions crowd her mind. Frustrated, she pushes them away.

In the second room, a double bed and wardrobe almost fill the space. A brightly-coloured patchwork quilt covers the bed. On the bedside table stands a vase of daffodils: Lanham's gesture of welcome. The bed has been made up with cream-coloured cotton sheets and pale blue feather-soft blankets. The pillows smell of freshly-cut grass.

She could indeed sleep here. If she can make up her mind. If she can bear the stark reality. The indisputable fact. Walter spent *years* here: asleep, awake, locked in a dream or a nightmare, talking, arguing, laughing … making love to the woman beside him. Whoever *she* was. *Could it have been Moira?* And if not Moira, how many *other* women had there been in his life?

In the third room, two easels with upright chairs sit in either corner. Rough yellowing sketches in crayon, charcoal and pencil are pinned to the walls, their edges curling with age: working drawings for both portraits and still lives. The uneven wooden floor glints back at her with its scent of beeswax polish. Through a small window, she glimpses more heavy cloud hanging over the sea.

But none of the rooms reveal a single solid clue about Walter's life. Their scrubbed tidiness has a chilling anonymity. She doesn't know what she'd expected – but it certainly hadn't been this.

She walks slowly downstairs, overwhelmed by loneliness. She doesn't want The Hideaway with its scraps of furniture, its sense of empty desolation. She hates being here alone, having to decide whether or not to sell it. She resents the demands of decision-making. She loathes the responsibility of keeping a roof over Anne's head.

She craves the impossible: to have Walter back in her life.

She'll race after Lanham, instruct him to sell the cottage. She doesn't give a jot about the price or who buys it. She'll go straight back to The Porthminster and leave for Woodstock in the morning.

She falls on to the sofa, her heart racing, fighting back tears, trying to stay calm. A small voice in her head says: You're being ridiculous. *Do not* make hasty decisions. Give yourself time to think. Recover from the journey. Regain your sanity.

She'll make some tea. The remedy for almost everything. Hot, sweet, refreshing.

She hauls herself to her feet. Her mouth tastes of rotting fruit, her head throbs. The paintings on the walls seem to crowd in on her: their colours shout, their faces leer, their lips curl in contempt.

Are they asking her to steer clear of them? To sell them as a package to the highest bidder? To give them away as a job lot as if they're merely decorative accessories? Not to inspect them too closely – because if she does, they might reveal something she'd rather not discover?

But isn't that precisely why she's here?

She begins to walk up and down the room, checking each portrait, really *looking* at them as if they're by a painter she's never met.

204

Three red-headed children play in a room.

An elderly man with gnarled hands grips his walking stick, his faded grey eyes full of memories.

A pair of burly fishermen drink tankards of ale in The Sloop inn on the harbour, elbows on tables, gathered fishing nets at their feet.

A mother and daughter, windswept and laughing, shelter beneath an umbrella that threatens to blow inside-out.

A young man with a baby throws her a winning smile. Wait a minute. The man …

Good God, it's *Daddy*. Younger, more vibrant than she'd ever known him: his eyes shine with happiness, his hair ruffles thick and dark. The baby boy he holds in his arms: is he Walter's *son*?

Eleanor's heart begins to thump with life.

On the opposite side of the room, Walter stares out at her again. Here he looks several years older. The baby is now a sturdy toddler with chubby arms and legs, hazel eyes and a mop of dark-gold hair. He's twirling a wooden top, painted with bright bands of colour.

And then her eyes meet those of a single woman. Walter has painted her three times. In the first portrait she stands in the basement kitchen, the enchanting porthole window behind her, wearing a navy-and-white-striped apron. Her sleeves are rolled up over her creamy skin as she stirs a fruity mixture in a bowl.

In the second, she sits in bed reading a book, her arms and shoulders bare, her head leaning against the pillows, the colours of her skin dappled, translucent. Through the open window shines a crescent moon.

And in the third, she perches out-of-doors on a wooden bench, backed by a scoop of sandy cove and a turquoise sea.

A silvery-blue cloak droops from her shoulders. Her eyes shine: wistful, cornflower blue. Her hair hangs long, loose and black as soot. Her face, its shape, the domination of those ravishing eyes, is extraordinarily beautiful.

Something about the colour of the cloak tugs at Eleanor's mind. She frowns, trying to remember. Then suddenly she's *there*. In Regent's Park Road, watching Walter hurl across the street to tap a woman on her shoulder. A woman wearing a cloak of silvery-blue.

Eleanor finds her voice: "Are you the woman Daddy was looking for? *Is your name Moira?*"

Now the questions spill out: "When did he paint you? Did you live here with him? Where are you now? When did you vanish from Daddy's life? Why was he still looking for you, up until the very night he died?"

A stony silence thunders through The Hideaway, but the sound of her own voice brings Eleanor to her senses, quelling her panic and despair. She has no intention of running away. She had planned a fortnight in St Ives, and that's *exactly* what she'll have. She'll prove to Anne, to Vera and to Jonny that she can be a responsible adult, make her own decisions, see her careful plans through to their conclusion.

Prove to *herself* she can do it.

Moira or no Moira. Determination will rule her days and nights.

Living in The Hideaway

1936

Eleanor can't make tea. The kitchen cupboards, although freshly scrubbed, are bare. On one of the worktops sits a set of crockery, a chunky teapot, cutlery and three small saucepans. But nothing to eat or drink.

She stares around the small space, trying to imagine Walter there. Putting the kettle on, shovelling the coal, taking a bath. Watching Moira while she stirred her cake?

No, there's something wrong. She can't fit *those* pieces together. Walter would never have done anything in such a tiny space. She can see him in his studio upstairs. Or playing with the child in the living room. Or standing on the balcony with the sea wind blowing through his hair.

But in this basement? It has a fusty smell to it. She wrinkles her nose. Are there *rats* in this kitchen? Behind the lavatory door? Hiding in the tin bath? She shivers. The room feels darker, smaller – and suddenly oppressive, as if it's a prison from which there's no escape.

A chill grips her by the throat. You could shriek your head

off in this basement. Scream for help. Nobody would hear you, not even upstairs.

But that's a crazy way to think. Why would she even have *imagined* it?

All she wants to do is climb those stairs to street level as fast as she can.

Her heart thumping, she pounds up to the living room, throws on her hat and coat. Then she remembers the red leather purse. She pulls it out of her handbag, removes its tiny key. She looks at the antique bureau standing in the corner, knowing in a flash where the key belongs.

She walks towards the bureau. Holding her breath, she slides the key into its lock.

It's the perfect fit. Quelling a flicker of hesitation that she's intruding into someone's private life, she turns the key and opens the flap.

The musty scent of cloves rises into the air from a bottle of perfume, long empty but clinging to its fragrance. On the right sits a jumble of papers, topped by a smooth grey-and-white pebble paperweight. She flicks through old invoices, a child's drawings, tiny ink-drawn sketches, recipes, details of commissions and their prices, shopping lists.

On the left lies a small straw basket filled with jewellery. She picks out a tarnished silver bracelet, dangling with chunky charms. A necklace with the initials *W* and *M* worked in turquoise stones. A plain gold band, wide but not inscribed, rubbed and faded, too heavy for a woman's finger. Could Walter have worn it?

But there are no diaries, no letters, no new clues – and certainly no clear answers to any of her questions.

∽

Flushed with disappointment, she closes the desk, leaving the key in its lock. She turns away, picks up her handbag and her set of keys. She'll explore the town, get her bearings, buy some provisions. Then she'll come back to light the fire, bring life and warmth into the cold silence. Forget her ridiculous forebodings.

She opens the front door and hears the murmur of the sea.

On her fingers she can smell the faintest scent of cloves.

In St Ives, she swiftly gets her bearings. Most shops cluster along Fore Street, which runs parallel to the harbour. She buys apples at Drews Fruit Store; succulent slices of ham from Tevorrow the Butcher; tea, milk, sugar, cheddar cheese, wholemeal bread, tins of soup, rich Dundee cake and firelighters from the International Stores.

She wants to explore the harbour, but the shopping is heavy, the sky streaked with darkening clouds and the air begins to fill with flurries of soft rain. She turns to scurry back to The Hideaway.

Then she remembers what Lanham had told her: that last December Walter had sold some paintings to The Portman Gallery. She asks directions. Five minutes later she peers into its window.

Propped on the left-hand side, one of Walter's landscapes glints back at her.

She stands transfixed. It's a view of Blenheim's lake at twilight. A full moon hangs in an aquamarine sky; the lake's waters pick up its reflection in a shower of light. Two patient fishermen in small boats, watchful, hopeful, dangle their rods over the water.

She remembers Walter's charcoal sketch for it. But she'd never seen the finished painting before. As she stands there, the lights in the gallery flick off, its door opens and closes.

Keys rattle. Humming to himself, the owner walks briskly away.

She watches as he greets a companion, a man wearing floppy blue trousers, a casual leather jacket and a straw hat perched at a rakish angle. Although she can't see his face, she has a peculiar feeling that she's seen him somewhere before.

But this time, memories of Regent's Park Road are no help whatsoever.

The Taste of Freedom

1936

When Eleanor draws back her curtains at The Porthminster Hotel the next morning, it's as if she's woken in a different world. A perfect sunrise lights a cloudless sky, projecting an orange ribbon across a calm and dazzling sea. Gulls preen and strut on her balcony. A ship crawls slowly across the horizon's delicately pencilled line.

Longing to walk on the beach, she's in St Ives by half-past eight, before many of the shops have opened. She walks all morning, taking the narrow path down to the stretch of Porthminster Beach, its mustard-yellow sand firm and damp beneath her boots. She explores the harbour and its cluster of small shops.

She watches the sturdy fishermen calling to one another, laughing, hauling their heavy nets. Their horse waits patiently, its legs deep in water, its cart filling with the morning's catch. An artist wearing a paint-stained smock and straw boater sits with his easel by the harbour wall, absorbed in his work.

She wonders whether Walter ever painted by this waterside.

She buys coffee from a stall, relishing its scent, warming her hands on the steaming cup. People nod and smile as they pass, but nobody speaks to her. They respect her solitude.

She walks to the end of the harbour, round its corner to the intimate semicircle of Porthgwidden Beach, with its smooth pebbles: granite-grey, pink, cream. Then she's at the top of the Island where she can see for miles, hear the ocean roar, taste the salt spray. Down again, and she's on the long strip of Porthmeor Beach, noticing how each of St Ives' beaches has its own character.

By one o'clock she's ravenous. She goes back to the café she found yesterday, choosing a leek-and-bacon pie, tea and a thick slice of Cornish fruit loaf.

And then it's time to return to The Hideaway – and to make up her mind.

The moment she steps inside, she wants to stay. The previous evening she'd left a few possessions scattered about. Her map of St Ives lies on the table, with her supper plates and the red leather purse. The coal fire has died but she can light it again.

She'll leave The Porthminster and make The Hideaway her home, if only for a few days. She relishes the challenge. It'll also save her a fortnight's hotel bill. Counting the pennies has become second nature.

She'll set up house here. Fill the tin bath every morning, keep the range alight, cook simple meals, read, walk, sleep in Walter's bed. She might never get another chance.

The furious manageress of The Porthminster Hotel faces her across the desk.

"Have you ever run an hotel, Miss Drummond?"

She shifts uncomfortably from one foot to the other. "I've never had the opportunity."

"Well, let me tell you that customers such as yourself are a *nightmare*. First you book two rooms for two weeks. Excellent. Delighted to have you both. Then you cancel one of the rooms—" she holds up a hand to stop an interruption. "I understand the circumstances. But now you wish to leave *tomorrow!*"

"I've inherited a cottage," she stutters. "Until I saw it yesterday, I'd no idea whether I could live in it, whether I'd even *want* to. But now I've seen it, I do."

"Right ... I'll have your bill ready for you after breakfast."

"I'm really sorry." She picks up the key to her room and turns away.

"Oh, and Miss Drummond." The manageress has flushed scarlet. "If you ever want to visit St Ives again, may I suggest you find somewhere *else* to stay?"

As she unpacks her suitcase the next morning in The Hideaway, a thrill of excitement grips her. A sense of holiday. It's Friday. She's free to do exactly as she likes all weekend – and the sun's still shining.

She'll walk along the beaches again, explore beyond the sands, eat lunch and supper in the Shore Café and the Copper Kettle. She'll buy fresh flowers to replace the wilting daffodils, a hot-water bottle to warm her sheets, gifts of Cornish fudge and shortbread for Jonny and Vera; and Walter's lake landscape from the Portman Gallery.

The Scala Theatre is showing *China Seas* with Clark Gable and Jean Harlow: *"a mighty melodrama of fierce lives, intense hates and dangerous intrigues on the seething China Seas"*. She'll buy a bag of toffees and go to a Saturday matinée. Pretend she has all the time and freedom in the world.

On Monday morning she'll go to Lanham's, phone Anne, make sure everything's fine. She'll ring Jonny, ask about Mrs Giffen, give him her news. How proud they'll all be of her. She feels so grown-up. She's in her own cottage, running her own life. In control of her destiny.

"Good morning!" A slim girl with a beautiful complexion and a mass of curly chestnut hair greets her at Lanham's. "How can I help you this bright Monday?"

"I'm Eleanor Drummond—"

"Of *course* you are! St Andrews Street. I'm Agnes, James's daughter. Have you had a lovely weekend?"

"Wonderful. I've been staying in The Hideaway. Yesterday I walked for miles on the cliffs and the weather's been perfect."

"And what can I—"

"May I use your phone?"

"There's one in the office at the back, through that door. Take all the time you need."

Eleanor walks through to a cramped room at the end of a narrow corridor. A black telephone stands on a dusty desk. She picks up the receiver and dials home.

"Vera? It's me."

"Eleanor! Thank *God* you've rung. We've been trying to get hold of you."

"What's happened? Is Mummy all right?"

"She's fine. We rang The Porthminster on Friday night but they said you'd left. They'd no idea where you were."

"I moved into The Hideaway."

"Ah … We thought you might have done."

"But it's got no phone. I'm ringing from James Lanham's office. You sound upset. Is anything the matter?"

"Not with us, dear heart. Your mother's shopping. She's fretting about you, but she's fine. It's Jonny. Bad news, I'm afraid. Mrs Giffen had to have an operation. The doctors thought she'd pull through. But there were complications. She died during surgery."

Eleanor stares blindly around the room, feeling sick and giddy.

"Eleanor? Are you there?"

"She was a sweet old lady, Vera. Jonny was devoted to her——"

"He's devastated. He told us on Friday afternoon, said he'd tried to ring you. Your mother was mortified when she didn't know where you were."

"Could you go to see him, Vera? Give him my love. Tell him I'll be home as soon as I can?"

"Of course, dear heart … As long as you're safe, we'll stop worrying."

Eleanor stands for a moment in the middle of the room. Summoning her courage, she dials both Jonny's numbers. The ringing tones scream through her head. There's no answer.

She walks back to the office.

Agnes looks up from a file. "Did you get through?"

"I did, thank you." She clears her throat, feeling as if she's swallowed a teaspoon of sand. "I've had some very bad news. I need to go home as soon as possible. Could we discuss money? I'd like to put The Hideaway on the market right now."

She walks down to the harbour, her head spinning. The fresh sunlight of early morning has sucked into a sullen sky. She feels so guilty. She should have rung Jonny from Exeter, or at least tried his number again at The Porthminster, later that first evening. It looks as if she's hardly bothered to think about him and doesn't really care.

She'd agreed an asking price for The Hideaway. It'll fetch at least eight hundred and fifty pounds, according to Agnes, who recommends she leave its furniture, but not the paintings. James has lots of contacts looking for such properties. There's no need to put up a FOR SALE sign. Keep the transaction private.

Could Eleanor be available to show people around? Only those they've vetted, of course. James will ring Michael Humphreys in Woodstock to put him in the picture.

Before she'd even had a chance to leave the agency, Agnes had picked up the phone.

"Mr Penrose? Agnes Lanham here. Good morning to *you*, sir. How are we today? … Excellent … And I have *such* good news. Just come on the market. Cottage. St Andrews Street. Great condition. Sea views. Private balcony. Fully furnished. Vacant possession. And, my dear sir, no onward chain!"

Eleanor asks directions to the Post Office, waits impatiently in a queue and writes out a telegram.

SHOCKED AND VERY UPSET TO HEAR YOUR NEWS STOP PUTTING COTTAGE ON MARKET STOP WILL BE HOME AS SOON AS SALE IS AGREED STOP THINKING OF YOU JONNY STOP LOVE ELEANOR

It's lunchtime, but she couldn't swallow a mouthful. She'll go back to The Hideaway, make the bed, wash the dishes, mop the kitchen floor.

Soon her little Cornish haven will belong to someone else.

By mid-afternoon the cottage sparkles and she's starving.

She eats high tea in the Copper Kettle, buys enough food to last the next few days, and two novels from the Fore Street bookshop: Jane Austen's *Pride and Prejudice* and George Eliot's *Middlemarch*. She knows them both from school, but it'll be good to read them again.

As she reaches the bottom of St Andrews Street, she stops in her tracks.

A man wearing floppy blue trousers and a leather jacket stands against The Hideaway's ground-floor window, shading his eyes with one hand and peering in. She'd seen him outside the Portman Gallery.

Before she can call out or catch him up, he turns, walks swiftly to the end of the street and disappears.

She should know who he is. But once again she hasn't seen his face. She can't place him.

Infuriatingly, she's back at square one, and none the wiser.

Meeting Felix Mitchell

1936

James and Agnes Lanham have lots of contacts.

By five o'clock the next day, twelve potential buyers have inspected The Hideaway. They arrive singly or in pairs, ask questions, open cupboards and mutter in corners. Some complain there's no bathroom, the bedrooms are small, the balcony lacks shade and privacy, the kitchen's dark and poky, its range old-fashioned. Eleanor is astonished by how passionately she wants to leap to its defence. But she bites her tongue.

Others exclaim at the beautiful sea view. They adore the cottage's location, admire its compact layout.

"You must have an artist in the family," one crusty old gentleman tells her, tipping his sailor's cap to the back of his head.

Bleakly, she agrees and shuts the door on him.

Everyone says they'll "think about it". They nod, smile and wander off. Nobody asks if they might see The Hideaway again. Nobody mentions money.

On Wednesday morning, a young couple with two small

children poke around. They tell her they need a large garden for their giant poodle and lots more space for their mother.

In the afternoon, nobody comes at all.

Eleanor paces up and down the living room. She washes some underwear and hangs it above the kitchen range, hoping nobody will notice dripping knickers. She makes more cups of tea than she wants, but can't be bothered to eat. She starts to compile an inventory of the paintings: *Man with a Walking Stick*, *Drinks with a Friend*, but stops when she reaches the portraits of Walter and the baby.

Wondering whether the child really *is* her own half-brother has become too painful to think about.

She picks up the novels, and puts them down again.

By half-past five she's had enough. Desperate to walk along the beach before the sun's guttering warmth has vanished, she pulls on her hat and coat.

She opens the front door.

The man wearing floppy blue trousers and a leather jacket stands on the doorstep, his hand raised, as if he'd been about to knock. His face is thin, with high cheekbones, and piercing hazel eyes. He pulls off his straw hat, flicking his dark-gold hair off his forehead.

A shock of recognition jolts her back to Woodstock, to St Mary Magdalene's. That bitterly cold, bitterly painful January day.

"Miss Drummond? My name's Felix Mitchell—"

"*What?*"

"How do you do? … I've come about the cottage."

Speechless, she stands aside. Felix pushes past her and steps over the threshold.

"I'm sorry it's so late."

His voice is dark and rich, with the soft Cornish burr she's heard so often since arriving in St Ives.

"I've been terribly busy. I ran into Agnes Lanham yesterday. She told me to get here as quickly as I could." He looks at her. "Your hat and coat ... Are you going out? Shall I come back tomorrow?"

She says, "My father left all his money to Felix Mitchell. Are you—"

"Yes, I am." He flushes. "Walter never breathed a word to me about his will."

"And weren't you at his funeral?"

Sorrow flickers across his face. "I wondered whether you'd noticed. I was standing at the back. In a terrible state."

"Why?"

He gives her a wry smile. "How could I *not* be there, sobbing my heart out? Walter was my father too." In response to her gasp, he holds up his hands. "For the first six years of my life, he looked after me in every possible way. My 'real' father was a French man, Pierre Tessier. I never met him – at least, not that I remember."

"And your *mother*?" Eleanor's tongue feels swollen with hope. "What's *her* name?"

"Moira Mitchell. Does that mean anything to you?"

A swell of relief seems to lift her body above the floor.

"Daddy made me promise to find her. Can you tell me where she is?"

"I wish I could. The fact is, I've no idea. But those three portraits over there are certainly of her ... Miss Drummond! You're not going to *faint*, are you?" He takes her arm, guides her to a chair. "Glass of water?"

She shakes her head, unable to speak. The room is full of bright swooping sparks diving towards her eyes.

"Something stronger perhaps?"

"I've got nothing here."

He crouches on his haunches, looking up into her face. The scent of turpentine rises from his hair. "Then may I take you for a drink?"

"That sounds wonderful." She hauls herself to her feet, desperate for the dizziness to pass. "What about The Hideaway? Can I show you around?"

He tilts his head and laughs. "I used to *live* here. I know every nook and cranny." He glances at the room. "Thank God you haven't changed anything." He walks towards the door. Then, abruptly, he stops, looking at the table, its clutter of maps, books, teacups – and the red leather purse.

He picks it up, then turns towards her, his face drained of blood.

"Where did you find *this*?"

"In Woodstock, in Walter's studio, when I was tidying up." Her voice trembles. "He'd stuffed it into a drawer. The key that was inside it fits the bureau over there."

Felix's hands shake. "The purse belonged to Mama. Walter found it on the floor, the night she disappeared. He always kept it in his pocket. He said it was his lucky charm that would surely bring her back."

He turns the purse in his palm, smoothing its rough edges, flicking at the rusty clasp, opening and closing it over and again.

"Would you like to keep it?"

He looks at her with grateful, tear-filled eyes.

"You've no idea what that would mean to me."

The first thing she notices when they are out in St Andrews Street is how good it feels to be beside him. They move in step, as if they've spent hours together as walking companions. She looks up at his profile, at the graceful slope

221

of his shoulders, and then sideways at the long, lean hands swinging by his side.

Her head clears. The narrow streets have a sharper focus. The murmur of the sea, the chatter of voices from people they pass, come clear and light. As they reach the harbour, a radiant cream and turquoise sunset takes her breath away.

He guides her along the harbour until its final dip by the pier.

"Let's drink here. I come to The Sloop a lot. It's a great haunt, particularly for artists. It'll get rowdy later, but for now we'll be able to hear each other speak."

The place is empty, but for the wooden tables and pungent aromas of beer and tobacco. She sits by a window, watching him order their drinks, share a joke with the landlord. He brings the glasses to their table.

"You look so like Walter it pulls at my heart. The colour of your eyes, the shape of your nose and mouth … Talk about 'spitting image'!"

They smile at one other.

He says, "I was too cut up to speak to you at the funeral. Anyway you were surrounded. It was hardly the place."

"I'd no idea you even existed."

"So Walter never talked about me?" His soft burr hardens with disappointment.

"Never." She sips her brandy. It burns her throat but revives her. "The first time I ever heard your name was at the reading of Daddy's will. Our lawyer wasn't allowed to tell us anything about you."

He bites his lip. "I'm sorry—"

"And the first time Daddy ever mentioned Moira to me was the night he died."

"So who did you think she was?"

She takes a larger sip. "Daddy's first wife? I think my

mother was his third. Am I wrong?"

"Only by a technicality. Walter and Mama never married. He wanted to, she always refused. Mama was very unconventional. But she and Walter lived as man and wife – and I was very much *their* child."

"Could you tell me the whole story? I loved Daddy more than anyone. I never suspected anything like this." She looks bravely into his eyes. "Begin at the beginning and don't stop until you get to the end?"

"That's a *very* tall order, Miss Drummond."

"*Please*, Mr Mitchell … I really need to know."

He says slowly, "I agree on one condition. That you sell me The Hideaway. I want to live in it again more than words can say." He moves his hand across the table to touch hers. "I agree to your asking price. Walter left me his money, and I've been saving like crazy. I had my first exhibition at the Portman Gallery last December—"

"So you're a painter, too?"

"How could I *not* be when Mama and Walter put pencils and brushes into my fist the minute I could hold them? Anyway, I'm not going to haggle when The Hideaway means so much more to me than its price. I had to leave it when I was six, twenty-two years ago. I've always dreamed of owning it. Will you say yes?"

She twists her hand in his. Their two palms meet. Her sudden wave of sadness disappears. "I will … That way, we can keep it in the family."

"Will you take it off the market? See James Lanham with me? Tell him the cottage is sold?" Felix's hazel eyes laugh into hers. "How can I ever thank you?"

"You can keep your side of the bargain."

"Only if you let me buy you supper."

"Go on then, Mr Mitchell. Twist my arm!"

Happy as Sandboys

1914

"Mama and Walter met in 1906 in Oxford."

Felix settles himself in his chair, long legs crossed, paint-stained fingers curled around his glass.

"I don't remember much before we came here. Mama loved it because St Ives was full of other painters. Walter had more commissions than he could handle, and Mama's work blossomed. The light, the five beaches, the way the sea curls around you everywhere you go. There's something very special about St Ives. The three of us were happy as sandboys."

A shadow darkens his face again.

"At least, I *think* we were. I was only a child. If Mama and Walter argued, they did so while I slept. They never shouted or threw crockery."

"But *something* must have happened."

He drains his glass, twists in his chair with a rapid, snakelike movement. "Let's go and eat. I'll tell you more when there's food inside me."

They walk back along the harbour, turn into the centre of town and up a narrow street called The Digey.

"I rent the top floors in Driftwood, over there." He points to a house in a dimly-lit alleyway. "The attic room has two enormous windows that give me lots of light. I love it, but my landlady likes to know what's going on." He grins. "And I don't always want to tell her … Anyway, I'm bursting at the seams. I moved in three years ago with almost nothing. It's amazing how much stuff you accumulate." He glances at Eleanor. "Aren't you at Somerville College?"

"I *was*, but I've given it up to look after Mummy. I work in an antiques shop." Suddenly she's gripped by a fierce dread of going home. "But my week in St Ives has been wonderful. A real taste of freedom."

"How long will you stay?"

She hesitates. She wants to say, "For the rest of my life." Instead she blurts out, "I'd love to stay another week." Her honesty takes her by surprise. "That's what I'd *planned*."

He stops in his tracks, his arm brushing her shoulder.

"Don't go home tomorrow. Your mother doesn't know I'm here. Nor does she know you've had an offer on The Hideaway."

She gets his drift. They became conspirators, playing for a brief window of time.

He says with studied nonchalance, "We've so much to talk about. Haven't we, Eleanor?"

It's the first time he's said her name. With her heart thumping so hard she's sure he'll hear it, she agrees.

They eat in a small restaurant overlooking Porthmeor Beach: watercress soup, poached bream in a delicate sauce. When their plates are cleared, he pours the last of the wine.

"Now for the hard part. I've never told anyone the whole story."

"I'm *longing* to hear it."

"The Great War was on our doorstep. Some Cornish men had already left to fight in the trenches. There wasn't much money around and certainly none to spare. If you qualified for an old-age pension, you were given five shillings a week. I made a friend of our St Andrews Street lamplighter. He worked a sixty-six-hour week, including Sundays, for twenty-four shillings. He had a wife, a mother-in-law and five children to support.

"Although we never had a lot of money, we survived. Mama's best friend, Lizzie Farrell, and her mother were both dressmakers, originally in Oxford with Mama, then in St Ives. Mrs Farrell's eyesight began to fade and Lizzie had to support them both on her wages.

"Mama had saved some money to give her on her birthday, Friday the 3rd of April. But that morning we woke to pelting rain, a thick mist and an evil-smelling fog. A thunderous storm had raged through the night. Five fishing boats had failed to return. People were waiting for news on the quayside. There was pandemonium.

"It was the Easter holidays. After breakfast I dashed out to play with my best friends, twins who lived up the road. At eleven o'clock, one of Walter's models arrived."

He gulps at the last of his wine.

"Mama said she'd take Lizzie's birthday money to her. According to Walter, she left The Hideaway without saying goodbye."

He gives a snort of bitter laughter, but his eyes are full of tears.

"Walter's model left at one o'clock. I came home for lunch, and then ran back to the twins. We thought Mama had taken shelter with Lizzie because the weather was even worse.

"Another model arrived at two o'clock and sat for Walter until four. Then she left, and I came home for tea. By that time, the rain had stopped, but the fog hadn't lifted. The streets were running with water and dead rats. Chimney pots and tiles had been washed off roofs. All five fishing boats were still missing. We were still waiting for Mama.

"At six o'clock, Walter decided to walk to Lizzie's and take me with him. He said he needed some air and exercise, but I knew he was worried sick.

"Lizzie and her mother were renting a couple of rooms in a boarding house on Westward Road, off Porthmeor Hill. Walter and I dashed through the streets and climbed the hill." His voice is very quiet. "I remember the wind pulling at my hair, the darkness of the sea. The storm lurked everywhere, as if at any moment there'd be more thunder and lightning. I clung on to Walter's hand, struggling to walk. We were determined to beat the elements."

He clasps his hands together. "Neither of us had the faintest idea what lay ahead. Lizzie and Mrs Farrell were astonished to see us. They'd been cloistered in their room, working on a trousseau. They hadn't seen Mama for a week.

"Walter and I stood dripping in the hall. Walter said, 'But Moira *must* be here. She left The Hideaway at eleven this morning. She had birthday money for you. If she's not here, where's she *been* all day? *And where is she now?*'

"Lizzie gave us some tea. She made Walter explain exactly what had happened. Ten minutes later, we raced down to St Ives. Lizzie took me home. Walter went straight to the police station. The search for Mama began in earnest."

∽

"She'd vanished from the face of God's good earth."

They are out-of-doors again, above Porthmeor Beach, the sea and sky inky blue, lights twinkling from a ship on the horizon, handfuls of stars trying to compete. Felix walks slowly, his head bent, his hands thrust into his pockets.

"The police questioned Walter for hours. They asked whether he'd quarrelled with Mama, how he'd spent the day. The fact that he and Mama were not husband and wife counted against him.

"Thankfully, Walter's models were his alibis. He hadn't been alone for a single minute. When two policemen brought him back to The Hideaway, he looked shattered. He told me he was sure Mama would be home soon. I knew he wasn't telling me the truth.

"The police searched every inch of The Hideaway. Walter found the red purse on the floor near the bureau, full of Lizzie's birthday money. He couldn't understand why Mama *hadn't* taken it to her.

"I sat up in bed, listening. Walter shouted at the police, 'What do you think you'll find? My beloved Moira's body underneath the floorboards? Why aren't you out there, looking for her in the town, on the beaches?' 'Because it's dark, sir, pouring with rain, and we'd be none the wiser.'

"Walter stayed up all night, by the front door, in the street, pacing around, praying for a miracle. The search in St Ives began at dawn. The police made house-to-house enquiries. They swarmed over the beaches, looking for clues. But nobody had seen sight nor sound of my beautiful Mama."

Felix quickens his pace, she struggles to keep up. They reach the bottom of The Digey and turn on to the harbour.

"Walter went to pieces. He couldn't eat or sleep or work. The police stuck **MISSING** photographs of Mama all over

228

town. Two days later, I spotted one, plastered to the harbour wall. It said **HAVE YOU SEEN THIS WOMAN?** I burst into tears and ran home. Walter and I sobbed in each other's arms.

"Meanwhile, Mama's Aunt Beatrice arrived from Newlyn. She and Walter agreed I should stay with her until Mama turned up – or until Walter could look after me properly. I didn't want to leave him – but I had no choice.

"After a month, the police stopped looking. They hadn't found a single trace of Mama or come up with the smallest clue. The morning she vanished, she'd worn a mackintosh with a hood. She hadn't taken an umbrella. The wind was so strong it would have ripped the thing to pieces. The only item we *thought* she'd been carrying was her purse."

He takes it out of his pocket.

"We had nothing left to look for. We knew Mama hadn't been robbed, but we didn't have any other answers. The police decided she'd left of her own accord and didn't want to return. Or she'd been murdered, and her body thrown into the sea."

He stands looking at the jumble of fishing boats, securely moored for the night. He holds the purse, turning it over and over in his hands.

"Walter couldn't prove whether Mama was alive or dead. And I was the most miserable child in the world."

"I never really lived here again."

They are drinking coffee in The Hideaway.

"Walter wasn't my 'real' father, so Aunt Beatrice became my legal guardian. Walter refused to believe Mama was dead. He chased off to Oxford to ask whether any of her friends had seen her. They hadn't. He even went to Paris where he was told Pierre Tessier was dead.

"One morning, Lizzie told Walter about a woman called Madame Thelma."

His voice hardens with contempt.

"She claimed to be a scientific palmist who could predict people's futures by looking at their handwriting and photographs. Madame Thelma looked at Walter's samples. She said she thought Moira was impulsive and untrustworthy, given to following her heart. She'd probably decided to 'go abroad in search of adventure and to find her fortune' that April morning.

"Walter screamed denial. That night, drinking with friends in The Sloop, he stood up to buy another round – and collapsed. He was taken to hospital in Penzance where a doctor told him if he didn't start eating and sleeping properly, he wouldn't survive. The warning seemed to bring my poor darling Walter to his senses."

Felix moves over to the French windows, stares out into the darkness.

"He decided to clean up The Hideaway, hang their paintings properly – and turn his back on St Ives. It was the summer of 1914. War was imminent, although Walter couldn't fight. He packed a small suitcase, left his easel and paints here, and caught the train to London."

No Last Goodbye

1936

"He met Mummy in Woodstock three years later." Eleanor is desperate to pick up the threads of the story.

"Daddy was staying at The Bear in the spring of 1917, on a painting holiday. He was sketching Blenheim's lake. Mummy stopped to admire his work. They started chatting. She fell in love with him at first sight. But he'd become a landscape painter. Why did he stop painting portraits?"

"Whenever he tried to paint someone's face, the only one he could see was Mama looking back at him. After Rebecca Holmes died, he decided that nudes were off his menu too. But he could get lost in landscapes. It helped to ease the pain."

"I hope meeting Mummy helped too!"

"I'm *sure* it did." Felix turns to face her. "Anne was exactly what he needed. He came to see me that summer, told me he'd fallen in love again. That he wanted to marry and settle down, out of London and away from Cornwall. I understood and I was happy for him. He'd begun a new life."

"How often did you see him?"

"Every year, just for a few days. He'd come to St Ives to check on The Hideaway. Sometimes I'd stay here with him. As I got older, it became easier. We'd talk about Mama, reminisce without the tears. When I went to art college, I'd show him my paintings. We'd discuss them, artist to artist. He was always so encouraging."

"One more question: when did you last see him?"

"In December. I had my first major exhibition at the Portman Gallery. He arrived for the opening. By that time, I was renting Driftwood. He bought one of my paintings, wanted to take it back to Woodstock. Then he decided it would be impossible to explain to Anne who it was by and where he'd bought it. It's hanging in my attic. You're welcome to have it.

"We had supper together that night, drank a glass of champagne to each other's success." Felix hesitates. "I'm glad about one thing, Eleanor. When we parted, neither of us knew it would be the last time we'd ever meet." He gives her a wan smile. "We never had to say a last goodbye."

They stand at the front door of The Hideaway.

"Tell me one last thing before you go ... Why all the secrecy? Why did Daddy never tell my mother about his past?"

Felix turns to look at her, tiredness etched around his eyes and mouth. "It's a very good question." He rubs a hand across his face, as if to soothe his weariness. "Walter and I were extremely close. I was the only person in his life who knew about most of his. But if I'm honest, I don't think he told me everything.

"Something terrible happened between him and Mama. Walter felt *guilty*. He'd say, 'If only I could turn back the clock, wipe the slate clean.' He never told Rebecca about

Mama. Years later, he said he couldn't tell Anne the truth because he'd left it far too late."

Felix runs his fingers through his hair. Standing there in the darkness, he looks thin, anxious, vulnerable.

"Sometimes the better you know someone, the harder it is to tell them the truth."

At eleven o'clock next morning they meet outside Lanham's agency. Eleanor had bathed in the tin tub, washed her hair, put on her best skirt and jacket, applied a bright coral lipstick, and dusted the sand off her shoes.

Felix had also dressed for the occasion in a cream lightweight suit and navy tie.

She holds out her hand. He raises it briefly to his lips.

"Did you sleep well?"

"Like a log." Her heart races with delight.

"And you haven't changed your mind?"

"I gave you my word." Her cheeks flame beneath his gaze. "And you kept yours. The Hideaway belongs to you."

"You've made me the happiest of men."

James Lanham can scarcely contain his delight.

"I can't believe I'm looking at the two of you together!" He pulls out their file. "Walter would have been *beside* himself with joy. I assume you'd like The Hideaway taken off the market? ... That's wonderful! I wish all my properties sold so fast."

Lanham looks at Eleanor. "Will you be going home to Woodstock immediately, Miss Drummond? Agnes told me you'd received bad news."

"I'll stay on for a few more days. Mr Mitchell and I need to discuss the paintings. I'm planning to leave on Wednesday."

"Then may I give you the inventory?" Lanham ferrets for a ream of paper. "Could you check through it? I'll write to your Woodstock solicitor again. The contract will be waiting for you when you get home." He holds out his hand. "It's been a pleasure doing business with you, Miss Drummond. Walter would have been proud of you."

Eleanor and Felix stand together in the street outside the agency.

"I feel like whooping for joy." The colour is high in his cheeks, his eyes shine. "Racing barefoot over the sands. Splashing in the sea. Drinking champagne."

"That sounds like a good idea – the champagne, I mean."

"Let's go back to The Sloop. And before we get too tipsy, I'll take you to my favourite café. Their chef will give us a proper Cornish lunch. I recommend the fishcakes and the treacle tart."

She looks up at him. "On one condition."

"Name it." He takes her arm.

"This time, I'm paying."

Red Taffeta

1936

As they settle in The Sloop, Felix looks directly at Eleanor.

"Are you really going to stay until Wednesday?"

"I'd always meant to have a fortnight's holiday, as well as getting through the business side of the trip. The minute I'm home, it'll be back to work, looking after Mummy, deciding what to do with the money from The Hideaway."

"Then I know how we could spend some of the time." He raises his glass. "I'd like to paint your portrait. Every morning, in my studio, let's say for five sittings – Friday, Saturday, Sunday, Monday and Tuesday – for a couple of hours each time. How does that sound?"

"I'd love it."

"Good. Wear something different every morning. I make dozens of preliminary sketches and choose the best. The light in my studio is different every day. I'll take you there after lunch. And on Saturday night we'll go to the *Palais de Danse* and jig up and down to the Rhythmonians Band. Do you dance?"

"I don't often get the chance."

"We'll pay ninepence each to get into the *Palais* and I'll dance you off your feet. In the afternoons we can walk along the cliffs. The path towards Zennor is my favourite. Its views are magnificent. You can almost get lost in the sky. And if it rains, we'll shelter in the picture house and listen to 'the incomparable tenor' Richard Tauber in *Heart's Desire*. We'll cram lots of good things into the next few days."

He clinks his glass against hers, inspecting her face as if he's already putting her image on to canvas.

"Whatever the weather, I promise you a week to remember."

An hour later they walk down The Digey, full of food and alcohol.

He marches up to the side of Driftwood. "This is my entrance." He pulls out his key. "It's more private, even though my landlady lurks by the window!" He unlocks a heavy oak door. "Welcome."

He leads her up a steep flight of wooden stairs into a narrow hall.

"Bathroom, bedroom, kitchen, in that order." He points towards them. "All pretty chaotic. My studio is on the next floor. Come on up."

A spacious attic room greets her, filled with light. The afternoon sun streams in from two large windows. It bathes the room in yellow beams dancing with motes of dust. She can see the harbour, the coastline, the sea and sky, racing clouds and the faint line of the horizon.

The room is sparsely furnished – a lumpy sofa, two battered armchairs, a screen embroidered with scarlet poppies, and the wild jumble of Felix's working equipment litter the floor – but it feels modern and stylish.

"What a fantastic place to work."

He stands behind his easel, checking his latest sketch. "I'll miss it when I move. But I plan to put a skylight in The Hideaway's studio."

"Good idea."

"Here." He beckons her to a far corner of the room. "This is the painting Walter bought. You can take it home."

She picks her way across the floor, trying not to tread on an assortment of empty cups, bottles of turpentine, paintbrushes and half-finished canvases. And then she's staring at a portrait of her father, so brilliantly lifelike it takes her breath away. Walter stands in this very room, looking out of a window. Felix sits behind him, sketching at his easel. The two men share a joke. Between them throbs an exquisite moment of harmony.

Tears spark in her eyes. "It's marvellous. I really love it."

"And what will you tell your mother?"

"The truth." She dashes a hand across her face. "The whole truth and nothing but the truth, so help me God."

"She won't like it much."

"She won't have any choice."

"Isn't that a bit brutal?"

"So what do you suggest? Either I invent a series of lies, which would be complicated and pointless. Or I don't tell her anything, which will look suspicious and underhand. It seems to me *I* don't have a choice."

He carries the painting to The Hideaway. They check through James Lanham's inventory. They agree that Felix should keep the furniture, Moira's watercolours and Walter's three portraits of her. Eleanor will take Walter's other paintings home.

He keeps glancing at the bureau. She asks him whether he wants to look inside. He nods gratefully.

"I remember Walter telling me it was Mama's special desk, that he'd locked it and hidden the key. Then he couldn't remember where it was!"

Together they rifle through its papers. Disappointed, he gives her a brief smile. "There's nothing here I haven't seen before. I'd hoped it might give me a clue to Mama's disappearance. I'll just have to stop hoping, won't I?"

They walk to the Portman Gallery, where he introduces her to the owner and she buys Walter's landscape. Felix tucks it under his arm as they return to the cottage.

"It's like retrieving the last piece of my father," Eleanor says. "I'll give it to a friend of mine in Woodstock. He was meant to drive down to St Ives with me, but at the last minute he had to pull out."

"Oh?" He guides her across Fore Street. "Is love in the air?"

"God, no … Nothing like that." She blushes. "I work in Jonny's antiques shop but he's only a good friend." She glances at Felix, half-frightened to ask. "I bet you've had a string of lovers in St Ives."

"I've had one or two affairs here, but nothing serious. There was a girl in Newlyn, older than me. I had a crush on her while I was still at school. Then at my London art college I met Rachel. I liked her, but she loved big cities. Coming to live down here with me was never on the cards."

They reach the bottom of St Andrews Street.

"The trouble is—" he hesitates. "I loved Mama so much and then she vanished. I'm frightened of falling in love in case the woman who steals my heart switches herself off like a light and leaves me on my own in silence and darkness."

That evening it rains.

They sit together in the picture house, watching Richard Tauber in *Heart's Desire*. Before the film, a Pathé Gazette newsreel, announced by the crowing cockerel, shows brief retrospective snippets of the Prince of Wales' life. Talking to soldiers on the Italian front in 1917. On tour in Canada in 1919, surrounded by adoring women. Visiting a miner's home in County Durham in 1929. Not only the people's prince but the people's friend, concerned about the problems of poverty, anxious to alleviate the miners' plight.

As they walk back to The Hideaway, Eleanor tells Felix how ironic it is that the new King is always shown on the British news *without* Wallis Simpson. Felix had never heard of her.

"The King will marry her *and* keep his throne," he says when she's described the royal affair. "He'll get the best divorce lawyer for Wallis and wriggle his way around the establishment's regulations. We'll have a Queen Wallis by this time next year, you mark my words. Edward's very popular in Cornwall. We'd *never* let him give up the throne, even if the woman he loves is an American divorcée."

Sitting as a model is a new experience for Eleanor.

She learns how to remain still and silent for several hours at a time.

She watches Felix, his face intent and serious, his hair flopping on to his forehead.

She listens to the scrape of his charcoal, seagulls calling to the wind and sky.

She imagines Felix and Walter walking and talking together.

And she wonders what might have happened if Moira

239

had returned. Would Walter have raced back to his first love, rejoicing? Saying to her and Anne as he left, *"Sorry, darlings. I really must be off. Things to do, people to see … Don't wait up."*

On Friday afternoon, after luncheon, they take the cliff path towards Zennor, returning an hour later for tea at The Hideaway, windswept and glowing. Eleanor's lips taste of the salt of the sea.

On Saturday afternoon, she catches the bus in St Ives. It rumbles through Carbis Bay, across the fields of Lelant and Hayle, to the boats and bustle of Penzance.

"If you want me to jig up and down with you, I'll have to go shopping."

She finds a small dress-shop on the High Street in Penzance and chooses a frock of red taffeta with a plunging neckline, tight sleeves and a full skirt. It swishes when she moves, filling her with excitement. Silk stockings and a pair of black patent-leather pumps complete the outfit.

Back in The Hideaway, she battles in the basement kitchen with hot water and the bath tub, washing her hair, scrubbing her back and singing *'If You Were the Only Girl in the World'* to the kitchen walls. She tries to banish the fear she always has the minute she climbs down the steps. There's a ghost lurking in the corner, ready and waiting to consume her soul.

True to his word, Felix dances Eleanor off her feet.

As he whirls her around the floor, his eyes shining with delight, his arm firmly around her waist, she realises that in the last few days he's taken over her world. She has scarcely thought about Anne or Vera or Jonny, and she pushes to one side all thoughts of her return to Woodstock.

But as Sunday drifts into Monday and then Tuesday, she

knows she'll have to tear herself away from him and go home sweet home.

They spend Sunday morning in Driftwood. He tells her that most people in St Ives are devout Wesleyans who assiduously keep the Sabbath, refusing to allow any boats to be launched, or artists to pitch their easels on the harbour. One miscreant who had disobeyed, and sat sketching the French crabbers with their bracken-coloured sails, was hurled unceremoniously into the Sunday sea.

She laughs. His eyes sparkle in response.

Monday's skies are dark. After luncheon they are forced back from their walk towards Zennor by driving wind and heavy rain. Thunder begins to rumble in the darkening skies.

He clutches her hand. "Storms frighten me. They remind me of the journey Walter and I made, stumbling home without Mama. Let's get back."

In The Hideaway, he flings off his raincoat, his face and hair drenched with rain.

She goes down to the kitchen to make a tray of tea. When she carries it upstairs to the living room, he's lying on the sofa, fast asleep.

For half an hour she sits looking at him, the long lines of his body, his slender hands. She wants the past few days to continue, exactly as they have, without change or interruption, never to end.

A seagull swoops on to their balcony, squawking for food.

He wakes with a start, meeting her gaze, smiling at her, stretching out his arms.

"How rude of me ... I'm so sorry ... You should have woken me."

And in that single fleeting moment, Eleanor falls in love.

On Tuesday afternoon, after her final sitting, they eat in the Copper Kettle. He walks her back to The Hideaway.

"I'll help you load Walter's paintings into your car. But I won't stay. I *hate* goodbyes. I'll keep everything short and sweet." He pushes his hair out of his eyes. "And please keep your keys. If you ever want to come back here, The Hideaway will always be your home."

She watches him walk down St Andrews Street, willing him to turn and wave, retrace his steps, run towards her, catch her in his arms.

But he does not look back.

She closes the front door, forces herself to climb the stairs. She opens the wardrobe, pulls out her clothes, folds them into her suitcase, the red taffeta frock on top. She'd worn it on Sunday morning, too.

"I must paint you in that!"

She cleans the kitchen, throws away some mouldy cheese and stale bread. She leaves the tins of tea, coffee and sugar, the ginger biscuits in their packet. She's handing over The Hideaway to him, not merely closing it down.

She dusts the living room, rakes the fire, fills the bucket with fresh coal. She stares at the gaps where Walter's paintings had hung, and rearranges Moira's watercolours on a single wall.

She hangs the last one, enchanted by its beauty. It's a still life of a melon, cut jaggedly in half, sitting in its oval dish beside two russet apples and some strawberries. The fruit gleams against a curtain patterned with climbing roses. She imagines Moira working on it in the studio, Felix playing at her feet, Walter beside them finishing a portrait.

A happy family on a normal day? Or one on the verge of disintegration?

Swiftly, uncomfortably, she turns away from the painting, trying to ignore her thoughts. The silence is deafening. The mantelpiece clock chimes six.

And suddenly she can't bear The Hideaway without Felix a minute longer. She sees him everywhere. His red woollen scarf, with its faint scent of turpentine, hangs on a peg. His notebook lies on the table, a box of charcoal beside it. His battered slippers crouch by the hearth.

She remembers him peering out of the window to check the weather. Rifling through the papers in Moira's bureau. Bending to light the fire, pouring a cup of tea. Lying on the sofa, asleep.

And then the moment he'd woken, stretching out his arms, smiling up at her.

That moment of certainty.

Perhaps she should climb into the Morris this very minute? Escape before she can say or do something she might regret?

She drags her suitcase down the stairs. She hesitates by the front door, paralysed, confused, her heart thumping with indecision.

And then she knows she's leaving – not for her car and the steering wheel. An inner voice says to her: *You have a choice. Choose. Quickly. This very minute. Take courage. Choose now.*

She releases the suitcase, flings on her coat, snatches up her bag. She closes the front door and locks it, trembling with impatience. She starts to race down St Andrews Street, along Fore Street, into The Digey, praying that Felix will be at home. If he's already in The Sloop, all will be lost.

But as she rounds the corner to Driftwood, she sees him hurtling towards her.

She says, "Thank God. There's something I meant to tell you—" but he takes her in his arms, pressing his fingers to her lips.

He says, "Let me speak first."

She struggles in his embrace. "I should have said—"

"I loved you from the moment I saw you in the doorway of The Hideaway."

She catches her breath with joy.

"I love you for listening to the story of my beautiful Mama. For the way you sat for me, in such stillness, lost in your thoughts. I loved dancing with you in that stunning red frock. And now I love you even more because you're leaving me."

"But not for twelve hours yet." She reaches up to him. Her voice is steady but her heart beats like a drum. "We have one entire night to spend together."

"Are you sure, my darling?" He holds her at arm's length. "Are you absolutely, one hundred per cent, rock-solid sure?"

"Yes, Felix, I am."

They walk the rest of The Digey in silence, only their fingertips touching, moving in harmony.

Driftwood feels quiet and private. He closes the front door. He gathers her into his arms, his lips on her forehead, in her hair, on her neck. He pulls away and then they kiss.

He follows her up the stairs. They stop outside the bedroom door.

"Wait here. I want to bring something to our bed."

She can hardly bear his absence. She looks across at a painting on the wall. It's a portrait of Moira she'd never noticed before: sad, stern, but hauntingly beautiful, signed by Walter.

She murmurs, "Give us your blessing."

He comes out of the kitchen, carrying a pair of candles and a box of matches.

In his bedroom, he draws the curtains, places the candles on the bedside table, lights each of the wicks. They leap into life. The smell of sulphur rises into the air.

He turns towards her.

He touches her cheek, smooths her hair, unbuttons her coat.

Candlelit shadows dance along the walls, flicker across his face.

They peel off their clothes.

"Come to me, my dearest girl, my darling Eleanor."

He holds out his arms.

And like a moth to a flame, she walks into them.

Letters from the Past

1936

She never remembered how she got from Driftwood to the end of The Digey. But she *does* remember coming to her senses, realising she's walking on her own in a cool, crisp dawn.

She's tired but exhilarated. She can feel his hands and mouth on every inch of her. His kisses flutter in her hair, sprinkle her face, open her lips and scald her skin. Her thighs burn as she walks. When she blinks, she sees beneath her eyelids the flickers of candle flame, the lights and shadows of his arms and legs, his face, his hands. She hears his voice. She remembers his words of love.

Halfway through the night he'd turned to her.

"Eleanor! Come closer. You'll never leave me, will you? Promise me."

"I promise. I'll be waiting for you in Woodstock. Come to me as soon as you can. Don't fret, my darling Felix. Sleep in my arms."

When she wakes at dawn, she knows that if she doesn't slip into her clothes and walk away, she'll stay with him for ever. With only one backward glance, her heart pounding with pain, she leaves him sleeping, his profile defined against the pillow, one arm flung out across the sheet, the candles burned down to their waxy base.

She opens the front door of The Hideaway and leans against it, trembling. The silence that greets her is comforting. She knows that Felix loves her. Meeting him has changed her life. And now she's sure that Walter meant it to happen. He wanted the two people he loved the most to meet and fall in love.

She patters down to the kitchen to make a cup of sweet black tea. She takes it upstairs, drinking it on the balcony, mouthing a silent goodbye to the early-morning sea and sky. Then she closes the French windows and forces herself to think about the journey home. Mummy, Vera ... She must face them. And Jonny. What on earth will she tell *him* about the most extraordinary two weeks of her life?

She stands in front of the paintings of Moira, looks into the cornflower-blue eyes. "I wish I knew whether you're still alive. I've only seen your image. It's not enough for me – and it's certainly not enough for Felix. If I were ever to find you, he'd be beside himself with joy."

She's standing at the front door with her suitcase when she remembers something Jonny had told her about antique bureaux. Some of them were made with secret drawers. She'd struggled with the one in Giffen Antiques for hours until she finally discovered its cleverly crafted 'bible well'.

She looks at Moira's desk. Might it have a secret drawer?

She walks towards the desk, opens its flap. She pulls a small table towards her and sits on a low stool. She removes the desk's paperwork, laying it in neat piles on the table.

Then she runs her hands over the flat inner surface of the bureau, feeling the grain of the wood underneath her fingers.

She was right. In the centre, flat and discrete, is the oblong shape of the section of wood sheltering the bible well. She opens the top drawer of the desk, pushing at the wood above it. With a faint splintering sound, the piece of wood rises into her hand. Beneath it she can feel some papers, tied together.

Her heart thumping, she pulls out the bundle.

Half a dozen letters lie in their envelopes, all addressed in a firm, black-inked hand: the first four to Moira at Walton Crescent, Oxford. A further two sent to Moira, but care of Lizzie Farrell to 6 Westward Road, St Ives. They are held together with a narrow blue-velvet ribbon, dusty, exquisitely soft to the touch.

In that moment Eleanor becomes a thief. She doesn't care. She's desperate to rip the letters from their envelopes. But if she reads them now, she'll want to show them to Felix. And if she takes them to Driftwood, she'll never be able to leave.

She makes a decision. She replaces the strip of wood in the bureau together with its papers, and closes the flap. She unzips her suitcase, lays the letters on top of her red taffeta frock.

She'll drive all day, stop at a guest-house and read the letters after supper. And then decide whether or not to tell Felix about them. They might contain information she'd prefer him not to know. They might tell her nothing useful at all. There'd be no point in raising his hopes – only to dash them again.

But suppose the letters contain information that *could* lead her to Moira. Maybe even reunite Felix with his long-lost mother?

She zips up the suitcase, and hauls it out of the front door. She staggers to the car and levers it into the boot. She sits behind the wheel, willing herself to turn the ignition key. And wondering …

Is the promise she made to Walter becoming an obsession?

Would he have asked her to make it unless he'd really believed Moira was alive?

She drives to Bath, her head buzzing with sweet memories. She finds a small hotel, eats supper, bathes, and climbs into bed, the bundle beside her.

She unties the ribbon feeling dizzy with hope.

The first letter, dated June 1911, was sent from the Randolph Hotel in Oxford.

My darling Moira

It was wonderful to see you again – you and now also my enchanting little boy. Thank you so much for agreeing to meet me. It has taken me months to summon up the courage to contact you, and my heart, it is full of sorrows and regrets and apologies. I have behaved like a drunken pig. Can you forgive me? I hope you already have. You could easily have told me you never wanted to see me again. That is exactly what I deserved.

But the moment we met again, I knew the old magic between us had returned – how you say? – with a vengeance. You are more beautiful than ever, chérie, and our adorable little boy, he has your smile and my eyes.

My darling girl, will you meet me again, tomorrow, here at my hotel? Without our enchanting Felix this time? Let me show you how much I love you. Let me for a few short hours take you in my arms.

You tell me you have decided not to marry Walter Drummond. He cannot love you as I do. I know that in so many important ways you are still mine.

And me, I am certainly, surely, without a single shadow of doubt

Your Pierre for ever

Eleanor longs to read Moira's reply, but the bundle only includes letters from Pierre. Frustrating, but better than nothing. There are two more from the Randolph in Oxford in the same vein, and then one from Paris dated August 1911.

I cannot believe you are planning to leave Oxford for Cornwall for a long holiday and – what is even worse – you say you do not wish to see me again. That my coming to Cornwall will be too difficult, that we shall not be able to keep our meetings a secret. I do not want *to keep them secret. I want to blaze our love loud and clear to the world.*

Please, my darling, think carefully about your move. I feel it will trap you all too firmly into your life with Walter. The last time we met, you told me you had many doubts about it. What has happened to make you resolve them? I beg you to open your heart to me.

If at any time you change your mind, I am ready to welcome you back into my life with our enchanting little boy.

Between that letter and the next, there is more than a year. By then, the tone of Pierre's letters is very different – and they come from Brown's Hotel in London.

I am a changed man. I have left Paris and the dissolute life entirely. My friends and family think I have died of poisoning by alcohol. I have done nothing to correct their assumption.

I was indeed very close to death. I do not want them to find me, to coax me back into my disreputable habits. My family have long since despaired of me and I have cut off all communications with them too.

I have moved to the Côte d'Azur, to Juan-les-Pins, where the air is clean and refreshing, the sea a sparkling blue and the surrounding hills, with their olive trees and magnificent cypresses, a peaceful paradise. I am building a villa for you and Felix. It will have a special studio – a room full of windows and wonderful light – where you can paint to your heart's content.

I live for the day when you will visit me, when we can spend more than a few snatched hours together and lead a proper loving family life.

And then, very close to Moira's disappearance in 1914, comes another letter from Brown's Hotel.

You say Walter will not allow you to visit me with Felix. I tell you that is grossly unfair. He has no right to keep you and our child captive. You have become prisoners in Cornwall. I only asked you both to come to the Côte d'Azur for a brief holiday. Already I am in London waiting for you. Surely it is within my rights to insist you join me?

You must know, my darling girl, there is a war coming. Some say it will be terrible, it will last for years. If that happens, we may never meet again. I have to spell it out, in case Walter is burying his head in the Cornish sand and you with it.

I am tempted to ask my solicitor to handle the matter. I long to come to St Ives and gather you in my arms. But I shall not do so. I respect your privacy too much. Also, I do not want to do battle with Walter. We have never met, and that is how I wish to keep it.

If you cannot come to see me with Felix, then come on your own. The villa, it is finished and ready for you. I have a chef, a housekeeper, a gardener. Your every need will be catered for. I can no longer live without you. I beg you: come to me. Please, my darling girl. Without you, I have nothing. No sunlight, no health, no joy in anything. There is only you.

⌒

Eleanor replaces the letters in their envelopes, her eyes burning with tears.

The picture Pierre has painted of Moira's relationship with Walter is nothing like the one Felix had given her. But then, as he admitted, he had been only a child.

What if Moira had used the day of the storm as a cover to leave Felix and Walter? Had she somehow, perhaps on the spur of the moment, travelled to London – and decided never to return? Had Pierre prevented her from leaving? Had he arrived unexpectedly in St Ives, snatched her from her Cornish home and set her, loved and pampered, in his villa on the Côte d'Azur?

She switches off the light, staring into the darkness, listening to the sounds of the hotel: the muted voices, the lilting laughter, the chinking glasses, footsteps passing her door, water gurgling in the pipes.

Should she send the letters to Felix? He'll devour them, passionate word by word. But what if she could do something more with them, that might surprise them both?

She makes another decision. She'll take them to Woodstock. Take them one stage further on her journey of discovery.

They lie on the bedside table, posing more questions than they answer. And, as if Moira were still very much alive, they radiate the faintest fragrance of cloves.

Act Four

Coming Home

1936

"Ah, Eleanor! At last! How *good* to see you!" Anne says. "How was your journey?"

Late the following afternoon, Eleanor limps into the hall. She'd slept badly and made a late start from Bath. Tired, unable to concentrate, she heard the sound of her lover's voice at every turn.

"You'll never leave me, will you? Promise me."

"It was easier driving home. The weather was better and I knew the way."

"Well, thank *heavens* you're back in one piece." Anne glances at herself approvingly in the hall mirror. She removes her feathery hat with the veil, smooths her gleaming hair. Eleanor hasn't seen her in that particular hat since Walter's funeral, nor the black suit with the tight jacket. And the Dior …

"Why are you wearing—"

"We buried Mrs Giffen this morning … *Such* a shame you couldn't be there … There was no wake. Jonny couldn't face it on his own. We stood around the grave and then everyone drifted away. All *very* sad."

"Oh, *God*, Mummy, I'm *so* sorry—"

"I had a *delicious* luncheon with Sylvia. We spent the whole afternoon playing bridge. Jonny asked when you'd be back. I said I'd no idea. It was so *humiliating*, Eleanor. First you go missing. Then you don't bother to keep in touch." Anne runs a delicate finger over her front teeth, removing their smudge of lipstick. "The shop's still closed, you know. Jonny's lost interest in everything."

"I should have been there for him."

"Too little, too late." Anne turns to face her. "Let me take a good look at you … You're *shining* with health. I'm *longing* to hear your news. Vera has the day off. Make us a pot of tea and some sandwiches. Bring them into the drawing room."

With a sinking heart, Eleanor walks into the kitchen. The house feels cold, full of silent shadows. Walter's ghost lurks everywhere.

"Isn't The Hideaway charming, Ellie? Now you know why I chose to live there!"

As she carries the tea-tray into the hall, the phone rings. She plonks the tray on the floor, snatches up the receiver, her heart fluttering like a wild bird.

"Felix?" She closes her eyes, praying.

"Hello, there! Is that Eleanor?"

That voice, clipped, cheerful. She hasn't thought about him in weeks.

"Bob Clark here … Forgotten all about me, what?"

"How nice of you to ring."

"Tomorrow at dawn. Gang of us off to celebrate May Morning. Simply spiffing if you could come."

She remembers standing on Magdalen Bridge with Walter, being crushed in the excited throng, the ravishing sound of the choir boys singing to the dawn.

256

"I'm sorry, Bob. I need to be at Giffen Antiques first thing tomorrow. I've just got back from Cornwall."

"That's *too* bad … Good hols?"

"Wonderful."

"Spiffing … Still miss you like crazy. Passed my exams, by the way. Worked like a Trojan. Midnight oil and all that. Thought my little head would burst."

"Congratulations." What were Pass Moderations about? They flutter in her head on some irrelevant academic cloud – yet only a few months ago her determination to conquer them had filled every waking hour.

"Thanks a million … By the way, *must* tell you. Covered Market yesterday. Bumped into a friend of yours. Guess who."

"No idea." She remembers her first kiss with Felix, standing in Driftwood, his hands stroking back her hair, the scent of turpentine.

"That Perdy girl. She's only Harry preggers! More ravishing than ever. Not a word about who's the father. Blushed, looked coy. Very cut up about your dad. She was off skiing when he died … Eleanor? You still there?"

She fights a flood of astonishment – and could it be envy? What might it be like to have Felix's child. "Lovely to talk, Bob."

"I must *fly*. *Tons* of stuff to do. See you in the summer? Do give me a bell. I *adored* our meal at The Bear."

"I'll give you the good news first." She puts the tea-tray on the low table and looks at Anne. "I've sold the cottage and its furniture for a great deal of money, so financially the trip was worth it."

"What a relief! Clever girl." Anne fills her plate with cucumber sandwiches. "Who's buying it?"

She licks her lips to little effect. "Felix Mitchell."

"What?" Anne spits a mouthful of crumbs. "The man your father left his money to? So some of it will come to us after all?"

"I suppose it will. Though I had no idea who might buy the cottage until he——"

"Have you *met* this Mitchell fellow?" Anne stuffs another whole sandwich into her mouth.

Eleanor is desperate not to give anything away. "He came to see the cottage. We agreed the deal. We met with the agent, settled the formal details."

"And the bad news?" Pink spots burn in Anne's pale cheeks. "What's *that* about?"

"The past, Mummy. About the life Daddy led before he met you."

Anne's cup rattles in its saucer. "You're going to tell me that Walter had three fat wives, six spotty children and a smelly Labrador. This will be *so* much better than another séance." Her hands fly to her hair. "Go on, then. Spill the sordid beans."

Eleanor tells Anne as little about Moira as she can get away with. Her mother's face hardens into a sulk as she pours herself an enormous brandy.

"I wish I could say I don't care. I suppose if the woman *had* come back, your father would have chased after her like a dog on heat."

A piece of ginger cake sticks in Eleanor's throat. "That's a shocking thing to say."

"Oh, don't be such a hypocrite." Anne brushes crumbs from her black skirt as if they were marauding mice. "Did you know that Rosie Perkins paid me a visit while you were away?"

Eleanor flushes with rage. "I gave her *strict* instructions to stay away."

"I suppose *you* thought I knew nothing about her squalid affair with your father—"

"I'd no idea you knew."

"Woodstock's a small place. People gossip. There are many other women, like our plump little Rosie, who'd have jumped at the chance of having Walter in their bed."

"Who told you?"

"Does it matter?" Anne shrugs. "You should never have given the hussy a single penny. She wanted another twenty-five guineas! The brazen cheek of the woman ... I sent her packing, and she *won't* be coming back."

Anne gulps the brandy, stands up and strides towards the door.

"I'm made of sterner stuff than you imagine, dear daughter of mine. You needn't spend another minute protecting me from the silly little Rosies of Woodstock."

Eleanor heaves her suitcase out of the Morris and trails it into the kitchen. She'd give anything to climb into the car and drive back to St Ives. Thinking about Felix is beginning to consume her, body and soul. What will she do without him? Write him a love letter every morning? Count the petals on spring flowers: *he loves me, he loves me not ...*

Dusk has fallen. The trees stand miraculously heavy with leaf. Spring has advanced since her departure. The air smells of newly-cut grass – the first cut of the year. A blackbird on the dry-stone wall sings blithely for its mate.

She unloads Walter's paintings into his studio, leans them against a wall. The one by Felix, of him and Walter in Driftwood's attic: that's too special to abandon. She hauls it up to her room and slides it underneath her bed.

Anne emerges from her bedroom wearing a turquoise

259

skirt and a pale blue cardigan. She throws a bundle of black clothes over the banisters.

"You can make a bonfire of those ghastly rags. My days of mourning are over." She gives Eleanor an empty smile. "And there'll be no more séances, either. Fat lot of use *those* were! I'm going back to Sylvia's. She'll be *desperate* to hear my news."

May Day dawns bright and clear. Eleanor lies in bed, imagining Felix beside her, wondering if he's awake, whether there'll be a letter. She'll have to tell Jonny about her trip. Open the shop. Pretend that nothing's happened.

But when she walks across the street at nine o'clock and rings the bell of Giffen Antiques, there's no answer. She peers in the window. The shop looks exactly the same, but at the first-floor windows the curtains are still drawn.

She races home and dials Jonny's number. She almost gives up, when a voice answers: "Giffen here … Hello?" He sounds as if he's been dragged out of a drug-filled sleep.

"Jonny, it's me. I'm so sorry I missed the funeral." She hears the sound of sobbing. "I'm coming over right now."

He shivers in the doorway in a crumpled dressing-gown, his face pale and tear-stained, his eyes bloodshot, his feet bare.

"Jonny Giffen! Look at the *state* of you!"

"Thanks for your telegram." He runs a hand through his tangled hair. "I managed to hold things together until after the funeral." He blinks back tears. "Then I came home and everything hit me. I can't stop crying. I'll never see Mum again."

She takes his arm. "Have you had breakfast?"

"I couldn't eat a thing—"

"Oh, yes, you could." She pushes him into the shop,

leaving the CLOSED sign exactly as it is. "Have a bath and get dressed. I'll make scrambled eggs and coffee. We can talk. And then we'll open the shop."

Jonny heaves himself upstairs. "I'll probably sell it. My life is pointless—"

"Don't talk rubbish. You adore your little haven and everything in it."

Jonny emerges in fresh clothes, clean-shaven, his hair wet. He starts to talk: all through breakfast; throughout the washing up; all morning in the shop; through the luncheon they eat at The Bear; and all afternoon when they walk around Blenheim's lake, its waters glittering beneath the May Day sun.

Finally they stop outside her door.

"Thanks for rescuing me, Eleanor. I was on the verge of giving up."

"Keep busy, every minute of the day. That's how I dealt with losing Walter. Time *does* heal."

"You're older than your years." Jonny smiles at her. "Shall I see you on Monday? Can you manage full days until I find extra help? I'll pay you three guineas a week for holding the fort."

"Of course." She hesitates. Soon she'll have real money in the bank. She won't need to work for Jonny. But now isn't the time to mention it. Not once has he asked her about Cornwall. "You should get away for a while. Drive to Aberystwyth. Take a few days off. Come home refreshed."

"What a *fantastic* idea!" Relief floods his face. "Can you manage without me?"

"I may have a long list of queries but yes, I'll be fine."

"You're *such* a wonderful girl. I'll tell Darren you're taking over."

"Give me a set of keys on Monday morning, show me how to work the combination for the safe. Then forget all about me."

He touches her shoulder. The Blenheim air has blown colour into his cheeks.

"I could never do that, Eleanor." He hesitates, as if he wants to say more. But he bites back the words and turns away.

She waits until they've eaten Sunday luncheon before she faces Anne with her extraordinary idea.

"I want to talk to you about Daddy's paintings."

Her mother wears a pink cashmere twin-set and a long plum-red skirt. Yesterday the Woodstock hairdresser cut and styled her conker-brown hair to curl down on her shoulders. She looks an attractive, stylish thirty.

"Which ones?"

"There are some finished landscapes in the studio, and one I bought in St Ives." She bites her lip, remembering having Felix by her side.

Anne looks bored. "Why don't you chop them up and make another bonfire? I'll dance around it, singing while they burn."

"Because I now have lots of Daddy's paintings I'd never seen before. They were hanging in The Hideaway, waiting for me."

"More of the same old stuff, I assume?"

"No, anything but. They're portraits. Wonderful, youthful work."

Anne frowns. "I never saw your father look at anything but clouds—"

"The landscapes came later." She keeps her eyes on her mother's face. "Daddy was originally a portrait painter. It wasn't until Moira vanished that he decided he couldn't handle portraits any more, because every face he looked at reminded him of her."

Anne flushes scarlet. "*Did* they indeed! How the *hell* do you know that?"

She'd almost given the game away. "Mr Mitchell told me. We were discussing the paintings he wanted to buy."

"Hmm." Anne relapses into silent hostility.

"The point is, I know how we could sell the portraits. They're in the studio."

Anne stands up, smoothing the imagined creases in her skirt. "Well, then, dutiful daughter of mine, you'd better let me see them."

"I want us to have an exhibition of them, right here," Eleanor says rapidly, before she loses her nerve. "We could have a two-day open-house, on a Friday and Saturday, as a memorial to Daddy."

"Good heavens, girl! When did you dream up *that* idea!"

"Last night. We could invite everyone we know, give them a glass of wine, label the paintings, put red dots on the frames when they're sold." She flushes with anticipation. "What do you think?"

"And what if nobody *buys* them?" Anne looks taken aback. "The event might fall flat as a pancake. It'll be too embarrassing for words. I'd *never* live it down."

"Come and look at the paintings before you decide."

She'd spent the morning in Walter's studio, leaving the door open so the mild spring air could flood in.

Anne looks straight at the self-portraits, catching her breath. "My God! Those *are* wonderful. Is the baby that Felix Mitchell fellow?"

"Yes." A giveaway blush stains Eleanor's cheeks.

"Aren't there any of Moira?"

"There were three, but Mr Mitchell wanted to keep them."

"What a *pity*!" Anne's voice rasps. "I'd have *adored* to see what she looked like."

Eleanor ignores the bitterness. "So, what's the verdict?"

Anne presses her lips together, holding back tears. "I suppose it's better to have money in our pockets than these portraits mouldering in this dump." Her eyes glitter. "Anyway, now you've told me your father's story, those murky shadows I've been doing battle with have given up their ghost. I'm in the mood to party."

"I *know* you won't be disappointed. Let's set a date. Shall we say Friday the 22nd and Saturday the 23rd of May? I think we should get a decorator for the downstairs rooms. Fresh, clean walls will give the portraits space to breathe. I'll organise a printed list. I want it to be a successful, professional event."

"You *have* thought it through, haven't you?" Anne gives her an appraising stare. "Could you afford to buy me a new frock for the occasion? So I can act the merry widow with a bit of style?"

At Brown's Hotel

1936

The mild May weather breaks on Monday morning. Eleanor waves Jonny goodbye as drizzle darkens the Woodstock sky and hangs in the air like soapsuds. She remembers racing back to The Hideaway with Felix through stinging pellets of rain; finding him stretched out on the sofa; watching him sleep.

She steps into Giffen Antiques. It's not the challenge it once was. Time to move on.

She plans the exhibition carefully, giving each portrait a name and price. She includes the landscape she bought in St Ives, deciding not to give it to Jonny, and five other paintings from Walter's studio.

The following Wednesday afternoon, she drives to a printer in Oxford with the list of paintings. She commissions a four-page leaflet, together with an invitation to the open-house event. They discuss a design and format; she arranges to see proofs the following week.

While Darren minds the shop, she meets with a delighted

Michael Humphreys to finalise the sale of The Hideaway, and with Robin Parker to tell him the good news. His beady eyes light up when she mentions the amount of money involved.

"If you're careful, it'll be enough to give you and your mother financial security for a good while yet. And Giffen Antiques can continue to be a useful, practical stepping-stone until you marry."

She flushes. "I'm not even engaged, Mr Parker. Jonny Giffen's taught me a lot about antiques, but I want to invest in my own venture."

Robin Parker squirms. "But not on your own," he murmurs. "Not without the help of a husband to support you."

"What's wrong with me supporting myself?"

"There's nothing *wrong* with it, Miss Drummond." He blusters, his fingers twitching over his tie. "It's an admirable ambition. It's just most unusual. As your bank manager, I'd *never* advise you to take unnecessary financial risks."

"I may take them anyway." She looks him in the eye. "But I'll be sure to let you know what I'm doing."

"*Before* you've done it, Miss Drummond?" Robin stands to shake her hand. "Give me a bit of warning, *there's* a good girl."

Eleanor grins at him. "It's a deal."

On Wednesday evening Eleanor meets Kath for supper at Fishery Cottage. They eat in the kitchen, Eleanor relaxed among the familiar pots and pans, the welcoming warmth of the oven and Kath's fragrant rabbit pie.

At last Eleanor can talk frankly about St Ives, the exhausting journey, finding Pierre's letters – and Felix. It's as if she's describing someone who's exploded into her life like an unexpected, dazzling firework.

"It was amazing. One minute I was free and single, with plans to sell The Hideaway and get back to Woodstock as fast as I could. The next, I was smitten. I can't get enough of the man. I want to listen to him all day long and all night. I liked Robert Clark in a sisterly way, and I've enjoyed working with Jonny. But I've never felt such physical passion before. Leaving Felix in St Ives was so hard."

"But what are you goin' to *do* about him? You've only known him for one short week. You've even been to *bed* with him. He hasn't written, he's not on the phone. He's hundreds of bloomin' miles away, Ellie. It's no use lovin' the man if you don't never *see* him."

"Oh, I'll see him again, I'm sure of that." Eleanor pretends to be confident. "I'm going to Brown's Hotel in London on Saturday afternoon. Will you come with me? I'll pay your train fare and everything. I really need your support."

"I'd love a trip to town. But what—"

"I want to ask the manager of Brown's whether he has an address for Pierre Tessier. Some of those letters were sent from Brown's. The hotel may know where he lives in Juan-les-Pins. Moira might be there with him."

"You could try. But don't be too disappointed—"

"And I'll ask Felix to the exhibition."

"If he comes, are you goin' to introduce him to your mother?"

"That's a difficult one." She frowns. "I'll cross that bridge when I get to it. Now, tell me … you and Sean. Have you set a date?"

"I fancy bein' a June bride. We're savin' every brass farthin'." Kath's voice darkens. "That's not somethin' Edward and Wallis have to do."

"What news?"

Kath takes a tray of custard tarts out of the oven. "Not good. Maud says Special Branch have been watchin' Wallis for months, tryin' to dig up the dirt."

"What *kind* of dirt?"

"Sexual, of course. Isn't that the worst for a woman? They're sayin' Wallis is havin' an affair with a man called Guy Trundle. He's married, in his thirties, and works for Ford motors. He's a charmer, a real ladies' man. Wallis has been seein' him at her dressmaker's. It's the only place where Edward can't follow!"

"Honestly, Kath! You'd think she'd be more than satisfied with the King."

"Indeed. She's askin' for trouble."

"What a *mess*. Why can't the royals keep their heads above such sordid waters?"

"I suppose they're only human—"

"But being human doesn't give us permission to behave like that. I could *never* be unfaithful. Can you imagine the lies, the pretence, the cheating?"

"Some people adore all that palaver. They've got time on their hands and nothin' better to do. No jobs, no money to earn, no shame! The secrecy, the cloak-and-dagger stuff, it makes 'em feel alive. Pathetic, ain't it? It's how they get their kicks."

"I prefer the dance floor." Eleanor remembers the swish of her red taffeta frock. "And being in the arms of the man you love."

Kath starts to clear the table. She looks down at her best friend. "Got it real bad, haven't you, Ellie?"

"No." Eleanor smiles up at her. "I've got it real good."

That Saturday afternoon, they take the train to London.

They walk from Paddington to Mayfair, relishing the

chance to window-shop in the milky spring sunshine, to check the latest fashions, to imagine leading affluent, leisured lives.

In Albemarle Street, they find Brown's Hotel, and settle in its soft leather armchairs. After they've ordered and eaten tea, Eleanor asks their waiter whether she might have a private word with the manager.

A portly man with flat grey hair and a fussy manner bustles up to her.

"Mademoiselle … Good afternoon." He has a charming French accent. "Everything it is to your liking, *non*?"

"Thank you, our tea was delicious. I need to ask you a favour."

"But of course … How can I help?"

"I'm trying to find my father's friend who disappeared twenty years ago. My father died in January. Just before his death, he asked me to find her. I've been reading some letters written to her by a Monsieur Pierre Tessier. He was a guest here at Brown's in April 1914." She pauses, her heart thumping. "Do you by any chance have an address for Monsieur Tessier?"

The manager's face tightens imperceptibly.

"Ah, *je suis désolé*, Mademoiselle, but I'm forbidden to give you information. We have the very strict rules here. Details about our clients, they would be confidential."

"But surely not for more than twenty years ago?" She gives him a smile she hopes will melt his heart. "Please, Monsieur? There's nobody else I can ask. I believe Pierre Tessier is living in Juan-les-Pins. All I need is confirmation, and the name of his villa. I made my dying father a promise I'd like to keep."

The manager pats her hand. "*D'accord*, Mademoiselle. I understand. April 1914, you say? I'll see what I can find."

He returns ten minutes later, brushing dust from his white

gloves. "I'm sorry, Mademoiselle, but our records, they do not go back that far."

"I see." She feels crushed by disappointment.

"If you really wish to find him, I'd visit Juan-les-Pins. It's not a big place. Monsieur Tessier, he might be well-known, *non*? And at this time of the year, the Côte d'Azur, it's so beautiful." The gloved hands circle the air in ecstasy. "You could take Le Train Bleu from Calais. It's expensive but you'll have a first-class sleeper and the food on board will be *magnifique*."

"That's a very good idea." The colour returns to Eleanor's cheeks. "Thank you for your help."

"My pleasure, Mademoiselle … And may I wish you *bon voyage*!"

"Well!" Kath says as they stand outside the hotel. "That wasn't exactly a success!"

"I'm not so sure. The manager was right. I'll have to go to the French Riviera."

"Even without an address?"

"Nothing ventured, nothing gained."

"And how will you explain the trip to your mother?"

Eleanor watches a horse pulling a heavy cart down Albemarle Street as if it were a straw basket. "I'll take her with me. She deserves a break. And when she's on the beach or at the bridge table, I'll search for Moira. Worrying about the woman is getting me nowhere. If I *do* something positive, I'll feel so much better." She pulls on her gloves. "Let's find a travel agent. I'll collect some journey times and prices. I'm sure there'll be a decent hotel in Juan-les-Pins."

"And if it's a wild-goose chase?" Kath looks at her. "If you don't find either Moira or Pierre, what then?"

Eleanor stares down the dusty road, at the lumbering traffic and the cloudy sky.

"I'll send Felix the letters, explain how I found them. Tell him I've done my best but I've reached a dead end." She grimaces. "Sorry, I didn't mean that."

She takes Kath's arm.

"You'll think I'm daft as a brush, but something in the back of my mind keeps telling me that Moira's still alive. All I need do is prove it!"

By the end of that week, Anne has arranged for a decorator to start on the ground-floor living rooms. She relishes the challenge of rearranging furniture. The house is in chaos as they eat their meals in the kitchen, then move upstairs to Anne's bedroom to read, talk and sew. The smell of fresh paint fills the rooms and lingers in corners.

"After the exhibition," Anne says to Eleanor one evening, "I think we should get the rest of the house decorated. It'll do me good." She steadies the tremor in her voice. "It's time I got rid of your father's clothes. I'll ask Vera to spring-clean my bedroom. We'll parcel up the suits and jackets, give them to charity ... What do you think, dutiful daughter of mine?"

Eleanor sighs with relief. "That's the best idea you've had in a very long time."

"You've coped magnificently, you and Darren," Jonny says. "I can't *tell* you how grateful I am. I stopped worrying about the shop. There were several afternoons while I was in the Cambrian Mountains when I almost forgot about Mum. I feel like a new man." He puts a velvet box into her hands. "This is for you."

Embarrassed, she murmurs, "You shouldn't have." Inside is an exquisite necklace. "Jonny! It's beautiful!"

"Stunning, isn't it? Late Victorian, stylish, elegant. I love those turquoise stones in the pendant. Put it on."

She fumbles with the delicate clasp, unable to understand why she feels so uncomfortable.

"Here, let me help." He stands behind her. For a moment his fingers brush the nape of her neck. He turns her to face him. "It suits you wonderfully."

She tries to hide her blushes. "I've got something for you, too." She ferrets in her bag, pulling out the leaflet and the invitation. "The printers in Oxford rushed these through for me. I'll send them out tomorrow."

He scans the list of paintings. "*Very* impressive. Was this your idea?"

"Yes." The necklace feels cold against her skin. "I hope you'll come to the Friday opening?"

"I can't really leave the shop." Jonny bends to unpack some ornaments he'd brought from Aberystwyth. "But I'll be free on Saturday afternoon." He looks up at her. "By the way, I met someone last week who's interested in helping in the shop. His name's Stephen. Turns out he's a distant cousin. He should be here tomorrow. You can meet him then."

That night, sitting at her desk, she writes a letter, letting the words tumble out, raw and honest.

My darling Felix

Leaving you in St Ives was the hardest thing I've ever done. You've been in my thoughts every minute since. I've organised this exhibition partly for you, so you can see more of Walter's work – and me at the same time.

I hope you'll be able to come.

All my love
Eleanor

She pushes the note inside the leaflet along with the invitation, addresses and stamps the envelope, throws a cardigan over her shoulders and slips out of the house.

At the postbox she whispers, "Wish I could go with you."

The ground-floor rooms of their house are soon transformed. The pale cream walls become an ideal showcase for Walter's people and places. Each painting is named and priced. Small piles of leaflets lie on low tables in the hall and the two living rooms.

On the morning of the exhibition, Eleanor pulls on a new dress in dark blue silk. Reluctantly, she adds Jonny's necklace. She has nothing else to wear at her throat, and the plain scooped neckline needs jewellery. She longs for her pearls.

She races downstairs to check everything one last time. She holds a piece of paper with a multitude of red dots. On an impulse, she uses two of them. The two self-portraits of her father with Felix are too dear to her heart to sell.

She'd been hoping against hope that Felix will come, but there's still been no word. She imagines him in their Woodstock doorway, his Cornish burr filling the hall; introducing him to Kath and Sean. To Vera. To Jonny. And to Anne.

She's decided what she'll tell her mother: the truth, the whole truth and nothing but the truth.

Except her plans come to nothing because Felix doesn't appear, either on Friday or Saturday. By three o'clock on Saturday afternoon, she realises he has no intention of being with her. She starts to worry. Perhaps he's ill? Maybe he's had an accident? She imagines him lying crumpled on his attic floor, unable to breathe.

Then she tells herself to stop being an idiot. The contract for the sale of The Hideaway has been signed and sealed. The money will soon be in her bank account. The fact that she'd rather see Felix again than have any amount of money is irrelevant. She must be strong, practical, realistic.

She refuses to contemplate the fact that Felix has decided to forget her. The time they spent together … their night of love … They'd meant something important, hadn't they? It had hardly been a casual dalliance.

So as the exhibition opens and closes, she disguises her disappointment. She concentrates on their visitors, helping them to coffee or wine. She talks vivaciously about the paintings, hiding the pain of missing Felix beneath a façade of enthusiasm.

By four o'clock on Saturday afternoon, red dots are studded across the walls. All Walter's paintings have been sold.

Eleanor pauses over a cup of tea, standing in silence, looking at the people around her. Anne, sprightly and glamorous in a tight oyster-satin frock, talking to Michael Humphreys, her quarrel forgotten. Vera sharing a joke with Jonny and Stephen. Robin Parker reaching for his cheque book. Sylvia and her gaggle of friends sipping wine. Kath and Sean admiring a Blenheim landscape she'd given them.

And it's then, as she stands there, looking and listening, that she has another good idea. She must *do* something with her life to prove she can survive without Felix. And she knows exactly what it'll be.

At The Trout

1936

That Saturday afternoon, Jonny asks her out to dinner. "You've worked so hard," he tells her. "This exhibition has been a triumph of courage, good taste, excellent work and inventive marketing. I've bought Walter's last remaining landscape … And you look *stunning* in that frock. The necklace has really come into its own. I'm so delighted you're wearing it."

She stands with him by the open front door. Her feet ache, her head throbs. All she wants is a bath and an early night, but she's desperate to discuss her latest idea. So she says, "I'd love to have dinner with you."

"Excellent … I'll pick you up at eight. Let's go to The Trout in Wolvercote. It's a magical place. After we've eaten, we can sit by the river and listen to the weir."

They settle at a corner table by the window.

Outside, candles flicker on the low stone walls. Peacocks strut and preen along the terrace, settling for the night in their favourite tree. Jonny orders parsnip soup and roast rack of lamb for them both.

She lays the menu aside. "I need your advice, Jonny … I had an idea this afternoon. I wanted to air it with you first."

"Sounds interesting, Eleanor … Fire away."

"You've had masses of experience of running a shop." She fidgets with her serviette, smoothing it over her knees. "I'm thinking of doing the same."

"Good *heavens*, Eleanor! I hope you won't be competing with me!"

"Of course not. I don't know enough about antiques and I could never afford to buy stock … But I *do* want to make use of our house. Next week, the money from the cottage will be mine. I want to invest some of it in my own business."

"How, exactly?"

Out on the terrace, peacocks scream by the river. Inside The Trout, the aroma of cigars drifts across the room. Spoons clatter against saucers. A group of guests laugh.

"I want to turn our two ground-floor rooms into a tea-room." She sits back. "What do you think?"

"Crikey!" Jonny flutters his eyelashes. "It's one *hell* of a commitment! You'll have to work terribly hard."

"That's exactly what I need. Something I can build from scratch and call my own … mine and Anne's."

"The trouble is that your house is your home. Those two ground-floor rooms are its heart … Where will you live?"

"On the first floor. It's what *you* do, isn't it? We now rattle around in a ridiculous amount of space. We hardly ever eat in the dining room: it's the kitchen for breakfast, and plates on our knees in the drawing room for luncheon or supper. None of us can bear to look at Daddy's empty chair." She flushes. "Missing him gets easier – but the pain's always there."

"Isn't it just!" Jonny makes an effort to finish his soup. "How will Vera fit in?"

"I'll ask her to cook. Soups, sandwiches, cakes, scones, shortbread. She'll love it. And I'll pay her a proper wage, not just the meagre allowance she's getting at the moment."

"What will *you* do?"

"Everything but cook. Plan the menus, manage the money, serve our customers. I'd like the tea-room to double as an art gallery. Walter's paintings sold so fast, I'm sure good work by other artists could do the same. Although that will take second place to the tea-room until it's up and running."

"Think very carefully." Jonny pushes his soup aside. "You'll need a downstairs cloakroom, comfortable chairs, good quality tables, sturdy crockery." He looks at her. "Is your kitchen large enough? You'll need extra staff to do the washing-up."

"I think we'll manage until we know how busy we'll be. If we want to expand, we could extend the kitchen into the garden. The cellar is dark and poky and I don't want Vera climbing stairs all day long. But there's always Daddy's studio. We could use it for storing fruit and vegetables."

He gives her an approving smile. "You sound pretty determined."

"Excited, too. It'll be a challenge."

"And I suppose I'll never see you again?"

She laughs. "You're welcome to come for luncheon five days a week."

"Hmm." He narrows his eyes. "You'll need Anne's permission. Don't count your chickens *quite* yet."

After supper they stand on the terrace, drinking brandy, looking out at the rush of flowing river. Eleanor shivers at the sound of the weir, thinking about Felix, longing for the sight, the sound, the touch of him. She imagines him standing beside her, scooping her into his arms.

Jonny moves closer. "Would you like my jacket?"

"Thank you, I'm fine. The weir reminds me of Cornwall. I miss the sea."

"I missed *you* while you were away." He stares straight ahead. "I love having you around, seeing you in the shop." He clears his throat. "What you've told me about the tearoom … It'll change everything, won't it?"

"I hope so." She laughs. "Sorry, Jonny, that sounds so ungrateful! I don't mean I want to get away from you—"

"The thing is." He swings to face her. "I could offer you a solid alternative. If Anne vetoes your plans, if you should change your mind." He swallows. "Damn it, I'm no good at this kind of thing … Look, I think you're a terrific girl. We make a marvellous team. It would be a great honour if you'd agree to marry me."

"What?" Prickles of shock flutter down her spine.

"You must have guessed how I feel." His voice tightens. "I told Mum I was in love with you before her accident. She gave me her blessing. I hoped you felt the same. You did ask me to go to St Ives with you."

She remembers how she'd scoffed at Kath's warning. "I wasn't making a pass."

"Forgive me." He steps away. "I assumed—"

"I only wanted us to share the driving. I didn't mean anything more."

"But you're wearing my necklace. It gave me hope."

"It wasn't meant to." Tears well up in her eyes. "It couldn't." She fights the choke in her voice, knowing she owes him a proper explanation. "I'm in love with somebody else."

She feels weak with longing for Felix.

Jonny gasps. "You've never mentioned another man." He frowns. "Was he at the exhibition?"

"No, he couldn't come. I met him in St Ives. I don't really want to talk about him … I might never see him again. But it wasn't just a holiday romance. I can't forget about him. I'm head-over-heels in love."

"You astonish me." Jonny's voice comes cold and flat. He moves away, thrusting his hands into his pockets. "And what can he offer you, this elusive, faraway beau you've only known for a fortnight? A comfortable home? Financial security and an established business? Total love and complete devotion?"

"Nothing like that." She swallows her brandy, puts down her glass, hugs her arms around her body, wishing Jonny's words fitted Felix better than they do. "He hasn't offered me anything. We were taken by complete surprise … I can't say any more. Thank you for paying me such an enormous compliment. You're a wonderful friend. But I can't marry you. I'm sorry, Jonny. Not now, not ever."

"I suppose I'm too old," he says gruffly. "I'll be thirty-nine next month, while you're still a slip of a girl."

"That's got *nothing* to do with it—"

"What else is there to say?" He fumbles for his keys. "The unhappy end of a not-very-romantic evening … I'll pay the bill and take you home."

"You won't *tell* anyone, will you? That I'm in love, I mean. Particularly my mother … I *really* don't want her to know. It's such early days—"

"I'd *never* betray you." His voice is icy. "What kind of a friend do you think I am?"

"Sorry." She bites her lip. "Oh, God, now I've made things even worse—"

"That," Jonny says, "would be quite impossible."

They drive back to Woodstock in uncomfortable silence. He parks his van in the Woodstock square and follows Eleanor to her door.

"See you Monday afternoon? I hope what's happened won't ruin our friendship."

"Of *course* it won't, Jonny."

"I'm delighted to hear it." But his eyes are cold. "Oh, and good luck with Anne. Let me know what she thinks about your grand idea."

He turns away. She stares after him, filled with remorse. Jonny's cheerfulness, his bantering tone, his ready laugh seem crushed: first by his mother's death, now by her own rejection.

But what else could she have said? Meeting Felix has shown her the difference between being fond of someone, enjoying their company – and falling deeply, desperately, in love.

The house is in darkness, Anne and Vera are in bed.

Eleanor turns on a small lamp in the drawing room. She falls into one of the armchairs, staring at Walter's paintings. Tomorrow she'll pack them, address them, arrange for their delivery. She'll give Jonny's landscape to him on Monday.

And tomorrow she'll talk to Anne.

She waits until her mother has returned from church. She brings her a cup of coffee in the drawing room and then explains her plan, calmly, quietly, spelling out the details. Anne sits in stony silence.

"So." Eleanor takes a deep breath, fearing the worst. "What do you think?"

"I've never heard such preposterous nonsense in my life." Anne is white with rage. "You may have money, now you've sold the cottage, but this is *my* house. I *forbid* you to mess about with it. A two-day exhibition's one thing. A permanent tea-room's completely out of the question. If you think I'm *going into trade*, you've got another think coming."

"A tea-room is a perfectly sound business venture." Eleanor's head aches, her throat feels raw, but she's determined to hold her ground. "I discussed the details with Jonny last night—"

"You had *no right* to involve an outsider!"

"Jonny's one of my best friends." Now her head's banging like a drum. "If you must know, he asked me to marry him."

Anne's face lights up like a struck match. "That's *fantastic* news!" She grabs Eleanor's hands. "Congratulations, darling! Jonny's a superb catch!"

Eleanor wrenches away. "I'm not in love with Jonny *or* his bank balance. I turned him down."

Anne stands up, stamping her foot.

"You're the most *infuriating* girl I've ever met. Here we are, fighting for survival. You dream up some crazy idea about our becoming shopkeepers, working our fingers to the bone, day in, day out, while you've had an offer of lifelong security."

"I want to open a tea-room, to give us financial stability. I'm fond of Jonny, but I don't want to marry him. It's perfectly simple. You must respect my decision."

"You'll live to regret it, Eleanor. You're looking the most wonderful gift horse in the mouth."

Anne flounces towards the door. She turns and glares at Eleanor.

"If *you* don't want our handsome Jonny Giffen, perhaps I should marry him myself!"

Compromise

1936

Over a ghastly Sunday luncheon in the kitchen, filled with icy silences, Eleanor perseveres, refusing to fall at the first hurdle. She describes her plans to Vera, who'd be delighted to help.

"Everyone says my shortbread's the best in Oxfordshire."

Anne stabs at a lettuce leaf. "I can see straight through your little plan, Eleanor. Or should I call it a crazy whim? It's pointless getting Vera on your side. I've said *NO*."

"In that case, I'll buy a tea-room in St Ives." She clatters her plate on the draining board. "I adored being by the sea. I'll sell delicious Cornish teas and make a fortune." She faces her mother. "What do you think of *that* crazy whim?"

Anne refuses to look at her. "You'd abandon me, wouldn't you? Leave me here without a backward glance."

"I'd have *lots* of second thoughts, but if you push me to the limit, I'll leave. I tasted freedom in St Ives, and it was very sweet." She makes for the door. "I'm seeing Robin Parker tomorrow. I'll find out what *he* thinks of my plan. *He* won't dismiss it as a crazy whim!"

But she stands rooted in the hall, preparing herself for another interview with her bank manager. If he tells her to get married, she'll stand up and punch him between his piggy little eyes. This new idea of hers: she could make it a success. She'll throw herself into the venture. She'll control it, watch it grow and flourish.

So what if she's "going into trade"? It's got to be more exciting than taking another exam. Or even than waiting to hear from the man she loves. At least she'll be *doing* something off her own bat.

Eleanor gets dressed the next morning in a smart suit, crisply-ironed blouse, with straight stocking seams, and highly polished shoes. Her sore throat has vanished. There's nothing like determination to kill a cold.

Anne taps on her door and pushes it open. Still in her dressing-gown, her hair dishevelled, she stands in the doorway, leaning against it as if she's too weak to support herself.

"You're looking very smart." Her tone is suspiciously conciliatory.

"You can never be too well-turned-out for your bank manager." Eleanor plays her one-upmanship card. "Wouldn't you agree?"

"Absolutely." Anne hurries on, "The thing is, Eleanor, I've been thinking about your idea … In fact, I was awake all night, mulling it over. Maybe I was a little hasty. I might have overreacted."

"What exactly are you saying?"

"I don't want you to leave Woodstock. You've been marvellous since your father died. Handled everything so well. What I said about marrying Jonny was very unfair. Before I met your father I had three proposals of marriage.

I turned them down. I understand exactly how you feel."

"I'm relieved to hear it."

"But these plans of yours. They came as a shock. I thought perhaps, as a compromise, I could meet you halfway?"

Eleanor picks up her hairbrush, pulling it through her hair with rapid strokes, trying to hide a tremor of excitement. "*Half* a tearoom? *Half* a business? Robin Parker will never buy it. I won't even waste his time suggesting it."

"I didn't mean half-baked." Anne sinks gracefully on to the bed. "I meant half the space. It's the idea of losing *both* ground-floor rooms that gave me such a fright. Suppose you started with the dining room? Leave me my drawing room until Christmas. If you make a success of the one room and need to expand, we could renegotiate." She folds her gown over her bare knees. "How's that for a plan?"

Eleanor smooths her eyebrows. "You think I'm going to fail."

"I didn't say that."

"Not in so many words. But you're hardly giving me a vote of confidence."

"I'm asking you to be prudent. The tea-room will be an enormous step. I don't want you throwing your father's precious money down the drain."

Eleanor stares at Anne's reflection in the mirror. Dishevelled, without make-up and wearing a shabby dressing-gown, she's still a remarkably attractive woman.

"I'm throwing more than money at this venture," she says coldly. "I'm starting a solid career, choosing to stay in Woodstock. I'm putting everything on the line: my energy, my reputation, my life. Drains of any kind are not an option."

"I admire your commitment. So: I agree you may have

the hall, the dining room, the kitchen, the garden and the studio. You may install a new cloakroom. You may have Vera – but I'll need a new housekeeper."

"That can be arranged."

"Then you have my blessing, dutiful daughter of mine. Is it a deal?"

Eleanor fixes her mother with a steely glare. "I hate compromise. If I decide to do something, it gets all my attention. But if it's either half or nothing, for the time being I'll settle for half."

She stands up. Facing her, above her bed, Felix's marvellous painting dances before her eyes. She'd hung it there the night before. Anne hasn't noticed it, but it spurs Eleanor on, gives her fresh heart. It reminds her of the urgency of her search for Moira, her need to prove to Felix and Walter that she can find her.

"And by the way, if Robin Parker approves my plan, before I open the tea-room I'm taking you on holiday. For agreeing to the exhibition. For giving me part of the house."

Anne's eyes light up like candles on a Christmas tree. "What a *very* sweet thought! Where are we going?"

"How does the French Riviera sound?"

Anne gasps with joy. "The south of *France*? We'll have sunshine and Mediterranean skies. It'll be *paradise*."

"Let's hope so … If he can forgive me for rejecting him, Jonny can drive us to Victoria to catch the boat train. We'll take the ferry to Calais, and that luxurious first-class sleeper, the Blue Train, down to the Côte d'Azur. We'll spend a week in Juan-les-Pins at the Provençal Hotel. And Vera can visit her sister in Bournemouth. God knows we all deserve a break."

"I'll need lots of new clothes." Anne glances at her shabby dressing-gown. "Summer frocks, sun hats, at least two evening dresses." She throws her arms around Eleanor, kissing her cheek. "That's for being the best daughter in the world."

As Eleanor goes down to breakfast, she sees an envelope addressed to her lying on the mat. She doesn't recognise the inky-black, slanting, slightly smudged handwriting. But the postmark is St Ives and the envelope smells of turpentine.

In the drawing room she closes the door, stands with her back against it. She mouths a silent prayer that the piece of paper doesn't spell rejection. Please, please, never ever that. She tears at the envelope.

My darling Eleanor

No doubt you think I couldn't be bothered to come to your exhibition. Nothing could be further from the truth. I was thrilled to get your letter and overjoyed to know that Walter's marvellous portraits will finally see the public light of day.

I'd been working in the studio, went downstairs to make some coffee and stupidly carried a stepladder up the kitchen stairs. I cricked my back. I've had to lie flat on my bed twenty-four hours a day for a whole week. It's been very frustrating.

I promise to see you soon. In among other commissions, and packing up the contents of Driftwood, I'm working on three portraits of you, all of them beautiful.

I remember our night together. Wasn't it truly full of wonder and wonderful?

I long to take you in my arms again. I promise it will be soon.

All my love
Felix

She falls on to the nearest chair, overwhelmed with excitement and relief. Felix loves her. There are the words, in black and white! She reads them over and again. She folds the letter into its envelope and pushes it into her pocket.

She realises that if Felix *had* come to the exhibition, she'd have introduced him to Anne.

"This is the man I love."

She'd have shown him Pierre's letters, told him about meeting the manager of Brown's, asked him to travel with them to France.

And, ironically, she'd never have dreamed up the tea-room. The weekend had been a turning point. Now there's no going back.

She walks into the kitchen where Vera's preparing breakfast. "You're going to be my tea-room chef. Mummy's agreed. We can use the dining room to start with. If we make a go of things, we'll expand after Christmas."

"That's marvellous news, dear heart." Vera puts down her wooden spoon, her forehead crinkling. "So why the tears?"

Eleanor stares across the kitchen, scrubbing at her face with her hand. She wants to say, "Because my lover should have been here on Saturday. I'm longing to see him, and I can't do anything about it."

Instead she says, "Because I've got to see Robin Parker with a serious business plan." Her voice has an infuriating wobble. "Pretend to know what I'm talking about. Mummy thinks I'll have shut up shop by Christmas and lost most of Daddy's money."

Vera wipes her hands on her apron. "You won't lose a brass farthing. You're the most determined young woman I know. Your tea-room will be a huge success and I'll support you all the way. Now dry your eyes, dear heart. Give your Vera the biggest hug in the world."

"As you know, Mr Parker, I've been thinking about making some real money." She wills herself to present her plans calmly, while her heart thumps with trepidation. "The success of my exhibition gave me a brilliant idea."

"Oh?" Robin Parker doesn't look particularly interested. "I hope it won't involve your investing large sums of money at great risk."

"It won't. It's only a small amount." *Go for it, girl. Spell it out.* "I want to open a tea-room. My mother has agreed that I can use our house. I'm still at the planning stage, but I'm going to open at ten and close at five."

She crosses her legs, her list carefully balanced on her knees. She talks fast, to prevent Robin Parker interrupting, outlining her plans in detail: to trade five days a week, to sell fresh produce and no alcohol, to use the space in the house. Half an hour later, she marches out of the bank with Robin Parker's blessing and the name of an accountant in her pocket.

"Never forget you're in business to make a profit, not merely to break even."

"Of course." Her heart throbs with excitement. Not once had Robin suggested her idea is a bad one, that she's too young to see it through, she doesn't have any experience, the venture might fail – or that she'll need a husband to hold her hand and offer a shoulder to cry on.

"I'll open a business account for you. The money from your cottage can go straight into it. And I'll give you a business-account chequebook." He gives her a direct look. "When do you plan to open?"

She explains about her short holiday. "After we're back,

I'll need a couple of weeks to get everything ready. I plan to open on Wednesday the 1st of July. That gives me a clear six-month run before Christmas."

Robin's half-smile flickers at her. "My most important advice to you is: don't turn yourself into a slave and work too hard."

She gives a nervous laugh.

"I'm serious, Miss Drummond. Remember: you're the boss. If you work yourself to death, nobody will be any better off. Stay fresh and rested. If you need extra help, consider it an investment, not a sign of weakness. You're bound to make mistakes. Be prepared to learn from them." He stands to shake her hand.

"I'd been prepared to do battle with you. I thought you'd tell me to go away and get married, forget the whole idea."

"That wouldn't have done me much good, would it?"

This time, she laughs with relief. "None whatsoever!"

"I admire your courage, Miss Drummond. And I wish you all the luck in the world."

"I've brought you Daddy's landscape," Eleanor says to Jonny in Giffen Antiques on Monday afternoon, "and I'm sorry about Saturday."

He touches her shoulder with a brief, conciliatory gesture. "Think no more about it, Eleanor. I hope we'll always be friends."

"Will you come to supper tonight? Mummy was very upset to hear I'd turned you down—"

"Thank her for the compliment!"

"But not because of that. She's given me the go-ahead for the tea-room. So has Robin Parker—"

"Congratulations, Eleanor!"

"Mummy took a lot of persuading and" – she blushes –

"a hint of blackmail. Would you take a look at our dining room, give me advice on the tables we could put in it? I want you to be involved."

"I'll help all I can." He runs his fingers through his hair. "Hell's teeth, I'm going to miss you. When do you want to leave?"

"As soon as you can find a replacement. And would you do me a favour? I'm taking Mummy on a week's holiday to the Riviera, before the tea-room opens. Would you drive us to Victoria station in the Morris? I hope you don't mind my asking—"

"I'd be delighted to help."

"And one more thing. What would you say if I asked you to give Mummy an afternoon job in my place?"

"Crikey!" His eyes spark with surprise. "What would *she* think?"

"I don't know. I'd like *you* to suggest it. If it comes from me, she'll kill it stone dead. But she likes you, Jonny. I have a feeling she might just say yes!"

Searching for Moira

1936

It's not until the last moment that Eleanor decides to take Pierre's letters with her to the Riviera. She'd written to Felix, telling him she's taking Anne on holiday – but not where they're going. She outlines her plans for the tea-room. He must come to Woodstock soon. She wants him to meet Anne.

But she tells him nothing about the letters. They shouldn't be hiding in her desk like a guilty secret. They belong to Moira. If by any miraculous chance Eleanor manages to find the elusive woman, it's her duty to give them back. So once again she slips them on top of the red taffeta frock.

Jonny drives them to Victoria that Thursday morning. His rejected proposal has brought him closer to Eleanor in a genuinely friendly way, for which she's exceedingly grateful. He could easily have turned his back on her in a huff of disappointment.

She sits in the back of the Morris, watching Jonny chat with Anne. He's persuaded her to work in the shop after their holiday. Anne protests: she knows nothing about antiques, she's hopeless with money. But she's looking forward to it. She enjoys being wanted – and she's so excited about the holiday.

They take the boat-train to Dover, and endure a rough crossing to Calais. The choppy seas make them both seasick. By the time they reach northern France, Anne looks pale and tired.

"This holiday had better be worth it, dear daughter of mine."

"Just think of the sunshine coming our way. From here on, our journey will be total luxury."

It is. The Blue Train proves immaculate. After chuntering through the Gare du Nord and the Gare de Lyon, they leave Paris in the early evening. Pungent cocktails and an excellent dinner follow – clear soup, sole in white wine sauce, roast duck, lemon soufflé, each course with wines to match. Anne looks younger by the minute – and she sleeps soundly through the night.

Eleanor listens to the whistle shriek and the wheels thunder as the Blue Train roars through Dijon, Châlons and Lyon to the coast and Marseilles. For the millionth time, she wonders what Felix is doing and who he's with.

Staring into the darkness, she's gripped by depression. She must be crazy, spending her precious money on this jaunt. It's sure to be a wild-goose chase. Nobody has had sight nor sound of Moira for twenty-two years. What are the odds on her still being alive? She could be anywhere in the world, with an altered identity, dead and buried in some foreign city – or, indeed, at the bottom of the Cornish sea.

She closes her eyes as the train rocks and grinds. The person who should be here with her, sharing her anxiety, having an equally sleepless night, is Felix. *He's* the one who should be looking for his mother. Moira's *his* responsibility. And yet, and yet … That ever-haunting voice echoes in her head.

"Find Moira for me."

She punches her pillow. "I'm doing my best, Daddy," she murmurs. "I'm doing my level best."

Juan-les-Pins is indeed filled with glorious sunlight, twinkling on to terracotta roofs, white houses, blue Mediterranean bays, green faraway hills topped with bright glints of alpine snow, sprays of delicate mimosa, stern eucalyptus and forests of dense pine.

The Provençal Hotel, an enormous white stone palace, overlooks its beach and curling sapphire seas. Eleanor and Anne have adjoining rooms on the third floor. Eleanor tips the smiling *garçon* and goes straight to the window with its spectacular view. She turns back towards the bed and catches her breath. Above it hang two exquisite still-life watercolours. Their resemblance to those in The Hideaway is too striking to be mere coincidence.

She inspects them more closely. They are both of tropical fruit in a bowl, but done with a brightness of colour and a confidence of touch that surpass the Cornish work.

Neither is signed.

She slumps on to the bed, her legs weak from the journey and the relief of being in Juan-les-Pins – and now the discovery of a first possible clue. Are the watercolours by Moira? If they are, might there be others in the hotel? Could she find them and ask about the artist? Would she be given a name – and even an address? Her mind whirs with possibilities.

∽

In the hotel's dining room, ready for a late luncheon with Anne, Eleanor stares across at a wall near the French windows that lead on to a glamorous terrace, filled with guests whose voices and laughter filter lazily into the room. The canvas hanging there is an enormous oil painting of a Parisian cocktail-bar dominated by a pair of lovers in full evening dress, looking into each other's eyes. No, not Moira's work, but there are many other public rooms in the hotel. The thread she's longing to establish could well be here.

Later that afternoon, while Anne is parked on the beach with an elderly English couple they'd met at the hotel, Eleanor walks back to the Provençal, bent on exploring as much of it as she can. She wanders into a half-empty lounge where, above a fireplace filled with mimosa, hang four watercolours. She stares up at them, positive they're Moira's work.

Her heart pounding with determination, she finds a young concierge in the hotel's foyer. In halting French, she tells him she admires the paintings in her room.

His face lights up. "But of course. They are very pretty. The Provençal is lucky to own them."

"Could you tell me who painted them?"

"No, Mademoiselle. The artist wishes to remain anonymous."

"So none of them are for sale?"

"Not here. But there is a small art gallery in Juan, called *L'Art sur la Plage*. I believe the same painter often exhibits there. The gallery is near this hotel on the right-hand side, along the Esplanade."

By eleven o'clock next morning Eleanor has escaped Anne and her new friends. She leaves them on the terrace and finds *L'Art sur la Plage*. It's closed, but will open again at four that afternoon.

While Anne is having a siesta, Eleanor changes into a fresh cotton frock. She slips out of the Provençal just after four. The gallery's owner greets her in English with a marked American drawl.

"Good afternoon! I'm Adam Selby. Welcome to *Sur la Plage*. Are you looking for anything in particular?"

"I'm staying at the Provençal. They have some exquisite still-lives of flowers and fruit, done in wonderful detail—"

"I know exactly what you mean." He adjusts the cuffs of his blue-silk shirt. "You're in luck. I have several by the same artist. I've hung them in this room here." He turns away to greet new visitors. "Excuse me … I'll be right back."

She wanders into the adjoining room. Its three white-washed walls gleam out at her, lit by porthole windows that remind her of The Hideaway kitchen. One of the walls is covered with pencil sketches of a male nude with a muscular body and a sweep of straight dark hair. A second boasts black-and-white photographs of Paris. But on the third are a dozen small paintings, split into two groups. Six are landscapes, done in smudged pastels, of narrow French streets leading to the sea.

And the other six? She moves closer. The painter has chosen a mahogany table placed beneath a window. Strong sunlight falls on to a crystal water jug, two wine glasses and a vase of crimson tulips, bending in full bloom.

Adam rejoins her. "What do you think?"

"They're beautiful. Are they all for sale?"

"Sure … I can give you a discount. How many would you like?"

"Only one, thank you … I'll have to carry it home." She points to the still-life in the centre. "That's by far the best. May I buy it?"

"Delighted!" Adam lifts it off the wall, reading aloud the

price tag on the back. "The artist *will* be pleased!"

"Does he have a name?" she asks as casually as possible, following him to his desk in the front room.

"No. No signature and no identity." Adam starts to wrap the watercolour. "Sorry, but the anonymity's important. It's a matter of trust. I have to honour the artist's request." He pulls an account book from a drawer and opens it. Eleanor spots a handwritten list of names – and details she longs to read.

The bell clangs at the gallery door. A woman in a long pale frock and wide-brimmed hat holds out her arms. "Adam! I made it!"

"Ingrid!" He dashes towards her. "*Wonderful* to see you! I wasn't expecting you until seven!"

In a flash Eleanor reaches for the book, rapidly skimming the list of names. Half-way down she spots:

Madame T. Cinq Saisons. Tulips in Full Bloom. Six, same size.

She marches back to the Provençal muttering *Cinq Saisons* under her breath, the precious watercolour under her arm, hatching a plan. She reaches her room without meeting Anne, and slides the painting into her suitcase. She'll hang it over her desk the minute she's back in Woodstock. Now she must put every moment of the next few days to good purpose.

First she'll find the villa. She's only guessing that Adam's "Madame T" is Moira Tessier, but that's what she'll assume until she has proof to the contrary. She'll leave the Provençal early next morning and ask directions to *Cinq Saisons* from anyone she meets. It can't be *that* far: Juan is hardly a sprawling town. If asked, she'll say she has an urgent letter to deliver.

At breakfast Anne plays into her hands, telling her she's been offered a lift to Cannes. "You won't mind my leaving you to your own devices for a few hours, will you? I'll be back in time for supper."

The minute Anne has left, Eleanor makes her first foray along the narrow villa-lined streets. They lead away from the Esplanade, up into the pine-filled woods, blessed with quiet shade.

She asks for *Cinq Saisons* from a gardener, a woman with a child, and a cyclist repairing his flat tyre. None of them recognise the address. She returns to the sea-front for a coffee in the beach café.

The waitress who serves her an iced lemonade and a black coffee says she knows *Cinq Saisons*. She worked there for a time: it's a beautiful villa, and Monsieur Tessier is the owner. She points Eleanor in the right direction. *Cinq Saisons* lies on the *other* side of the Provençal, half an hour's walk into the hills.

She waits until mid-afternoon to avoid the noonday heat. She walks fast, following the waitress's instructions to the letter. Finally, with enormous relief, she finds the sign above a pair of wrought-iron gates:

Cinq Saisons

She hesitates on the opposite side of the road, trying to decide what to say if and when somebody greets her. But even before she's crossed the street, the front door opens and the iron gates swing wide. A woman in a crisp nurse's uniform pushes a bath-chair down the villa's drive. In it sits an elderly, frail-looking man whose white hair sticks out beneath his Panama.

Eleanor stands in the shade of the pines as the couple move down the hill. Is that really Pierre Tessier? In her imagination he's still the passionate young lover writing to Moira, begging her to join him. But those letters had been written twenty-five years ago.

She looks across at the villa again, alerted by voices. A garage door opens, and a wine-red Daimler emerges. The front door opens again. A woman in a dark suit steps straight into the car. Doors slam. The car purrs down the drive, through the gates, and past Eleanor.

Desperate to see the woman in the back, she flings out an arm in a wild attempt to stop the car. The chauffeur, wearing his regulation cap and jacket, ignores her. She only manages a brief glimpse: the woman's face is hidden behind the veil of a fashionable hat.

Over supper, Anne chatters excitedly about her day.

"You look a bit peaky." She sips her wine. "What have *you* been doing?"

"Nothing in particular. It's been too hot to think."

In bed, sleep eludes her. Tomorrow she'll make the same tracks to the villa. She rehearses what she'll say when the villa door opens. But what if Madame Tessier never entertains guests? What if, the moment she knows who Eleanor is, she's told to leave? She needs a cast-iron excuse to visit *Cinq Saisons* that has nothing to do with Walter or Felix.

She sits up in bed. Of course! She'll take the watercolour with her, give herself a new identity. She'll pretend to be the owner of an Oxford art gallery. She can ask, if indeed Moira *had* painted it, whether she'd sign it. A few brief moments with the woman is all she'll need to confirm her identity.

Towards dawn she falls asleep. A strange dream troubles her. The Daimler stops outside the villa. The woman in the back seat rolls down the window, reaches out a hand to touch her shoulder. "I've something to tell you." Her voice is soft, her face hidden by the veil. "It's most important. It can't wait."

Felix emerges from behind the car. Eleanor gasps with surprise and joy. He kisses her cheek, lifts her hand to his lips. "Mama's message," he says, "is for me."

She jolts awake, her head aching, her heart lonely, tears scalding her eyes. If only Felix were in bed beside her.

She eats breakfast before Anne comes down, leaving a note propped on her mother's coffee cup:

Gone for an early walk before it gets too hot. See you at luncheon.
Love E

She tucks the watercolour under her arm. It's half-past eight. She aims to be at *Cinq Saisons* by nine.

As she reaches the villa, she hears a distant church bell chime the hour. She waits until its echoing clangs fade. Then she presses the button, watching as the iron gates swing open. She marches up the drive.

The villa, with its pale grey stone and arched windows, looms ahead of her. She notices flowerbeds filled with a limited palette of white and pink. In the distance a gardener stoops over his spade.

Without her ringing another bell, the front door opens. A maid stands waiting: young, neat, wearing her cap and apron.

Trying to quell her nerves, Eleanor speaks in halting French. "Good morning. I'm sorry to disturb you so early—"

"Good morning, Mademoiselle. Not at all."

"Please may I have a word with Madame Tessier? I collect paintings." She holds out her watercolour, swiftly unwrapping it. "This is by her, isn't it?"

"Yes, indeed. That's Madame's work. It's most clever of you to find her. She never tells anybody she's an artist."

"Then may I—"

"Alas, no. I'm so sorry. Monsieur and Madame Tessier are not at home."

She's stung by surprise. "But I saw Madame leaving the villa yesterday. And Monsieur Tessier, in his bath-chair, with a nurse—"

"Indeed. He goes out every afternoon. But he's not well. He and Madame have gone to Germany, to take the waters at Baden-Baden. They left last night."

Eleanor's mouth tastes bitter with disappointment. "When they will be back?"

"Not until August or September. It will depend on what the doctors advise."

Tears of frustration burn her eyes. "I urgently need to see Madame. To sign my watercolour. I'd love to have more of her work for my gallery."

The maid smooths her skirt. "Would you like to leave a message?"

"No, that won't be good enough. I'm leaving for England myself." She looks over the maid's shoulder into a marble-tiled hall. An enormous mirror reflects a vase of lilies whose cloying scent drifts out to her. "But if I write Madame a letter and leave it with a small parcel, would you make sure she gets them on her return?"

Back in her room, she grabs a piece of hotel notepaper. She writes as fast as her shaking hand will allow.

AS FROM: 20 High Street Woodstock Oxfordshire England
3 June 1936

Dear Madame Tessier

I was devastated to hear that you and your husband had left for Baden-Baden. I have travelled to Juan-les-Pins expressly to find you, and to return these letters to your safe keeping.

My father, Walter Drummond, died in an accident in January. Just before his death, he begged me to find you. Now, it seems I've gone some small way towards doing so. Luckily, the Provençal Hôtel and Sur la Plage have some of your watercolours, though neither of them gave away your identity. I know that as a painter you wish to remain anonymous.

I should love us to meet. When you get this letter, would you write to me? Felix has told me so much about you. But not enough. I found these letters in your bureau in The Hideaway. Nobody else knows about them, not even Felix. I'm sorry if I've intruded on your privacy.

I shall not tell Felix I've found you until you give me express permission to do so. Knowing you are still alive will give him the greatest joy.

Yours
Eleanor Drummond

She puts the note on the bundle of Pierre's letters, takes the lift down to reception and asks for a large envelope. She addresses it, labels it **STRICTLY PRIVATE AND CONFIDENTIAL,** asks the receptionist to stamp it with sealing wax. Then she hurries back to the villa. The same young maid opens the door.

Eleanor makes her promise that nobody but Madame will see the package, that it will be safely hidden until her return. Whenever that will be.

301

The maid gives a bob of curtsey. The sealing wax glitters in her hands like dried blood.

Eleanor stands at the bottom of the drive as the gates of *Cinq Saisons* clang behind her. The midday sun beats down from a blinding white sky. Heat from the ground burns into her face, making her limbs throb, her forehead drip with sweat. Above her tower the pine trees, still and silent in the heavy air.

She's done everything she can. Now she must be patient. But she won't wait for ever. She'll give Moira until the end of August to reply. If she hasn't heard from her by then, she'll write to Felix. Tell him how much she's managed to achieve.

If only she'd arrived one day earlier ... She might never get an answer to her letter. The whole trip could have been a waste of time.

She takes off her sun hat, rakes her fingers through her damp hair.

She starts to walk down the hill towards the sea, longing for Woodstock's cooler days, the freshness of its twilights and its frosty nights.

And for the man who in a single week has changed her life.

Act Five

The Naming

1936

June flashes by in a whirlwind of activity, heralded by the
arrival of a substantial sum into Eleanor's new business
account.

Her relief and excitement – and her pleasure at seeing
Anne relaxed and happy – are tempered by knowing that
The Hideaway now belongs to Felix. In her room, at her
desk, she holds its keys, wondering whether he'll invite her
to visit him – and imagining what he'd say if he knew she'd
found Moira. In a letter, she tells him only that they'd had
a good holiday and the date for the tea-room's opening.

She's much too busy to brood.

The Woodstock house is flung once again into chaos, as
the decorators finish work on the first and second floors, and
spruce up the exterior paintwork. Builders install a
downstairs cloakroom. Dirt flies everywhere; dust follows.
Plumbers and electricians arrive, bringing a lavatory, a
hand-basin, taps, and terracotta tiles for the cloakroom floor.
A safe is installed in her bedroom.

Deciding she's better off out of the noise and dust, Anne
disappears to Giffen Antiques. At first she's too scared to do

anything but watch Jonny, get to know his stock, and make tea. When he gives her money at the end of the week, she spends it at her dressmaker's, telling Eleanor she can hardly wait for Monday afternoon.

Relieved to see Anne occupied, Eleanor concentrates on her own plans. She meets her new accountant. After consulting Kath, she chooses local suppliers of fresh produce, discussing her requirements and their prices.

Jonny helps her to buy new furniture. They drive to a warehouse near Banbury to find six round tables and twenty-four comfortable wooden chairs, as well as accessories for the tea-room. Her excitement quickens with each day. She discusses the menu and price list with Vera. Jonny takes a photo of the tea-room. Eleanor gives both the list and the photo to her Oxford printer, together with copy for a handbill announcing the tea-room's opening. She and Jonny plan to push it through every letterbox in Woodstock during the last weekend in June.

With Anne's agreement, she names the tea-room *Eleanor's*. A local craftsman makes a sign to hang above the door. Interested neighbours gather in the High Street to watch it being fixed into place.

Anne squeezes her hand. "Your father would have been proud of you."

It's the first time Anne has mentioned Walter in many weeks.

The night before the tea-room's opening, Eleanor unhooks Felix's painting from above her bed and staggers downstairs with it. She hangs it in prime position in the tea-room. In the stronger light, it looks better than ever. She notices the delicate lines Felix has traced around Walter's eyes, how he's captured the set of his shoulders, the determined thrust of his chin. The colours of the portrait sing against the smooth cream of the wall.

She's just finished hanging the portrait and jumped down from the chair when Anne walks into the room.

"That's not Walter's work, is it?"

"No." Her face feels flame hot.

"So who's it by? Who's that, sitting behind your father?" Anne looks directly at her. "Who painted that portrait?"

"Felix Mitchell." Beads of sweat crawl down Eleanor's neck like flies on a horse's nose. "He's an accomplished portrait painter."

"*Is* he indeed?" Anne inspects her face as if she's looking for the tell-tale signs of measles. "Did you get to know him well, this Mitchell fellow?"

Eleanor walks rapidly to the window to flick at the new chintz curtains, hiding her face from Anne's much-too-curious gaze. "Not particularly. We hardly had time to say hello." She looks back at her mother.

"Hmm." Anne gives her a suspicious look. "I'm relieved to hear it. You wouldn't want to get mixed up with him on a *personal* level, now, would you?"

Eleanor wakes early next morning, terrified. She's checked everything a hundred times: the sparkling kitchen with its shining pots and pans; the new cloakroom; the tea-room itself with its elegant tables and chairs; the fresh white roses in each of the vases; the sugar bowls and menus; the new wooden till.

Today she and Vera will become a professional working team. Anne, whose interest in the venture has grown, hovers in the background in case she can help. Now, all Eleanor needs is customers.

The postman hands her a bundle of bills, which she'll

open at the day's end. But on another envelope she recognises the handwriting: Felix has sent her a hand-made card. On the front is a tiny black-ink sketch of her, standing on the St Ives harbour in her raincoat, looking out to sea: her hair windswept, her mouth slightly parted, her eyes full of laughter. Its likeness is breathtaking. Inside, he's written:

To my one and only Eleanor—

Good luck for your grand opening! Wish I could be with you, but I'm renovating The Hideaway: tiny new bathroom upstairs, freshly painted studio, wonderful new skylight, lots of clean white paint. Exhausting but rewarding. Hope to see you when the chaos has subsided. Don't work too hard. And don't stop thinking about me.

All my love
Felix

She slips the card into her apron pocket where it sits, brushing against her thigh, making her feel loved.

At ten o'clock, Eleanor and Vera look at each other, smile anxiously – and open the tea-room door.

Nothing happens. There's nobody in the street. The silence is frightening. Eleanor prays that *somebody* will come in. She wants to rush outside shouting, "We're giving free coffee to our first customers."

"Be patient, dear heart." Vera straightens her spotless apron. "They'll come flooding in by lunchtime, you'll see."

A figure appears at the end of the street. Then another. Rosie Perkins and a friend march past with their noses in the air. Rosie talks loudly about people who are too poor to do anything but sell their own breakfasts.

Vera looks at Eleanor's face and pulls her inside. "Always ignore mindless tittle-tattle. It's a waste of God's good time."

An hour of nerve-wracking patience pays off. At eleven o'clock a family of four come in, closely followed by an elderly couple. By lunchtime the tea-room is crammed. Eleanor closes its doors at five o'clock, exhausted but triumphant. She hugs Vera, tells Anne she knew she could do it, and shakes Jonny's hand.

Anne opens a celebratory bottle of wine. "I hardly slept last night for worrying."

"You should have had faith in me from the start," Eleanor says. "Fresh scones, pungent coffee, fragrant tea … How could we possibly fail?"

But she drinks the wine with a glad heart.

The following Wednesday evening, at the end of her first week in the tea-room, Eleanor goes to see Kath. Her feet are sore but her sense of triumph overwhelming. Kath meets her in the Fishery Cottage garden and flings out her arms.

"Congratulations, Ellie! How did it go?"

"It's exhausting, but because it's *my* enterprise, it feels worthwhile. Of course, I've got a long way to go. At the moment everything's new and exciting. Customers are trying us out. They may or may not come back. I'm sure we'll have days when the tea-room's empty and I'll wonder what I'm doing with my life!"

"You'll never guess what I've been doin' with mine!"

"Forgive me, Kath … I haven't even asked how you are."

"I've been entertainin' royalty. It's been top secret in case the press got hold of it. The King and Wallis Simpson came to Blenheim Palace for a long weekend. Ernest Simpson came with 'em, though *he* slept in a separate room. There were other guests, too, very distinguished ones. Winston and

Clementine Churchill, Lady Emerald Cunard, Duff and Diana Cooper, the Duke and Duchess of Buccleuch … It were hard work, but the Duke and Mary Marlborough were happy with how everythin' went."

"How did your guests spend the weekend?"

"We organised a picnic for 'em on the lake by Rosamond's Well. The King played the bagpipes after dinner, until Wallis asked him to stop. They danced in the Long Library, had drinks on the terrace, ate the best food Blenheim could offer … I heard Mary Marlborough sayin' she liked Wallis Simpson!"

"Did you *see* her, Kath?"

"Several times. She were always very well turned-out, in her high heels, tight-fittin' frocks, expensive jewellery. Her voice is hard as nails, but Edward hangs on every word. But listen … You must promise not to tell another livin' soul. There were a secret reason for the weekend's fun and games. Wallis is divorcin' her husband. Edward insists on it, and he paid Ernest a lot of money for her."

"So now the King has bought somebody else's wife!"

"He intends to marry Wallis if it's the last thing he does. I looked at the Visitors' Book after they'd signed it. Edward took the left-hand page to himself. Everyone else put their signature on the right-hand side. Wallis placed hers at the top. She comes first with Edward and neither of them care who knows it."

"But you don't believe we'll have a Queen Wallis next year."

"Can't see it happenin' myself. The church, the establishment, the government … None of 'em will allow it." Kath shivers. "It's gettin' chilly. Come inside and let's eat. By the way, did I tell you what Wallis calls the King when he's out of the room?"

"I can't imagine."

"She calls him Peter Pan."

"Honestly, Kath! You wouldn't catch *me* calling my beloved Felix silly little names behind his back … Wallis Simpson doesn't deserve to *have* our King!"

"No," Kath says. "I don't suppose for a single moment that she does."

A Midnight Feast

1936

"Close your eyes," Edward VIII says with all the authority he can muster. He'd been drinking heavily since breakfast and it's now five o'clock on a balmy June afternoon. His hands shake as he opens the large red-velvet box.

"Oh, *David!*" Wallis Simpson tightens her white leather belt. She might use it on her besotted lover tonight if she feels in the mood. "Not *another* surprise!"

"The biggest of your life!" Edward cannot undo the clasp of the stunning necklace of emeralds he'd commissioned specially from Cartier. Wallis has to do it for him.

Even so, when she sees the gift around her neck, her jaw drops, her eyes glitter, her pulse races with delight and triumph.

"*David!*" she drawls. "How *perfectly marvellous!* How can I *ever* thank you?"

Edward kneels at Wallis's feet. "You know how, Wallis, darling," he says.

And then he passes out.

Wallis stands there, looking down at him, caressing the emeralds. Eventually she rings for her maid, pointing in silence to the disaster flopped out over there.

"Deal with him," she says, her lips hardly moving, the manicured nails pointing. "And fast. You know the drill. We take cocktails with the bigwigs at seven."

Wallis had planned her wardrobe for this June's Friday-to-Monday at Blenheim Palace with her usual obsessive care and attention to detail. Her maid, her jewels, her clothes are all near at hand. She likes to have such things as maids close by, just in case, and for the flimsiest of reasons.

But for the Friday evening dinner, fully dressed, stunningly bejewelled, as she checks her appearance she's apprehensive. The list of distinguished guests is a little overwhelming.

Of course, her Aunt Bessie's so proud of her! But something's not quite right. Perhaps it's that she's been driven *out of London*. She's definitely *not* in her natural milieu.

She glances out of an elegant window on to the stretch of glittering water: the "marvellous lake" as David calls it. Shivering, she loops her arms around her body. The trouble is: *there's no escape* in Blenheim. She *admires* the building, of course, but what if she suddenly decides to *leave*? Where have they parked David's car? She has absolutely no idea how the layout of this formidable Palace works.

It's all right for the others, she thinks bitterly. They've been *born* into a life of luxury and privilege. None of them knows what it's like to go hungry, the humiliation of having to earn one's living by—

Snap! She shuts down her memory bank. She tightens her lips and tries to smile. The result is not a success.

∽

313

Her maid manages to haul the new King of England to his feet. He looks the colour of freshly mown grass. She dumps him in a tub of cold water where he comes round, apologises, tells Wallis she looks ravishing and gets dressed in his own room. Other flunkies take over while Wallis, breathing a sigh of relief, paints her lips a lurid shade of purple.

On the dot of seven, their mouths stretched into two emptily loving smiles, their fingertips touching, the King and his rake-thin, snake-thin consort glide carefully down the stairs. They make for the already crowded Long Library where cigarette smoke wafts into their eyes and the pungent aroma of gin belches from every nook and cranny.

Half an hour and several glasses of pink champagne later – Wallis cannot get enough of it – she has a biting headache. Her eyes feel dry and sore. David has once again thrown caution to the Blenheim wind. He's almost rolling around the room. Quite honestly, she can hardly bear to be within *sight* of him.

She eats half of whatever is put in front of her. The headache eases, her thin stomach feels bloated. Suddenly there she is, in a room filled with women who are all smiling at her. What are they smiling *about*? It's as if they've spun a web and trapped her in it. As if they've conspired to keep her occupied, made sure she eats just a tiny bit more: cheese and fruit, petits fours, mint chocolates, coffee.

Heavens above, now she feels *sick*.

She looks over the creamy shoulders of the women surrounding her.

Where the *devil* is David?

And where's that sensible husband of hers?

Where the hell's teeth is Ernest?

314

When she asks one of the pair of creamy shoulders, they shrug. The men have gone off with their brandies. Give them an hour. They'll be back.

Wallis excuses herself. She strolls up to her room. Eyes follow her ascent. So does a sudden hushed silence. Somebody breaks it with a mirthless snort of laughter.

David is neither in their suite, nor in his. Wallis calls for her maid and some whisky. She's just stepped out of her frock and silk underwear when the King of England and ruler of Empire comes thrashing in.

He catches Wallis in his arms, burying his head in her unpinned hair.

He says, *"Now you are really mine!"*

Wallis draws carefully away. The emeralds bask in their glory on her dappled skin. "And what *exactly* do you mean by that?"

Her sickening headache has returned, her maid will need to find those special tablets. David can forget about the white-leather-belt routine: tonight it will be cuddles only and he'll be darn lucky to get *those!*

The King stands straight-backed in front of her, his large eyes wistful.

"Your husband has sold you to me for the largest sum of money in the world."

It is now Monday evening. The guests have gone, piling into their cars with their summer furs, holding their cigars, smiling and bobbing and whispering in corners.

Servants have spent the entire day wiping every fingerprint from the Friday-to-Monday visit. It never happened. Nobody was here.

∞

Except, wait a minute. Not so galloping fast.

There is the record of the Friday-to-Monday weekend in the red-leather tombstone of a volume: the signed Visitors' Book.

Edward's signature sits on the left-hand side.

And Wallis Simpson's? Why, if that isn't a sight for sore eyes!

Proof, if ever it were needed, that the whole darn thing *did* happen. The whole darn thing.

There she is, sky high, riding the crest of the potentially royal waves.

Top of the Blenheim list. Ten out of ten. More distinguished than any of the other guests.

The King's favourite.

If that doesn't take the biscuit and a very large sherry!

There she is. Consort, queen, ruler of the Empire, Hitler's bosom pal, and seducer of every creature on God's earth …

Now it's midnight. The clocks chime the hour. One by one the lights in Blenheim Palace flick out. The sky holds on to its last slivers of crystal light.

There is the sound of horses clopping. They pick up the pace, impatient to arrive.

Four of them.

They gallop in, very fast, from four different directions: Bladon, Oxford, Combe, and Witney.

Their riders wear leather. They each carry a bottle of something celebratory.

They tether their foaming steeds to the pegs along the stable wall.

Nobody has noticed their arrival. There's nobody else about.

∽

One by one, they walk silently out of the stables, across the marvellous space of the Blenheim courtyard, down to the glittering lake.

They're big men – tall, sturdy, strong – but they move like silent panthers, reeking triumphantly of the successful kill.

"We've achieved everything we could possibly have hoped for," their leader says.

"He's bought her. Now she can only be his. He will have to abdicate. We are home and dry."

Birthday Surprise

1936

Running the tea-room becomes the most demanding work Eleanor's ever done. Getting a place at Somerville had been tough. Coping with her father's death was emotionally crippling. Handling her mother was difficult. But she's never had to deal with so many people before, make daily decisions, be a continual part of the busyness of life.

She'd worried that "going into trade", as Anne had so patronisingly put it, would leave her feeling like a second-class citizen. But she can't be bothered with the occasional snub from her customers. The cut and thrust of the tea-room's challenge is exciting and rewarding. The days fly by in a blur of activity.

Eleanor's, from the day it opens, is a resounding success. But she knows that its standards need maintaining, its menus must be altered and refreshed, and that only her own vigilant eye will ensure its success.

Kath asks what else she's been doing. She sighs and laughs.

"No time for anything else, Kath. My life's been taken over by the tea-room. I feel as if I've been eaten by a shark."

"And how's that Felix of yours?" Kath asks. "Any signs of *him* on your horizon?"

"He must be terribly busy. His paintings, The Hideaway … He'll soon find time to be with me."

Every day she prays he'll appear at the door of *Eleanor's*, and every night she dreams of being in his arms.

July tumbles into August. Regular customers go on holiday. Tourists arrive. Eleanor hires Fran, a pleasant young girl with a ready smile, who cleans the kitchen while Vera cooks. When a fortnight of sultry heat arrives, Eleanor looks at the garden with a business-woman's eye, planning an extension in the spring. The tea-room generates its own energy. Her exhaustion is replaced by feelings of satisfaction and achievement. Anne treats her with a new respect.

Sometimes at the end of a particularly busy day, Vera gives her a hug.

"Always knew you could do it," she says briskly. "Now, how much shortbread do you want for tomorrow? And shall we try a new rhubarb crumble?"

Eleanor's nineteenth birthday, on the 22nd of August, falls on a Saturday. She wakes dreading the hours ahead, remembering the same day last year; thinking about Walter's gift of the beautiful pearls.

Anne and Jonny have invited her to a birthday dinner at The Trout. She hasn't been back to Wolvercote since the evening Jonny proposed. She glances across the room at the exquisite painting of the tulips. Wouldn't it be a wonderful birthday gift if a letter from Moira arrived?

Anne makes a special effort. That afternoon, while

Eleanor is working, she goes to the hairdresser, coming home at four o'clock looking sleek and glamorous. She dashes upstairs for a bath.

Eleanor's feet ache. It's been a long, hot day; she's jealous of Anne's leisured freedom. She walks into the kitchen with three orders for Vera, and collects a plate of sandwiches for two young tourists. She carries them into the tea-room.

Sitting at the corner table by the window is a man in a loose linen jacket and pale blue trousers. His hair flops on to his forehead. He looks up and across the room – directly at her. The hazel light from his eyes seems to create a rainbow between them, shimmering with astonishment and desire.

She manages to put the sandwiches on the right table. She moves towards him, as if a giant magnet is pulling them together.

"Good afternoon, Eleanor!" Felix says. "And a very happy birthday!"

She falls into a chair opposite him. "How did you know? When did you *arrive*?"

He laughs. "Walter told me the date of your birthday a month after you were born. He came down to Newlyn to tell me he had a daughter. I was so jealous. I realised you'd see him every day, and I'd take second place. The date stuck in my head. Last week I promised myself: however much I had to do, everything could wait until I'd seen you again."

Her heart races with delight. "And when——"

"An hour ago. I'm staying at The Bear, but not for long. I must go home on Tuesday."

She feasts her eyes on his face, his hair, his hands, longing to kiss him.

"I'll bring you the most delicious tea you've ever had!"

She dashes into the kitchen, emerging with a tray

crammed with cucumber sandwiches and strawberry tarts.

"You look so professional." He watches her laying out the food. "What time do you close?"

"At five. I have to go to a birthday supper with Anne. I'd ask you to come, but she doesn't know anything about you yet—"

"I understand." He drops his voice. "I'm the big bad wolf. The villain who stole Walter's money and snatched his daughter's heart."

She blushes. "I'll get away as soon as I can and meet you at The Bear. Will you wait for me?"

"All night, if I have to." He touches her hand. A stab of desire surges through her body. "Now go and serve those customers before there's a riot in the aisle."

They drive to Wolvercote in the Morris, Jonny at the wheel, Anne beside him in her oyster-satin frock. Eleanor sits in the back, burning with impatience for the meal to be over. Anne and Jonny talk endlessly about Giffen Antiques. Eleanor eats rapidly, hardly noticing the food, barely listening.

On their return, Anne and Jonny disappear into the kitchen to make coffee. Eleanor says she's off to meet Kath for a drink. She makes a dive for the door, racing towards The Bear, charging through the crowds. Felix has changed into his cream linen suit. He is pacing up and down outside the hotel.

She hurtles into his arms.

"The trouble with being in Woodstock is that everyone knows me."

She sits beside him at a small table in the bar, drinking champagne, surrounded by the buzz of voices and laughter.

"In St Ives I was blissfully anonymous. But here ..."

"If I invite you to my room," he says teasingly, "the whole village will notice and be aghast."

"Exactly." She laughs with him, but her heart stabs with disappointment. They clasp hands under the table. "It doesn't matter. As long as you're here … Sunday and Monday are both days off for me. I'll spend as much of them with you as I can."

"I've brought your birthday present. It's one of the portraits. I finished three, but this one is the best. It's in the car … Drink up. I'm longing to show it to you."

They walk slowly through to the car park behind The Bear.

He stops beside his Austin Seven. "How do you like *this* little beauty? I bought it second-hand, so I could drive to Woodstock." He opens the boot, lifts out the wrapped painting.

"We can take it to Walter's studio. It's still a mess, but Anne never goes there."

"So you can't even hang it in the house?" He slams the boot. "Are you *frightened* of your mother, Eleanor?"

"Not exactly." She slips an arm through his as they walk towards the studio. "But I'm still treading on eggshells. Maybe I'll always have to."

"You can't let the shadows of the past cloud everything." He glances down at her. "Sooner or later, Anne has to know about me."

"Of course. But not yet. She's happier than she's been for months. We have money in the bank and the tea-room's a success. She even has a part-time job in a local shop. But I keep an eye on her all the time."

"She's lucky to have such a devoted daughter!"

"I'm doing it for Walter. When he was alive, I needed his approval for everything. I can't suddenly switch off that habit like a lamp."

"Do you think *he'd* approve of your loving me?" His voice is light and mocking but it's a serious question.

She reaches up to kiss him. "He'd be over the moon … Let's get that painting inside before we get hit by a car."

Eleanor switches on the light. Felix stares around the studio, absorbing every detail.

"So this is where Walter worked."

"This was Daddy's world."

"It's marvellous! I can almost see him sitting at his easel."

"I sold some of his paintings of Blenheim at our exhibition. Otherwise, the room's pretty much as he left it."

"Here." He bends to unwrap his gift. "For you, with all my love."

She catches her breath. She's wearing the red taffeta frock, sitting in Felix's attic, one of the windows behind her, a band of sunlight streaming over her shoulder. There's a marvellous thoughtfulness about her eyes and face, the placing of her hands, the turn of her head.

"I *love* it. I'll smuggle it into my bedroom. If Anne sees it, I'll tell her the whole story."

"And face the consequences?"

"There's nothing she can do to stop me loving you. Kiss me again, so I can show you how."

A few minutes later she picks up a blanket from the corner of the studio and throws it over the chaise longue. Then she leans past her lover to turn out the light.

On Sunday morning she leaves Anne a note telling her she's gone out for the day. She meets Felix at The Bear, blushing beneath his gaze. They drive into Oxford, walk across the University Parks, eat luncheon at a small restaurant and return to Woodstock.

They spend the afternoon in Blenheim, walking again, the sky overcast, the early sunshine gone. They'd talked all morning. Now, as four o'clock approaches, they keep a new, companionable silence, as if there are no more words to be said because none are needed.

They reach Blenheim's marvellous bridge for the second time. He tugs at her hand, drawing her closer to the stone parapet. They stand together, looking over the calm, grey-green water.

"Summer's nearly over," he says. "Those leaves are beginning to turn. It must be beautiful in the autumn."

"Will you come again soon?" She leans her head on his shoulder. "To see the colours for yourself?"

"No." He stares over the lake. "I'm not driving to Woodstock again. That is, not until you've given me an answer."

"But you haven't asked me anything!"

"Haven't I? I've been asking you a question since the moment I saw you yesterday." He turns to face her. "I want you to come back to St Ives with me. I want you to be my girl, every minute of the day and all night long. Will you, Eleanor?"

She catches her breath, unable to speak.

"The work I've done to The Hideaway ..." He lifts her hands to his lips. "It's all been for you. I'm longing to share it. I want you to look at my paintings every evening. I want to take you dancing on Saturday nights, to walk with you on Sundays. To have you in my bed again." He smooths his fingers over her hair. "Give me your answer, my darling Eleanor. Will you come back to St Ives with me?"

Her eyes fill with tears. "If you only knew how much I'd love to say yes."

He stares at her, his face dark with disappointment. "Are you turning me down?"

"How can I simply pack a bag and leave? Abandon Mummy, Vera, the tea-room?"

"You're not indispensable. Someone else can run it. You can't live in your mother's thrall. You need a life of your own—"

"Of course I do. But not yet!"

"So what are you saying? That you want me to wait?"

"Exactly that—"

"For three months? Six months? A year?" His voice hardens. "Month after month with nothing but scraps of paper full of loving words? Snatched days like these when we skulk around, hoping nobody will see us together? Half an hour of love-making, sliding off an old chaise longue on to a dusty floor?"

They laugh shakily but he perseveres.

"Maybe we'll have a week together at Christmas. It'll fly by, then leave us apart again." He shakes his head. "I can't live like that. Love such as ours is as rare as a wild orchid. It has to be honoured and obeyed. We should thank our lucky stars that Walter's death brought us together, and *do* something about it."

"But we've only known each other a few months—"

"I've known you for years. That's what it feels like. As if I've been waiting for you all my life."

"Then wait a little longer." She strokes his forehead with her fingertips. "Please, Felix, I beg you … Give me" – she thinks rapidly – "until Christmas. To make sure the tea-room will survive. To look after Anne a while longer. Give me time talk to her, tell her about you. I can do all that when the time is right."

"The time never will be right unless you *make* it right! Do it this afternoon. Go home now. Tell your mother everything. Meet me at The Bear and bring her with you.

325

When she sees us together, she'll see how happy we are."

"All right," Eleanor cuts in. "I'll do it now. At least, I'll try." She glances at her watch. "We'll meet you at The Bear at seven. How does that sound?"

His arms close round her in a suffocating hug. For a moment he lifts her off her feet. She sees the sky swaying, the lake's waters lapping, the sun dying among its gold-stained clouds.

"That's my girl!" he says.

Tomorrow

1936

She drags herself away from the warmth of his arms.
She starts to run: over the bridge, past the Palace, down the gravelly path and out of the Triumphal Arch into Woodstock. Her breath pounds in her ears. She knows she has to get away from Felix, put space between them, give herself time to think.

She must be mad even to *contemplate* abandoning everything. The tea-room will never survive without her. She and Vera work as a team because they know each other so well, because Vera's loyalty knows no bounds.

And how on earth will Anne react to being told that her daughter is about to disappear to Cornwall with a man whose very name is enough to turn her pale with shock?

And yet, and yet ... She longs to be with Felix, to live with him, have time to relax into his love, to stop looking over her shoulder, counting the hours before they have to part. Their love *is* a rare orchid. If she turns him down, she might never find anything as wonderful with anyone else.

∞

She crashes into the house.

Voices and laughter come from the drawing room. She peers in. Anne and Sylvia Dunkley are taking tea together, nodding and laughing like middle-aged conspirators, relishing the gossip of the day.

"Ah, Eleanor!" Anne reaches for the teapot. "*There* you are! I was just telling Sylvia about your lovely birthday supper. It was so sweet of Jonny. It was his idea, you know. And he paid for everything. He's so *considerate*, isn't he?"

"I suppose so." She gulps her tea, standing up.

"Vera's gone out for the evening but she made us all this before she left. Do you want a sandwich or a slice of her delicious lemon sponge?"

"Neither, thank you."

"*Do* sit down, darling—"

"I need to tell you something."

"So spit it out!" Anne pats the sofa. "Don't just *stand* there like a waif in a storm. Sit down and be friendly."

She says through clenched teeth, "It's a bit private, Mummy—"

"I'm sure Sylvia wouldn't mind listening."

"No, that's impossible—"

"You do look a bit flushed, dear. Your hair's all *over* the place and your shoes are terribly muddy. I hope you're not ill."

"I'm fine." Her courage evaporates. "It's not important. Tell you later. Sorry to interrupt."

She clomps upstairs to her room.

She paces the floor. The clock on her bedside table ticks relentlessly. She leaves her door ajar, straining to hear what's happening. When will Sylvia *go home*? And what exactly will she say to Anne? She rehearses it in her head.

"You remember Felix Mitchell? I told you we never met

properly? Well, we *have*, and we've fallen in love. He's asked me to go to Cornwall, to live with him. He's staying at The Bear, and he'd like to meet you. Could we all have supper tonight?"

She can almost hear Anne's shriek, her sobs, her words of disbelief and ridicule.

Downstairs, a door opens.

Anne calls up, "Eleanor? ... Sylvia's very kindly asked me to supper. We'll talk in the morning."

The front door slams.

Eleanor flounces back into her room, furious with herself for not insisting that Anne listen to her there and then. The house is empty. Seizing the opportunity, she races downstairs and out to the studio. It feels different. From now on, its battered chaise longue will always be the place where she and Felix made love. She picks up the blanket they'd lain on, folding it into her arms, remembering.

Then she grabs the painting of the girl in the red taffeta frock, staggering for a moment beneath its weight. She hauls it through the garden, into the house and upstairs. She lays it on her bed. How confident and composed she looks in her scarlet finery: her skin creamy and smooth, her hair neatly combed back from her forehead, her eyes tranquil and shining.

The calm before the storm?

"So where's your mother, then? You haven't told her, have you?"

Felix sits at the same table in The Bear, a half-drunk glass of beer at his elbow. He stares at her, his eyes cold and disappointed, his voice accusing.

She slumps beside him, her legs trembling. "Anne was having tea with a friend. I couldn't interrupt."

"And when they'd finished their precious sipping?" His voice is acid with sarcasm. "Why didn't you talk then?"

"She went out to supper before I could say anything."

"*Really?*" He gulps his beer. "You *amaze* me."

"There's no need to be like that."

"So how should I be? You obviously haven't tried very hard."

She murmurs through clenched teeth, "I said I'd do it when the time was right——"

"No, you didn't. You said you'd do it *now*." He swallows the remains of his drink. "I need another beer. Would you like anything?"

"A glass of red wine would be wonderful."

He buys the drinks, plonks them on the table. "So where do we go from here?"

"I *promise* I'll talk to Anne tomorrow." The wine slices at her throat.

"Tomorrow? Really? When exactly?"

"At breakfast. Or during the morning. We shop in Oxford on Mondays. I'll talk to her in the car." She gives a shaky laugh. "Every mother wants her daughter to be happy, doesn't she? Anne can hardly complain I've neglected her since Daddy died. I can leave with a clear conscience——"

"Are you *sure?*" He swivels towards her, clasping her hand. "I don't want you having second thoughts in St Ives, worrying about Anne, wondering whether you've made the right decision."

"I *know* you're the only man for me. And I *so* much want you to meet Mummy. I want you to *like* her. I'm *longing* for her to like you. It's just——"

"Go on."

"I wish Daddy hadn't left you his money. That Moira hadn't been your mother." She swallows her secret with the utmost difficulty. "I wish Anne didn't hold so much against you."

"But she does." He shrugs. "All I can do to 'mend' things is to love you and offer you everything I have." He adds quietly, "All that is mine, from this time forward, until death us do part."

She catches her breath. "The words of the wedding ceremony."

"Indeed." His hand slips to her wrist. He tightens his grip. "Perhaps you're wondering why I haven't asked you to marry me? I don't believe in it. I want us to be together because we *want* to be, not because some silly little civil servant has made us sign a piece of paper. Do you understand?"

"*I* understand." She gulps at her wine, her heart thundering with disappointment. "But it won't help your case with my traditional, conservative mother one little bit."

That night, in bed, alone, she lies awake, worrying. Something nags at her. Something Felix has said reminds her of someone else, somewhere else, in a similar predicament, but she can't think what or who it is.

Towards dawn she drifts into sleep. She wakes with a start an hour later, remembering. Moira had left Oxford to go to France with Pierre without telling Walter. She'd vanished on the spur of the moment, after only knowing Pierre for a few days – and with disastrous consequences.

Now Felix is asking exactly the same of her.

She sits up, her head pounding. She wonders whether he really understands what he's expecting her to do.

Give up everyone and everything for him.

Eleanor faces her mother over the breakfast table, her hands clammy.

"I need a new frock, dear daughter of mine." Anne flaps through a copy of *Vogue*. "Something glamorous for the autumn. Could we search in that nice little dress shop in Turl Street? We've got plenty of time. Jonny's not expecting me until two."

Eleanor's heart sinks. Anne has her day mapped out. She's looking forward to the new season. There's colour in her cheeks, sparkle in her eyes. Working with Jonny is doing her good. She looks younger, happier, contented. In one fell swoop, Eleanor could destroy all that and so much more.

She takes a deep breath, buttering a piece of cold toast. "That'll be fine as long as we're back by one." Another deep breath. "Look … there's someone I'd like you to meet."

"Oh?" Anne pours a second cup of coffee. "Is that what you wanted to talk to me about? Sorry I couldn't get away. You know what Sylvia's like."

The toast stares at Eleanor, slimy with grease. She smothers it with chunky marmalade. "Of course I do."

"So?" Anne glances at her sharply. "Who *is* this mysterious person?"

Eleanor stares at the coffee pot, unable to meet Anne's eyes. Suddenly she understands how many times her father must have tried to tell Anne about Moira: must have promised himself that, today, it would be different. This time he'd *force* the words out of his mouth. But always, at the last moment, his courage had failed.

So does hers. The words she's rehearsed so carefully teeter on the tip of her tongue but somehow they can't escape. Everything's so difficult, so complicated. She owes her mother so many explanations she hardly knows where to start. She's waited too long. What if, having heard what Eleanor has to say, Anne barges over to The Bear and orders Felix to leave Woodstock?

She clears her throat, babbling rubbish. "Oh, he's not a bit mysterious. I've been thinking about cleaning up the studio so we can expand the tea-room. It might be a good idea if we went to see Robin Parker together."

"Good heavens, Eleanor! Is *that* all?" Anne scrapes back her chair, stretching slim arms above her head. "*You're* the business woman. Go and see Robin on your own. Let me know how you get on." She turns at the door. "Can we give Sylvia a lift into Oxford? She has an appointment with her dentist in Beaumont Street."

Eleanor trudges into the hall and picks up a couple of bills. And a letter, on expensive, ice-blue notepaper, addressed in a clear, round hand. Its postmark is Juan-les-Pins.

She'd almost given up hope. She leaps upstairs, stands by her window, rips at the envelope.

Cinq Saisons, Juan-les-Pins 19 August 1936

My dear Eleanor

It was such an extraordinary surprise to get your letter and the small bundle of letters from my beloved husband. I was sorry to hear of Walter's death, but overjoyed to learn that Felix wants to see me.

I returned to the Riviera last night, alas without my Pierre. He died in Baden-Baden, in spite of everything the doctors tried to do. So now I am without him in this huge villa, with so much time on my hands and only my painting to fill the long hours. I'm dreading the months ahead.

Please tell Felix I should love to see him again, more than he'll ever know. I never meant to abandon him, only to leave Walter, but I couldn't do one without the other. It's a long story and not one I can explain in a letter.

Congratulations on discovering that bible well. Nobody else ever managed to.

And thank you for finding Pierre's letters and returning them to me. They are all the more precious to me now. And of course thank you for travelling to find me. I hope one day we shall meet face to face.

Au revoir
Moira Mitchell

Five minutes later, Eleanor races out of the house, Moira's letter in her hand, no coat, no hat, nothing in her heart but her burning desire to find Felix. She stands in the foyer of The Bear, asking for him, her breath stabbing her ribs.

He emerges from the dining room, clutching his serviette and newspaper.

"Eleanor! Whatever's the matter? Is it Anne? Have you told her? Oh, God, is it the worst? Did she throw you out?"

She tries to catch her breath. "This has got nothing to do with Mummy. It's the most *wonderful* news. You'll never guess."

"So tell me, for God's sake."

She pulls him into the empty bar and shuts the door.

"My darling Felix, I think you'd better sit down."

He flops into an armchair. She stands beside him, clasping his hands.

"That holiday I took with Anne a couple of months ago … Remember?"

He nods. "But what——"

"I went to Juan-les-Pins to find Moira." She swallows. "It was one of the craziest things I've ever done."

His eyes fill with amazement. "Why *there?*"

She crouches beside him. "I found some letters from Pierre in Moira's bureau."

"You never told me."

"I wanted to prove they could lead somewhere. And they have."

Disbelief, joy and triumph flash across his face as he listens to her story. He grabs the letter from her shaking hand. He reads it, tears sparkling on his cheeks.

"Mama is alive ... I can't believe it. How can I ever thank you?"

"She might have returned to St Ives to find you. Now that Pierre is dead—"

"But she might not."

"We'll never know. Things have changed for her—"

"And for me." He wipes his face. "Out of all recognition."

"What will you do?"

"I've no idea ... I can't think straight."

She glances reluctantly at her watch. "Will you forgive me? I have to go. I'll meet you back here for luncheon at one o'clock. And I hope Anne will be with me. I can't promise, but—"

"Yes, of course." For a brief, wonderful moment he takes her in his arms. "You'll *never* know how grateful I am and how much I love you, my darling. Hurry back."

Anne spends an hour in the dress shop, trying on half their stock.

Eleanor paces around, trying to be patient. When Anne can't decide between two outfits, Eleanor buys both and hustles her into the street. She's decided to tell her mother about Felix as they drive back to Woodstock. Anne will *have* to listen. She won't be able to flounce away or call for Vera.

"Thank you *so* much," Anne says happily. "I adore *both* frocks. I shan't know which one to wear."

Eleanor mutters, "I wish *my* problems were as easy to solve." She takes her mother's arm, guides her through the traffic. "I have something extremely important to tell you. We're going straight home, fast."

But when she tries to start the Morris, the engine coughs and dies. She stares at the dashboard in disbelief. There's no mistaking that crashing red finger on the dial. No petrol.

"Honestly, Eleanor! This isn't like you at all. You're usually so well organised!" Anne grabs her handbag. "I can't be late for Jonny. He's leaving for Wales this afternoon. I'll run for the bus. Ring the garage from that shop over there. They can send a mechanic."

In tears of frustration, Eleanor stands in a cramped back office, ringing first the Woodstock garage, then The Bear.

"Could I leave a message for Mr Felix Mitchell, please? My car's broken down and I'll be late. *Very* late ... Could you ask him to meet me for tea at four o'clock? My name's Eleanor Drummond."

The day becomes a nightmare of waiting. And then it gets worse. The mechanic says she'll have to wait for at least an hour.

She leaves the shop and the car, and wanders into town. She might as well have a sandwich in the Covered Market. Thinking about Felix, longing to be with him, she finds herself at the Cadena Café.

As she pushes at the door, she hears a baby crying. Sitting in a corner, rocking the handle of a fashionable perambulator, is Perdita Willoughby-Jones.

They stare at each other.

Perdita turns scarlet. She jigs the pram up and down with increased fervour. Its hood is decorated with a flapping pink-satin bow.

Eleanor says, "My *God!* How wonderful to see you again!"

Perdita gives her a crimson smile. "You too."

"May I join you?"

"Of course." Perdita can hardly refuse. "This is my daughter, Rosemary."

A violent wail comes from beneath the pram's hood. Eleanor pokes her head around to take a good look. The baby opens her eyes to take a good look back. Her eyes are Walter's violet-blue eyes, her nose is Walter's nose.

Eleanor straightens her back and takes a deep breath. She touches Perdita's shoulder. She says with all the courage she can muster, "Your daughter looks very like Walter." She can hardly get the words out. "Is she … Did you … Is it possible? Tell me I'm wrong, Perdy. *Please* tell me I'm talking nonsense."

She collapses on the nearest chair.

Perdita looks down at the baby, then at Eleanor. "It only happened once. We'd been to the picture house on Walton Street. You were with us. You went off to powder your nose. Your father invited me out. We were in the back row and we'd been holding hands. It was extremely stupid of me to respond, to flirt with him, but I did. There was something irresistible about him.

"We went to a small hotel in North Oxford." Her eyes fill with tears. "I thought maybe we'd have a late supper, a glass of champagne, a romantic kiss and cuddle. But Walter had only one thing on his mind. At the last moment, I panicked. I tried to stop him, but he was surprisingly strong. He didn't *threaten* me, exactly, but he told me I knew what I was doing and he certainly didn't give me a chance to get away. I risked my neck for him, too. I nearly fell, climbing a wall, getting into College after midnight."

"Is that why you chose to leave Somerville?"

Perdita gives a sharp, high laugh. "I didn't *choose*, dear little naïve Eleanor! I was pushed. Somebody must have spotted Walter and me together. It might have been Scroggs. He's always been a bit of a spy as well as Head Porter. I was summoned to see Miss Darbishire. She was absolutely vile. She told me I was a total disgrace, that I'd let everyone down, that I didn't deserve a place at Somerville. Ten minutes later, Scroggs helped me pack."

"But what did you——"

"Tell my parents? That I'd had enough of College life. That I wasn't a bluestocking. When I discovered I was pregnant they were furious. So was I. I wrote to Walter but he didn't bother to reply. I never saw him again. He'd had his way with me and it was obvious he didn't give a damn. My parents packed me off to Paris. I had Rosemary there."

Eleanor clenches her fists. "I'm so terribly sorry, Perdita. I can't *believe* my father could have behaved like——"

"Can't you? Miss Darbishire knew all about him. She implied I was having an affair with a well-known philanderer."

"Perhaps it's just as well I've also left Somerville!"

"I'm married now, you know. No more Willoughby-Jones for me. I'm Mrs Martin Travis. We own one of those swanky houses in Park Town – and we put up a decent pretence that Rosemary's *our* child. I married one of my father's friends, see? Second wife, young, glamorous, all that twaddle. Martin's stinking rich and if I'm perfectly honest a bit of a bore. He loves horses and golf. But he's safe."

Perdita glances at the wailing infant thrashing her arms and legs around like a tiny windmill. "A safe pair of hands. That's what my manipulating mother said I needed. And that's what I've got!" She starts rocking the pram again to drown the noise. "We'd better go. The only thing that stops

Rosemary bawling is being on the move."

Eleanor watches Perdita stand up, pull on her hat, and wheel the pram away.

Sick to her stomach, she finds she has no appetite.

The car mechanic gives her a lecture about always carrying a spare can of petrol in the boot. When she finally climbs into the Morris to drive home, the traffic on the Woodstock Road has slowed to a snail's pace. There had been an accident at the roundabout. The usual twenty-minute drive extends like loose elastic to an hour.

By the time she gets home, tired, frustrated and famished, she has to face a list of queries from Vera. At a quarter-past four, she slams out of the house and makes a dash for The Bear.

Felix is nowhere to be seen. He's not outside the hotel, or sitting in the bar, or reading a newspaper in the lounge. The restaurant is empty apart from an elderly waiter polishing glasses and humming a weary tune.

She stands at reception and asks for Felix Mitchell. Frowning, the receptionist consults her list. "I'm sorry, Miss. Mr Mitchell has checked out."

"I'd arranged to meet him here for tea."

"May I have your name?"

"Eleanor Drummond." Her mouth is so dry she can hardly speak. "I rang—"

"Ah, yes, Miss Drummond. Mr Mitchell left you a note."

Her heart skips several beats and then seems to freeze before thumping into overdrive, leaving her breathless.

"Thank you." She stares at the envelope. There's no mistake. It has her name on it.

She sits at a table in the empty bar. The black letters jump up and down in front of her eyes. She tries to steady her hands.

My darling Eleanor

I feel so humiliated. You haven't told Anne about me. About us. I just know in my heart you haven't. I understand – or I'm trying to! But I couldn't bear to listen to any more of your excuses today. Or tomorrow. Or the day after that.

I've laid all my cards on your table. I can't do any more than travel to Woodstock to offer you everything I have. Now I'll drive home without you, because I can't bear another night here with you so close to me and yet so far.

I love you. Look at my portrait of you in your scarlet frock. See the love in it, in every single swirl of glorious paint. Remember how we danced together when you wore it. Please remember me.

I shall be leaving for Juan-les-Pins to see Mama as soon as I can. Thank you from the bottom of my heart for bringing us together.

Always your loving
Felix

Reaching Cinq Saisons

1936

Felix Mitchell swings himself on to Le Train Bleu. He wears his cream linen suit, a blue paisley scarf instead of a tie, new patent leather shoes and crimson leather gloves. He looks a real dandy. He *feels* a real dandy. He's beside himself with joy.

Felix springs up and down Le Train Bleu, tipping his hat at the ladies, grinning benignly at the gentlemen.

"*Bonjour, Madame … Bonjour, Mademoiselle …*"

The fact that it's early evening doesn't bother him. He never wears a watch.

The ladies gasp, whether they want to or not. Who's that *ravishing* man, they ask each other, fluttering their fans, murmuring like turtle doves.

Mon Dieu! Those eyes! That hair! So comme il faut!

He sits down to dinner on Le Train Bleu, alone at his own table.

Beneath the cream linen suit, he's skin and bone. He

never knows when it's time for lunch or supper. But a dinner like this – wafer-thin smoked salmon with cool cucumber, roast duck, creamed potatoes fluffy as air, goat's cheese with delicate oat cakes, raspberries with the lightest touch of cream – well! He savours every morsel. He drinks every glass of whatever is offered with a graceful gesture of gratitude, slinging it down his throat as if he were a parched well.

He's ravenous with excitement and joy.

After the meal, ignoring several silently implied requests from three splendid-looking women, he lurches back to his compartment, clinging to the sides of the train as if they were his boon companions.

He manages to take off his suit and hang it up. Placing both hands on the window, he gazes out. It's twilight. He has no idea where he is, only that soon he'll meet his Mama again. The woman he hasn't seen since the day of the storm.

It feels like yesterday.

He collapses on the lower deck of the bunk bed.

He's asleep before he can say goodnight.

Le Train Bleu rocks and hisses on its way. He hears only that marvellous voice in his ears. His Mama's voice, when she sang him lullabies, when his skin itched until it bled – but her singing made it all better.

He wakes to the glow of dawn: a pearly sky, lit with bands of sapphire. He wants to paint it. He needs his brushes, his smock, his easel. He longs to capture for immortality this most special of dawns.

Over scalding black coffee and three croissants, so light he feels he's hardly eaten anything, his fingernails immaculate, his scarf at an oh so debonair angle, Felix Mitchell decides he's the happiest man alive.

He steps on to land at Juan-les-Pins.

He knows exactly where he needs to go.

He'd asked Eleanor for directions. His one and only Eleanor …

Heavens above! What a find *she's* been. So swift, so easy. So *interesting*. Her *face*. Her *mannerisms*. Her beautiful slim body.

He swallows a lump in his throat.

Then he moves on.

It's still early morning, not yet hot enough for a baking sun. He's aware of being surrounded by tall green trees. Enormous pines. He can smell them, their high yet musky scent. He walks and walks. He's in a trance. He moves through an air that nurses the sweet scent of oleander.

Is it really oleander? Or lavender? Or something like it?

He stands still for a moment to sniff the sky.

He shivers.

He can smell cloves.

O God, dearest God above, he can smell the scent of cloves.

He looks above his head to a sign swinging in the newly sprung breeze:

Cinq Saisons

He's here. Where he should have been years ago. He wants to bow to the powers of the green hills that have led him safely thus far to such miraculous purpose.

He adjusts his scarf, flicks back his hair, licks dry lips.

He reaches out to press the bell.

The gates swing open.

The villa's front door opens.

There stands a pert little maid in an adorable ice-white apron with frills at its adorable edge.

"*Bonjour, Monsieur.*" Her voice is sweet, high-pitched, like a child's.

He stutters and stammers. He speaks in English, because he has no idea at that moment how to use any other language: "Madame Tessier?"

Then he clears his throat. He sounds like an ageing parrot trying out a new set of words.

"*Madame Tessier ... Please ... Is she at home?*"

He has to ask the question with great care in case it comes out backwards.

The maid answers him in good clear English. "Yes, sir. She is. Who shall I say is calling?"

He says, "I am her son." He swallows. Tears well up from his entire body.

"Could you tell her, please? *My name is Felix Mitchell and I am her son.*"

A New Partner

1936

"So *then* what did you do?" Kath asks.

Eleanor and Kath walk together in Blenheim two days later, on Wednesday evening, the air sharp with a first touch of autumn chill, the path wet with the previous day's rain.

"What *could* I do? Climb into the Morris and follow Felix to Cornwall? I wanted to, I can tell you. I was furious he'd assumed I'd said nothing to Anne. What if I *had*? She'd have been upset, maybe devastated – but I hope prepared to meet him. And I'd have looked a complete idiot."

"But he was right, Ellie. You hadn't told her anythin'."

"No, and by the time I got home, he'd vanished and I'd lost my nerve. I felt so appalled by my father's behaviour with Perdita that I could hardly think straight. Baby Rosemary is my half-sister! Darling Daddy indeed ... How can you go on loving somebody who behaves like that?

"I went up to my room, shaking like a leaf. And there was Moira's painting, hanging on my wall. I'd forgotten to tell Felix I'd bought it."

"So what *will* you do?"

"Give myself until Christmas. I need the autumn to make sure the tea-room will survive. And I need time to tell Anne about Felix."

"And what do you think *he'll* do?"

"First he'll find his Mama. When he gets home again … Well, they say absence makes the heart grow fonder, don't they? If he really loves me, a few short months of waiting won't make any difference."

"But what if they *do*?"

"They won't." Her voice shakes. "He bought a little two-seater Austin Seven, specially to drive to Woodstock. He spent weeks finishing my portrait. I've got to risk it, Kath. I must be able to *trust* him."

Kath sighs. "I don't know how I'd survive without knowin' Sean and I will be neighbours until we're wed. We see each other every day, even if it's only for half an hour."

"I wanted to talk to you about that. Well, not about your wedding, but your plans for the future. Vera wants a holiday in September. Would you like to take her place for a fortnight? Come to work with me?"

"Ellie! *There's* a surprise!"

"Actually, I want to ask you a lot more than that. Vera started up the tea-room with me, and I couldn't have done it without her. But by the end of the day, she's exhausted. I don't know how much longer she'll want to go on working so hard. She has the money Walter left her—"

"What exactly are you saying?"

"I'd like you to join me as my partner. Those two weeks in September could let you find out whether you enjoy it. You'd have your own kitchen. You could choose your staff. You'll earn more than the Palace pays you. And when I manage to scrape up the courage to move to Cornwall, you'd be in sole charge. I'd have a partner who could share the responsibility – and the rewards." She throws an arm around Kath. "Are you interested?"

Kath looks at her with shining eyes. "Of course I am! That Palace kitchen is so hot and crowded. I'm sick of Cook bossin' me around when I know I can prepare any food you name better than she can ... I'll have to tell Sean, but I'm sure he won't object."

That night Eleanor sits at her desk, writing Felix a note of apology and explanations, disappointment and longing, promises and passion.

She waits for his reply. It arrives a fortnight later, full of love. He's ecstatic about Moira, her villa and the beauties of the Riviera. Eleanor burns with jealousy. She longs to be back at Juan-les-Pins, sharing the joy of his reunion.

She hides the painting of the girl in red taffeta under her bed. If Anne sees it, a string of questions will follow. When the showdown happens, she's determined to plan its time and place.

Every Saturday afternoon, when she closes the tea-room, she longs to climb into the Morris and drive to St Ives. Surely Felix must be home by now? She imagines travelling through the night, sleeping for an hour in a lay-by, pushing on again until she reaches the sea – and the love and reassurance of his arms. A briefly snatched day and a single night with him would be better than this silence: a chance to pledge their love, make plans for the future.

But at every Saturday's end, she hesitates. She busies herself with the chores – and lets the brief opportunity slip away into the dusk.

On the Riviera Terrace

1936

"I'm so glad you told me." Felix swings one lean leg over the other. His long fingers hold the dainty glass of the best champagne.

He and his beloved Mama have talked for hours. It's time for luncheon on the Riviera terrace, but neither of them have an appetite.

She says, "It wasn't easy. But I wanted you to know. And about time."

"Of course. But what happened wasn't *your* fault." He swallows back the bile which had fought its way up his throat in spite of the bubbly. His stomach wants to retch, his mouth to spew vomit. "Walter was a monster."

"Many are."

"But he *hid* it so well." Felix drums his fingers against his glass. "When I was a child, growing up without him, the highlights of my little life were seeing him again. For the snatched weekend in Newlyn, then in St Ives. *I had no idea.*"

"Secrets and lies, my darling boy!" Moira pushes herself from her low wicker chair. She raises her arms to smooth

348

her hair. Her body is slim and taut; she has the exquisite posture of a dancer.

He runs his professional eye over the widow's black lace dress, the narrow waist, the straight back, the shining hair, the extraordinary poise.

"I should love to paint your portrait, Mama. You're still very beautiful."

A deep blush rises from Moira's throat to her cheeks. She smiles at him, but there's more than a flash of sadness in her cornflower-blue eyes.

"When Walter called me beautiful I used to *resent* it. I'd think, oh God, here we go again. It'll be another ghastly night. Me saying no, please *no*. Walter denying I had a choice." Her voice darkens. "Denying I no longer wanted him."

He stands to take her in his arms. "But it's all over now, isn't it, Mama?"

She pulls away. "No, darling boy. That's the whole point. It's *never* over, even though it happened so long ago. Memories like mine never fade." She hesitates. "Besides—"

"Yes? Tell me."

"There was worse." Her voice chokes. "I could tell you, but I never want you to know."

"But I'm here precisely to be *told*—"

"No." She takes his hand. "It would be pointless. Let's go and eat."

He raises her hand to his lips. "Come back to The Hideaway with me in a few weeks' time. I want you to see what I've done to it. You surely can't be planning to stay here on your own?"

"I promise to visit you. But I won't ever live in The Hideaway again."

"You mean there are too many ghosts?"

She looks past him, out to the blue of the Mediterranean Sea.

"I mean," she says, "there are too many ghosts – and worse."

The Engagement

1936

Having Kath in the tea-room kitchen during the two mid-September weeks comes as a revelation. She works at twice Vera's speed, invents fresh recipes, gives Eleanor ideas for their winter menu, introduces her to new suppliers, adjusts the tea-room's prices slightly upwards – and even makes her laugh at the end of the day when they're both exhausted. Their partnership, born of years of friendship, now has the excitement of a new challenge.

"I wish I'd brought you in at the very start," Eleanor says.

The fortnight's over. They're sitting in the kitchen on a Saturday evening over fresh sandwiches and a bottle of Chablis. "But back in July, I had no idea whether this would succeed. I had so much to learn. I couldn't have asked you then to take the risk."

"I've had the happiest two weeks of my workin' life. It's hard and fast – but it's so much fun."

"So where do we go from here?"

"I'll have to give the Palace proper notice, but I could be

free to join you at the start of November. How does that sound?"

"Perfect. It'll give me time to talk to Vera, who can go back to being our housekeeper. And I'll get the legal stuff signed and sealed with Michael Humphreys."

"Have you told Anne about me joinin' you?"

"Not yet." She refills their glasses. "I hardly see her these days. She's either working for Jonny or gadding about. But she always leaves the business side of things to me."

At the end of September, Maud visits Blenheim for a week's holiday, looking smarter than ever. She's bursting with royal news.

"Edward and Wallis spent all summer cruisin' the Mediterranean on a yacht called the *Nahlin*," she tells them on Sunday evening over supper at Fishery Cottage. "The King walked around those small seaside towns stripped to the waist, with Wallis in tow. He ain't got no royal dignity."

"With everyone snapping their cameras?" Eleanor asks.

"Of course. The papers in America and Europe are *full* of the scandal. They said that Wallis seemed fed up with Edward. She travelled to Paris on her own. Then she told him she wanted to go back to her husband. The King went crazy. He said he couldn't live without her and threatened to slit his throat. Now her divorce is goin' through, exactly as he'd planned. God only knows where it'll end."

"At least he knows what he wants."

"But what does his *country* want? The minute Wallis is a free woman, I can see everythin' coming to the boil. Just you watch and wait."

Eleanor's doing the same: watching and waiting.

At the end of September a letter from Felix finally arrives.

He'd spent a glorious month in Juan-les-Pins. Now he has a ton of work to do. He loves her. His bed is cold and lonely. He's eternally grateful to her for finding Moira. But he makes no mention whatsoever of their future.

She's suddenly filled with dread. She may have kept her promise to her father. But in the process, has she lost the man she loves?

Both Robin and Michael approve her plan for Kath to join as her new partner. One Wednesday afternoon at the end of October, after she's signed the contract in Michael's office, Eleanor rushes to the drawing room to show Anne the document.

"It's done and dusted, Mummy." She throws open the door. "I'm *so* excited. I have a new partner—"

Anne stands beside the fire in Jonny's arms. Her lipstick is smudged, her hair tumbles around her shoulders, her eyes glitter with happiness.

"Congratulations, Eleanor," Anne says. "And I have a new fiancé."

"I *beg* your pardon?"

Her mother grips Jonny's hands. "We're engaged. You're the first to know. Jonny asked me to marry him on Saturday. I couldn't *wait* to say yes. I'd been *longing* for him to ask. We *adore* one another."

"Good God, Mummy." She clutches the back of the sofa. "You hardly *know*—"

Jonny breaks free of Anne and moves swiftly towards his future stepdaughter. "I hope you don't mind, Eleanor." His voice is thick with emotion. "I made a complete fool of myself with you, but the fact is that my darling Annie and I are much closer in age. We've both lost someone we love and we turned to each other for comfort." He glances lovingly at Anne. "After we started working together, we realised how well we fitted into each other's lives … I'm a *very* lucky man."

"I've been so busy I didn't notice." She flops on to the sofa. "I don't know what to say."

"That you're happy for us." Anne sits beside her. "You can stop worrying about me now. Jonny will take care of me."

"Care for you *both*," he says quickly. "Not that you need it, Eleanor, you're so independent. I could never replace Walter, but——"

"No, indeed, thank you." Her mind fizzes with shock. "You could never be my ..." She tries to control her voice. "So when——"

"We're planning to marry on Saturday the 12th of December." Anne looks at Jonny for confirmation. "We'd like to spend our honeymoon in Europe. I'd love to go to Paris, and Jonny wants to visit Florence and Rome. We'll ask Stephen and his wife to run Jonny's shop over Christmas."

"And where——"

"We'll hold the ceremony at the Register Office in Oxford and have a small party here in the tea-room, if that's all right with you. We don't want to make too much of a song and dance."

"And where will you live?"

Jonny sits down the other side of Eleanor. "We thought I could move in here, after we're married. But only with your approval."

"We'll keep this drawing room for ourselves," Anne says. "But next summer you could certainly expand into the garden——"

Eleanor stands up, desperate to be on her own. "I'm

delighted for you both. I hope you'll be very happy together." She drops the new contract into Anne's lap. "If you could read this, make sure you've no objections—" She makes a dash for the door.

Jonny says, "Before you go …"

She turns to face him. He looks young and buoyant. His coppery curls gleam. His eyes shine with a gratitude both infuriating and disarming.

"Thank you for giving us your blessing, Eleanor. I *promise* you won't regret it. I intend to make your mother the happiest woman in the world." He slides towards Anne, flinging an arm around her. "Don't I, my darling girl?"

Anne lifts her face for Jonny's kiss, as if there's nobody else in the room.

Eleanor crashes into the kitchen.

Vera says, "Good *gracious*, dear heart, whatever's the matter? Have you seen a ghost?"

"I think there might be one in the drawing room."

"In the—"

"My father's ghost … Mummy will explain. Jonny's in there with her. Could you take them a tray of tea? If I do it, I might throw it at them."

"Eleanor!" Vera almost drops a plate of cakes. "What on *earth* has happened?"

"Can you manage without me for half an hour? There's something I must do."

She marches out of the house and starts to run. Through the Triumphal Arch and the sweep of Blenheim's parkland. Up to the front of the Palace, round the side to the stables. She even startles the horses.

Sean emerges from behind a black mare he'd been

355

grooming. "What's the matter, Eleanor?"

"Where's Kath?" She has a stitch in her side; she bends double to get rid of it. "I must talk to her."

Sean strokes the mare's nose to keep her calm. "She's at Fishery Cottage. It's Wednesday afternoon. Remember?"

"Of course." She pushes her hair out of her eyes. "Sorry, I forgot." She starts to run again.

Sean stares after her, shaking his head.

"I don't understand why you're makin' such an almighty fuss." Kath takes a tray of scones out of the oven. "Way I sees it, your mother's engagement's got to be good news."

"But Jonny proposed to *me*——"

"You turned him down, Ellie. It's not as if he's been seein' Anne behind your back! She and Jonny are both old enough to know what they want. It may not be love's young dream, but I reckon they're lucky to have found each other. It gives your mother a second chance of happiness. And it gives you a wonderful opportunity."

"To do what exactly? Be maid of honour at some stupid ceremony? Smile, throw confetti and eat their disgusting wedding cake? The whole thing's obscene."

"Can't you see? It gives you a chance to escape."

"You want me to climb into my Morris and disappear in a cloud of October dust?"

"Not *now*, course not. But *after* the weddin', when your mother and Jonny are on honeymoon, after we've closed the tea-room for Christmas, what's to stop you leavin' then?"

"What indeed? Mummy only wanted me here because she couldn't face life on her own. Now she's got Jonny to pay the bills, she'll hardly notice I've gone."

"I know someone who *will* notice."

"Who?" The knot of anger in Eleanor's stomach feels the

size of a melon. "Who the *hell* will either notice or care?"

"*I* will, you silly little lump of lard! Give me a hug, for heaven's sake. I'm goin' to run that tea-room of yours whether you're here or not – and don't you never forget it. But I'll be missin' you loads and I ain't afraid to say so."

The two girls stand for a moment in each other's arms.

"I'm sorry, Kath." Eleanor's voice comes thick with tears. "This has happened so *fast*. I can't keep up."

"Oh, yes, you can. We've got until the weddin' to make our plans ship-shape. Don't you go sayin' nothin' to Anne about any of 'em. When she and Jonny have gone, you can leave a letter explainin' everythin'. And *then* you can go down to Cornwall, and claim that man of yours who's waitin' so patiently for you by the big blue sea."

"Do you think we can plan everything without Anne finding out?"

"She'll be far too busy to think about anythin' besides her trousseau."

"That's *certainly* true—"

"But I'll only do this on one condition. I want you back here in Woodstock with me for a whole week every three months. So you can keep an eye on the tea-room. Check the books. Talk about any changes we need to make. I ain't prepared to do this on my own. Your tea-room is called *Eleanor's*, after all. Remember?"

"That place has cost me blood, sweat and hundreds of worried hours."

"That's settled, then. We're goin' to need someone to replace you as a waitress. I'll ask around, unofficial like. By the way, I'm goin' to make two hundred small Christmas puddin's and wrap 'em as gifts. We'll make a profit of five pence a puddin'. How does that sound?"

"What *would* I do without you?" Eleanor straightens her

shoulders. "I'm going home to write to Felix. He'll be over the moon."

By the time Eleanor gets back, a small crowd of well-wishers have gathered to drink Anne and Jonny's health. Unable to contain her joy, Anne had rung Sylvia to tell her the good news.

Vera, flushed and happy – "You've got it wrong, dear heart. It's *wonderful* news. I've always liked Mr Giffen. He's a real gentleman" – makes sandwiches and cuts slices of her best cakes.

Tired and ravenous, Eleanor sits in the kitchen. She drinks a pot of tea and crams two cucumber sandwiches down her throat, tasting nothing. She can't face the hubbub of voices, the radiance in Anne's eyes, the bursts of Jonny's laughter. She disappears to the silence of her room.

Her anger subsides. A wild jealousy of her mother's happiness replaces it. The celebrations *should* have been for her and Felix. His arrival had given her a chance of happiness, but she hadn't been brave enough to take it.

She could still find an opportunity to tell Anne about him. While her mother's so happy on her own account, might she not greet her daughter's news with unusual tolerance? Isn't the time to tell her exactly *now*, before she's become too entangled in wedding preparations?

Kath's suggestion that Eleanor should say and do nothing until Anne is on her honeymoon is a practical solution, but it's also a coward's way out. To hide behind a letter when it's too late for talk, for explanations – indeed, for Anne's improbable but not impossible blessing – makes Eleanor feel uncomfortable. She should want to shout about Felix's love from the rooftops, not mope around, keeping him a secret.

One reason she doesn't discuss her love life with Anne is

358

that she's no longer sure how Felix feels about her. His letters are full of love, but they are also few and far between. She only hopes that no news is good news.

Writing to him now with news of Anne's engagement might break his silence. A week later it does. He sends her an ecstatic card: he's delighted that Anne will soon be off her hands. And then he asks again: "Have you told her yet about *me*?"

The atmosphere in the Woodstock house changes from muted sadness to gentle joy.

Anne herself is increasingly absent. Often entire nights go by when she doesn't come home. Eleanor is only too aware of her mother's empty bedroom, but she makes no comment. Anne is perfectly entitled to spend the night in Jonny's arms. Eleanor doesn't have a querulous leg to stand on. And she's reluctant to start talking about herself in case the temptation to tell Anne about Felix overtakes her, leaving her in deep water. She prefers to flounder in the shallows, talking about the wedding party, frocks and flowers, while she plans her letter to *Dear Mummy*.

Then she starts to worry about Vera. She doesn't dare tell her about her plans until after Anne and Jonny have left for Paris. Vera might disapprove, or feel it's her duty to tell Anne. And how will she feel about Kath taking over the tea-room? About Eleanor becoming a sleeping partner?

At the end of October, in preparation for Kath's permanent arrival, and after a meeting with her accountant when he tells her she can never be "too professional", she buys an Underwood typewriter for thirty pounds, carries it up to her room and plonks it on her desk. Between now and Christmas, she'll teach herself to type.

On Sunday the 1st of November, the day before Kath takes over the kitchen, Eleanor makes herself clear out Walter's studio, insisting on doing it without Vera. Anne is in Aberystwyth on a shopping trip with Jonny.

The job is depressing. She gets halfway through and decides to call a halt. Kath has enough space to store preserves, bottles and Christmas puddings. Eleanor pushes the chaise longue against the wall, remembering her precious hours of love on it. Throwing out Walter's half-finished paintings is unbearable. Instead, she stores them in neat piles at the far end of the room.

She collects the paintbrushes he'd used, sorts out the best dozen, cleans them, wraps them in her handkerchief and puts them in the desk. A gift for Felix …

Her last chore is to find the old broom. The floor is thick with dust. Two old rugs lie on it, their corners frayed. She rolls them up, intending to throw them away. She starts to sweep the floorboards and notices a small metal rung attached to a board beneath the chaise longue. Curious, she pushes the furniture aside. She tugs at the rung. The floorboard lifts immediately. Beneath it lie two large sketch pads. Her heart thrums as she pulls them out.

The first is filled with charcoal drawings of a naked woman. Eleanor flushes with shock and recognition. A single face looks back at her.

It's Moira's. She's lying in bed and out of it, on the floor with cushions behind her. Eleanor flicks through the pages. Detailed drawings of arms and shoulders, legs and thighs, hands and faces follow.

Eleanor closes the sketch pad and opens the second one. She gasps. Perdita Willoughby-Jones looks back at her, stark naked.

Eleanor's stomach churns. Without turning another page, she stuffs both sketch pads back into their hiding place. She has no idea when Walter drew them, or that he'd managed to get Perdita to pose for him. She doesn't want to see any more. Part of her never wants to look at Walter's work again. She'd like to hurtle out of the studio and never come back.

Trembling, exhausted and overcome with sadness, she closes the trapdoor, pushes the chaise longue over it, and makes sure that a couple of old cushions nestle together on the floor. Nobody else will find that tell-tale rung, or bother to lift it to discover its secret.

The following day, Kath arrives to check Vera's stock, bringing the two hundred Christmas puddings with her in Sean's van. They unload the fragrant gifts and store them in the studio. Eleanor is heartily relieved when she can close its door again.

At noon, Maud appears unexpectedly. She invites them to luncheon at a small restaurant in Woodstock, relating more anecdotes about the King.

"Wallis Simpson's divorce was heard in Ipswich on the 27th of October," she tells them. "God only knows what's goin' to happen next."

That night, Eleanor flicks through *The Times*, thinking how ironical it is that the King has never been so popular, and how much he'll be missed if he does abdicate.

On the 27th of November, a morganatic marriage is finally opposed by the Cabinet. By early December, news of the dangers that Wallis poses have become public knowledge. Customers in *Eleanor's* gossip about it, scandalised by the news.

Wallis receives poison-pen letters. When a stone is thrown

through the window of her London flat, Edward insists that she leave immediately for Fort Belvedere. On the 3rd of December, grim-faced, without a word of thanks to her staff, Wallis leaves for the south of France, taking with her one hundred thousand pounds' worth of jewellery: gifts from her blond, blue-eyed and besotted King.

On the 9th of December, Edward is officially asked one last time to reconsider his decision to abdicate: to wait for a year, during which it's hoped that his passion for Wallis will cool. He's asked to attend his Coronation, to accept his role as King without Wallis, and then possibly marry her at a later date.

Edward rejects every suggestion. Many of his advisers think he's losing his mind as well as his throne. They monitor his every move and phone call, looking to his younger brother, Bertie, with his embarrassing stammer, strong-willed wife and pretty daughters, to inherit his title and restore sanity to the Empire.

Meanwhile, Anne plans her wedding outfit with extreme care and a lot of help from Eleanor. They shop in Oxford and buy a cream velvet suit with a tight, low-cut jacket and a long flowing skirt. Anne looks stunning in it: slim, elegant and glamorous. Eleanor chooses a pale pink satin frock. She doesn't really like it, but Anne does. For the moment, keeping her mother happy is Eleanor's top priority.

On the eve of the wedding, Jonny puts a beautifully wrapped box into Eleanor's hands. "Anne told me how much you loved Walter's pearls," he says awkwardly. "You've been wonderful to us, you've organised our party so brilliantly. I can't wait for the three of us to be a proper family. But I want you to have this, to wear at the wedding. Don't open it now. You'll only embarrass me."

Alone in her room, Eleanor opens the gift, her fingers trembling. Jonny has given her another necklace: three strands of perfectly round natural pearls finished with an emerald clasp. They are breathtakingly beautiful and must have cost a fortune.

She bursts into tears. She doesn't want jewels or a pink frock or a new stepfather; nor to have to make complicated decisions that will affect the rest of her life. She wants her father back in Woodstock, in spite of everything – and Felix by her side.

Later that night, on Friday the 11th of December at ten o'clock, Eleanor sits in the drawing room with Anne, Jonny and Vera. She turns on the wireless. Sir John Reith, Director of the BBC, announces, "This is Windsor Castle. His Royal Highness, Prince Edward." And the sad, quiet voice of the Prince of Wales takes up his story:

"At long last I am able to say a few words of my own. I have never wanted to withhold anything, but until now it has not been constitutionally possible for me to speak. A few hours ago I discharged my last duty as King and Emperor, and now that I have been succeeded by my brother, the Duke of York, my first words must be to declare my allegiance to him. This I do with all my heart.

"You all know the reasons which have impelled me to renounce the throne, but I want you to understand that in making up my mind I did not forget the Country or the Empire, which, as Prince of Wales and lately as King, I have for twenty-five years tried to serve. But you must believe me when I tell you that I have found it impossible to carry out the heavy burden of responsibility and to discharge my duties as King, as I wish to do, without the help and support of the woman I love. I want you to know that the decision I have made has been mine and mine alone.

"And now we all have a new King. I wish Him, and you, His people, happiness and prosperity with all my heart. God bless you all. God save the King."

There is a long silence. Eleanor switches off the wireless, her heart racing.

Jonny says, "Crikey! I bet that brother of his is having sleepless nights. Poor old Bertie can hardly get a word out without stammering. How on earth is *he* going to speak to the nation?"

Vera says, "The one *I* like is Elizabeth. She's such a sensible little girl. She'll make the most dignified Queen. Not like that snooty American. Never trusted her further than I could spit. Edward must be out of his mind. Imagine spending the rest of your life following Wallis around."

Anne says, "Well, *I* think it's so romantic. Fancy giving up a throne for your girl! It's the love story of the century." She turns to Jonny. "What would *you* give up for *me*, my darling boy?"

Jonny gazes into Anne's eyes. "Pretty much everything," he says. "But luckily for me, that won't be necessary."

Eleanor bites her lip and stays silent.

Spelling It Out

1936

The morning of Anne's wedding dawns clear and surprisingly mild – unlike Eleanor.

She feels jealousy, relief, resentment, and a grudging admiration for her mother, about to step into the arms of a second husband with such elegance and ease.

"I'll never forget your father." Anne adjusts her glorious hat, checks her flowing hemline one last time. "We had some good years together before he decided to sample the delights of other women. But Jonny's such *fun*. He makes me feel *young* again. And I'm not going to give him a chance to be unfaithful." She turns to Eleanor. "How do I look?"

"Beautiful. Now hurry up. Jonny's waiting for you in Oxford. You'd better not give him the chance to marry anybody else."

The ceremony goes without a hitch. The luncheon party in the tea-room is gentle and merry. If anyone apart from Eleanor remembers Walter, nobody mentions him.

By three o'clock the guests have eaten the delicate cold

meats and salads, drunk more than is good for them, and devoured Vera's succulent wedding cake. In their hats, coat-tails and rustling skirts, brushing away the crumbs, murmuring good wishes, they drift away.

Jonny, intoxicated and beside himself with happiness, flings an arm around his bride. He beckons to Eleanor and pours three glasses of champagne.

"Before we leave, a final toast to my two girls ... Here's to love."

Anne smiles up at him, raising her glass. She looks at Eleanor. "To love such as Jonny's and mine," she says. "I hope you'll find it one day."

"Oh, didn't you know?" Jonny grips Anne's hand. "Eleanor's already found the love of her life."

"I *beg* your pardon?"

Eleanor signals to Jonny to keep quiet. He doesn't register her frantic appeal. He's looking at the rise and fall of Anne's breasts above the low-cut jacket.

"It's one of the many reasons," Jonny continues blithely, "that Eleanor turned me down. And I'm so glad she did!" He glances at Eleanor's face, abruptly realising he's said too much.

But it's too late.

Anne says, "What the *hell* you are talking about?"

Jonny comes to his senses. "Crikey!" His eyelashes flutter. "So you *still* don't know?" The champagne froths in his glass. "Eleanor met someone in St Ives, darling. She told me months ago that she was head-over-heels in love." He sways on his feet. "Now I'm *in loco parentis*, I feel you ought to know." He takes another swig. "Oh Lord! Have I let the infernal cat out of its bag?"

Anne takes Eleanor by her pink satin arm and pushes her upstairs, into the untidiness of her bedroom. Closing the door, she kicks off her shoes and collapses on to the bed.

"Right, dear daughter of mine. Exactly what cat and what bag?"

For a moment Eleanor stands there, feeling like a schoolgirl caught playing truant. She could deny everything. Pretend that Jonny had misunderstood her. She'd invented a lover in order to turn him down. There *had* been somebody special, but not any more.

Then she decides: the moment of truth has arrived. She'll come clean. It's too late for Anne to do anything about it – and it's too good an opportunity to miss.

She crosses the room and stands looking out of the window, her face turned away from her mother's furious stare.

"If you must know, I'll tell you … I'm in love with Felix Mitchell."

"*What?*" Anne hoists herself upright, making the bed springs creak.

Briefly, Eleanor spells everything out.

"After Daddy died, I felt so lonely." She fights the tears, overwhelmed by memories. "Meeting Felix allowed me to share Daddy's life." She swallows. "And then we became lovers."

"You went to *bed* with him?" Astonished, accusatory, the shrill words hang in the stuffy air.

"Yes." Her confession brings a deep blush to her cheeks. "He came to Woodstock on my birthday. I *tried* to tell you about him but you were always too busy to listen." *Go on, girl, tell the whole truth.* "We're planning to live together in St Ives. I'm going to open a tea-room there. I wanted you to meet him but—"

"I'm more shocked and appalled than I can possibly say." Anne chokes. "Of all the men in the world, you had to fall for *him*." She unbuttons her jacket. "And what a time to tell me!" Her hands shake. "There's no time to talk properly, no time to discuss this, no time for *anything*." She steps out of her skirt. "You're *unbelievable*."

"Thank you for being so understanding." Eleanor's sarcasm echoes in her ears. Her story has emerged as lame and ridiculous. She curses herself for not finding the right words, for making Felix sound like a shadowy, underhand figure who lacked the courage to appear in person. She wishes she hadn't told her mother a single honest word.

Anne rustles over to her wardrobe in her long silk petticoat. "I *forbid* you to go anywhere with anyone – let alone Felix Mitchell – until Jonny and I can discuss your future."

"I'm nineteen years old, Mummy, not nine. You can't forbid me to do anything—"

"*Can't* I just!"

"No, you can't." A savage anger bubbles in Eleanor's heart. "It's all right for me to take responsibility for our family's finances, run a tea-room, look after you, be your ridiculous bridesmaid." She looks down at the pink frock, longing to rip it off. "But the minute I want to do something for *myself*, something I've waited for with all the patience in the world …"

Her voice breaks. She turns to face Anne.

"Then it's a predictable, 'Good *grief*, Eleanor, you can't *possibly* do that. You're to stay put and do the dreary chores while I swan around Europe having the time of my life.' God *forbid* I should have a life of my own!"

Anne stares into the mirror, inspecting her smudged lipstick. "What on *earth* do you think your *father* would have said?"

"Do you know what?" She can see Walter lying on the

bed, blood seeping through his bandage, his violet-blue eyes clouded, his hands burning hot. "I think Daddy *meant* me to meet Felix. That's why he left me The Hideaway. He sent me to St Ives to find Moira's child – *his* child – the man he loved with all his heart." She throws back her head in triumph. "And find him I did."

Anne puts down her powder-puff. "So you found him." She starts to brush her hair. "It doesn't mean you have to spend the rest of your *life* with him, does it, Eleanor?"

Anne disappears with Jonny at four o'clock, making it clear she can hardly wait to get away, with only a perfunctory kiss for her daughter.

"You'd be *out of your mind* to go chasing after that man. When it all goes *terribly* wrong, don't say I didn't warn you ... I'll send our honeymoon postcards to Woodstock, hoping you've changed your silly little mind. Give Kathleen my regards. I'm *amazed* that such a sensible girl has given you her support."

A sobered-up Jonny grasps her hands. "Whatever you decide, don't burn any boats. You can *always* come back to Woodstock. We won't be on honeymoon for long, and we'll be here for you, no matter what."

She turns away, flushing with humiliation, as the cab carrying Anne and Jonny trundles off. It would serve them both right if they never saw her again.

Eleanor and Vera change out of their wedding finery. They spend three hours clearing and washing dishes, sweeping floors, tidying rooms, making sure that Anne and Jonny's bedroom is pristine, ready for their return.

Then Eleanor sits down with Vera over supper.

"I've something important to tell you." She brushes a

handful of confetti from her sleeve. "Listen to the whole story. Don't say anything until I get to the end."

"Of course, dear heart. Your mother said you wanted to talk to me ... Hasn't it been the most wonderful day? Anne is Mrs Giffen now. You're the last of the Drummonds. I'm so delighted to still be here for you. Your dear father would have been *so* proud, God rest his lovely soul."

Return to St Ives

1936

"'Course," Maud says with a contemptuous toss of her curls, "none of Edward's servants would leave England with him, even though he asked 'em."

They're in the Woodstock kitchen, sitting around the table, eating Sunday luncheon the following day.

"Fred Smith, he's been with Edward for donkey's years, told him straight to his face, 'Your name is mud.' Craig, his valet, didn't want to leave his wife. The junior piper said he couldn't go because if he did, his parents would die of shock." Maud nibbles at some lemon-meringue pie. "Edward said he'd make sure they got jobs with other royals, but I don't know they'll be able to. He's got a nerve, walkin' out of everybody's life as if he couldn't give a brass farthin'."

"Steady on, Maud," Kath interrupts. "He didn't take his decision lightly——"

"What he said on the wireless about not havin' a wife and family. Are we supposed to feel *sorry* for him? Edward could have married any decent single good-lookin' woman and had a load of children. But oh, no! He has to mess about with

371

other people's wives and then drop 'em like hot potatoes. Talk about abusin' his power." Maud dabs her mouth. "Anyway, he was driven out of Fort Belvedere in his Buick and plonked on to HMS *Fury* at two in the mornin'. He'll be somewhere in Europe by now, and he won't be comin' back. Not if the royal family has anythin' to do with it."

"But surely," Eleanor says, "they can't just turn their backs on him."

"All kinds of rumours have come creepin' out the woodwork. People are sayin' it's good riddance because Edward and Wallis are Nazis. The government stopped lettin' him see confidential documents way back in the summer. They reckoned Wallis had access to 'em and that *she* were spyin' for the Germans." Maud starts to clear the dishes, rattling them around. "It were only in January that Queen Mary were commendin' us to 'her dear son'. I wonder whether she'd any notion what the year would bring."

"Nobody *ever* knows." Eleanor helps Maud with the plates. "All we can do is to handle the things that happen to us as best we can. Trust people to understand us. Do as you would be done by. That's the only way to live. Don't you agree?"

The tea-room opens again on Tuesday the 15th of December for five days before it closes between Christmas and the New Year. Counting the days to her departure, Eleanor plans to leave for St Ives on Tuesday the 22nd of December. That'll give them the previous Sunday and Monday to spring-clean the kitchen, make sure everything's shipshape before they take a break.

"You *must* write to that Felix of yours," Kath tells her on the Sunday afternoon.

"I've been waiting to hear from him. But yes, of course, you're right."

"Well, make it sharp, Ellie. It'll soon be Christmas. He needs to know about your plans as soon as possible. He might be going back to Juan-les-Pins for the holiday."

"I'll send him a Christmas card with a message. If I post it today, he'll have time to answer."

But he doesn't.

Eleanor convinces herself that he's delighted she's finally told Anne about him. He can't wait for her arrival. He's longing to hold her in his arms again. He's finished The Hideaway, ready for her return. He's done it all for her …

Three days into that last week, Vera gets a telegram from her sister, telling her she's been diagnosed with cancer and asking her to come to stay until the New Year. It might be their last chance to spend the festive season together. Eleanor agrees to let her go.

Vera vanishes in a cloud of worried panic. They soldier on without her, very relieved when they close the tea-room's door on Saturday afternoon.

In the doorway, Eleanor takes Kath in her arms. "I couldn't possibly leave if you hadn't agreed to take over." Her eyes fill with tears. "I'll write from St Ives the moment I get there."

"I just want to know you're happy with that man of yours. Be sure to tell him what a lucky fellow he is." Kath hesitates. Then she says, "If anythin' goes wrong, Ellie, anythin' at all, you know where I am. And don't you never forget it."

Later that same evening in the silent house, Eleanor digs out the painting of the girl in the red taffeta frock. She hangs it in pride of place in the tea-room. Now she wants the whole world to see it and admire.

Her drive to Cornwall is swift and easy. The weather is unexpectedly kind and the Morris behaves impeccably. She's surprised at how many details of the journey she remembers, but she props the list of towns on the dashboard just in case.

In her handbag nestle her keys to The Hideaway.

She'd packed her entire wardrobe into two suitcases and is even taking her typewriter. She wants to find premises for a tea-room in St Ives. Once she's installed with her lover, she'll meet with James Lanham to discuss the location and price of a suitable property. She wants something small, preferably on the harbour and close to St Andrews Street.

She's also taken Jonny's pearls. In January, she'll travel to London and sell them in Bond Street to finance her new deal. When her plans are in place, she'll meet Michael again, ask him to act as her legal adviser. She'll keep Robin up-to-date. And Felix is bound to have friends who'll be interested in working as cooks, waitresses, suppliers.

Deep in thought, she reaches Exeter and finds a small guest-house. Her dreams are filled with the sounds of Felix's Cornish burr and the excited flapping of gulls.

She arrives in St Ives the following afternoon, just before two. She drives straight through the town to the car park, leaving her luggage in the boot of the Morris. Her head down, her heart thrumming, she walks as fast as her legs will carry her to St Andrews Street.

The front door of The Hideaway has been painted a shiny green. It has a new nameplate and a circlet of holly, whose spiky leaves glisten with red berries. The wooden window frames sparkle with fresh white paint. New muslin curtains hang at the windows.

She knocks on the door. At last! Any minute now and she'll be in his arms.

There is no answer.

Her mouth sour with disappointment she knocks again, stepping away from the cottage, glancing up at the bedroom. She presses her nose against the window, taps at the pane. He must be shopping for their supper. Perhaps if she does the rounds, she might find him coming home? Hunger makes her stomach growl. She'll have something to eat and come back in an hour.

She turns and marches swiftly towards Fore Street. A gruff voice calls to her, making her jump.

"Miss Drummond? Why, bless my soul! If it isn't Miss Drummond!"

She spins round to face James Lanham. He doffs his hat, gives an elegant bow, holds out his hand.

"How wonderful to see you again, Miss! You're looking *very* smart. What brings you to our lovely seaside town?"

"I'm here for Christmas, Mr Lanham, and I'll be staying on. I've only just arrived."

"Splendid news! Quite splendid." Lanham's voice falters. A shadow flickers across his eyes. "And are you staying at The Porthminster?"

"No." She blushes. "I'll be living with Felix ... Mr Mitchell ... in our ... in The Hideaway... as his guest."

"I see." The corner of Lanham's right eye twitches. He steps away from her. "Well, I suppose if that's all right with *him*—"

"Why shouldn't it be?"

"No reason at all, Miss Drummond. You know me. Never interfere." He crams his hat back on. "Apologies. Must be on my way. Things to do, people to see ... May I wish you a *very* Merry Christmas."

The Thunder of Waves

1936

Eleanor watches James Lanham limping up the hill. The sky has darkened. A cold wind whistles in from the sea, almost blowing her hat off. She clutches at it, shivering. She seems to have lost her appetite. She'll walk down to the harbour, fill her lungs with sea air, pull herself together.

Of course, she has the keys to The Hideaway. She digs for them in her handbag, making sure. If the worst comes to the worst – she sidesteps a group of drunken Christmas shoppers who sway past – *if*, when she returns, Felix is *still* not there, she could always let herself in. Give him a joyful surprise.

For a single black moment, she wonders who she's trying to convince.

God Almighty … What if Felix really *has* found somebody else?

She hears Kath's voice in her head. *I tried to warn you, but you wouldn't listen.*

The scent of hot pasties drifts into the air. Her stomach growls, as if it too is taking sides against her.

Her tongue numbed by scalding tea, she reaches The Hideaway again. She leans against the stable door, banging her gloved fist against it. She wants to wail like a neglected child. *Daddy, Daddy … Felix, Felix …*

Where on earth *is* he? Shopping for their blissful reunion? Back in Juan-les-Pins with his beloved Mama? Hiding behind the door?

She stops banging. An elderly couple who live three doors down stare at her as they walk past. She drags her freezing feet towards the Morris, flings the door open, climbs in and huddles like a foetus in the back seat.

A child peers in at her, squashing his nose against the window, misting it up. "Mam, Mam! Look in there! There's a funny lady in there, Mam!"

A woman's voice orders the child to come away.

Her stomach grumbles again, more loudly. For God's sake! She's behaving like a criminal. She'll get out and crawl back to the cottage. *Use* those keys before she freezes to death. Not that anyone will care if she does.

This time, she looks neither right nor left. In St Andrews Street, a gang of children fling themselves past her, laughing and shouting, tossing a ball over her head. She stomps through them, scrapes her keys in The Hideaway's door, opens and closes it and switches on the light.

The cottage smells of paint and turpentine; a meaty fragrance wafting from the basement; the cloying scent of stale hyacinths.

The room looks larger and wider than the image she's held in her mind for many months. Its walls glitter, pristine white. She recognises the screen with the scarlet poppies, the portrait of Moira that had hung outside the Driftwood bedroom. But the painting beside it is new work: Moira sits on the terrace of her Riviera villa, wearing a skin-tight, low-cut, black-lace dress.

Moira's delicate watercolours have disappeared. In their place hang three new ones: larger, bolder, more clearly defined, filled with tropical fruit and sunflowers painted in the dazzling hot colours of the Mediterranean.

She looks around the room. A white cloth covers the dining table which has been set for three. At its centre sits a vase of pink winter roses and three candles. Who's the third guest?

Still in her hat and coat, clutching her bag, she climbs the stairs. Directly ahead of her is a new small bathroom. The bedroom is untidy: the bed's unmade, clothes clutter the floor. The new skylight in the studio opens it up to a swirl of darkening clouds and the shadows of swooping gulls.

She moves across the studio to the easel to look at the portrait Felix is working on. A girl's face stares back, seductive, alluring. In her early twenties, she has chubby cheeks, a sensuous mouth, laughing blue eyes and a mass of bright chestnut hair curling to bare shoulders.

A jealous knife stabs Eleanor's hungry heart.

She's seen that face before, but she can't remember where.

She glances along the walls, longing to see her own portrait. Hadn't Felix said he'd worked on three and given her the best? Is it terribly vain of her to hope he'd finished them all? Perhaps he'd hung the others in the living room?

She's about to go downstairs to check when she hears the sound of a key in the front door. Her heart thumps with delight. He's back.

Then she freezes. A girl's voice calls, "Felix? Hello, honey, I'm home!"

She backs into the studio, her head fizzing with anxiety. Who the hell is *that*? Why has some girl let herself into The Hideaway with such familiar ease? Felix must be expecting her. Is she a maid, a neighbour, a friend – or, God forbid, something more?

She hesitates. Should she make herself known? Explain her presence with as much poise as she can muster? Go on hiding until he *does* return?

She's behaving like a petty thief, caught red-handed over the silver spoons. She must go downstairs, explain who she is with quiet dignity.

Gritting her teeth, she steps on to the landing. She hears the chink of plates and cutlery.

Guilt and fear suddenly overcome her. Maybe if she moves really fast, she can slip downstairs and out to the street without being seen or heard?

Except she can't. She hears the key in the door again – only this time, she also hears Felix's soft, much longed-for and so dearly remembered Cornish burr.

But it's not *her* name he's calling.

"Agnes? I'm back! Phew! What a drive! Sorry I'm so late, darling."

Feet pound up from the kitchen.

"Welcome home!" A smacking kiss, then another quieter one. "Let me take your coat … I was lonely without you, honey. It feels like you've been gone forever. How was your trip?"

He groans. "A *total* waste of time, Aggie. I got there, but there was nobody in. I hammered on the door, went back several times. Everything was closed. In the end I had to leave another letter. Remember the one I wrote in November, how I struggled with that? It took me four drafts before I was happy with the second one!"

379

"You said you never wanted to write to her again—"

"I didn't! *Truly* I didn't. I'm no good with words on paper. I sound pompous and absurd. And it's so cowardly to hide behind a letter. But I had no choice. I didn't want to hang around a minute longer than I needed to."

Another kiss, this time lingering.

"Anyway, it's done and dusted … She'll have got my *second* letter last night. How've you been?"

"Busy in the office, as usual. But I took an hour off this morning to make us a casserole. Best beef with red wine and garlic, just as you like it."

"It smells delicious."

"Good. Are you hungry?"

"Ravenous … But there's something even more tasty we could do before we eat."

The girl laughs. She sounds joyful, confident, flirtatious. "You *are* a naughty boy! I wonder what *that* can be." Another kiss.

"Are there any candles in the bedroom?" Felix, his voice muffled.

"Yes. We only burned half last time before I blew them out."

"Excellent … Come on then, my darling Aggie … Show me how much you've missed me."

Eleanor backs into the studio until she can go no further. For a wild moment she imagines making a leap for the skylight, pushing it open, slithering over the rooftops, vanishing from everyone and everything into the churning belly of the sea.

She hears footsteps climb the stairs, push into the bedroom. The door shuts. The girl laughs. Felix chuckles. She hears a match being struck, the scuffle of clothes being pulled off eager bodies. She tries not to listen, pressing her hands over her ears, standing there, paralysed.

Then she can't bear it a moment longer. She bolts through the door, out of the room, across the landing. Halfway down the stairs, she hears the girl cry out with joy. Instantly Eleanor loses her footing and slips. Now she's tumbling – heavily, clumsily, noisily – down the stairs. She lies at the bottom in a crumpled heap, pain screaming from her right wrist, her ankle throbbing, her head banging like a drum. She wants the earth to swallow her in one all-consuming gulp.

Felix flings the bedroom door open.

"Who's there? What the *hell* is going on?"

He stands at the top of the stairs, his dressing-gown flapping around his body. She gazes up at him. He's older and thinner. A dark, well-trimmed beard and moustache give his face a new authority. He stares down at her.

"Eleanor?"

She heaves herself to her feet, trying to rescue her dignity.

"I'm so sorry, Felix. I didn't mean to intrude. I never meant ... I'll leave immediately."

The pain in her ankle shoots up her leg. She clamps her lips together to stop herself crying out in agony.

"What in God's name are you *doing* at the bottom of the stairs?" He turns away to call into the bedroom, "It's all right, Aggie ... It's Eleanor Drummond! There's been some terrible muddle."

She clings to the banister to take the weight off her ankle, flinching from the echoing pain in her wrist. She says through clenched teeth, "I wrote and told you I was coming. Didn't you get my card? I sent it last week—"

"I only got it on Monday. It must have been delayed in the Christmas post. I left for Woodstock immediately. To find you. To explain. But the tea-room was closed and there was no answer from your house."

She gasps, remembering he'd said, "It's done and dusted." He'd been talking about *her*, about being in Woodstock. "And you left me a letter?"

"Yes." Felix helps her towards the sofa, his arm around her. He'd knotted the belt of his gown but she can smell his musky scent. She wants to bury her face in his chest, but he draws away.

"I hadn't heard anything from you for months. You never came to St Ives. You never told me Anne knew about us. I assumed you were never going to tell her. I wrote to you in November, calling the whole thing off, and telling you why."

"I never got the letter." Her heart thumps with despair. "Do you really think I'd be here if I had?"

"No, maybe not." His face is ashen. "When you never replied, I had to assume you'd decided to forget me. Then I got your card. I panicked. I'd assumed Anne would never know about us because you didn't want us to be together."

"Far from it." Her voice shakes. "I've been *longing* to hear from you. I had to assume no news was good news. I've thought about little else."

Felix says flatly, "I'd no idea."

"So now you're with … Who's the girl upstairs?"

"Aggie. Agnes Lanham. James Lanham's daughter."

Of course! She'd met her at the agent's office. She'd recognised her face on Felix's canvas. And *that's* why Lanham had greeted her so nervously.

"I've known Aggie for years." He swings into a chair, folding his gown over his legs. "Walter and James Lanham were friends from the moment they met, but Aggie's five years younger than me. *We* didn't meet properly until I moved into Driftwood.

"Nothing happened between Agnes and me for ages, but in October we saw each other again at a party. We just hit it off."

Eleanor wants to spit with jealousy and anger. "So it's serious?"

He lowers his voice. "Who knows? She's still terribly young. And beautiful, of course. We have *fun* together." He looks her in the eyes. "I need a woman in my life. Someone to talk to, walk with, dance with. Someone I can paint. You understand."

"*Of course* I understand! I thought that someone was *me*!"

"It *was*, Eleanor. I loved you very much. I drove to Woodstock but you refused to come back with me. You dithered around so half-heartedly. In effect, you turned me down."

She's on the verge of tears. "It wasn't as *simple* as that!"

"Oh, but I think it was. It is. Or it *should* be. You work out what you want in life and who you want. Then you go for it. You let nothing stand in your way." He gives her a wry smile. "Look at the Prince of Wales, at the complications *he* faced. But he made everything simple. He loved Wallis. He said she was as necessary to him as the air he breathed. That's real love, Eleanor. You move heaven and earth for it—"

"But I *did*!" She's blazing with indignation. "I *have*. I've planned *everything* … I'm free to *be* with you. I've turned my world upside-down to be here. My friend Kath will run the Woodstock tea-room. I want to open one here, in St Ives, and live with you … But Mummy was right. I shouldn't be here. I feel like an idiot. You're telling me it's already too late, aren't you? I was willing to give up everything for you, but you don't give a damn."

He says nothing.

She reads his answer in his eyes. She can't bear to see it a moment longer. She wills herself to stand, fumbles in her bag. "I've brought you some Christmas presents." She throws them across the room into his lap.

He stares down at them, sucking in his breath. "You *shouldn't* have, Eleanor … I'm so *sorry* about all this."

"I hope you'll enjoy them." Her anger mounts. "I rescued some of Walter's paint brushes." Her voice sharpens. "And I bought you a *very* expensive watch." She swallows back the vomit lurching into her mouth. For a terrible moment she almost bursts out laughing. "Now, I hope you'll spare me a single moment's thought!"

Defying the pain in her leg, she hobbles to the front door. She dips into her handbag for The Hideaway's keys and drops them on the table.

Then she's standing outside in the frosty night. She slams the door. A bitter wind blows into her face. Her eyes stream with tears.

The only thing she can hear in her head is the thunder of waves.

The Nature of the Beast

1936

She limps to the corner of St Andrews Street.
She hears Felix open the door, shout, "Eleanor! For
God's sake, don't just *leave* like that! Have supper with us …
There's plenty of food. It's Christmas!" His voice fades.
"Now I feel terrible!"

She glances back at him. He's standing in the doorway,
his legs sticking out from beneath his gown. She sees him
turn to talk to the girl at his elbow. Then Agnes pulls him
back into the warmth and light, into her arms.

Eleanor takes a shaky breath. She waits until the door
clicks shut. Her wrist and ankle throb with pain. St Andrews
Street blurs through her tears, huddles in thickening
darkness. A group of carol singers stand three doors down,
valiantly singing *"Away in a Manger"*, their voices almost
drowned by the wind.

She starts to hobble into town, with no idea where she's
going or what she intends to do. Sobs surface from the
depths of her lungs. A dreadful self-pity grips her – and then
an almighty fury. With herself. And with Felix.

He has utterly betrayed her.

So has James Lanham. She finds herself limping past his office. She stops in her tracks. Lights still burn inside the agency. Anger bubbles into her mouth. Damn it! She'll confront him, tell him *exactly* what she thinks about how he's behaved.

She flings his door open.

Lanham is sitting at the far end of the office, opposite a woman wearing a luxurious fur coat and a dark, wide-brimmed hat. Her back is towards Eleanor.

He leaps to his feet. "Miss Drummond!"

"You might have told me." She flings out the words. "You might have *warned* me Felix and Agnes were having an affair. That I was about to walk into *their* little world, instead of meeting up again with the love of my life!"

"I'm terribly sorry." Lanham is scarlet with embarrassment. "I thought you knew … I assumed you were here as their guest."

She stands in the freezing doorway. The pain in her ankle snakes ferociously up her leg.

The woman in the hat stands up and turns to look at her.

"Eleanor Drummond!" she says. "How wonderful … We meet at last."

Her voice is low, with a sweetness about it that makes Eleanor want to cry. Cornflower-blue eyes stare into hers as the woman moves towards her, gripping her hand, seeming to notice how Eleanor flinches with pain.

This time, it seems – at last and properly – she has kept her promise.

"I can't believe it."

Eleanor looks into the face she feels she knows so well. Lines hover around Moira's eyes and mouth. They crease her forehead and her hands. But her poise, the elegant way she wears her clothes, her air of serenity and confidence: all make her undeniably beautiful.

"I never thought I'd find you," Eleanor stutters. "I got so close in Juan-les-Pins, and then you vanished."

"But I'm here now." Moira makes her sit down. "What have you done to yourself? Are you in pain?"

She explains. "I feel *such* a fool. I've come all this way for your son, only to find him in Agnes Lanham's arms."

"Instead you've found me. Let's hope *something* good comes from this fiasco." Moira turns to Lanham. "Could you do me a favour? Nip over to St Andrews Street. Tell Felix I won't be joining him for supper. Eleanor and I have our first real chance to spend a few hours together. It's an opportunity neither of us wants to miss."

The next thing Eleanor knows she's sitting in Lanham's dusty back office, her throbbing ankle propped on a low chair. Moira holds a cool damp handkerchief to her forehead. The scent of cloves hangs in the air, sharp and refreshing.

"That's better. I thought you were going to faint. Here, drink this. Hot sweet tea. Then I'll take you to my hotel. You can stay there as my guest for as long as you need. Your ankle's swollen. And your wrist, I can see that's also painful. Am I right?"

Eleanor nods. "But there's no need—"

"There's *every* need! What on earth do you plan to do? Drive to Woodstock in the dark? Fall asleep at the wheel? I'd never forgive myself."

"You're right. I'm in no fit state to drive."

"So drink up. I'm staying at The Porthminster—"

"They don't like me there."

"So what? The place is half empty. You can stay as my guest. They'll prepare a bedroom for you, close to mine. We'll get a doctor to strap up that ankle of yours, and we'll enjoy supper together. Where's your luggage?"

"In my car."

"So, we'll walk slowly to find it, and I'll drive us to The Porthminster." The cornflower eyes flicker at her. "Finally I'll have a chance to say I'm sorry."

"You? Sorry?" Eleanor gulps the tea, her head spinning. "Whatever for?"

"If I'd looked after my son better, you wouldn't be in such a predicament. I'm staying in St Ives for Christmas. I'm going to buy a holiday home here. James and I were discussing various properties."

She soaks the handkerchief in water, wrings it out, turns to Eleanor.

"But I'm *bitterly* sorry because your affair with Felix has obviously come to an end." The colour rises in Moira's cheeks. "He's behaved atrociously. And if I'm completely honest, I have to tell you something. This is hard for me, but if I don't say it, nobody else will."

"What is it?"

"I think you've had a lucky escape."

Eleanor feels the breath catch in her lungs. "Why?"

Moira presses the handkerchief to Eleanor's forehead. "Do you want the truth?"

"Of course." But she grits her teeth against another wave of pain.

"Felix doesn't *love* Agnes. Oh, *she* adores *him*, that goes without saying. She's hoping for wedding bells. She's pretty, charming and convenient, and Felix is enjoying her. But their affair won't last. By the spring, he'll have thrown her over."

388

Eleanor says breathlessly, "Then is there still hope for me, do you think? Should I stay here, wait for him to come to his senses?"

"No, absolutely not. I *beg* you to go home to Woodstock." Moira bites her lip. "I need to tell you something else, to prove my point. While Felix was in Juan-les-Pins with me, for those few weeks, he seduced a pretty young woman he met while we were having drinks at The Provençal. She owned a small yacht moored off the coast. Felix used to swim out to meet her. Even if you *had* moved in with him this afternoon, you'd have discovered he has a roving eye. He can't help it. It's the nature of the beast."

Moira hesitates. Then she says, "Walter was just the same. I failed to change him, and neither you nor I nor any other woman will ever change Felix." She looks at Eleanor, her eyes filled with regret. "Much as I love him, I believe he'd have made your life a misery. You don't need that, Eleanor. You deserve so much better."

They have supper by the fire in Moira's suite at The Porthminster. Moira had summoned the local doctor to examine Eleanor's wrist and ankle. He'd strapped them with bandages, given her strict instructions to have them X-rayed as soon as she got home, and had offered her a sleeping tablet.

Moira looks up from her soup. She says with a calm directness that Eleanor has already come to appreciate, "I gather that Felix told you what happened to Walter, Felix and me when we lived together. Back then in St Ives, Felix was only a child. He knew very little about what was really happening. I suppose you want to know *why* I disappeared from his life that terrible day in the storm?"

Eleanor flushes. "You don't have to tell me. My mission

389

was to find you, to keep my promise to Daddy, to reunite you with Felix." His name sticks in her throat. "As for what happened … I've no wish to pry."

"You deserve to know, even if what I tell you about your father will *not* be music to your ears. But if I *don't* spell it out, the wondering will always be at the back of your mind. Am I right?"

"Yes. The picture Felix painted of your life together, the affection and happiness he described … None of it tallied with Pierre's letters."

"Felix so much wanted us to be a happy family. We weren't. It was partly my fault. I was the odd one out. The cuckoo in the warm and cosy nest. But Walter's love for me changed from devotion and affection into something so monstrous that, in the end, he gave me no choice but to leave."

Moira stares into the fire, remembering.

Eleanor sits back to let her talk.

Act Six

On the Beach

1911

With as much grace and dignity as she can muster, Moira Mitchell lowers herself on to the tartan rug that Walter has spread out for her on Porthmeor Beach. Little Felix is already stark naked, the skin behind his knees and on his arms and chest so red and blotchy it seems to be on fire beneath the sun.

"*There*, my angel face." Walter opens the picnic-hamper lid. "Cake, biscuits and some lovely fish-paste sandwiches that your Auntie Bea made for us yesterday. You just make yourselves comfortable while I go and find us somewhere to live."

Moira looks up at him. She unties the wide ribbon underneath her chin, raises her arms, takes off her driving hat. Dust falls off it on to her skirt. She coughs. She wipes her face with the back of her gloved hand. The fingers of her gloves are stained with dirt. Her hair is flat with sweat.

She says, "You've got three hours."

"I *beg* your pardon, dearest?"

"*Three hours!*" Moira raises her right hand. Three grubby

fingers point upwards to the sky. "Three hours in which to find us somewhere to live. If, by the end of this afternoon, we've nowhere to go but your dusty, noisy, *intolerable* little sports car, we'll get the next train out of here—"

"Oh, *don't* say that—"

"And what's more, Walter Drummond, you'll never see us again. The journey down here was bad enough. The heat, the dust, the traffic ... Staying with Auntie Bea was a *nightmare. Do* this, *do* that – poor little Felix was hardly allowed to *breathe.* If you think this has been a holiday, you're very much mistaken."

Walter opens his mouth to argue. Then he changes his mind. He drops a hot, wet, conciliatory kiss on Moira's forehead. She does not enjoy the experience.

"Never fear, my *sweetest* girl. I shall find the three of us the most *adorable* little cottage you ever did see."

"I'll believe *that* when you've got it." Moira looks across the beach. Felix is waving his wooden spade at a seagull, laughing with delight. "And not so little, Walter, please. We need space, remember? Space to eat and sleep and work and paint and be separate people. I'm not living in some pathetic cramped seaside caravan."

"I wouldn't *hear* of it, my angel—"

"So go on then ... *What are you waiting for?*"

Moira watches Walter lurching across the beach.

She turns her attention to the sea, taking great breaths of salty air into her dust-filled lungs. She allows herself to lie down, but all the time she keeps Felix in the frame. She never takes her eyes off him, not while she's in charge. Not for a moment.

If it weren't for Felix, Moira wouldn't be here in Cornwall. She'd be in France with the love of her life. Pierre hadn't liked the sound of this holiday. He hadn't wanted her to go. He'd written to her just before they left:

"What if that Walter Drummond does not allow you to return to Oxford? What then? Shall I never see you again? How could I bear my life without you?"

Moira asks herself the same question as she lies on the beach. The trouble is, Pierre doesn't understand what her life in Oxford had been like. So overlooked and overheard. So little freedom. It's partly wonderful to be here. To escape the ferocious heat of Oxford. The stinking drains. The parched river beds. The *stench* ...

But what if Walter keeps her a prisoner in St Ives?

What will she do then?

She'll cross that bridge when she comes to it.

Two hours later, Moira and Felix, ravenous for anything but sand, are holding their noses and eating Auntie Bea's stinking sandwiches.

Walter comes puffing towards them. He squats on his haunches, pats Felix on his silky head, raises Moira's hand to his lips.

"I've found," he says, his heart beating so fast that his words sound like small explosions, "the most *divine* little cottage. It's *just* the right size. It's in St Andrews Street, the most wonderful central location. We'll be in the very heart of St Ives. It's perfect. The cottage has everything we need. There's even a balcony overlooking the sea. It'll be our paradise, just for the three of us."

"How much will it cost?"

"Don't you worry your pretty little head about *that*." Walter assumes his best paternal, authoritative air. "We can rent it for as long as we want."

Moira clambers to her feet. Her back aches. Sand rustles in her hair, clings to her lips, scratches at her throat. She longs for a bath. She's dying for Pierre.

"So, Walter …" She stands with her hands on her narrow waist, her cornflower-blue eyes flashing. "If this is the start of your brave new world, why don't you take us there right now." She bends to pick up her naked little boy. "And be quick about it."

Turning a Blind Eye

1913

It's a sunny August afternoon two years later.

Felix, who's now five, plays marbles, skips with ropes, and bowls the red wooden hoop down St Andrews Street with his two best friends, the twins Rupert and Victoria, whom he adores.

In his studio upstairs, Walter is painting a deliciously attractive young model.

Moira hunches at the table in the living room. A recent, half-finished sketch of summer fruit is laid aside at her elbow, but she's peeling potatoes. On the chair beside her in a wicker basket lurks a pile of damp clothes waiting to be ironed.

The sheen has disappeared from Moira's hair. Her skin, given the intensity of Cornish sunlight currently available, is surprisingly pale. She wears a high-necked blouse and long skirt, both of which have seen better days.

Moira's paintings make pin money which she spends on Felix and food. Walter's paintings make him a lot more money. He disposes of it partly in The Sloop, partly on his models – "My *dear* girl, you look *ravishing* in the new hat!" – and partly on oils, brushes, elaborate smocks and enormous canvases. And sometimes, when he's nagged into it, on household bills. He seems to have forgotten he has a family.

Lizzie Farrell pokes her head around the top of the stable door.

"It's only me."

Moira puts down her paring knife. "Lizzie, darling. How nice. Come and sit down."

Lizzie rustles in. She wears a crisp new summer frock she made herself the night before. It's simple, stylish, full-skirted and delightful.

"I've got wonderful news." She strokes the pale curls beneath her straw bonnet.

"I could certainly do with some of that!"

"What's he done *now*?"

"Only the usual." Moira inspects the face of another potato.

"God, Moira. Why on *earth* do you put up with it?"

Moira pushes at her hair with the back of a wet hand. "You know why. Felix is happy here. He's healthy. His skin is clear as a bell. He eats like a horse, swims like a fish. He has friends. People in St Ives *like* me. Not in the political, challenging way we had in Oxford with our Votes-for-Women group, but artistically. They buy my paintings." She puts down the potato. "I have *you* …"

Lizzie grasps her hands. "Listen to me. Things might get better. *So* much better. I've found us a house to rent."

Blood rushes to Moira's face. *"What?"*

Lizzie pulls a piece of paper from her skirt pocket. "Here. Take a look. It's on Carbis Bay, right on the beach. It's called Spindrift. It's big enough for you and Walter, me and

Mother, Felix and any friends he might ask to stay the night. At the side there's an annex that sleeps six people. We could rent that out in the summer months and make good money."

"God, Lizzie, it sounds *perfect*. Is there room for—"

"Yes, darling. You and Walter could have separate studios *and* separate bedrooms."

Moira murmurs, "Lizzie Farrell, you're my saviour and I love you."

Upstairs a door opens.

Walter says, "Thank you *so* much, Amanda, darling. You've been *so* patient. Same time next week?"

A blonde girl, hardly more than seventeen, wearing a turquoise suit and a mind-blowing scarlet hat drifts slowly down the stairs. A smile hovers on her painted lips. Without acknowledging either Moira or Lizzie, she lets herself out.

Moira swallows her feelings. A year ago she'd have burned with fury and resentment. Now a dull apathy has taken over. She *wants* to feel more, to bubble with jealousy. But she no longer cares what Walter thinks of other women – or what he does with them.

Walter remains at the top of the stairs. "I'm absolutely parched. Would there be a cup of tea available? Could you bring it up?"

"Good afternoon, Walter." Lizzie stands to challenge him. "I've something very important to show you."

"I'm terribly *busy* at the moment—"

"But not too busy, I hope, to look at a house on Carbis Bay."

"Why on *earth* would I want or need to do that?"

Moira picks up the saucepan of peeled potatoes. She wishes Walter were on her level. Then she could empty the pan over his selfish head. "Because, Walter, as you very well know, *we need more space.*"

Walter stares down at her. "You mean *you* do. You're one of those women who never has enough. If I gave you the moon, you'd demand the stars as well."

"How *dare* you be so rude!"

"Just bring me my tea, Moira, my dear sweet angel face. And by the way," Walter swings one dapper leg over another, "yesterday morning I signed a new five-year lease with James Lanham. We're now committed to renting this adorable, *perfect* little cottage until 1918. I want Felix to have continuity in his young life. I want my clients to know they can always reach me here. And I *love* living at the heart of our extraordinary artistic community. I've even managed to get our landlord to agree to my giving our cottage a name."

Moira's heart bubbles with anger. "Without at any time consulting me about anything? I suppose you've called the cottage My Blue Heaven."

Walter snorts with laughter. "Not quite, although of course it *is* heavenly. No, its name is now The Hideaway. Close to the centre of St Ives, and yet our own private, gloriously intimate little world. Isn't that a marvellous choice?"

He turns to walk back into his studio.

"Oh, and with my tea, could I have some of your delicious lemon-drizzle cake, please? A *very* large slice."

The End of the Line

1914

Moira walks alone along the harbour. It's Easter 1914, and early afternoon. Back home, she has the usual tidal wave of chores. They're so boring and repetitive she can't find the energy to face them. She has a painting to finish. She longs to work on it, but once again her space in their small studio has been invaded by one of Walter's models.

She sees Lizzie walking towards her. Gratitude floods her heart.

"Has anything come?"

"Yes." Lizzie digs in her pocket. "This arrived for you yesterday morning."

Moira grabs the letter. "You're an angel. Let's go and have some tea. I'll read it in the café."

Moira tears the envelope open. Her cheeks flush with excitement.

"Pierre's coming to London. He's made all the bookings. He'll be staying at Brown's Hotel."

Lizzie drinks her tea, her eyes on Moira's trembling hands. "And he wants you to join him?"

"He wants to see *both* of us … Felix *and* me." Moira chokes. "What am I going to do?"

"Do you *want* to see Pierre again?"

"You know I do. More than anything."

"So make it happen, Moira. Heaven knows, you've been patient enough."

Moira takes a deep breath, willing herself to find the courage to speak.

"I'd like to spend a few days in London over Easter."

She's having supper with Walter three days later. Felix is in bed, fast asleep.

"Why on *earth* do you want to do that?" Walter helps himself to a slice of fresh white bread, spoons a large portion of chicken casserole on to his plate. Moira's is empty but he doesn't notice or care.

"There's a dealer who wants to meet me. He owns an art gallery in Bond Street. He's asked to see some of my work."

"Oh, *really*," Walter sneers. "So the little shops and galleries in Cornwall aren't good enough for you any more. Is that what you're saying?"

She ignores the question. "And I'd like to take Felix. Just for a few days. In all the time we've spent in St Ives, I've never had a holiday. I need one." She puts some food on her plate although she's never felt less hungry in her life. "A break from the chores. A chance to do some shopping."

"Sorry, Moira, it's *out of the question*. I need you here, *both* of you. I can't sleep unless you're by my side, my sweetest girl. And Felix is *much* too young to travel to that big black city. Besides, who'd cook for me? Keep this place clean? I've got clients coming out of my ears. I haven't time to travel with you."

She stares at her empty plate. A year, maybe even six months ago, she'd have accepted Walter's unbelievable selfishness. She'd have been too tired to argue, too resigned to his patronising attitude.

But something in her has changed. She feels as if she's climbed to the top of a mountain and for the first time she can see the spectacular view on the other side … A vision of what her world *could* be like if only she can find the courage to make it happen.

She'd like to pick up her plate and smash it over Walter's head. She wants to get up, scoop Felix from his bed, carry him in her arms, slam out of the door, run hell for leather to the rail station and climb on to the next available train.

"Is there something wonderful for pudding? I must keep up my strength." Walter raises his head. "Jesus Christ, will you listen to that rain. And the wind … There's a really nasty storm blowing up. You'd better close the windows, Moira. We don't want those gusts knocking anything over, do we, now?"

She says, "I'm going to Lizzie's tomorrow for lunch, whatever the weather. It's her birthday. She's expecting me. I've saved up some money for her, as a gift. Mrs Farrell's having problems with her eyesight. Lizzie's been finding it terribly hard to keep up with the work."

"God Almighty!" Walter digs a large spoon into his apple crumble. "Lizzie this and Lizzie that! I wish you cared as much for *me* as you do for your little friend. Just make sure you leave me some lunch tomorrow. I've a *very* busy day ahead."

All that night Moira lies in bed beside the snoring Walter. He murmurs in his sleep, snuffling like a warthog, gurgling in his throat. Now and then he mutters a name: "Rowena," or "darling Jenny," or "Meg, Meg, Meg."

Never "Moira, Moira, Moira …"

When he moves towards her in the middle of the night, flinging his arm around her, lifting her nightdress, she turns away, dreading his touch, the smell of his breath, the feel of his fingers on her skin.

"No, Walter, *no* …"

She thinks: *Don't touch me. Don't ever touch me again.*

She can't sleep. She can't close her eyes. She can't even blink. Her face feels cool and waxy, as if she were lying in a closed mausoleum that nobody will ever bother to open.

She knows she's reached the end of the line. Soon, very soon, something is going to tip her over it.

Who cares?

Doesn't anybody *care*?

Next morning the storm continues unabated. Walter sleeps like a dead man. Moira eats breakfast with Felix. As she lifts his bowl, scraped clean of porridge, she kisses his cool round cheek. She's never loved him more than at that single moment.

Neighbours come crashing on their stable door with the news. Boats have been lost at sea. Fishermen are feared drowned. It has been the most terrible night.

Moira doesn't need to be told.

She wraps Felix in warm clothes and lets him go to play with the twins up the road. Before he races out of the stable door, she hugs him tightly to her heart. He smells of honey and oatmeal.

She grabs a set of clean clothes, carries them down to the basement. While Walter's sleeping, she'll take a bath. Try her best to wash away the despair and exhaustion of the night, the smell of Walter's fingers on her skin.

The water's warm and wonderful. She slips her naked limbs beneath it, bobbling the sponge with soap, relishing the scent of coal-tar, its sunshine-yellow colour, closing her eyes.

Something cold presses against the back of her neck.

"My *darling* girl." Walter's icy fingers lift her hair. "How marvellous to see you naked again after all these months! Our bedroom's always so dark and mysterious. A fumble beneath the sheets hardly counts. But now, I have you completely to myself."

"No, Walter." Moira opens her eyes, clutches the sides of the bath. Her wet hands slip and slide. She's completely at his mercy. "Please ... leave me alone."

"Why should I, when you look so adorable, so vulnerable ... so *delicious*?" He moves along the floor at the side of the tub. He throws off his gown. He's stark naked.

"Now, I want you to do *exactly* as I say, exactly when I say it. Are you ready for this, my angel face?"

"*No, Walter. No, no, no…*"

"Oh, *yes, yes, yes,* my beautiful angel. I've waited for this moment long enough."

An hour later, Moira stands in the kitchen. She's emptied the bath, dried her battered body, pulled on her clothes. She's also been sick down the lavatory.

With a ruthlessness she'd never have thought possible, Walter has raped her repeatedly, pushed her over the line and vanished upstairs.

Moira collapses on the basement steps, too weak to move. A pair of Felix's small blue-leather shoes look up at her. She holds them to her face, weeping into them. Rain pelts down against the porthole window. On a gush of filthy water, a dead rat floats by.

She closes her eyes, wanting to forget everything and everybody.

Longing to die.

Someone knocks at the stable door.

Moira puts down the shoes, one, two, side by side, straight and even on the steps.

She listens as Walter greets the newcomer.

"Amanda! My *darling* girl! How *brave* of you to tackle the rain and wind on my behalf. Come up ... Let's get you out of your lovely clothes and dry you all over."

She climbs the basement stairs slowly, one at a time. She hears Walter and his model laughing together. Anger grips her heart, a mounting fury she no longer wishes to control, even if she could. She clenches her fists, making herself stem the tears.

She tells herself not to look at anything in the room that belongs to Felix. Not to think of him. Not to remember.

She moves towards her bureau. From it she removes some money and her passport. She looks at the red-leather purse with its birthday gift – and throws it on the floor.

Then she flings on her raincoat. Her body shakes with pain. Her heart thunders with fury.

She hurls herself at the stable door.

A Thousand Pieces

Christmas Eve 1936

"I can't believe it." Eleanor's voice trembles with shock. "I can't *believe* my father could have done that to you."

"I'd hardly have made it up." Bitterness sparks Moira's voice. "I knew I was reaching the end of my tether, but I hadn't anticipated being treated with such cruelty and contempt."

"Daddy ..." Eleanor chokes, "when he was dying, after his accident, he asked me to tell you something——"

"Oh?" Moira looks across at her. "And what was that?"

"He said, 'Tell Moira I'm sorry.' Of course, at the time I'd no idea who you were or what he was talking about."

Moira gives a half-smile. "Well, now you do. And an apology, however abject, is hardly enough. So much too little, and so much too late!"

"I wish it had never happened."

"In ways neither of us had properly intended," Moira's voice shakes with her memories, "both Pierre and I managed to lose ourselves in France. His Parisian friends assumed he'd died of drink. He hadn't seen his family for years. And if I never returned to St Ives, I thought Walter would either assume I'd drowned in the storm or that I'd left him because I couldn't tolerate his obscene behaviour a minute longer."

Eleanor watches as Moira stands to clear the soup bowls. She brings slices of roast turkey and green vegetables from the trolley. Her body is still slim but strong. Her blue silk frock fits her perfectly. She moves with a riveting ease and grace.

Eleanor wills herself to ask, "How did you manage to escape St Ives?"

"There was a horse and cart waiting outside the baker's. The delivery man was inside the shop. I threw myself into the back of the cart and covered myself with a bundle of old sacking. I knew the cart would be returning to St Erth. Once it was there I'd be able to catch a train to Paddington.

"I bribed the inspector on the train. He agreed I could hide in a carriage that was carrying parcels and post. The journey was horrendous, but I didn't care. My only mission was to get as far away from Walter as I could, as quickly as possible. I knew that I'd never go back to him.

"Of course, I ached for Felix. I worried about him all the time. But the weeks slipped by. In August, war broke out. It became too dangerous to travel. Every time I even mentioned returning to St Ives to find Felix, Pierre raged and shouted – and then refused to look at me. So I stopped talking about the possibility. In effect, I gave Felix to Walter. I knew he adored the boy. I didn't have the heart to take him away."

Eleanor watches as Moira picks at her food. "Were you happy with Pierre?"

"We'd loved each other from the moment we first met in Oxford. Pierre's drinking got in the way. I think he was frightened by how much he felt for me. And he wasn't ready to be a father. But once I'd left Paris, my absence came as a shock. Although it took him time to repent, he really did mend his ways.

"During the war in France I kept my head down, learned to speak fluent French, and stayed safe. Afterwards, I had all the time in the world to paint. Pierre encouraged me in ways Walter never had. For Walter, my talents were second-rate – or at least, second to *his*. Pierre spent his time sailing, meeting friends, looking after me.

"I'd made my choice. We married in a simple ceremony in Cannes, a year into the war. I never doubted it was the right thing to do."

"You were so lucky. I'll have to go home now, my dreams shattered, my life in pieces."

"Nonsense." Moira looks sternly across at her. "Felix tells me you thrive in Woodstock. Your friends, your tea-room. Build on what you've already achieved."

"Without Felix."

"There'll be other men. You'll see."

"But I want – I wanted – your son. We slept together. That was such a huge step for me. The fact that Felix and I were lovers committed me to him as seriously as if I'd married him."

"It may have done once, but the world is changing fast. The established patterns are breaking into a thousand pieces. People are finding new freedoms. Look at how your Prince of Wales found his."

"I suppose he's lucky to have found love."

"Do you think so?" Moira raises her eyebrows. "Consider what he's given up for it. The throne, the Empire, his family, his home, his country. Wallis has lost everything *she* ever had, except for money, and she'll never have enough of that. Do you really think that's a good basis for a relationship?"

Moira pushes her plate aside, looking all the time at Eleanor.

"When you find your new man, make sure he loves you for what you *are*, not for what he can make of you. Don't give up anything you're passionate about because he asks you to. Stand on your own feet through thick and thin. And make a choice you'll never live to regret."

Eleanor swallows the sedative.

She has vivid dreams, full of light and colour. She's standing in Walter's studio. Anne walks through the door, holding her baby son in her arms.

"His name's Walter Giffen," she tells Eleanor, giving her the child. "But Jonny and I are going to call him Jay."

Eleanor looks down at her little brother. He has wisps of red hair and shining turquoise eyes. He smiles up at her, stuffing a fist into his milky mouth.

She wakes early before it's properly light.

The pain in her wrist and ankle have subsided. With the greatest care, moving slowly, she slips out of bed, pulls back the curtains and opens the balcony window. She steps into the cool air of the Christmas Eve dawn.

The faint roar of the ocean takes her in its arms.

Be patient, it seems to say, be calm. All will be well. Go home to Woodstock, to the life you created there. It waits for you. So does something else. You thought long and hard about it. Now it becomes crucially important …

Sobs rise to her throat but she swallows them into silence. Something in her has changed. When she thinks about Felix, instead of flutters of excitement and longing, she feels only relief that she's managed to escape.

410

She never wants to see him again.

As for Walter, when she thinks about *him*, she feels nothing but a terrible numbness. What Moira had revealed amounts to a gigantic leap too far.

With the sudden clarity born of deepest sleep, she knows what she's going to do.

She'll drive home immediately. She'll take the letter from Felix waiting for her on the Woodstock doormat and burn it, unopened, in the fire. She'll find a cottage to rent, begin to live an independent life away from Anne and Jonny.

And in the spring of the New Year, she'll slay Walter's ghost and have his studio demolished. In its place she'll build a small art gallery, with high windows for good honest daylight, wide shelves to support the work of sculptors, white walls to showcase the painters of Oxfordshire.

She'll write to Moira, asking her to bring new paintings to Woodstock. She'll commission fresh work from her, establish an ongoing relationship, do everything she can to heal the wounds of the past.

And she will indeed do something else.

Within the hour, she has bathed, dressed and packed.

She taps on the door of the room next to hers. She bends for a moment over a sleepy Moira, reaching for her hand, murmuring, "My wrist and ankle are much better. I can cope with the driving. I'm going home. Write to me. Come to see me. Take care of yourself. And thank you for everything."

Eleanor hauls her overnight case out of The Porthminster Hotel.

She stands for a moment on the steps, feeling the sharp sea wind against her face, gulping the cool air into her lungs.

Then she makes for the Morris, climbing into it as an old friend, grateful for its sense of privacy, its boot piled with all her worldly possessions.

The car hums into life.

With a new resolution in her heart, she drives out on to the empty road.

She glances for a moment at the sea.

Then she turns right and starts to climb the hill away from St Ives, out of Cornwall, towards home.

Behind her, the figure of a man races up to the hotel.

His dark-gold hair flaps across his forehead.

His coat flies open in the wind.

A new watch sparkles on his wrist.

He sees the car, he waves wildly, he sees Eleanor.

But she does not see him.

And within minutes, she is out of sight.

Burning Bright

January 1937

Eleanor parks the Morris in Beaumont Street. She checks her make-up in the mirror, smooths the sleeves of her new coat, picks up her leather gloves and immaculate handbag. She climbs out of the car and walks briskly towards Somerville.

It was the first thing she'd done on her return to Woodstock: crouched by the freshly-lit fire in the empty house, shivering but determined, she'd written to Helen Darbishire:

"I expect you thought you would never hear from me again. A lot of water has flowed under my bridge since we last met. I wondered whether you could find the time to see me in College before term begins. I have a very great favour to ask you.

I only hope I'm not too late."

The Principal's reply came by return of post. She'd be delighted to see Miss Drummond again and sends her best wishes to Eleanor's mother.

Nothing ever changes here.

Eleanor checks in at the porter's lodge, feeling as if *she*, however, has changed beyond all recognition. She has enough confidence to take on the world. But these walls are the same, the staff at the College are the same, dear old Scroggs is still giving students his immaculate, sympathetic help, and she's sure the kitchen staff are about to prepare the same menus for the New Year. The College library will have the same layout, perhaps with a few new books. The bedrooms will be just as Spartan, with maybe a few new blankets.

The sense of continuity is brilliantly reassuring. She needs to rely on nothing changing at Somerville so that she can pick up the threads of her old life and make something entirely new of them. Not immediately, of course. She has many other things to do, some more important, others less so. But in the autumn, when the leaves begin to turn ...

Eleanor taps on Miss Darbishire's door and waits with her heart thumping, listening for the familiar, *"Come!"*

"Last year," she says quietly, "was the most difficult of my life." She shifts her position, the silk-covered cushions behind her back. "Nothing prepared me for it. I'd never had to live without my father. I hadn't realised how much I depended on him. I was in deep shock. My mother needed a lot of support, more than I could give her. I had to take financial control of our lives in ways that seemed completely beyond me."

She swallows. How much should she tell Miss Darbishire? The Principal's eyes never leave her face. She feels encouraged by the quiet, devoted listening. She feels free to talk.

"But I discovered they *weren't* too difficult. If you're

414

desperate for money and really single-minded about making it, you can. And then I kept finding out things about my father that I should have much preferred never to have known—"

"I entirely understand, Miss Drummond." The Principal's eyes are full of sympathy.

"Did you *know* about him? About his vile reputation? About—"

"We did, Miss Drummond. We also knew that you weren't involved in any way whatsoever. You've risen to every challenge."

"There were times when I didn't know what to do next, when I made the wrong decisions, when I put my trust in someone who didn't deserve it."

"But that's all in the past, Miss Drummond. It's too easy to dwell on what's happened, to ask, 'What if I'd done things differently?' You can't *change* anything that's happened. All you can do now is move on."

The Principal pauses.

"So how *do* you wish to continue with your life? What are your plans for your future?"

"I'd like to finish what I started. Go back to my books, take those exams again. My academic energies are burning bright. I'd like to return to Somerville."

The Principal clasps her hands together. "I'd *so* hoped you'd tell me that, Miss Drummond. Are you *sure?*"

"Quite sure. If I don't, I'll always regret the missed opportunity. My Woodstock tea-room makes enough money to cover my College fees. My best friend's now running it with me. It gives me time to study, get back to my books. I've got plans to use the tea-room as a showcase for local painters. And maybe to travel while I have a chance. I feel I could drive anywhere, see new places, breathe fresh air, meet new people. Take on new challenges."

Miss Darbishire stands up. She moves towards the window to look out at the College gardens. Then she turns to look at Eleanor: a long, cool, appraising stare. "I'll give you this, Miss Drummond. You have the courage and determination of someone older than your years."

"Thank you."

"And your mother? Will she let you make your choice?"

"My mother has married again. She and my stepfather are still on honeymoon. Once they're home, they'll hardly notice my absence. I'm no longer my mother's chief protector, for which relief much thanks."

"You realise – and I must warn you – you may find it hard, returning to your studies after this extraordinary intermission."

"It can't possibly be as difficult as the year I've just had."

"Perhaps not. But the world is changing around us with disconcerting speed. Because I'm a Wordsworth scholar, and I look after the welfare of Oxford students, people often assume I live in an ivory tower. That I know nothing about affairs outside my little life.

"That's not true. I keep in close touch with friends in many different parts of the world. One of them spent Christmas with me. She's just returned to her diplomatic work in Berlin." Miss Darbishire pushes impatiently at her hair. "Her news from Germany is bleak. She thinks – and many agree – there's going to be a Second World War. It'll be dark and dangerous, far worse than the Great War. Its consequences for our country may be dire."

"Then we must fight for its survival." Eleanor straightens her back, as if in preparation. "My father was a pacifist. I understood his beliefs, but I don't share them. If push comes to shove, I'd be willing to do anything for England."

"Your studies might be interrupted by the war, Miss Drummond. Would that make a difference?"

416

"Not in the least." Eleanor shrugs. "The past year has taught me you can't predict the problems you might have to face. You can only deal with them on a daily basis as best you can."

"By putting your shoulder to the wheel."

"Exactly." Eleanor realises that she and Miss Darbishire are having a real conversation. They've forgotten they're teacher and student. Instead, they're two women talking together. And they have the experience to know what they're talking about.

"What this country will need," Miss Darbishire says, "are young women who can carry their weight alongside our men. Who can be clever, resilient, honest and strong."

"I can be all those. Let me win back my place at Somerville and I'll show you how."

"I'm very inclined to." Miss Darbishire's eyes light up with her smile. "Are you *ready*, Miss Drummond? The long hours of study, those examinations, the competition, the new friends – and certainly new enemies – the energy and commitment you'll need.

"Are you ready for all that and a great deal more? Our beloved country will need young women such as you who can work in many different and unusual ways. Secret, underground ways. Who can say one thing and do another without anybody noticing how brilliant they are."

There's a pause, a silence in the conversation which could turn it different ways. Helen Darbishire makes up her mind.

She says quietly, "How is your French, Miss Drummond? How would you deal with taking a particular assignment abroad?"

"My French could be quickly improved." Eleanor feels a thrill of new excitement throbbing through her body. "And I know somebody – in many ways she's a member of my family – who has excellent French. She has more than that. She has a home and contacts in Juan-les-Pins. An artistic network of people she can trust. She also has friends in Paris she's known for many years."

"She could be very useful to us then … When it comes to planning against Herr Hitler. When it comes, as it surely will, to fighting a Second World War."

"Yes," Eleanor says. "I'd trust her with my life."

"And I'd trust you with mine … Are you ready for that and a great deal more, Eleanor Drummond?"

She stands to shake the cool, steady hand of the Principal of Somerville College.

"Yes, Miss Darbishire," she says. "I'm ready for everything."

Acknowledgements

Daddy's Girl is a new and revised edition of *The Choice*, which was published by The Book Guild in 2017. In July 2020 I decided to launch my own imprint, VMBooks. I have taken the opportunity to give this novel a radical edit and an entirely fresh look.

I am most grateful to the brilliant Paul Downes, Creative Director of GDAssociates, who created its stunning new cover and who has worked with me for the past seven years on my website, continually updating and refreshing it.

My original ideas for *Daddy's Girl* sprang to life in 2008 when I had lunch with John Forster, then the distinguished Archivist at Blenheim Palace. John's extraordinary knowledge of the history of Blenheim and Woodstock helped to give my work confidence and accuracy. John allowed me to see the unique Visitors' Book, signed by Edward VIII and Wallis Simpson in Blenheim Palace that weekend in June 1936, which made history and led directly to the abdication of the King.

I am also indebted to Captain Philip Moran, former head of the RNLI in St Ives, Cornwall, who knew more about the place than anyone else in the world, who meticulously read an early draft of my novel and also graciously allowed me to use his own cottage as my fictional The Hideaway.

419

I could not have written *Daddy's Girl* without the marvellous help of the Principal and Staff at Somerville College, Oxford. They not only talked me through a host of details of College life in 1936, but also allowed me and my photographer, the wonderful Chris Challis, to roam around its rooms and gardens to give me an accuracy of perspective and detail so crucial to an historical novelist's needs.

In July 2021, Blenheim Palace very kindly allowed their brilliant Historian, Antonia Keaney, to make a video with me as part of her work for the Palace. Antonia is not only a wizard with the high-tech knowledge this involves, but she is marvellously easy to talk to. Her poise and confidence are contagious. She knows when to let her guests talk joyfully about their special fields, and exactly when to ask a question that will fill a gap or point a different way in the potentially swirling maze of dialogue.

Such double-handed skills are exceptionally rare and only polished after years of dedication and experience. I cannot thank either Antonia or Blenheim enough for allowing me at a critical moment in my career as an author and indie publisher an opportunity to explain, discuss and illuminate a complicated, innovative and courageous novel. To be able to do so from the peace, warmth and tranquillity of my beloved cottage was little short of miraculous. Thank you all so much.

Valerie Mendes
28 September 2021
Woodstock

www.valeriemendes.com

Printed in Great Britain
by Amazon